THE RITES OF MAN

By Meg Bortin

Published by Ten16 Press, an imprint of Orange Hat Publishing

www.orangehatpublishing.com
Wauwatosa, WI

Cover design by James Eric Jones

This book is a work of fiction. Names, characters, places and incidents are the product of the author's imagination or are used fictitiously.

Early praise for *The Rites of Man*

"Meg Bortin's *The Rites of Man* is a cautionary tale about what happens when ambition trumps love. Set in New York in 1996, the novel brilliantly captures the spirit of the age. But at its heart is a vital interrogation of the writer's craft, which remains even more relevant today in our online world driven by AI and social media."

— Anne Penketh, author of the *Brittany* murder mystery series

"In *The Rites of Man*, the best-selling writer Thomas G. Paine has left the city for his refuge by the sea with the hope of overcoming writer's block. Into his life walks Sherry McManus, a lively woman in her mid-forties who cherishes her independence, won through her cosmopolitan life as an artist photographer. She is an inspiration for Tom, who in no time starts writing the long-expected masterpiece. But this is only the premise of the novel you're going to read, and you're in for a great ride of twists and turns. A novel for our time. Irresistible."

— Odile Hellier, author of *Village Voices*

"Meg Bortin pulls you right in with compelling characters, great dialogue, plot twists, scenes that transport you to another era and iconic places this well-traveled author knows intimately. *The Rites of Man* is an original, fun and surprising read."

— Eleanor Beardsley, Paris correspondent, *NPR*

"*The Rites of Man*, set in 1996, tackles the question of creativity with captivating detail. An enthralling novel, not without its moments of comic relief."

— John Tagliabue, former *New York Times* correspondent

"Beware of books."
– *Erica Jong*

PART I / THE GAME

July 1996

Chapter 1

The game began in earnest on July 12, 1996, eight days after they'd met. The participants, Sherry and Tom, had discussed the idea the night before and had even made a feeble attempt at a first round before being overcome by their mutual attraction and engaging in what most people in a similar situation would do upon finding themselves together in bed.

Now, in the predawn half-light, Sherry considered her options. She was quite aware of the risks. Their second morning together, and she already felt the beginnings of a fever she'd forgotten about, or tried to. She could imagine seeking happiness with Tom. He was witty, kind, and seemed touchingly vulnerable. But—and she'd learned this the hard way—it was far from self-evident that the pursuit of happiness would lead to a happy conclusion.

The thump of breakers against the shore rolled into the room. Tom was still sleeping. If she could just ease out of bed without waking him, she could escape back to Manhattan. She held her breath, barely moved, but Tom stirred, blinked, saw her.

"Sherry."

All thought of leaving dissolved at the sound of his voice.

"Tom," she said, reaching for him.

"Not yet," he whispered, and she felt the fever mount.

He rolled her gently onto her back.

"Your turn," he said.

Her turn. Well, she had a thousand stories.

"Get me started," she said.

The game was on.

Tom pushed aside the sheet. The light was just strong enough to make out the dark tangle of her hair against the pillow, the slope of her cheek, the slight downward turn of her mouth. He wanted to know every curve of her body, every thought in her mind. In the newness of their relationship, he wanted to know everything about her.

"Then tell me this," he said. "You're a beautiful woman. You've clearly been around, but you never settled down. Why not?"

He'd wondered about it. How could a woman like Sherry McManus have stayed single? At forty-four, she radiated charm. Half Jewish, half Irish, she'd told him. The combination was a knockout.

"I tried," she said.

"And?"

"It's a long story…"

"We have time," he said. "Tell me. Who did you try with?"

She raised an eyebrow.

"Just how much time do we have?"

Tom laughed, and Sherry had to smile. Only a week, and he got her. Thomas G. Paine, prize-winning author and former darling of the chattering classes, the man whose sandy hair and chiseled features had graced the cover of *Time*. He had some Native American blood, he'd told her—hence his middle name, Geronimo.

"Come on," he pressed her. "Who?"

"Well, there was the revolutionary…"

"Wait—don't tell me. A Black Panther. No, I know. A Cuban. You met cutting sugarcane with the Venceremos Brigades."

"Yeah, Rick would have loved that," Sherry said. "He actually signed up one time, but he was too busy organizing."

"This sounds very sixties."

"Early seventies, actually. We were at Berkeley."

"I know," Tom said. "He spotted you across a crowded classroom."

"No, not really." Sherry sat up in bed. "We got gassed together."

Tom sat up beside her, settling in against the pillows. His hand drifted onto her thigh.

"Tell the story," he said, knowing she'd spin it out, taking her time. There was only one rule to their sporting collusion: to pit wit against desire in expectation of a climax.

"It was an anti-war demonstration," Sherry said. "I was really young, eighteen. The police were out in riot gear. Everyone was shouting. You know, 'Ho Ho Ho Chi Minh, Vietcong are gonna win.' That sort of thing."

"Yeah, we had demos like that at Columbia, too," Tom said. "The leaders chanting 'Ho Ho Ho Chi Minh!' and 'Che Che Guevara!' and everyone getting into it."

"Well, no one was mentioning Che that day," Sherry said. "It was all about Vietnam. Some of the kids were throwing rocks, and it got ugly. I had my Pentax with me and started taking photos. I didn't see the police fall back to charge. There was a bang and a cloud of smoke, then more bangs. Everyone was screaming and running for cover. My eyes were burning. I couldn't see what was happening. Then someone grabbed me. 'Come on,' he said. 'They'll smash your camera!' We ran into the nearest building—it was a dorm—and he led me into the men's room. Tears were streaming down my face. I was actually blinded. He doused my face, then his. I told him I'd caught some great shots if the camera wasn't ruined. 'Fucking pigs,' he said. 'That was pepper gas.' Then he stripped to his shorts. I could see by then, so I asked what he thought he was doing. 'Just give me the camera and get out of your things, or you'll cry all day,' he said. So I went into a cubicle and stripped to my bra and undies. I was still crying. 'By the way,' he said, 'I'm Rick.' He handed me some paper towels under the door. 'You can come out,' he said. 'I won't bite.'"

Sherry laced her fingers through Tom's.

"But he did," she said. "Revolutions are sexy."

Tom smiled, anticipating the endgame.

"What happened?" he asked. "Did he seduce you right there on the bathroom floor?"

"No," she said. "He got us some clothes from a friend in the dorm, and we both went home. But a couple days later, we went to the movies. It was an outdoor cinema on campus. Rick took me to see *Breathless*. His cover was that Godard was political, but in fact Rick was in love with Jean Seberg. Especially that scene where she's out on the streets of Paris hawking the *New York Herald Tribune*, with her hair cropped short. It was like the fifth time he'd seen the movie, just for that scene. I'd never seen it before, and Belmondo was a revelation. You know, the way he runs his thumb over his lips. Then we went to Rick's." She paused, remembering.

Tom brought her thumb to his lips. She felt a rush as their eyes met.

"Go on," he said.

"We smoked a joint on the couch. He had a record playing, 'Season of the Witch' by Donovan. He started kissing me."

Tom could visualize the scene: Sherry drawing Rick in with her dusky eyes, yielding to the kiss. He fought to control the wild feeling rising inside him.

"Sounds very sexy," he said.

"It was," she said. "He was my first lover."

"At eighteen? You're joking."

Sherry slipped down on the bed, pulling Tom with her.

"Rick refused to believe it," she said, "but one thing led to another. We helped each other strip. After all, we'd already done that. But this time it was hot, and—well, it was just immense..."

Tom was kissing her breasts, her neck, moving on top of her. Taking him in her arms, Sherry wrapped herself around him, parting her lips, yielding to his kiss.

When they rose, sunlight was filtering through slatted wooden blinds into the second-story bedroom of Tom's clapboard house overlooking the beach. They went downstairs and took their coffee out to the deck. It was a windswept, glorious day.

As she contemplated her lover across the weathered picnic table, Sherry thought back to the night they'd met. She hadn't recognized him. At forty-three, Tom Paine hadn't published a word in years, and his name had slipped from the bestseller lists, along with his photo.

What kind of serendipity had brought them together, chance or fate? A Fourth-of-July barbecue, a throng of guests, couples dancing under the stars. Tom had been standing alone, drinking a glass of wine. She'd caught him in her lens. If she hadn't brought the Pentax, he might not have approached her. They wouldn't have started talking about photography, about nothing in particular, about would you like to dance? While the others were waving sparklers, they wouldn't have wandered down to the beach and, on a mutual dare, dived into the waves. And when they'd come up, laughing and shivering, they'd kissed.

The memory of that kiss made her shiver again in the sunshine.

When they'd gone their separate ways that night, Tom had slipped her his card, scribbling his phone number under his name. Until that moment, he'd been an anonymous partygoer. He had clearly come to the barbecue alone. But once she realized who he was, it had taken her only a split second to remember that he had a wife—or had had a wife.

"Call me," he'd said as he pressed the card into her hand.

She hadn't planned to. But when she got home to the city, she'd pulled one of Tom's books from her shelf and started to read. As she'd turned the pages, she could hear him telling the story. In the end, curiosity had overcome her common sense. She'd called.

As it turned out, Tom and his wife had separated a year earlier, he told her. He lived alone at the beach house, trying to write, to break through a seven-year dry spell.

A couple days later, she'd taken a train back to the island, and now she'd disregarded her personal declaration of independence to chance a second visit...

The sound of Tom pushing his bench out against the deck brought her back to reality. He walked around to her side of the picnic table and kissed the top of her head.

Keep it together, she told herself, as he took their mugs back to the kitchen.

He held the screen door open for her, tilting his head in invitation. Barefoot, she followed him into the house and up the stairs.

Later, they took a walk on the beach, hand in hand near the water's edge. The tide was ebbing, the waves lapping the shore.

"Finish your story," Tom said.

"Nothing special," Sherry said. "We were in love. Then we weren't. It's boring."

"No, it's not," Tom said, stopping to look at her—her hair wild in the wind, gray eyes squinting against the sun, her freckles an endearing imperfection. "Sherry, I love your stories."

"You just like them for the sex."

"No. I want to know you."

Sherry touched his face. How could she have thought of slipping away?

Now he was skipping stones across the water.

"We lived together for three years," she said. "The house was filled with music. Rick played the cello—he said it was like making love to a woman."

"Nice line."

"What can I say? It felt like home. I grew up surrounded by music. My mother taught piano. And Rick reminded me of my father. They're both lefties, baseball fans, news junkies."

"Sounds like a perfect childhood."

"It was uncomplicated," Sherry said. "My parents were very loving, and I was their only child. I guess I felt secure."

"You're lucky," Tom said, reflecting on her choice of career. Why a woman who grew up in such happy conditions preferred to view life through a lens was a question not easily answered. He studied the beach for another stone, chose a flat one, and let it fly.

"What does your father do?" he asked as they set off again along the shoreline.

"He taught history at City College, but he's retired now. They both are—Rose and Bernie. Anyhow, on Sunday mornings, Rick would go out and get the *Times* and bring it home with some lox and bagels. Then after breakfast, and you know, whatever, he'd play the Bach cello suites for me."

"And you wanted to get married…"

"He didn't want to have anything to do with that. Rick said marriage was a capitulation to the values of the ruling class. You know, a cop-out."

"Sure. The campus radical."

"Other people were saying the same thing," Sherry said. "The women's movement was taking off at Berkeley. We were in the streets, demanding liberation, even though no one knew exactly what that meant. In my women's group, married women were looked down upon as an inferior species who had allowed themselves to be indentured to men. To become their property. But at the same time, most of us had boyfriends…"

"Yeah, I remember those days," Tom said. "Women wanted to have it both ways. Free love, with commitment."

"And what about men? Think about it, Tom. That was twenty-five years ago, and we still haven't come to terms with the way the women's movement played out for all of us. And so-called sexual liberation. The pill freed us, but it also freed men to sleep around without having to worry about the consequences."

"I never thought about it like that," he admitted.

"We saw ourselves as pioneers," Sherry said. "But looking back, we were guinea pigs."

"That's pretty negative."

"Yes and no," she said. "It was a crazy ride. We were—we felt like we were changing the world. And in some ways, we were."

"Yeah, sure. Peace and love. What a joke that turned out to be. All the radicals who turned into brokers with houses in the suburbs…"

"Now you're being negative," Sherry said. "Those years changed your life, Tom. I mean, didn't you write a book about it? They changed all our lives."

"Yeah, and look at us now. Almost everyone I know has sold out, gone crazy, or died."

Far offshore, a sailboat was skimming across the waves, its spinnaker billowing brightly in the wind. Sherry followed it with her eyes, thinking about the seventies, wondering how to reply to Tom's dark take on the aftermath.

"You know," she said, "our generation—it's like we were standing on a fault line through the heart of America. There was a shift in the way the country conceived of itself, and out there in Berkeley, we were right on the edge. Mentalities changed. We'll never go back to the black-and-white way our grandparents saw the world."

"Christ, I hope not." Tom picked up another stone and skipped it, flipping it out beyond the frothy edge of the waves.

"For me, the real earthquake was Vietnam," Sherry said. "I mean, it was so blatant that everything we'd been taught in school about being on the side of the angels was total bullshit. It's like the movement opened up a moral chasm, and those of us on the front lines, well, we had to jump. Some got scared and jumped back, but some jumped forward."

"What about you and Rick?" Tom asked.

"That's what's so odd," Sherry said. "I mean, there he was, the big revolutionary, reciting Mao and criticizing me for being too straight. But in the end, he jumped back, and I jumped forward—for better or for worse."

The sun was high now, and families were arriving at the beach. Tom checked his watch. They'd have to hurry to make Sherry's train back to Manhattan.

"We'd better get going," he said.

With the weekend looming, they said little on the drive to the station. It was Friday, and Tom would be joining his wife in the city on Saturday for a visit he'd described as keeping up appearances. He kissed Sherry goodbye on the platform and waved as her train disappeared.

Back at the beach house, Tom felt distracted. He put some coffee on, hoping to clear his head. There was something out there—if only he could grasp it. But every time he tried to zero in on whatever it was, the image of Sherry rose up. He missed her already. What was it she'd said about making love for the first time? That it was colossal? No. She'd said it was just immense.

The sound of coffee percolating brought him back to the present. He poured himself a mug and went out to the deck.

Don't think, he told himself, gazing out across the dune. That was how ideas used to come to him, before writer's block derailed his life. It was always when he wasn't thinking about anything in particular, while he was under the shower, or jogging in Washington Square. Let it happen again, he thought, willing his muse to return. For the first time in too long to contemplate, he could feel her presence, as if floating on the breeze caressing the deck.

Tom went back inside. Taking the stairs two at a time, he went up to his study. There it sat: his Olympia portable. He approached it warily. Friend or foe? He rummaged in his desk, found a ream of paper, grabbed the typewriter, and took it all out to the deck.

Beads of sweat pearled on his forehead. On the picnic table, everything stood ready. The typewriter, the paper. All he needed to do was sit.

Gulls swooped overhead, their cries seeming to mock him: "Do it. Do it. Ha ha ha ha ha."

Wild feeling rising, Tom straddled the bench.

Could he do it?

He drew a page from the ream and rolled it in.

Sherry's cat Max was waiting to be fed when she entered her apartment. Afternoon sunlight slanted through tall windows overlooking Riverside Drive, noisy with Friday rush hour. Everyone else was leaving the city to which she'd just returned. Typical, she thought, as the handsome tabby turned circles around her legs, waving his tail like a flag.

"I missed you too," she said as he led her to the kitchen. She filled his dish and unpacked her minimalist travel kit—a toothbrush—and returned to the living room to check her messages.

It was a large, bright room, one wall hung with framed black-and-white photos of musicians performing in concert. The display spanned the two decades since Sherry had turned her love of photography and music into a career embracing both.

The light on the answering machine was flashing. Two messages: her photo editor wanting her to shoot a rehearsal next week and Anouk confirming their date for tomorrow.

Anouk Saint-Clair had flown over from Paris to sing jazz at Carnegie Hall, a rare honor for a French performer. Sherry was looking forward to the concert, and even more to their dinner afterward. They'd been close friends since meeting at Berkeley in the seventies, but these days they crossed paths only occasionally. It would be good to talk.

Chapter 2

They ordered Manhattans when they arrived at the steakhouse on Saturday night. Anouk was in an ebullient mood. She'd received a standing ovation for her rendition of the songs of Ella Fitzgerald, and when the drinks arrived, she raised her glass.

"Here's to your city," she said. "It's *fan-tas-tique!* I love it—the energy, the people, the creativity." With that, she broke into a trill: "New York, New York…"

Sherry laughed as diners turned their heads to see who was singing.

"Yeah," she said. "It's dirty and gritty and noisy. What's not to love?"

"You're proving my point, darling," Anouk said. "Don't you see? That's what New Yorkers share with Parisians. A sense of irony."

"Paris," Sherry said. "It's been so long."

"You should come over. But I understand you've been busy. So, tell me, darling—who is this new man in your life?"

Sherry lowered her voice.

"Nobody knows, so please be discreet. He's a writer. Tom Paine."

"Really? Thomas G. Paine? I'm impressed," Anouk said. "Didn't he win the National Book Award? But I haven't seen his name recently."

"Tom has writer's block. That's kind of how we met. He's been living out at his beach house on the island, trying to start a new novel. I went out to the Hamptons with Lou for a barbecue on the Fourth, and Tom was there. We just connected. When I was leaving, he slipped me his phone number."

"And you called him."

"Not right away," Sherry said. "But when I got back to the city, I took a fresh look at his first novel. Maybe you remember it. *Common Sense.*"

"That's his trademark, isn't it, taking the works of Thomas Paine the revolutionary and writing a novel under the same title."

"He seems to have made it work. Anyhow, you probably never read the original, but it's effectively a call to arms. Tom Paine called on the American colonists to rise up and fight for independence from Britain. He published *Common Sense* in January 1776. Six months later, America declared independence."

"Really, darling?" Anouk said. "What a powerful book."

"It was a pamphlet at the time, but yeah, it was powerful. So when my Tom wrote his *Common Sense*, he added a subtitle, *Independence Revisited.* The theme was that things were off track in America and we needed to do something about it as a matter of common sense. He wrote it during the Reagan presidency, when a lot of people felt the same way."

"I never read it," Anouk said, "but I do remember that it made quite a splash."

"I'd forgotten what a great read it is. You get swept up in the love story between Nick and Kate, but it's really about young people challenging the United States to get back to its founding values. I haven't finished rereading it yet—I'm making it last."

Sherry reached into her bag and drew out the novel, its cover emblazoned with an American flag. She flipped to the epigraph page.

"It's right here, from the original *Common Sense.* 'The cause of America is in great measure the cause of all mankind.' Which is still true today, by the way."

"So you put down the book, rushed back to Long Island, and fell into bed."

"No," Sherry said. "When I called, he was leaving for the city."

"Okay," Anouk said. "He rushed straight to your place and you fell into bed."

"He couldn't. Tom's still officially married. Some weekends he spends with his wife."

"Are you serious?"

"It's actually not a problem," Sherry said. "They split up a year ago, and they haven't had sex in ages. They sleep in separate bedrooms."

"How do you know?"

"He told me."

Anouk raised an eyebrow.

"Okay, okay," Sherry said. "I know—he specializes in fiction. Doesn't matter. First, I like him. Second, I believe him. And third, at least I'm safe this time, if you see what I mean."

"I'm not sure I do. Safe from what?"

"Come on. You know my track record. Do I have to spell it out? With Tom, there's a built-in barrier against expectations. I won't get carried away."

"I'm not sure that's the way love works," Anouk said.

"Who said anything about love?"

The food arrived: thick T-bones, the kind you couldn't find in Paris. It was Anouk's favorite New York dinner, as long as it came with a decent bottle of Bordeaux.

"I need to hear more," Anouk said. "After you called, when did you see him?"

"It was Monday. I took the train out to the shore. We sat around on the deck and talked politics. You know, would Clinton be re-elected, that sort of thing."

"Very romantic."

"I guess you had to be there. I told Tom how much I was enjoying rediscovering *Common Sense*, and he got out his second novel, *The American Crisis*—the one about the Weathermen, in which Nick and Kate rob a bank and go into hiding. I'd already read it, of course, but that was a long time ago, so he read me an excerpt."

Sherry dropped her voice a couple of tones and recited from memory, mimicking Tom: "'These are the times that try men's souls.' Nick scrawled the phrase on the cellar wall. He was bitter. They hadn't meant to kill anyone."

"At least he's got a sense of humor," Anouk said.

"It gets better. I can hear him reading to me. Something like: 'They were freedom fighters, robbing the rich to help the oppressed. And now he and Kate were stuck here, in Brooklyn, underground. Literally. It was so unfair.'"

"Is his voice really that deep?" Anouk asked.

"Mainly when he's aroused..."

"Oh my god. So he read to you and he took you to bed."

"Uh-huh. All afternoon."

"No wonder you like him."

"Darling, give me a break," Sherry said. "Tom's creative and funny and tender..."

"And great in bed. I get it. But all afternoon? What about your second date?"

"That was Thursday. We slept a couple of hours. The rest of the time..."

"Stop—I can't take it," Anouk said. "But what do you do when you're not having sex?"

"We tell each other stories. You know, true stories. It's kind of a game we play."

"And?"

"It's hard to describe. It's like, we're in bed, and we're already turned on, and instead of making love, we tell stories."

"Really? And that's what you like about him?"

"It's edgy," Sherry said. "I feel a rush just talking about it. It's like foreplay. We get high on each other."

"Well, he must be a powerful guy if he can make you high telling stories. And he dreamed this up?"

"No, it was my idea. I've actually played this game before, but with Tom being a writer, it's more interesting. Wordplay before sex play, if you see what I mean."

"I see only too well," Anouk said. "But you've known him for what? Ten days?"

"It's only a fling," Sherry said. "And Tom's great. You'd really like him."

"Maybe."

"Although I do feel a little conflicted about the wife."

"Don't," Anouk said. "If there's a problem, it's between her and Tom. It's not your problem."

"That's so French."

"Just be careful, darling. Enjoy it while it lasts. But stay focused."

"That's my specialty," Sherry said, raising an imaginary camera.

As she clicked the shutter, her mental lens saw Tom—out on the deck in his faded cut-offs, tall, tanned, and infinitely desirable. But he wasn't at the beach house now, she knew, and when she tried to picture him with his wife, the image blurred.

Three miles downtown, Jessica Franklin was serving boeuf bourguignon as Tom filled crystal glasses with the expensive bottle of 1989 Nuits-Saint-Georges Premier Cru they'd been saving.

At forty-three, Jessica was in her prime: cropped dark curly hair with a dramatic streak of gray, the plunging V of her Donna Karan dress revealing more than a hint of breast.

With them at their West Village townhouse were Steve Lifshitz and Marilyn Mulligan, their closest friends—close enough to know that Tom had moved out, and that writer's block had something to do with it.

As Tom handed the glasses around the vintage oak table, Jessica took her seat, confident that the conversation opener she'd been saving couldn't fail to make an impression.

"Tom says he's started a new novel."

"Far out," Steve said with a genial nod to his friend.

"Tommy, that's fantastic," Marilyn said. "Tell us about it."

"Not much to tell," Tom said. "I'm just playing around with ideas."

"It's a big secret," Jessica said. "He refuses to discuss it. I'm not even sure it's true."

Tom shot his wife a glance. This was just like Jessica, to mock him in front of their friends. As if that would teach him a lesson for not meeting her expectations.

"Come on, man—give us a clue," Steve said, swirling his glass. He worked as a Wall Street lawyer and had acquired a taste for fine wine.

"Guys—I'm not ready to talk about the book," Tom said. "I don't know where it's going."

Marilyn raised her glass with the encouraging smile she'd perfected as a Montessori preschool teacher and mother of three.

"Still, getting started is a real accomplishment," she said. "A toast to Tom."

Tom couldn't savor the moment. He sensed what was coming.

"Yes, here's to my husband," Jessica said. "Thomas G. Paine, writer-in-residence at the beach, who hasn't published a word in seven years."

Tom's eyes flashed a warning, but Jessica was on a roll, her resentment overpowering any pretense of keeping up appearances.

"Who's still playing around with ideas after a whole year out on the island. It makes a woman wonder what he's really been doing out there."

"Just getting some air, Jess," Tom said.

"Air, schmair. You're supposed to be working. And what have we seen for it? Nothing."

Steve and Marilyn exchanged a glance. It was often tense when they crossed from the East Village to see their friends, but tonight the atmosphere was toxic.

"The bourguignon's fabulous, Jess," Marilyn said. "Is this the Julia Child version? I tried it once and it took two days. How do you find the time?"

"I simplified," Jessica said. "I had to. I've been tied down at the paper. We're working on a special issue."

Marilyn's face lit up.

"Tell all," she said. "What's it about?"

Jessica wrote about art at the *Village Voice*. She always knew which obscure New York painter or sculptor would be the next big name. Just by choosing which artist to cover, she could make a career or break one. Marilyn liked to be first to know, but Jessica wasn't talking.

Instead, she slipped a morsel of beef to the large poodle waiting patiently by her side. With his curly salt-and-pepper fur and jaunty bandana, he was a perfect match for Jessica.

"Hey," Tom said. "Don't feed Che at the table."

"Don't give me orders," Jessica said coolly. "You lost that right when you moved out of our bedroom."

"Only because you prefer to sleep with the poodle."

"Guys," Steve said. "Take it easy. This should be a celebration. Right, Tom?"

"Excuse me." Tom pushed his chair back from the table and slouched into the study, which now doubled as his bedroom. He closed the door, went to the phone, and dialed a number. No answer.

"Sherry, it's me," he said when the answering machine clicked on. "Can we meet up tomorrow? I need to see you. Don't call me back, right? Jessica's on the warpath. I'll phone you in the morning."

Tom quietly replaced the receiver in its cradle and returned to the dinner party, where Steve was holding forth about the Yankees. Marilyn was a Mets fan. That always made for lively repartee. At least they were no longer talking about his novel.

The blinking light of the answering machine caught Sherry's eye when she came in from the steakhouse. It was late—she and Anouk had closed the place. She admired her friend's stamina. A concert singer who could perform at Carnegie Hall, knock back a couple of Manhattans and half a bottle of Bordeaux, and still be fresh the next day. Anouk was heading to Tanglewood in the morning.

"Now who could that be?" Sherry asked as Max jumped onto the couch. To be honest, she'd been hoping for a message. She sat down to create a lap and pushed the button.

Yes, it was Tom.

But as his words spilled into the room, their urgency surprised her. And did he have to mention his wife? The last thing Sherry wanted was Tom's marriage invading their courtship.

Chapter 3

Tom phoned Sunday at nine, and by ten he was at Sherry's door bearing a bouquet of feathery peonies. He held them out to her.

"They're gorgeous, Tom," she said, kissing him on the cheek. "Come in."

Tom strode into the living room, where Max was asleep on the couch.

"Hey, who's this little guy?" he asked, approaching to stroke the puss. Max opened a resentful eye and went back to his catnap.

"Max is my constant companion," Sherry said. "Except when I abandon him to go see you. He's been talking about divorce if this continues."

"You could bring him."

"Nope. When we're at the beach house, I want you all to myself. Come on, let's make some coffee."

On their way to the kitchen, Tom stopped short at the wall of photos.

"Wait a minute," he said, sweeping his gaze across the wall: conductors, their hands a blur of motion; pianists bent over the keyboard, their faces rapt with emotion; a dramatic shot of a singer onstage, arms thrust out, head thrown back, her African robe illuminated against the black of the theater; hands, just hands, delicately bowing a violin, grasping the neck of a cello; musicians imparting their passion to youthful students. Tom recognized Leonard Bernstein in one shot, Jessye Norman in another. Then there were photos of ordinary people, at work or at rest; photos of New York and Paris; photos of Sherry with friends; and photos of Sherry herself.

Sherry stood back to let Tom discover her work. He approached the wall for a closer look, then turned to her with new eyes.

"You said you were a photographer," he said. "You didn't tell me you were an artist."

"It's what I do," Sherry said. "It keeps me off the streets."

"Don't joke about this. I'm serious. Your work is awesome."

"It's not just my work. It's my life."

Sherry started for the kitchen, but Tom called her back.

"Wait a second. Tell me about some of these people," he said, approaching the wall again. He zeroed in on a photo of a young Black man with a cocky smile, his arm slung around a younger Sherry. "Now who would this be?"

"That's Granville, around the time I first met him," Sherry said. "Granville Macks. He's my partner—we shoot together a lot."

"Should I worry?"

"Not really. He's gay."

But Tom had moved on to another photo.

"Has he seen this one? You look like an artist's model."

The shot showed Sherry lying nude on an old-fashioned sofa, a silky cloth over her loins. Perched on one elbow, she smiled beguilingly into the camera.

"Of course," she said. "Everyone's seen it. Everyone who comes here. All my friends."

Tom was still studying the photo.

"Don't get me wrong," he said, "but you were pretty hot when you were younger."

"So I'm told," she said drily.

"But even better now that you've mellowed," Tom added quickly.

"Mellowed? You wish."

She headed for the kitchen, leaving Tom alone with the photos. He was having a rethink. He'd been so caught up in their romance on the island that he hadn't stopped to consider Sherry's life in New York. What did she do in the city while he was out at the beach? She was a free-spirited woman. Could he trust her? And her photos—the collection was mind-blowing.

When he joined Sherry, she'd arranged the peonies in a vase and a pot of espresso was gurgling. She filled two cups, placed them on a tray, and led Tom back to the living room, setting the tray on the low table in front of the couch. When they were settled, Sherry dived in.

"I wasn't expecting to see you today," she said. "What's going on?"

Tom set his cup aside.

"I'm going back to the beach," he said. "Come with me."

"Really? I thought you were spending the weekend in town."

"That was the plan. But things got a little tense last night."

"What happened? You mentioned Jessica..."

"We had some friends over for dinner, and she started in on me," Tom said. "What have I been doing at the beach house, like that."

Sherry felt a flicker of alarm.

"Does she suspect you're seeing someone?"

"Hell no," he said. "How could she? But she loves giving me a hard time, mainly about my failings as a writer. She seems to thrive on embarrassing me."

"Then why do you still see her, Tom? Why continue with the charade?"

"It isn't that easy. Jessica and I go back a long way."

To her dismay, Sherry felt a pang. She got up to take the cups back to the kitchen, but Tom rose and caught her by the waist. He took the tray from her and set it aside.

"It isn't easy for anyone—I know that," he said. "What matters is, you and I have started something, and I want it to continue. I want that more than anything."

Conflicting feelings cascaded through Sherry as she searched his eyes. It's a fling, she reminded herself.

"I want that too."

When their lips met, her doubts slipped away.

"Let's get out of here," Tom said. He released her to check his watch. "Come on, get your things. If we hurry, we can make the 11:45."

"Now? No, I can't. I have to work today."

"Seriously? It's Sunday."

"My photo editor is expecting some prints tomorrow," Sherry said. Her editor at *Musiques*, the magazine she shot for, was on deadline for a spread on Juilliard, and Nan Gillette would not tolerate breaking a deadline. Sherry took Tom's hand and led him to the door.

"But before you go," she said, "let me ask you something."

"Anything," Tom said.

"Last night, when you called, you said it was important. Did you just want to ask me to come to the beach, or was there something else?"

The shadow of a smile crossed Tom's face.

"Possibly…"

"Tell me."

"After you left on Friday, I got an idea."

"An idea—for a book?"

"Seven fucking years of nothing. And then you walk into my life and…"

"Tom, that's huge."

"So I'm going back to the beach to write," he said, "and this time it's for real. When you're done with your work, can you join me?"

"Tomorrow?" Sherry said. "Sure."

Chapter 4

Sherry switched on "Morning Edition," keeping half an ear on the news as she sorted through the photos she'd printed: musicians teaching at Juilliard, their emotions on full display. As she worked, she reran the tape of her conversation with Tom the previous day. She knew of other separated couples who stopped short of divorce, presumably out of loyalty, if that's what was going on. The upside was that it clarified matters. Her affair with Tom would remain one—even if she already sensed that this affair had staying power. Hadn't she just bought a toothbrush to leave at the beach house? She chalked that up to the triumph of hope over experience.

Sherry slipped the photos into a manila envelope and went to her closet. The radio was still talking about Hurricane Bertha—the storm had pounded the entire East Coast, a surfer had died off the Jersey shore, and Fire Island got socked. With rain still spattering down outside, she chose an embroidered Mexican tunic and jeans. In any event, she thought, even if her affair with Tom had staying power, there was a limit to how far they could go, and that was deeply reassuring.

It was noon when she went out. That left plenty of time to deliver the photos to *Musiques*, schmooze with Nan, and make it to Penn Station for the 2:35. Protected by her yellow slicker, armed with the toothbrush, she ducked into the subway at 96th Street and headed downtown.

≈

Jessica was having one of her days. She'd felt it as she walked Che through Washington Square on her way to work, shielding herself with a stylish umbrella. The way he had to sniff at every bush and check out the particulars of every female hound. It could drive a woman crazy.

Now, at the Monday meeting of the *Voice* culture section, she struggled to pay attention. Joe Reilly, the casually hip New Yorker who ran the section, was fretting about the line-up of their special issue on the decline and fall of the New York arts scene. Everyone was dying of AIDS. Or heroin. Or both.

"Now what about Julian Schnabel?" Savannah Banks asked. "The Basquiat film comes out next month, and I just saw the preview. Downright brilliant."

"Yeah, Schnabel's still around, but Basquiat's dead," Joe said. "Art killed him. That's what I'm talking about." He swept a hand through his dun-brown hair as he looked around the table, settling his gaze on his favorite columnist. "Where can we go with this? Jessica?"

"Same old shit," she said.

Everyone laughed.

"No, really," Jessica said. "I mean—"

"She means SAMO," Joe interjected, and the room fell silent. A journalist of the seen-it-all school, he did not suffer fools gladly. He nodded approvingly at Jessica. "Go on."

"Same Old," she said. "Basquiat's early trademark. We peg the piece to his start as a graffiti artist and how he inflected the creative life of the city. And how that energy has dissipated and how to get it back."

"I like it," Joe said, his eyes lingering on Jessica a little too long. "Okay, everyone. Think it over, and we'll take it further next week."

When the meeting broke up, Jessica and Savannah strolled to the Cooper Square café where they often lunched on Mondays. They chose a table with enough space for Savannah to slide in comfortably. She was eight months pregnant.

"How are you feeling these days?" Jessica asked when they'd ordered. "You're looking great, by the way."

"I do feel great," said Savannah, flicking aside a strand of ash-blonde hair. She'd come north nearly a decade ago but hadn't lost her drawl. "My mama always told me that a man can't resist a pregnant woman. Something about the pheromones. I reckon I know what she means. Phil can't keep his hands off me."

"Well, lucky you," Jessica said. She'd been weighing whether to tell Savannah what had gone on after the guests left on Saturday. It had been brutal. Tom berating her for wrecking the evening, and what she'd replied.

"Oh my," Savannah said. "I guess I should learn to hold my tongue."

"Forget about it. I had a bad weekend."

"Do you want to talk about it?"

"No, not really," Jessica said. "Listen, I'm really happy for you. It's just hard hearing about your pheromones when I'm too old to get pregnant."

"Why, honey, don't talk like that. Of course you're not. Women our age are in the prime of life. I mean, look at you— you're a sexpot."

"That's not the point," Jessica said. "You're thirty-eight. Fine. I'm forty-three. For women my age, getting pregnant is as likely as a bear walking into a bar. And that's if you're having sex."

"But don't you want to have children?"

"I do. I mean, I did. To be honest, things haven't been going so well with Tom."

"What do you mean? That gorgeous old hunk of yours?"

Usually, Jessica concealed her feelings, sticking to the version that Tom was spending time at the shore merely in order to write. But as Savannah drew her out, she felt an irrepressible need to drop the veneer.

"He's a loser." There, she'd said it. "We had a big fight this weekend. He can't get it up. He hasn't fucked me in—well, I'm not going to finish that sentence. It's too embarrassing."

"Are you trying to tell me Tom Paine is impotent?" Savannah asked. "I don't believe it."

Realizing she'd said too much, Jessica called for the check and changed the subject.

"Jean-Michel Basquiat—now there's a hunk," she said. "I used to see him at parties."

"Really? That's awesome," Savannah said. "I wish I could have met him, but he died too soon. Isn't it a shame he didn't make it past twenty-seven? Now tell me, honey, are you going to be okay? Can you patch things up with Tom tonight?"

"Not tonight," Jessica said. "He's out at the shore, allegedly writing the next Great American Novel. He'll be out there all week."

The rain had stopped by the time Tom and Sherry drove up to the beach house, but the deck was wet, so they went inside. On her two previous visits, Sherry had barely noticed the layout of Tom's hideaway, going directly from the bedroom down to the deck and back again. Now, as he sat down to roll a joint, she took a look around.

The ground floor was one large room, the kitchen separated from the sitting area by a butcher-block counter. The place had a comfortable feel, with pine flooring and a wide, faded couch facing a flagstone fireplace. A low wooden table sat before it, magazines spilling over the bottom shelf. Floor-to-ceiling bookshelves lined the side wall, and large windows looked out over the deck to the dunes and the ocean beyond.

Sherry went to the windows to watch the waves roll in, the light playing off the water in shades of gray too varied to count. A lone brave soul on a kayak paddled by just offshore.

The sound of Tom piling wood into the grate made her turn her head. In his worn work shirt and jeans, he looked more like a backwoodsman than a writer. She joined him as he lit a match, and the fire crackled to life. New York felt a million miles away.

"One match only—I'm impressed," she said.

"It's just practice," Tom said. "Living out here on my own, trying to write. A fire makes the place feel less empty. Besides, I guess I'm kind of a pyromaniac at heart."

They stood side by side, watching the sparks dance. Pale flames licked at the kindling and rose to embrace the logs. As the wood snapped and caught, the sweet odor of burning hickory wafted into the room.

Tom lit the joint he'd rolled, passed it over, and led Sherry to the couch. Daylight was fading, and the fire cast a rosy glow.

"Now where were we the other day?" he asked as they settled into the cushions. "You said you jumped forward and Rick jumped back..."

"Don't even think about going there," Sherry said. "It's your turn."

"Okay," Tom said. "But first, we need to get comfortable."

He leaned down to unlace Sherry's sneakers, removed them, and kicked his off.

"I want to look at you," he said, delicately lifting the edge of her tunic. "Could you, ah, slip out of this overcoat?"

Sherry smiled as she pulled it off.

"More," Tom said, leaning in to remove her bra.

As they kissed, Sherry unbuttoned his shirt and helped him shrug it off. She looped her arms over his shoulders, enjoying the sensual charge of her breasts meeting his skin.

"It's getting hot in here," Tom murmured, reaching down to unzip her jeans.

"Aren't you forgetting something?" Sherry said as she stopped him.

She stretched out on the couch, propping herself against the armrest, folding her arms behind her head, exposing herself to his gaze.

Watching the play of the firelight over her naked torso, Tom realized that she knew how erotic he'd find it. He stretched out in the other direction.

"I'm going to tell you about the first time I got laid," he said. "And when was that?"

"In 1970, when I was seventeen."

"And you expect me to believe you were a virgin…"

"Well, yes. It was after my junior year in high school. I'd gone over to Scotland on a summer study program, and when the Edinburgh festival opened, we went to see *As You Like It*. The actress playing Rosalind just blew me away. So I went back the next night, and the next, and finally worked up the courage to go backstage and say hello to her."

"What was she like?" Sherry asked. "Describe her."

"She was blonde, an English Rose type," Tom said. "Very different from the girls back home. Her name was Fiona, and she was twenty."

"An older woman…"

"It was her first starring role," Tom said. "I'm sure you know the play. She spent most of it disguised as a man—an incredibly sexy man."

"How did you get her into bed?" Sherry asked.

"You probably won't believe me, but it was her idea. We went out for coffee, and afterward, she invited me up to her room. Then one thing led to another."

"I need details," Sherry said.

Tom smiled and caught hold of her hands.

"Come here," he said. "I'll show you."

Only embers remained by the time they rose, and night had fallen. Tom flicked on the lights and walked naked to the kitchen as Sherry dressed. She joined him at the butcher block, where he was opening a bottle of red.

Sherry looked him up and down.

"Are you planning to dress for dinner?"

"Sure," he said.

He looped a chef's apron over his neck, tying it neatly around his waist.

That was the thing about Tom, Sherry thought as he set to work, broad-shouldered and tanned except for his buttocks. He could make passionate love to her and then stand there cooking unselfconsciously in the nude, a paragon of cool. He seemed totally together, except when it came to his writing.

He hadn't said anything more about his idea, she realized. If she mentioned the writing, it could spoil the moment. But if she didn't, he might think she didn't care.

"Tom," she said finally, "have you made any progress? With your idea?"

He looked up from his cutting board.

"It's coming along," he said. "But I'd rather not discuss it— putting it into words might block me again."

Sherry nodded. She felt the same way when she had an idea for a photo. Making it too specific could interfere with the artistic process.

"I get it."

Tom shot her a grateful look and went to fetch his clothes.

"Candlelight?" he asked as they brought the food to the table.

"Whatever, Tom," Sherry said. "As you like it."

After supper, Tom stoked up the fire, put on an old Marvin Gaye album, and rolled another joint. They danced as they smoked it, singing along when they remembered the words. After a couple of numbers, they collapsed laughing onto the couch.

"Now it's your turn," Tom said. "Tell me what happened with Rick."

"I'm kind of stoned," Sherry said. "It was a long time ago…"

"And you were so young. Become that Sherry. I'd like to know her."

As she gazed into the fire, Sherry let the present slip away, transporting herself back to her Berkeley days with Rick. She'd seen him as her soulmate, her partner for life. Even in the aftermath of the sixties, she'd still honestly believed that the Hollywood version of love could translate into reality. Well, she thought wryly, that Sherry no longer exists…

"We don't have to do this tonight," Tom said, sensing her shift in mood.

"No, I want to tell you about it. It's kind of a major event in my life."

She took another hit of the joint, set it aside, and went to stand before the fire, creating the distance she needed to keep it together while telling this story.

"When Rick graduated, he went out to Ann Arbor to study politics," she said. "This was back in '72. I was still at Berkeley, finishing my degree and trying to figure out how to make it as a photographer. We kept in touch by phone. I missed him, but I wasn't worried about it."

"And?"

"And I heard through the grapevine that he'd started seeing a woman we knew," Sherry said. "So I flew out there and confronted him. Rick didn't deny it. He said he still loved me—he actually cried—but it was too late. I didn't believe him. So we broke up."

"Just like that."

"Yeah, I dumped him."

"Is that what you meant by jumping forward?" Tom asked.

"No. I was too wrecked to jump anywhere. I just flew back to Berkeley and tried to keep it together. A couple months later, Rick phoned to tell me he was engaged to that woman. I didn't know whether to laugh or cry."

Sherry picked up the fire tongs and stabbed at the logs, sending sparks flying.

"So I just wished him well, you know? But it destroyed me. Can you imagine? Mr. Marriage-Is-A-Cop-Out getting married?"

Backlit by the fire's red glow, still wielding the tongs, she had the look of a virago, Tom thought, a female warrior incensed by the ways of men.

"I thought Rick's rules were the right rules for people like us in our time, and I played along. But he'd been bluffing—I'd been not just betrayed but outplayed."

She hung the tongs on their hook and returned to the couch.

"That was the toughest part," she said. "How were women supposed to be liberated when men still held all the cards? I decided I needed some distance from America's sexual revolution. That's when I jumped forward."

"What did you do?" Tom asked.

"I flew to Paris."

"Interesting choice. Sexiest city in the world..."

"It was liberating," Sherry said. "Have you been there?"

"Only once. A long time ago."

He rose, flipped the record over, and held out his hand.

The strains of Marvin Gaye followed them up the stairs, just audible over the rumbling surf. Moonlight filtering through the blinds cast pale blue stripes across the bed. They stripped and climbed beneath the sheets.

When "Heard It Through the Grapevine" came on, Sherry felt a little frisson. Was this Tom's idea of a joke? But he was kissing her, wanting her, and the thought slipped away.

Chapter 5

The sun was over the treetops when they rose, and it was already hot. They skipped breakfast. Instead, Tom drove Sherry to Gosman's, a dockside joint near the tip of the island. They ordered lobster rolls and coffee, then lingered over a chilled bottle of white, enjoying the sea breeze and the harbor activity.

Watching the seagulls squawk and dive, Sherry felt relaxed enough to return to their fireside conversation.

"You said you were in Paris a long time ago," she said. "How long is long?"

"It was back in '76," Tom said.

"So we were there at the same time. We could have crossed paths."

"I knew it. You were that intriguing woman in the leather jacket smoking Gauloises."

"Gitanes," she said. "But I did have a leather jacket."

"What did I tell you? We're cosmically linked."

"That jacket was my disguise," Sherry said. "I wanted to blend in with the French. To pass, if you see what I mean."

"Did it work?"

"Sometimes. If I kept quiet. I never lost my American accent."

"But you did speak French…"

"I studied it at Berkeley. I always had a thing about France—probably because of my dad. He fought on the Normandy beaches during the war."

"Really? That's awesome."

"He told me stories about it when I was a kid. Not the fighting, but the villages and the people. He fell in love with the place, and I was impressed. So when I wanted to get out of the States, I chose France," she said. "And what about you? What took you to Paris?"

"It was Jessica's idea," Tom said.

"You've been together twenty years?"

"Even longer. We met at Columbia in '73. But you don't want to hear about that."

"Actually, I do," Sherry said. "How did you get together?"

"Well, Jessica was a kind of firebrand. I'd seen photos of her speaking at demonstrations, and she wrote for the campus paper. So I already knew who she was when she turned up in my Shakespeare class. We flirted a little, and one day she suggested I come with her to a Vietnam protest. I'd been a quiet English major up to that point, not really involved in politics. She couldn't believe it. She made it her personal project to raise my consciousness, and along the way we fell in love."

"So you were, like, twenty?"

"Yeah. It was my first serious relationship," Tom said.

"Your only one, from the sound of it."

He smiled.

"Until now, you mean…"

Sherry glanced out at the harbor. Boats were sailing toward each other, passing and moving on—like lovers, she thought.

"Let's get back to your trip to Paris," she said.

"I was living in England at the time. I went over as a Rhodes scholar, and after my year in Oxford I moved to London. Jessica was in New York—she'd been hired as a cub reporter at the *Voice*—and we wrote to each other constantly. She liked my style, so she got the *Voice* to let me write a sample column. Our man in groovy London, that sort of thing."

"By Thomas Paine," Sherry said.

"Yeah. That's why she came over. It was the bicentennial of American independence, and Jessica thought it was a good time to take me on a tour of memorials to my revolutionary name-sake. She thought it would inspire me."

He poured them each another splash of wine.

"First, we went up to Norfolk. Not everyone knows this, but Tom Paine was actually from England. He was born in a little place called Thetford. They have a bronze statue of him holding *The Rights of Man* in one hand and a quill in the other. It was powerful. I felt—I don't know—awed in his presence. Then we went over to Paris."

"And this was all Jessica's idea?" Sherry asked.

"She's a very determined woman."

I bet she is, Sherry thought.

"Go on," she said.

"We went to see the plaque commemorating Tom Paine over by Odéon. It's on the building where he stayed during the French Revolution. Did you know he got elected to the body that abolished the monarchy? The Convention. Even though he didn't speak French…"

"Do you?"

"No," Tom said. "Never learned it. Anyhow, Tom Paine got kicked out of the Convention for speaking out against the guillo-tine. They threw him in prison. He was already a hero here in the States, and that made him even more of a hero, but the French still kept him in jail for over a year. In the end, he became a hero there, too."

"But why did Jessica think this would inspire you?" Sherry asked. "Are you actually related to Tom Paine?"

"No, not at all. I've looked into my roots—we just share the same name," he said. "Anyhow, from Odéon we took the metro down to the Parc Montsouris. Jessica wanted to show me another statue: *Thomas Paine, Citizen of the World*. We sat on the grass and talked about the future. I said I wanted to move on from the column and try to write a novel. Jessica said she thought I should use the Thomas Paine connection—you know, pick up his titles."

"That was her idea, too?" Sherry asked.

"It was brilliant. That evening I took her to dinner at Lipp and asked her to marry me."

Sherry had heard enough. She finished her wine and stood up.

"Want to walk down to the water?" she asked.

"Yeah, sure," Tom said. He signaled to the waiter and paid.

They strolled across the parking lot to a narrow strip of sand. Sherry slipped out of her sneakers to dip her feet in the sea. She jumped back, laughing, as a wave splashed up to her knees. Tom extended a hand, and they set off, their arms forming a bridge across the water's edge.

"Now tell me about your Paris," he said. "When you went over, where did you stay?"

"At first with my friend Anouk," Sherry said. "She's the singer I had dinner with the other night. I was pretty broken up about Rick, and she took good care of me. She had a great multi-culti circle of friends—musicians and artists, like that—but eventually I had to move out. So I found a maid's room on the Rue des Ecoles."

"A garret in Paris. Very romantic. And you had a lover..."

"Of course."

"Don't tell me. He was a Parisian with a beret who spent his days in cafés reading *Le Monde* and debating the relative merits of Sartre and Camus."

"Parisians don't wear berets," Sherry said.

"But he was a Frenchman..."

"Sort of," she said. "He was actually born in Algiers when the country was still French. His family was Jewish, and when he was a teen, they fled to Paris. That was during the Algerian War, in the late fifties. Later, he moved to Israel and worked on a kibbutz for a spell. When he came back to France, he became a TV journalist. He traveled a lot—kind of a man of the world. But his passport was French."

"And you were in love."

"Well, it was rocky," Sherry said. "We had what he called an open relationship. Raphael was the kind of guy who insisted on separate bedrooms but always wanted to know what was going on in mine."

Tom smiled, amused at her turn of phrase. He looked back to see how far they'd gone. Gosman's was a small point on the horizon.

"How did you handle that?" he asked as they reversed course. "Did you sleep around?"

"Not my style," Sherry said. "And Raphael—I never asked, because I didn't want to know. Things were great when we were together, but I had no idea what he was doing on the road. And sometimes that was really hard to take. Near the end, we had this big blowup over at my place. I told him the relationship wasn't going anywhere, and if he kept spending so much time away, it never would."

"Did you want it to?" Tom asked.

"Raphael was very—well, I know it sounds old-fashioned, but he was very dashing. He had this kind of flair. Not that tall, but dark, with laughing eyes. We would have had beautiful children. But he didn't want to be tied down. At first, that was fine by me. After the breakup with Rick, I told myself I'd never trust another man. But you know, things happen. I think it's actually a chemical reaction, at least for women. Once you start having sex, you get attached. That's why it's called making love."

Tom picked up a stone and sent it skipping across the waves. He was impressed by her observation, and more than a little turned on.

Sherry leaned down to splash some water on her face. They still had a few hundred yards to walk, and the sun was hot.

"Why don't we take a swim?" she said.

"I've got a better idea. Let's go back to my place."

L'Amour l'après-midi. Who shot that film? Sherry was entangled with Tom on his bed in the afternoon heat, but her mind was elsewhere. Their conversation had taken her back to Paris in the seventies. No air conditioning anywhere, and in her room beneath the roof, not even a fan. In summer, it had been positively steamy. They would spend the day in the nude, she and Raphael, feeding each other the plump raspberries she brought home from the market, drinking water because they were high on each other and had no need for wine.

Now her body rose and fell in rhythm with Tom's. Love in the afternoon. He was forcing her out of her thoughts and into the moment.

"You're beautiful," Tom said when they finished.

She'd heard it before—that was the kind of thing men said when they were happy in bed with a woman. But still, it made her smile.

"I have to go," she said.

"I know."

The sun was beating down on the deck when they emerged. Squinting, Tom waved to an elderly woman in the next yard.

"How's it going, Mrs. Johnson?" he asked, and the woman approached the wooden railing that separated their property, a neatly tended herb garden running along Tom's side.

"Well, Tom, I was wondering if you could spare a branch of rosemary," she said.

"Sure, help yourself. By the way, this is Sherry."

Mrs. Johnson peered suspiciously at Sherry through thick glasses.

"Hello," Sherry said, feeling mildly affronted. She hurried across the deck to the drive, where Tom's Jeep stood waiting.

"What's the deal with your neighbor?" she asked as they pulled away. "I don't like the way she stared at me."

"Don't mind her," Tom said. "She doesn't see very well."

"She looked at me as though I shouldn't be here."

"Forget about it. She just wanted to check you out. Who wouldn't? Anyhow, I rely on Mrs. Johnson. She looks after the house when I'm away. I don't mind if she's nosy."

Fair enough, Sherry thought, but the incident had unnerved her. As they drove along, she wondered how comfortable Tom felt about having her in his life. How did he negotiate the reality

that he was still married to another woman? And then it came
to her.

"Eric Rohmer," she said.

"What about him?"

"Do you remember his film *L'Amour l'après-midi*? They called
it *Chloe in the Afternoon* in English."

"Vaguely."

"It was one of his so-called 'Moral Tales.' I saw it with Rick
before we split up."

"Why do you mention it?"

"It popped into my mind," she said. "I don't know why. I've
always detested Rohmer."

But thinking about the film, she did know why. Odd the way
the subconscious works, she mused. It was a story of temptation—a married man's temptation to stray with another woman.
But if Tom's marriage was over, she reasoned, then he wasn't actually straying...

"When will I see you again?" Tom asked as they pulled up to
the station.

"I don't know," Sherry said. "I'm shooting a concert tomorrow. Soon. Good luck with the writing."

Chapter 6

Sherry emerged with Granville and Lou from the darkness of Avery Fisher Hall into the midday clamor of Broadway, the music still echoing inside her. The rehearsal had been brilliant. Kurt Masur conducting the New York Philharmonic in three versions of *Romeo and Juliet*—by Prokofiev, Tchaikovsky, and Bernstein. Three versions of love and death.

"How many stars will you give it, Lou?" Granville asked as they strolled uptown to Mort's, their regular lunchtime joint. At forty-two, Granville still got a charge from walking the streets of New York. He'd moved east with his battered Minolta more than two decades earlier, when tensions in Oakland were high and getting away was the best hope for talented young Black people.

"I'd say three-and-a-half, maybe four," Lou said. "They nailed the Prokofiev. I've heard the suites many times, but this was magic—so menacing. The Tchaikovsky was a little slow. And *West Side Story*, well, that's been played to death."

Lou Karmitz, music critic for a morning tabloid, often accompanied Sherry and Granville to rehearsals. His appraisals, written in gruff Brooklynese, were watched closely by the New York music world. He had a late afternoon deadline, so lunch wasn't a problem. They entered the bar and chose a table near the back.

"I'm glad we had a little time with Masur before they got started," Granville said. "I think we got some decent shots. His face is so expressive."

"He's like so serene in private and so satanic on the podium," Sherry added.

She and Granville weren't competitors. There was enough demand for both, and over the years they had bonded. The fact that he didn't come on to her made everything easy.

"What'll it be?" Lou asked. "The usual?"

At fifty-four, Lou was getting a little paunchy around the middle. He knew he should work out more, but God how he hated the gym. And these lunches were sacred. He ordered the usual: a Cobb salad for Sherry and porterhouse steaks with onion rings for himself and Granville, with beer all around. That's what they always had at Mort's, ever since they'd first wandered in— when was it? He made a quick calculation.

"I was just thinking," Lou said. "We've been bumming around together for nearly twenty years now. We should organize a little celebration."

"It can't be that long," Sherry said.

"'Fraid so, kid. Even if you don't look any older than the night we first met, at that gallery thing."

"What gallery thing?" Granville asked.

"It was the opening of a photo exhibition," Lou said. "In Soho."

"Seriously? How can I not know this story?"

"Well, Lou and I actually crossed paths earlier," Sherry said. "It was when I'd just come back from France. I was waiting tables at Caffe Dante. Lou and his music friends were regulars, but they never noticed me. I was invisible then."

"You invisible? Don't make me laugh," Lou said. "You looked like a cross between Grace Slick and Janis Joplin. We used to fantasize about you. And then you turn up at that opening..."

"The theme was musicians in concert," Sherry said. "Anouk took me along."

"Yeah, Anouk," Lou said. "She comes up to me and says in that sexy French voice of hers, 'Lou, darling, I'd like you to meet my very dear friend, Sherry. She's a photographer.' And I thought, aha, the waitress from Dante."

"You said something original like, 'Haven't I seen you somewhere before?'"

"I couldn't believe my luck," Lou said. He turned to Granville. "So I took her by the arm and introduced her to a few people. We stayed at the gallery schmoozing until the champagne ran out. Then she seduced me."

"That's his version," Sherry said. "In fact, he invited himself up to my place for a drink."

"That's how I discovered her work. I told her she was too talented to be waiting tables. She had these huge photos from Paris all over the wall. Terrific faces. And this banner with a saying by some French writer."

"André Breton," Sherry said. "The surrealist. He had this theory about crazy love and wrote a phrase to describe it. '*La beauté sera CONVULSIVE ou ne sera pas.*' It's kind of hard to translate. I think he was saying something like, 'Without passion, beauty cannot exist.'"

"Nice," said Granville. "I like that."

"It was her prize possession," Lou said. "Hand-lettered. She said she made it with some artist she knew in Paris."

"With Jacques," Sherry said. "He took me around to museums and introduced me to the surrealists. I got my first look at art photography—you know, Man Ray, Dora Maar..."

"My, my, girl, you do get around," Granville said. "You never mentioned any Jacques."

"You never asked. Anyhow, it wasn't like that. Jacques was very charming and also very married. We weren't lovers. But we became close friends."

"Hey—I was married too, but that didn't stop you," Lou said.

"That was different," Sherry said. "Don't take this badly, but I saw you as an older man."

"What?" Lou said. "I was only thirty-four."

"And I was twenty-four," she said. "The difference seemed huge at the time. You were so sophisticated. You acted like you owned the city. And you and your wife—come on. You both saw other people. We knew it would just be a fling."

"Then I made the mistake of taking her to that club where Jimmy was playing," Lou said. "You remember that night, Granville?"

"How could I forget it?" he replied. "That was the first time we all met."

"Lou was such a sweetheart," Sherry said. "He took me everywhere and introduced me to everyone."

"You were such a wannabe," Lou said.

"I'll just ignore that," Sherry said. She turned to Granville. "Lou can say what he wants, but in fact, he gave me my start. I'll always love him for that."

"Aw, quit it," Lou said. "You're making me blush."

Sherry returned her attention to Granville.

"So one night Lou told me he'd heard about this very young, very hot sax player who had a gig over at Sweet Basil. So we went to check him out, and there you were taking pictures when we arrived."

"I saw you come in with your camera," Granville said, "and I thought, hey, that looks like competition. Better get to know her."

"It was very cool, the way you just asked to join us," Sherry said.

"Well, I wanted to know who you were shooting for."

"And you looked so surprised when I said I didn't know."

"The kid was just getting started," Lou said. "She was taking photos and trying to hawk them wherever she could. Anyhow, we were blown away by Jimmy. He had that special sound. Kind of like Coltrane channeling Eddie Shaw."

"James McCoy Robinson," Granville said. "He was one of a kind."

"When you told us you knew him, I was super impressed," Sherry said.

"Talk about impressed," Granville said. "I couldn't believe I was sitting there with Lou Karmitz, no less. The hottest critic in town. And I thought Jimmy ought to meet him too."

"So you had to go and invite him to join us during the break," Lou said.

Sherry smiled. "That night was the start of so many things."

"And the end of our romance," Lou said. "How could I compete? As soon as Jimmy set eyes on you, I knew I was finished."

Sherry planted a kiss on Lou's cheek.

"You're so finished that we've been sitting here having lunch together for the past twenty years."

"Okay, kid, have it your way. But that ain't romance in my book."

"Jimmy and I—it was the last thing I expected," Sherry said. "But I guess that's the way it always happens."

"You just scooped that boy up," Granville said. "I would have liked to get it together with him myself. But he preferred the ladies."

"You know, being with Jimmy was great while it lasted," Sherry said. "But you—well, I don't want to get all serious and everything, but I just can't imagine not having you as a partner. It's been so much fun. So that night is mainly special for me because it gave me you."

"Now you're making me blush," Granville said. "If I could blush."

Lou called for the check.

"Enough of the love fest," he said. "I gotta go. Time to commit a few words to paper."

Granville turned to Sherry. "Where are you heading?"

"Up to my place to develop the pix," she said. "I need to get the prints over to the magazine tomorrow before catching the train to the island."

"The island?" Lou asked. "You don't mean to tell me you're having a thing with that burned-out writer you met at the barbecue?"

Sherry smiled.

"He's not so burned out."

Chapter 7

Tom was waiting at the station the next evening when Sherry's train pulled in. He greeted her with a kiss.

"What took you so long?" he asked, slinging an arm around her shoulder.

"I was working."

"Me too."

"Writing? That's great, Tom."

They climbed into the Jeep and drove off toward the beach house.

"How's the novel going?" Sherry asked after a while. "Sorry, but I'm dying of curiosity."

"It's taking shape."

"Can you give me a hint?"

He didn't answer, so they rode in silence past the Fort Pond, barely visible in the fading light, and down the coast along the Old Montauk Highway. They could hear the ocean crashing as they approached the beach house. Lights beckoned from inside.

"Smells delicious," Sherry said as they entered. She lifted the lid of a Le Creuset pot. "Spaghetti sauce?"

"Bolognese," Tom said.

He passed a glass of New York merlot across the butcher block.

"So you want a hint…"

"Forget about that. I heard what you said the other night."

"It's a real problem. I'm afraid that talking about the book could jinx me."

"Then don't say anything, Tom. It's all right."

"Here's what I can tell you," he said. "The title. It will be called *The Rights of Man*."

Sherry smiled.

"Very original."

"See? Four little words, and you're already making fun of it."

"Don't be like that," she said. "I know you have a trademark. The question is, what are you putting under that title?"

"Patience, my love. Give me a little more time."

They made small talk over dinner and then took the rest of the wine upstairs. When they climbed into bed, Tom dimmed the lamps and rolled a joint.

"This could be habit-forming," Sherry said as she took a toke.

"Don't believe what you hear about marijuana. It's not like nicotine."

"I wasn't talking about the weed."

"Aha," he said, leaning in to kiss her. "You mean…"

"Uh-huh." She stretched out luxuriantly, looking up at Tom in the lamplight. Beneath his halo of sandy hair, shadows obscured his features, the darkened planes of his face taking on an almost diabolical look. The duality was so intriguing that she wished she'd brought the Pentax.

Tom took another hit of the joint. Sherry looked radiant— seductive and expectant. He stretched out alongside her.

"Now where were we?" he said. "You were telling me about Raphael."

"You want to hear about Raphael…"

Tom smiled. She was interfering with him, and he liked it.

"Ah… yeah," he said.

"Like what he was like in bed?"

"If you want to tell me…"

"Well," Sherry said, "he was French… so… you know…"

"Ah. Like…"

They kissed for a while.

"Any other questions?" Sherry asked as Tom tossed the pillows aside.

"Yes," he said. "More?"

Smiling, she took him in her arms.

"Yes."

Sherry showered and came down wrapped in Tom's terry robe to find him serving up scrambled eggs and toast. He handed her a mug of coffee, and they carried their breakfast out to the deck.

They sat quietly for a moment, listening to the surf crash and recede, content to be in each other's presence. A gentle wind ruffled the dune grasses.

"You know, I think I could stay here with you forever," Tom said.

"That's so romantic, Tom. But we're still just discovering each other."

"And that's the best part. Sherry, I love your stories. They're— well, they're delectable. Delectable and delightsome."

"Delightsome? You're just trying to get me to tell you another one."

"Will you?" he asked.

"For a price."

"Name it."

"One kiss."

Tom ambled over to Sherry's side of the picnic table and straddled the bench. Her lips were warm against his in the morning sun.

Hand in hand, they moved to the chaises longues and stretched out side by side.

"I met your price," Tom said. "Now let's see. When we left off, you and Raphael were doing French things together in bed…"

"Tom—last night was fabulous…"

"It was, my love. But you're stalling. Tell me about Raphael."

"I already told you," she said. "He was on the road all the time and I got tired of it, so I wished him well and went home to New York. He lives in Israel now, with his family."

"Didn't you miss him?"

"Not really," she said. "I started meeting a lot of men. Mainly musicians."

"Musicians like who?"

"Isn't it your turn now?"

"Nope. Still your turn," he said.

Sherry felt too good to object. Besides, she thought, if Tom wanted to hear about her former lovers, she could play that game.

"Well, there was Jimmy," she said, lingering over the name. "He was fantastic in bed…"

"I think I'm jealous. What did he do when you weren't in bed?"

"He'd get out his saxophone."

"A sax player. Now I'm really jealous."

"So young, and he played like an angel…"

"What did he look like?" Tom said. "Describe him."

"He was beautiful—like an African prince. He'd get this far-away look when he played, no matter where he was. He could be in a club, but the world was elsewhere. He dipped down into his soul, and the music came out through his fingers."

"Hang on," Tom said. "He was young, he was Black, he played the sax in clubs, and his name was Jimmy? You're not talking about James McCoy Robinson?"

"Actually, yes."

"You had an affair with him?"

"We saw each other for a while. It was a long time ago."

"What was that like, dating a Black guy?" Tom asked.

"He took me into his world," Sherry said, "up to Harlem to meet his family. He was the oldest son, and the younger kids looked up to him. We'd take them to church on Sunday mornings. There was this gospel choir raising the roof, with everyone singing along. It was incredibly powerful—so joyous. Then we'd go back to his place, and he'd play for me…"

"How'd his folks take it when he brought a white girl home?"

"They were warm people—they treated me well—but they warned us things wouldn't be easy," Sherry said. "You know, you read about the problems Blacks face in America, the legacy of slavery and all that, but it's impersonal. Spending time with Jimmy's family opened my eyes. They had, like, this sense that the doors that were closed to them would never open. That's why, when Jimmy started to make it as a musician, his parents told him not to get his hopes up. He'd opened a door, but they already saw it slamming shut. It was, you know, a defeatist psychology, bowing down to what they saw as inevitability, but it wasn't their fault. I don't know how many generations we'll need to get past that."

"James Robinson didn't bow down to anyone, as far as I know."

"Well, he left the States. He lives in Switzerland now."

"Yeah, so I heard."

"Jimmy said it was easier being Black in Europe, where people didn't have the same prejudices," she said. "Not that there isn't racism in Europe. But Jimmy said Europeans saw him first and foremost as an American, and that was a revelation. For the first time in his life, he was identified by his nationality, not by his color. It was like a liberation from history."

"But isn't it sort of a cop-out for an American jazzman to move abroad?"

"Well, Jimmy was hardly the first. Look at all the American Blacks who went to Europe seeking exactly that kind of liberation. Bud Powell, Dexter Gordon. And of course, Miles Davis fell in love with Paris. He went back again and again. And it wasn't just musicians. James Baldwin and Richard Wright moved to Paris. They needed the distance from America to get in touch with their anger and write about it. And just like Jimmy, they found a kind of respect they couldn't get back home."

"Weren't you tempted to go join him?"

"Jimmy fell in love over there, Tom. When we'd been together about a year, he got invited to the Montreux Jazz Festival. He wanted me to come, but I had to work. One day, he phoned to tell me he'd met a woman. I could tell from his voice—it was over."

"And you just let him go without a fight?"

"What could I do?" Sherry said. "She was a French jazz singer, and she was gorgeous. I looked her up in the photo files at *Musiques*. Jimmy said he was sorry, but he never came back. Now they've got three kids and a house on Lake Geneva. And you know? I'm happy for him. Which is not to say I wasn't brokenhearted. For a while…"

"Do you stay in touch?"

"He gives me a call from time to time. All my exes do."

"So I should be jealous."

"Should you?" Sherry asked. "Or should I? After all, it's Friday. Are you heading back to the city? We could take the same train."

"No, my love, that won't work," Tom said evenly. "Jessica's joining me here with a couple of friends."

Sherry felt her face flush.

"Jessica? I thought you were hardly on speaking terms."

"It's her house, too. I can't stop her from coming."

"I guess," she said. "It just makes me feel funny to think of her sharing your bed."

"Ain't happening."

Sherry said nothing. She did feel jealous, she realized with dismay.

Tom tried to gauge her reaction, but Sherry's face was a mask. Her eyes were following a pair of gulls swooping high over the house.

"Hello?" he said. "Earth to Mars…"

She glanced at him, then back at the sky.

"Your turn," she said.

"I really don't have many stories," Tom said. "It's different for you. You're out having adventures, living your life, while I'm sitting at my typewriter, living in my imagination."

"That is such horseshit," Sherry said. "I'm nobody special. You're the famous writer. You're full of stories."

"It's just that you're so sexy I always get sidetracked," he said, adding hopefully, "Want to go back to bed?"

"No way."

"Okay then. But I need help. Ask a question."

"Sure," she said. "But it's a tough one."

"Uh-oh."

"You and Jessica have been together for more than twenty years, right?"

"Right."

"Why didn't you ever have children?"

"Yeah, that is a tough one," Tom said. "We talked about it early on. We both wanted to have a family, but we were young. Then our careers took off, and we put that on hold. And then I stopped writing, and our sex life went on the rocks. So nothing happened."

"How does Jessica deal with that? Does she still want a family?"

"I don't think she cares anymore. She used to. She went to get a fertility test before I moved out of the bedroom. When it was normal, she asked me to get tested too."

"Did you?"

"No. I didn't want to. I just figured nature would take its course. But it didn't."

"That's funny," Sherry said.

"What's funny?"

"No, I mean it's odd because I can picture you so easily as a father."

"Well, I'm not," Tom said, "and to tell you the truth, I think it has something to do with creative energy. You know? The way writers get so absorbed in their work that there's not enough juice left over for other forms of creation. That's what I tell myself, anyway, when I'm feeling down about it."

"Oh. Sorry, I didn't realize," Sherry said.

"And you," Tom ventured. "Don't you want children?"

"It's a little late now. I don't even want to think about it."

The conversation had rambled beyond Sherry's comfort zone. Making an excuse, she went upstairs and dressed quickly.

They made small talk on the way to the station.

"When will I see you?" Tom asked as they pulled up.

"I don't know," she said.

A light kiss, and she was off.

Watching the trees flit by as her train rumbled toward the city, Sherry tried to suppress the thought of Tom and Jessica together at the house she'd just vacated. But doubts kept surging up. She'd seen photos of Jessica from Tom's glory days—a beautiful woman. The idea of Tom even touching Jessica made her cringe.

Trying to steady her nerves, Sherry formed a mental picture of the beach house. There were two extra rooms upstairs: a guest room, presumably for their friends, and Tom's study with what looked like a sofa bed. For Jessica, she hoped. But the closer her train got to Manhattan, the worse she felt. She wondered how she'd make it through the weekend.

Back home, Tom hastily straightened the house, changing the sheets and giving the bathroom and kitchen a quick once-over. As he moved from room to room, he could feel Sherry's presence. Spending the weekend with Jessica felt too much to bear.

But he couldn't lie to himself. If Jessica was resentful, he was the cause of it. Their life had been on an upward track before his writing problems set in. Remembering Jessica's charm back then, her pride in him as he conquered the world, he felt a pang of remorse. She'd stood by him, believing in his talent even while he floundered. She'd stood by him for years, even when he lost his ability to satisfy her in bed. He still felt ashamed about that. Well, she'd clearly lost her esteem for him now, and he'd moved on. With Sherry, he'd proved to himself that he could still be a capable lover. The problem was that Jessica's opinion still mattered. He couldn't shake the need to prove to her that he could still be a capable writer...

Pull it together, Tom chided himself. He ran the kitchen tap, splashed cold water on his face, filled a glass, and drained it. He still had several hours alone in the house, and he intended to use them. He fetched the Olympia, carried it out to the deck, and sat down to write.

Late afternoon shadows were slanting across the dunes when Jessica's hatchback crunched up the gravel drive. Out bounded Che, followed by Marilyn and Steve.

Tom had been writing for hours—he hadn't felt the time slip by. Startled, he grabbed his manuscript and hurried inside to stash it. The deck's screen door banged shut behind him.

"Nice welcome," Jessica said as Tom re-emerged. She brushed past him carrying an overstuffed brown paper bag of food from the local market stand.

Steve and Marilyn were unloading the hatchback.

"Here, let me give you a hand," Tom said, striding across the deck to help them with the travel bags.

"Hey, man," Steve said, sweeping his gaze across the dune to the ocean. "This is such a great place. No wonder you spend so much time out here."

"I guess he's been writing," Marilyn said. "Look, there's his typewriter."

Tom held the screen door open, and they took the bags inside.

"Let's have some beers," he said. "Then we can stoke up the barbecue."

"Great idea," Steve said. "It was hotter than hell on the road."

Jessica tossed her shoes into a corner by the fireplace.

"Count me out," she said. "I'm taking Che for a run."

Before anyone could object, she was gone, jogging barefoot to the shore as the pooch darted ahead, prancing and leaping in the joy of the open air.

"Don't mind Jess," Tom said. "She's not really into hospitality these days."

"Yeah, we noticed," Steve said. "What's going on with you two? That dinner the other night was just insane."

"We were afraid you might come to blows," Marilyn said.

Tom winced.

"Only verbal blows," he said, handing them each a beer.

As they settled into deck chairs to enjoy the sunset, Tom wondered how much to confide. This weekend by the shore had been planned long ago. He hoped it would go smoothly. Yet he felt the need to open up—and Steve and Marilyn wouldn't take sides.

"The other night, after you left," he said, "Jessica called me a loser. That's how bad things are. As far as she's concerned, I'm just a commodity. If I'm not producing books, I lose my value."

"She loves you, Tommy," Marilyn said.

"No way. That light went out long ago."

"Then why are you still together?" Steve asked.

"We're not. We've been living apart for a year."

"We thought that was so you could write," Marilyn said.

"That's what we tell people."

"Well, that sounds kind of crazy," Steve said. "I mean, we love the both of you and we wish you could work it out, but if your marriage is over, why don't you get a divorce?"

Swallows were flitting across a lavender sky as the dusk deepened.

"One explanation might be that Jessica doesn't want to lose the material comforts we've acquired," Tom said. "Our place in the Village, and the house out here. The fine wines, the two cars, the designer clothes—all the perks of being the wife of a best-selling author. If we divorced, she'd have to start life all over again, and it might be a very different kind of life. I think she's afraid of that—otherwise, she would have packed up and found another guy by now."

He got up to light the barbecue.

"A less cynical answer," he said, "is that we both still need each other in an odd way. But Jessica's been so difficult lately, I don't know how much more I can take."

"Careful—here she comes," Marilyn said.

Jessica jogged up to the deck and tore off the navy bandana she'd tied around her head as a sweatband. She sank onto a chaise longue.

"Were you talking about me?" she said, accepting the beer Steve handed her. "I'm sure that must have been fascinating."

"You're always fascinating, Jess," Steve said.

Che dashed from Tom to Jessica and back, wagging his tail and sniffing the deck to rediscover the familiar scents. He found his water dish and lapped noisily.

"What's going on with the barbecue?" Jessica asked. "Don't tell me you're just getting started. Tom, go put some water on for the corn." She turned to Marilyn. "I have to tell him everything. He's totally out to lunch, wasting his time out here."

"I'm not wasting my time, Jess," Tom said, allowing himself an inner smile at the thought of Sherry. He rose and went in to deal with the corn.

"Yeah?" Jessica called after him. "Well, you used to be somebody. Somebody very special. And now who are you?"

She turned to her guests.

"He can't even manage to get dinner on the table. It'll be dark before we eat."

"Hey, Jess, ease up," Steve said. "We're out here to relax, remember? Who cares if it's dark when we eat?"

Chapter 8

Jessica was sipping coffee on the sun-splashed deck when Tom came down. The pot was empty, so he started a fresh one.

"Want some breakfast?" he called through the screen door.

"You know I don't eat breakfast," Jessica said.

Tom stepped outside.

"Hey, Jess," he said. "Don't use that tone with me."

"What are you going to do? Divorce me?"

"I might," Tom said mildly, "if this continues…"

"Well, go ahead. I'm tired of spending my life with a has-been."

Jessica studied her fingernails, fully expecting Tom to slink back into the kitchen. She knew how defensive he felt about his career. But when she looked up, he was still standing there, surprisingly unruffled.

"And what about when your has-been makes a comeback?" he asked.

"Don't fuck with me, Tom. I know you're not writing."

"Do you think I had my typewriter out just for show?"

"Probably. You are indeed the master of invention."

"Actually, you're wrong," Tom said. "I'm onto something, and it's going to make waves. I can feel it."

He went back into the kitchen and cracked a couple of eggs into a bowl. What a difference a day makes, he thought, remembering his morning with Sherry.

Jessica followed him into the house.

"Okay, big guy," she said. "If you've started writing, then prove it."

Tom weighed his options, but not for long.

"Excuse me," he said, going upstairs to his study.

When he came back down, he handed her a couple of pages. Jessica scanned them quickly.

"All right. And you're calling this *The Rights of Man*?"

"That's the idea."

"Wasn't that Tom Paine's book about the French Revolution?"

"Yup."

"From what I can see in two pages, it's more like *The Rites of Man*. R-I-T-E-S."

"Interesting," Tom said. "But that would mean tweaking the Tom Paine gimmick."

"So what?" she said. "You're not Tom Paine, you're Thomas G. Paine, and you can do whatever you want. It's perfectly legitimate. I like it."

Tom turned away and busied himself with the eggs. Unless he'd misunderstood something, he'd just received Jessica's stamp of approval. And her new take on the title was intriguing enough to consider.

"So you've finally put pen to paper," she said, joining him at the butcher block as he scrambled the eggs. "I thought you were shitting me."

"No, this is the real thing."

"Well, that's a different story. Maybe I'll join you for breakfast after all."

"Okay," he said. "We can share."

Tom poured two fresh cups of coffee and divided the eggs.

"By the way, I just might pick up your title idea," he said as they carried their plates outdoors. "I appreciate it, Jess. It's not the first time you've inspired me."

She glanced at him over her coffee.

"I know," she said.

⌀

It was going on noon when the four of them trooped down to the shore, armed with beach umbrellas and huge, bright towels. Che romped ahead, scampering back to run circles around them, herding them toward the water.

"Looks like your poodle must have some sheepdog in him," Steve said.

Tom laughed.

"I always knew the dog was a mutt," he said.

"He's pure poodle," Jessica protested. "I've got the breeder's certificate. Tell them, Tom."

"Yeah," he said, "the mutt's a purebred."

He grinned at Jessica. Steve and Marilyn exchanged a glance.

"Well, how about that," Steve said. "Looks like everyone's in a better mood this morning."

They found a spot beneath the dunes, up the beach from the waterline. At the height of vacation season, the shore was overspilling with families. High-pitched shrieks filled the air as children dashed in and out of the waves.

This was Tom's least favorite time of year on the island. He preferred empty stretches of sand where he could roam and think. But today it didn't bother him—the tumult, the crowds. He was feeling surprisingly great.

"Come on, Steve," Tom said when they'd unfurled the parasols and arranged their towels. "Let's see if Che remembers how to play frisbee."

The two men jogged off, and at the sight of the frisbee, Che sprang to follow. Soon he was racing up and down the beach, leaping to snatch the flying saucer from the air, then trotting it back to Tom or Steve.

Jessica peered over the cover of her paperback to watch them play. She was wearing oversized sunglasses and a striped beach hat over her dramatically cut black one-piece. Tossing the hat aside, she jumped to her feet.

"Why should boys have all the fun? Come on," she said, spraying sand on Marilyn as she ran off to join them.

Marilyn adjusted her polka-dot bikini and made her way across the sand. She was hardly an ace at frisbee, but she was game. When Che dropped the plastic disk at her feet, she picked it up, straightened her Mets cap, and let it fly. Tom caught it and flung it back to Jessica, who grabbed it, laughing, and tossed it back.

Steve and Marilyn tried to intercept, but Tom and Jessica kept control of the disk, flinging it back and forth as Che raced between them.

"Hey, you two," Steve called out. "This is a foursome, not a twosome."

"Yeah, that's cheating," Marilyn said.

"Yeah?" Tom said as he captured the frisbee. He glared at Marilyn. "Nobody calls me a cheat."

Throwing the frisbee into the waves for Che to retrieve, he strode off toward the house.

The living room was dark when Tom came in from the noon-time brightness, and it took him a moment to see clearly. He felt abashed for losing his cool in front of his friends. Maybe he was cheating, even if he and his wife were estranged. But being with Sherry didn't feel like cheating. It felt like his life was finally back on track. So why did he feel so hot and bothered?

Pull it together, he again admonished himself.

He looked out the screen door to see if anyone had followed him back. The coast was clear. Picking up the phone, he dialed Sherry's number.

The line was busy.

He waited five minutes and tried again. Still busy.

Who can she be talking to, he wondered.

About to dial a third time, he hung up as he heard the others arriving. They came in noisily, chatting and making as though nothing had happened.

❧

Sherry had been on the phone for half an hour. Before it rang, she'd been turning in circles in her apartment, unable to work. When the bell jangled, she didn't pick up, fearing it might be Tom. Damn straight she wouldn't talk to him while he was out there cavorting with his wife. But when the answering machine clicked on, the French-accented voice that came through most certainly wasn't Tom's. She snatched up the phone.

"Jacques? I'm here," she said.

"Sherry—I thought I'd missed you," Jacques said, his voice crackling across the transatlantic line.

The way he said her name still charmed her: "*Chérie*," French for "darling."

"No, I'm here," she repeated, seeing her friend in her mind's eye—his tousled black hair, his ironic smile, his artist's gaze.

She curled up on the couch, relieved to have someone she trusted to talk to. Although she and Jacques hadn't crossed paths in the twenty years since she left Paris, they'd stayed in touch by phone, and their intimacy had grown with the passage of time. Every so often, he sent her a postcard-sized painting with a message scrawled on the back. She replied with a postcard-sized photo, usually of a musician. He'd followed her career with interest, proud of his small role in setting her on her path. He also liked to follow her love life.

"Can you talk?" Jacques asked. "Are you alone?"

"Yes. I mean, no. I'm home alone with Max, but I'm not alone, if you see what I mean."

Jacques laughed warmly down the phone line.

"I know you too well, Sherry. You mean you have a new man in your life, *n'est-ce pas?*"

"Sort of," she said. "It's complicated."

"Meaning?"

"He has a wife. They're separated, but they're still married."

"*Ooh-là*. But are you in love?"

"I don't know," Sherry said, although the thought of Tom made her pulse race. "I've been telling myself it's just a fling, but it may be more."

"So you're giving your heart to another man. I don't know how I feel about that."

Sherry smiled into the phone. Flirting was part of their routine.

"Part of my heart will always belong to you, and you know it. But please don't joke with me now. I can't take it. I'm too confused."

"Ah yes—men. We are very confusing creatures."

"Stop teasing and help me. You're married. What goes on in a married man's mind when he's seeing another woman?"

"That is a very delicate question," Jacques said. "As if I should know…"

"I know, I know. You and Sophie don't fool around. How is she, by the way?"

"She's away for the summer. In Provence, with her sister. But getting back to your question, I would say it depends on the situation. Do they have children?"

"No."

"Does he still love her?"

"No. I don't think so."

"Then it is very dangerous," he said. "Imagine. He meets you and finds you attractive. When he makes love to you, his heart goes boom. Passion takes over. He cannot be rational. He doesn't want to be rational. All he wants is to experience your touch, your taste, your kiss, over and over again. He is crazy about you, and he is thinking, 'What can I do to keep her with me?' But he also has feelings for his wife. He doesn't want to hurt her."

"You sound like you know a lot about this. Is something going on?"

Jacques paused.

"Let's just say that Sophie and I have traveled a long road together, and it's only natural that we might want to explore other possibilities from time to time."

"You're kidding. Are you saying you have an open marriage now?"

"It's best not to define it," Jacques said. "Sophie has wandered, and I've, let's say, allowed myself to be tempted. But I still love her…"

The tremor in his voice gave Sherry pause as compassion took over. Was he calling to talk about his own heartache? She'd been too self-obsessed to realize.

"Then I'm sure you'll work it out," she said. "Just give it time."

"And that's my advice for you, precisely."

"I wish you were here now. We could go out for a beer and laugh about this together."

"Be careful," Jacques said. "I might take the next plane to New York."

"Or I could come over to Paris…"

"That's a pleasant thought. Could you?"

"In my fantasy life, maybe," Sherry said. "But in real life, I'm going out to Aspen for the music festival in August, and I can't leave now. I can't leave Tom."

"Tom? Is that his name?"

"Yes," she said. "Tom Paine."

Tom's little outburst went unmentioned throughout the day, and by evening it had been forgotten. During the afternoon, they'd all trooped over to the seafood joint down the road to buy some steamers. When the clams were ready, they took everything out to the deck.

"You'll never guess what I saw today," Jessica said as Tom poured the wine.

"Uh—a shark?" Steve asked.

"Bigger than a shark," Jessica said.

"What—a whale?" Marilyn asked.

"You're on the wrong track," Jessica said. "Think big as in bestseller."

"Quit it," Tom said.

"No—spill," Steve said.

"Well," Jessica said, "you know how Tom kept saying he'd started a novel and I didn't believe him? He showed me the manuscript this morning. It's a winner."

"She only saw two pages," Tom said.

"Doesn't matter," Jessica said. "I can tell in the first few paragraphs if a writer is faking it. My nose starts to twitch—I call it my bullshit detector. Well, it didn't happen."

For the first time in longer than he could remember, Tom let himself feel good in Jessica's gaze.

"Thanks, Jess," he said.

"Just keep writing," she said.

After dinner, the men offered to do the dishes, but Jessica sent them back out to the deck.

"Here," she said, handing Marilyn a dish towel. "I'll wash, you dry."

Marilyn was dying of curiosity, but she didn't want to get too personal—that could backfire. And the men were right outside the screen door. She spoke softly, hoping the running water would muffle the conversation.

"I'm so glad to see you and Tommy getting along together again. Things were so tense last night I thought you two were finished."

"Appearances can be deceiving," Jessica said.

"It wasn't just appearances. Tom told us you'd called him a loser."

"Well, he won't be when this book comes out."

Intrigued by Jessica's breeziness, Marilyn switched tacks.

"What got Tom started writing again?" she asked.

"I don't know. He refuses to talk about it. But you know, it's not just the writing. He's been useless for so long, and now he seems to be back. Like a different man..."

During the night, Marilyn stirred in bed, then woke. She nudged Steve.

"Listen," she said. "Do you hear anything?"

From the bedroom next door came the sound of rhythmic creaking—or was it just the wind against the shutters?

Chapter 9

Tom helped carry the bags out to Jessica's car. Che bounded into the rear and Steve settled in beside him, with Marilyn up front. It was early Sunday afternoon, and they were heading back to the city, hoping to beat the inevitable traffic jam.

Tom opened the door to the driver's seat for Jessica.

"It's been a good weekend," he said.

"Wait a second," she said. "I forgot my toothbrush."

Jessica ducked back into the house. Her toothbrush was where she'd left it, on the edge of the bathroom sink. But as she popped it into her bag, something caught her eye. There, in the plastic cup behind Tom's green toothbrush, was another one. A pale blue one.

She picked it up. Was that son-of-a-bitch cheating on her?

She took a moment to collect her thoughts. Should she confront him? No, he didn't need to know she knew. But if he was two-timing her...

Joe Reilly flashed through her mind—Joe, running a hand through his hair as he checked her out. He'd been coming on to her for months...

She stuck the offending toothbrush back in the cup and went downstairs.

"Be careful on the road," Tom said as she slipped into the driver's seat.

Jessica banged the door shut.

"You be careful," she said, curtly enough for Tom to wonder what she meant. She revved the motor, spraying gravel as she pulled out of the drive. Steve and Marilyn waved from the back seat, and they were off.

Tom watched until they were out of sight. He had plenty of time, but somehow he didn't feel like writing. He went inside and tidied the house. He made himself a cup of tea. Finally, he took the Olympia out to the deck and inserted a clean page.

He typed a few words. Stopped. Typed a few more. He stared into space.

"Shit," he said, tearing the page off the roller and crumpling it into a ball.

He inserted a fresh page and stared at it.

Nothing.

He got up and paced the deck, hoping that inspiration would come. Sat down again. Watched the gulls swoop above.

By late afternoon, the deck was strewn with balls of crumpled paper. Tom was still sitting at his typewriter, facing a blank page.

Sherry was having dinner with her parents at their place on the Upper East Side. It was a Sunday tradition: her dad in his Eames chair watching the news when she arrived, her mom sitting down at the baby grand after dessert.

Rose waited until the food was on the table to dive into her favorite subject.

"So what's new in your life, dear?" she said. "You're looking great—so suntanned. Have you been to the beach?"

"I've got a friend on the island, so I've been spending some time out there," Sherry said. She hadn't told her parents about Tom.

"A man friend?" Rose's eyes lit up. "Bernie, Sherry's got a boyfriend. Here, have some chicken. Who is he? When can we meet him?"

"We're just friends," Sherry said. The last thing she needed was her parents on her back about her clandestine affair.

"Anyway, he doesn't come into town," she lied.

She'd been distracted all evening by the phone call she got

from Tom just as she was leaving for dinner. He was coming into Manhattan in the morning and wanted her to meet him at noon in Central Park. That was odd in itself—he never came into town on weekdays as far as she knew—and his voice sounded strained.

"Doesn't come into town?" Bernie said. "What is he, a beach bum?"

"Don't mind him," Rose said. "He's been grouchy since the game ended."

"The Yanks got their asses whipped by the fuckin' Brewers," Bernie said. "Two runs in the second and it was all over. Couldn't do any better than that. They lost, three to two. To Milwaukee, for Christ's sake."

"Sorry, Dad," Sherry said. "I thought the Yankees were having a good season."

"Yeah, the bums are at the top of the standings. But then they go and let a rinky-dink team like the Brewers walk all over them. It's humiliating."

"Well, you know what you always say," Sherry said. "It ain't over till it's over."

She brushed her mouth with her napkin and stood up.

"I've got an early start tomorrow," she said. "Thanks for dinner, Mom."

"Leaving already?" Rose said. "But I made apple strudel. And you haven't told us about your friend."

Sherry's eyes flashed a warning, but Rose ignored it.

"Okay, so you don't want to tell us about him," she said. "That's all right, dear. But if this fish looks like a keeper, don't let him get away. Remember, you're not getting any younger. And we still want grandchildren. Don't we, Bernie?"

"Aw, give the kid a break," Bernie said.

He walked Sherry to the door and gave his daughter a hug.

"Don't mind your mother. So long, kid."

Chapter 10

Murray Thompson, trim and balding, looked up from his reading and beamed.

"You're back!" he said, setting aside a sheaf of typewritten pages.

For seven years, as the literary agent of Thomas G. Paine, he'd been waiting for something new. Now Tom was sitting across from him in his book-lined midtown office.

"Not so fast," Tom said. "I've only written a couple of chapters."

He'd been facing Murray for twenty minutes, long enough to get into a state of nerves.

"I wouldn't worry about that," Murray said. "Just keep going."

He was fond of Tom. Over the years, their agent-client relationship had morphed into a friendship. They'd socialized during Tom's heyday, attending literary events with their wives and going on as a foursome to dinner. They'd stayed in touch during Tom's protracted dry spell, playing tennis from time to time or going out for drinks and talking about the writing life. He'd encouraged Tom to keep at it, while secretly fearing the hiatus might never end.

"Murray—what if I can't keep going?" Tom asked. "I kind of hit a wall yesterday. That's why I wanted to see you."

Murray peered at Tom over his reading glasses.

"After you called last night, I phoned Helen," he said.

Helen Nussbaum, Tom's editor.

"We're seeing her at four o'clock. She won't want to hear about any walls."

"Jesus, Murray—it's too early," Tom said. "Helen hasn't seen the manuscript yet."

"She'll have read it by the time you arrive. I'm meeting her for lunch, and I'll hand it to her. She's going to love it."

He checked his watch.

"In fact, we'd better get going, or I'll be late."

They rode the elevator down in silence.

"I think you're missing my point," Tom said, nodding at the doorman as they exited onto the street. "This is a very unusual book. I'm not sure I can pull it off."

"Sure you can," Murray said affably. "Where are you heading?"

"Uptown."

"Then we can't share a cab."

Murray raised his arm to hail one. Yellow taxis were streaming past, but they all seemed to be taken.

"I'm not even sure my friends will like it," Tom said. "Or my wife."

"Jessica?" Murray said. "If the book makes money, she'll like it."

A free cab drew up, and he ducked inside.

"See you at Fitzgerald & Fitzgerald," he said. "Four o'clock. Don't be late."

Tom walked along 48th to Madison, stopping on impulse at a flower stand. He took a cab uptown and was waiting by the tennis courts at noon when Sherry arrived, flushed from jogging to the park. She was wearing a striped tank top and shorts.

Tom handed her a long-stemmed red rose.

"My, my," Sherry said. "What's the occasion?"

She kissed him on the cheek.

"More," he said, taking her in his arms.

"Tom," Sherry said. "We're in public."

But as they kissed, the joggers in the park didn't give them a second glance.

Sherry had more than a few questions for Tom about his weekend with Jessica, but she didn't want to rush it. She led him to a bench. Players were lobbing balls back and forth across the courts.

"You know, I could have come out to the island later," she said. "What's so important it couldn't wait?"

"I just needed to see you. Call it an animal urge."

This wasn't like Tom, Sherry thought. He was usually so controlled about his comings and goings.

"And?" she asked.

"Actually, I've just seen my agent."

"That's excellent, Tom. Did you show him your work?"

"Yeah. He seemed to like it."

"Fantastic. I'm happy for you," she said.

"I'm too nervous to be happy. We're meeting my editor at four."

"Oh, I get it. You're here because you need to kill time."

"As if…" he said.

"As if what?"

"As if anything could stop me from seeing you when I get a chance."

They embraced in the doorway of Sherry's apartment as if they'd been apart for weeks, not days. Then Sherry ushered Tom in and went to put her rose in water.

While she was busy, Tom approached the wall of photos for a fresh look. He returned to the photo of Sherry posing nude on a couch, then scanned the wall as if hunting for something. When Sherry joined him, he was examining a shot of a striking young man in an Afro, an alto sax tucked under one arm.

"Is this Jimmy?" he asked.

"Bingo," she said.

Tom ambled over to a large portrait of a violinist.

"And who's the fiddler?" he asked.

"That's no fiddler—he's a virtuoso. It's Jerzy Gregorski. Don't you recognize him? Of course, he was younger then…"

Her tone caught Tom's attention.

"Just how well did you know him?" he asked.

"We were close for a while," Sherry said.

"What? Have you been involved with every musician on this wall?"

"Not all of them…"

Tom clasped her shoulder possessively.

"Let's go to bed," he said.

Sherry led him to her room. A satin quilt lay across her bed. Above the headboard stretched her banner with the words by André Breton: "*La beauté sera CONVULSIVE ou ne sera pas.*"

Tom ran his hand over the quilt, silky under his touch.

"I want to look at you, my love," he said. "Pose for me like you did in that photo."

They helped each other strip, and Tom watched as Sherry arranged herself on the bed, propping herself on one elbow, camping the artist's model. She pulled the quilt vaguely over her loins, her cinnamon tan interrupted only by the two pale triangles at her breast where her bikini had blocked the sun.

Through the open window, the muffled roar of traffic rushed into the room, ebbing and flowing like waves.

Tom pushed aside the quilt, revealing a third pale triangle.

"Lie down, my love," he said.

Dressed in a flowered kimono, her hair still wild, Sherry slipped a disk into her CD player and turned up the volume. Tom was in the shower, and she wanted him to hear it.

She was in the kitchen, wondering how she'd broach the subject of his weekend with Jessica, when he emerged looking relaxed and happy, a towel wrapped around his waist.

She felt a pang when she saw him—him and his Kirk Douglas smile. Don't fall in love, she warned herself, although her body was still humming.

"This music," Tom said. "Pretty magnificent. What is it?"

"It's Bach," Sherry said. "The Chaconne in D Minor for solo violin."

"And the violinist is, ah, your friend?"

"Yes. It's what Jerzy was playing the first time I saw him."

"And when was that?"

"It was at Tanglewood in 1980. The Boston Symphony was rehearsing in the Shed one morning. We went in to take a look, and Jerzy was playing the solo. To die for."

"I can see why you fell for him," Tom said. "I just don't like the idea of sharing you."

Sherry thought about that while Tom dressed. His possessiveness was absurd under the circumstances. The time had come to have it out with him.

She found some Brie and a bottle of white in the fridge. When Tom joined her in the dining nook, he poured the wine and touched glasses with her.

"You've been around, my love," he said. "I'm lucky to have you."

"While it lasts…"

"Don't talk like that," Tom said. "We're just getting started. Of course, it'll last."

Piqued by his nonchalance, Sherry looked at him pointedly.

"You have a wife, Tom," she said. "You just spent the weekend with her."

A shadow crossed Tom's eyes.

"Don't let this become a problem. It doesn't matter that she came out for the weekend. Jessica—"

Sherry cut him off. "It matters to me. I wish it didn't, but it does. You said you didn't want to share me. Well, the more time we spend together, the less I want to share you."

Surprised at her tone, Tom took a moment to consider his reply.

"We've never really had this conversation, so let's have it," he said.

"Yes, let's. There are three of us in this relationship. I think I deserve to know what's going on."

"There's something you need to understand," Tom said. "I know it may be hard, but please try. Meeting you, getting to know you, is the best thing that's happened to me in years. Suddenly everything's coming together. But I'm indebted to Jessica. I owe my career to her."

"That's nonsense," Sherry said. "You created your career."

"No, not entirely. When I was struggling to make it as a writer, Jessica worked to support me. She was the breadwinner. She never let me down. And during all that time, she believed in me. In fact, I think she still does."

"That's pretty ironic, given that you're deceiving her."

Tom chose to ignore the barb.

"I've been going through a rough patch, and it took a toll on the marriage," he said. "And now you're in my life. But I can't just walk out on her. It's not that easy."

"I'm not asking you to divorce her, Tom, if that's what you think."

"And I'm not saying I'll never divorce her. But I need time to work things out. Please be patient."

Sherry looked away. She had known from the start that Tom was married, even if he'd been living alone for a year. She had not only accepted the limits to their relationship—she'd welcomed them. But now, as their attachment grew stronger, she felt the need to protect herself, to create some distance. Yet every time they were apart, she ached for him.

"What are you thinking?" Tom asked. "Speak to me."

The question hung in the air as Sherry wrestled with her feelings. It wasn't a moral dilemma about being involved with a married man. The sexual revolution had seen to that: the notion of one person as another's property for life had been rejected by an entire free-thinking swath of her generation. The issue was rather whether the situation was wrong for her.

Telling herself she could change her mind later, she forced a smile.

"I'll try to be patient," she said.

"Good," Tom said fervently.

As he lifted her hand to his lips, his eye fell on his watch.

"Shit, I'd better go." It would take him half an hour to get to Fitzgerald & Fitzgerald, and Helen Nussbaum didn't like to be kept waiting.

Feeling drained by the conversation, Sherry accompanied him to the door. She needed some time alone, she realized.

"When will I see you, my love?" Tom asked. "Can you come out tomorrow?"

"Not tomorrow. I have to shoot a concert."

"Then when?"

"Maybe Wednesday."

"It's a date," Tom said.

Helen Nussbaum was waiting with Murray when Tom arrived at her office. She was a formidable woman—tough, smart, with the face of a bulldog and a personality to match. Tom's manuscript lay on her desk.

As he took a seat, Helen lifted the title page and frowned.

"*The Rites of Man?*" she said. "R-I-T-E-S? You're taking a risk with this title."

Tom didn't let her frown worry him. He had never seen her smile.

"It feels right," he said. "Have you had time to take a look?"

"She read it, Tom," Murray said.

"Twice," Helen said. "It's very—original."

"Well, it's been seven years," Tom replied. "I thought I could try something new."

He steeled himself for her verdict.

"You thought right," Helen said.

"You like it?"

"Wait till the public gets hold of this," she said.

Tom broke into a grin.

"You like it," he said.

"You bet I do. Perfectly in tune with the times."

"What did I tell you?" Murray said.

Helen passed the manuscript over to Tom.

"How soon can you finish?" she asked.

"I don't know. It's going pretty quickly now."

"Keep going," Helen said. "If you can get me a draft by the end of summer, we can polish it up and crash it into print in time for Christmas."

Tom felt a rush of elation.

"I'll try," he said.

"Good," she said. "And Tom—don't show it to anyone. People will be curious when they hear you're making a comeback. We need to make the most of that. Let's keep this under wraps."

Tom left Murray and Helen chatting about the advance. Back on the street, he headed for the nearest phone booth. When Jessica didn't answer at home, he tried her at the *Voice*.

"Have dinner with me tonight," he said when she picked up. "I'm in town, and I've got news."

"Really?" Jessica said. "I thought you were busy writing."

Joe Reilly was standing beside her desk, a question in his eyes. She covered the receiver and mouthed a word: "Tom."

"I just left Fitzgerald & Fitzgerald," Tom said. "I saw Helen."

"And?"

"I'll tell you over dinner."

"Sorry, I can't do dinner tonight," Jessica said. "I'm tied up at the paper. Tell me now."

"At the paper? All evening?"

"Don't give me a hard time, Tom. We're trying to get the special edition together. Joe, ah, wants to discuss a few things over drinks. It could take hours."

"It could indeed," Joe said softly.

"Hey—is someone with you?" Tom asked.

"Just tell me," Jessica said. "What did Helen say?"

"That's the news. She loves the title. In fact, she loves the whole concept. She wants to get it out by Christmas. Just thought you'd want to know."

"Listen, we're under pressure here," Jessica said. "Keep writing. Without distractions, if you see what I mean."

"I don't," Tom said, but she had hung up. "See what you mean."

What was that about, he wondered as he strode the few blocks from Helen's office to Penn Station. Jessica had an uncanny knack for taking the wind out of his sails. But there wasn't time to worry about that now—he had to get back to work. If he caught the next train, he could be back at the shore in time for a late supper. Then tomorrow, a full day at the typewriter. No, not just tomorrow. All week.

Outside the station, he found another phone booth and slipped a quarter into the slot.

"Sherry?" he said when she picked up. "About Wednesday— something's come up."

"Really? What's going on?"

"My editor's hot on the book. She wants more, like suddenly."

"That's great, Tom," Sherry said cautiously.

"But I'm going to have to work all week. No interruptions."

"So I'll come out this weekend?"

"Let's see how it goes," he said.

Surprised, Sherry kept silent.

"Sorry, my love," Tom said. "But don't worry. I'll make it up to you."

Chapter 11

Sherry felt a familiar thump in the gut when she saw Tom jogging to meet her train, as though no time had passed. But six days had gone by since their afternoon tryst in Manhattan, and for Sherry the wait had been hard. The conversation about Tom's marriage had left her feeling unsettled enough to consider calling the whole thing off. It didn't help that she was about to leave for a month to cover the music festival in Aspen.

Tom had called once a day, but he'd been preoccupied with his writing. Toward the end of the week, when he'd asked her to come out for a couple of nights, she'd agreed to come on Sunday, hoping that the visit would provide some clarity.

Now, as they embraced, she was glad she'd made the trip.

"I've missed you, my love," Tom said, standing back to look at her.

In the early evening light, Sherry had never appeared more desirable to him, her tan set off by the beige-on-beige stripes of her summer dress, her hair swept up with a clip, rebel wisps escaping to frame her face. She had the Pentax slung over her shoulder.

They stashed her bag in the Jeep and headed to Gosman's for an early supper. Tom had reserved a table overlooking the harbor, and when they were seated, a waiter appeared with a chilled bottle of white.

"How was your week?" Sherry asked as they touched glasses.

"I've been pounding it out," Tom said. "I have to turn in a draft by September."

"That sounds brutal. Why the rush?"

"My editor wants to publish before Christmas. They want to make a splash with my comeback. I'm excited, Sherry. I can't believe I'm finally making progress with a new novel. And it's all thanks to you, my love."

"Me? That's absurd," Sherry said. "I haven't even seen it."

"I know, and I'm under orders not to show it to anyone. But Sherry—if we'd never met, I'd still be looking at a blank page. Being with you has inspired me."

"Is that a metaphor for sex?"

Tom smiled.

"That's part of it, but not all. It's who you are. Your spark, your spirit…"

"And I'm good in bed."

"You can joke about it if you like," Tom said, "but for me, this is serious. I've got my creative juices back. After seven years in the wilderness, I've found my direction. I'm just scared that when we're apart next month, I'll lose it again."

"Tom, you're not going to lose it. You're an author. If I've had something to do with getting you started writing again, that's great. But it was bound to happen in time."

Over dinner, Sherry brought Tom up to date on her festival plans. The lineup was impressive, with Michael Tilson Thomas as composer-in-residence. She was flying out with Granville, Anouk was arriving from Tanglewood to perform, and Lou would be passing through.

"So you'll be having fun, but what about me?" Tom said. "I don't know how I'll make it through August."

Sherry hadn't planned on mentioning her own qualms about August, but when Tom brought it up for a second time, she couldn't stop herself.

"You'll have Jessica," she said.

For a split second, Tom was taken aback. He'd been so caught up in his work that he hadn't revisited their discussion about his marriage. But it was clearly still worrying Sherry.

"My love, Jessica won't be here. She's going to Maine."

"Really? For the whole month?"

"That's what she told me," Tom said. "She and some friends from the *Voice* are renting a cottage."

As he spoke, he thought back to Jessica's phone call informing him of her plans. She'd been rather vague, but that didn't bother him. He'd be able to write, with no interruptions.

"Won't you be lonely out here on your own?" Sherry asked.

"Not at all. I'm an old hand at that. And what about you? You'll be with your friends all month. Think you'll forget about me?"

"Probably," she smiled. "Let's go home."

The first thing Sherry noticed when she awoke the next morning was Tom's scent: a mix of sea breeze and something wilder, almost animal. It contrasted with his patrician persona. Or how patrician was he? She thought about that. Tom hadn't said much about his family.

Out on the deck later with their coffee, they considered how to spend the day. Tom proposed going sailing—he knew a man with a boat. Sherry was up for it. Once the matter was settled, she stretched out her legs on the weathered bench to catch some early rays.

"You mentioned that your father was a broker," she said. "Tell me about him."

"There's not much to tell," Tom said. "I guess you could say we're estranged."

"Really? What's that about?" As an only child, same as Tom, Sherry could no more imagine being estranged from her parents than she could life on Mars.

"It's complicated," Tom said.

"We have time."

"Not if we're going to make it to Shelter Island by lunchtime."

He took their mugs inside and headed for the shower. But Sherry wasn't about to drop the matter. She thought it over while dressing. What about Tom's mother? She could ask later, she decided. They had all day.

They piled into the Jeep with a beach blanket and a cooler and hit the road for Sag Harbor. When they reached the marina, Tom's friend with the boat was shooting the breeze with a lanky man in sunglasses. Sherry noticed the Leica slung over his shoulder.

They exchanged the usual pleasantries, Tom handed over some dollars and, hand in hand with Sherry, made for the boat.

The lanky man followed them with his eyes until they were out of earshot.

"Who's your friend?" he asked the boatman. "I'm sure I've seen him before."

"That's Tom Paine."

"The author?"

The lanky man pointed his Leica in their direction, clicking the shutter a few times.

"Yeah," the boatman said. "He lives out here now."

"But he hasn't written anything for a while, has he?"

The boatman shrugged.

"He says he's working on something new."

"Interesting," the lanky man said, firing off a few more shots. "I might be able to use that. And who's the babe?"

"Don't know. Not his wife, that's for sure."

The sun was glinting off the water as Tom maneuvered their day-sailer out of the harbor and into the bay. It was an easy-to-handle Catalina 16.5. Sherry perched on the edge, enjoying the spray as they cut through the water. Tom was an experienced sailor, and the breeze was light, just brisk enough to make the crossing enjoyable.

"So, about your family," Sherry said after a while. "I don't even know your parents' names."

"Anne and Henry," Tom said. "Anne Havelock and Henry Paine. The all-American couple."

"And which one has Native American roots?"

"Do you really want to have this conversation?"

"Yes, absolutely," Sherry said. "Tom, I want to know you. And it will give me something to think about while I'm on the road for a month."

"Okay then," Tom said. "But I'm warning you, it isn't pretty."

"I can take it. Tell me why they named you Geronimo."

"Yeah, well, we have to go pretty far back in time for that," he said. "I'm one-eighth Apache, and it's on my mother's side. She's actually descended from a Mayflower pilgrim, Peter Browne—that's Browne with an 'e'—but things happened."

"The Mayflower? You're kidding."

"No," said Tom. "So, by the time my mother's grandfather was born, the family had dropped the 'e.' Her grandfather was William Brown, of Boston. He married a woman named Susannah Whitestone and they had three sons: George, John, and Thomas, named after the first three presidents of the United States. That was back in the 1890s. I was named after my great-uncle Thomas, by the way."

"And what about the Apache blood?" Sherry asked as the Catalina skimmed the waves.

"I'm getting to that. William Brown headed west to look for gold in 1897. He went out to New Mexico, leaving Susannah behind to care for the three boys. It wasn't a state yet, just a territory, but news had traveled east that there were gold nuggets lying right out in the open along creeks in the mountains south of Santa Fe. He thought he could strike it rich. But this was Apache territory."

He paused to steer the daysailer through the wake of a passing motorboat.

"Now, from what I hear," Tom continued, "my great-grandfather William was quite a looker, a smooth-talking fellow with plenty of charm. He made friends with the people in the area, and in due course, he got friendly with a young Apache woman, very beautiful, so the story goes. When she got pregnant, William had to flee for his life, and he took the girl with him to save her. Susannah knew nothing about this, of course. William stayed with the girl, and she bore him a daughter. But there were complications, and three days after giving birth, she died. So there was William, out in New Mexico with a rough bunch of gold seekers and a newborn infant on his hands. He found a local woman who had just given birth, and she agreed to nurse the baby. And after thinking it over long and hard, he sent for Susannah."

"Geez, what a story," Sherry said. "You should make that into a novel."

"Maybe someday. So, Susannah joined him in New Mexico, leaving her sons in the care of her sister. Needless to say, she was shocked when she found William there with a baby. But she was a kind-hearted woman, and once she got over the shock, she accepted the situation. A year later, they returned to Boston with a small fortune in gold and the child. They had named her Rebecca, after Rebecca Browne, a daughter of Peter Browne, William's Mayflower ancestor."

"So Rebecca was your grandmother," Sherry said.

"Wait. We have to dock. I'll finish later."

Tom steered the boat up to the edge of the Mashomack nature preserve. A blue heron rose from the surrounding marshland, startled by their arrival. Turtles basked lazily on the sunlit sand. Tom knew the area and suggested they take the Yellow Trail, an easy three-mile hike.

The island was pristine. Dragonflies flitted over the meadow as they made their way along the trail, beautiful in the noonday sun. Clouds of swallowtails appeared from time to time. Tom had brought binoculars, and they took turns looking for the osprey and red-tailed hawks that nested on the island. By the time they returned to the boat, Sherry was famished.

They spread the blanket on the sand, and Sherry stripped down to her bikini.

"You were telling me about your grandmother," she said as they unpacked their lunch.

"Yeah. Rebecca Brown."

"And she was half Apache. How did that go down in Boston?"

"She was easily accepted into the family," Tom said. "She was a bright girl, the apple of her father's eye, and nobody knew her mother wasn't Susannah. The Brown family thought the girl's exotic looks came from a hidden gene on her mother's side, and Susannah's family thought the opposite."

"Go on," Sherry said, as Tom opened a couple of beers.

"When she came of age, Rebecca married a man named Joseph Havelock. On the eve of the wedding, her parents told her the true story of her origins. It came as a shock, of course, but Rebecca was a sensible young woman. She decided to keep the knowledge to herself."

"That's not surprising," Sherry said. "Given the era."

"My mother, Anne Havelock, was born two years into the marriage," Tom said. "She was a bookish girl and became a schoolteacher. When she was twenty-six, she met my father on a blind date. This was in 1948, and he had just graduated with an MBA from Harvard."

"Henry Paine? Your estranged father?"

Tom nodded.

"They married quickly, and on the eve of her wedding, my mother was told of her Native American heritage."

"That she was one-quarter Apache."

"Yes. But instead of hiding the knowledge, she decided to investigate her roots. They moved to New York, and my father went to work on Wall Street. My mother gave up teaching; she wanted to start a family. While waiting to get pregnant, she enrolled at NYU to study Native American history. Within a couple of years, my father started making good money. The only problem in their marriage was the lack of a child."

"And then you came along…"

"Well, yeah. She finally got pregnant in the spring of '52, about three years into the marriage. That doesn't seem long now, but the waiting had been unbearable for my mother. My father, too, apparently. He was so grateful when I was born that he let her name me."

"Thomas Geronimo Paine," Sherry said. "Great byline. I wonder if she thought about that."

"She wanted to make sure I didn't forget I was part Native American," Tom said. "My mother was proud of her heritage. When I was only knee-high, she started telling me stories of the Apache. Little things—you know, how they lived, their myths. I don't know how much of it was fact and how much fiction. She actually fantasized that she might be descended from Geronimo. She described him as a great Apache fighter, not a bloodthirsty murderer. What fascinated her most were his supposed super-powers. He was thought by the Apache to be able to read the future and to have the power to heal. When I was a kid, she made me believe I might have the same powers."

"Do you?"

"Try me."

"Okay. Let's see," Sherry said. "Where will we each be a year from today?"

"Hmm. I see… I see… Well, it's blurry."

"What a load of bullshit."

"Yeah, I never believed in that special powers hocus-pocus my mother fed me," Tom said. "But she did spark my powers of imagination. I guess that may be why I became a writer."

Sherry said nothing for a while, lazing in the sun, watching Tom as he squinted out to sea. When she reached for him, his skin was hot beneath his T-shirt. She slipped out of her bikini. There was no one around to see except for a couple of egrets.

"Now?" Tom asked. "Let's wait till we get home."

"No way," she said. "I'm totally turned on by your story."

They said little on the sail back. The wind had picked up, and the Catalina clipped through the waves. They made good time, getting thoroughly drenched in the process. Back at Tom's place, when they'd dried off and had a cup of tea, Sherry got out her Pentax. It was their last evening together before the August hiatus, and she wanted some photos of Tom.

"Just pretend I'm not here," she said as he set to work making dinner. He'd brought some rosemary in from the garden to use in a marinade for chicken.

Sherry kept her lens trained on his hands as he chopped the herbs. They were practical hands, strong enough to control a boat in a stiff breeze but so very gentle when they caressed her. The memory of Tom stroking her breasts in the afternoon heat on the beach made it hard to keep her focus. In her mind, she knew she had to control her emotions. But in her heart, she could feel herself cascading to that place where everything shifted, where the sound of a voice could spark a rush of yearning, where its absence could fuel a desperate ache.

"There," Tom said, turning the chicken over in the marinade. He looked up and seemed surprised to see that Sherry was still behind her camera. "Have you got enough pictures now?"

"Sure," she said.

"Then let's have a drink. Margaritas?"

They took the drinks out to the deck to enjoy the sunset. Sherry stretched out on a chaise longue while Tom fired up the barbecue. She ran her tongue around the salty edge of her glass, wondering how they'd both manage being apart.

"Let me tell you a story," she said as Tom came to sit beside her. "I once got a Christmas card that said, 'Wishing you peace and joy in the new year.' When I opened it up, there was a hand-written message inside: 'But if you had to choose, which would it be—peace or joy?' It's something I've thought about over the years."

"So, which would you choose?" he asked.

"No, you first."

"I guess it would have to be peace," Tom said. "I've got some demons, you know. I mean, when I can't write, it's hell. I've spent seven years longing for the kind of peace that comes when you know you're creating something that means something. You know?"

"I do," she said.

"Okay, your turn. Peace or joy?"

Sherry didn't hesitate.

"Joy. Moments that make my heart sing."

"And you'd give up peace for that?"

"I think peace is an illusion," Sherry said. "After all, we're going to die. How can you make peace with that unless you're a saint or the Dalai Lama? Maybe he can achieve true inner peace. Maybe. The rest of us go on from day to day, muddling through in an imperfect world. But every so often comes a moment of transcendence. I live for those moments."

"Like what?" Tom asked.

"Like today. A perfect day."

"But joy is fleeting," he said. "Tomorrow, when you leave, joy disappears."

He got up to check the fire. The coals were starting to glow.

"Let's have another drink," he said.

Sherry followed him into the kitchen, needing to stay in his presence. He mixed two more margaritas and took the chicken out to the grill. They moved a couple of deck chairs over to the barbecue so he could keep an eye on things.

Neither of them noticed the lanky man pointing his Leica in their direction from a second-story window of the house next door.

"So, about our perfect day," Tom said. "I've got a special bottle of wine for tonight. When the sun's down, we'll have dinner and then, you know…"

Sherry smiled at him serenely. It was another perfect moment—the waves lapping against the shore, the warmth of the evening breeze, her lover beside her.

"You look happy," Tom said.

"I am. Right here, right now."

"Then let's not talk. Let's just be together."

They watched orange streaks form in the sky as the sun dipped lower, washing the deck in a rosy blush. From time to time, Tom checked the barbecue. When the last rays had vanished and the chicken was ready, they gathered their empty glasses and went inside. Tom opened the wine, a 1990 Pomerol. When they were seated, he raised his glass.

"To you," he said. "My inspiration."

"Tom, that's intense."

"I'm a changed man, my love."

"No more demons?"

"Well, they're not bothering me as much these days."

"Demons is a colorful word for someone like me with a visual imagination," Sherry said. "I can picture little red devils with pitchforks dancing around your typewriter."

Tom laughed.

"Don't be so literal," he said.

"Well, what is it then?"

"It's hard to talk about. I guess it started around the time I fell out with my father."

"So spill already," she said. "What happened between the two of you?"

Tom hesitated for only a moment.

"Well, he came to see me one day. This was back in '89. My second novel had just come out, and Jessica and I were moving into our place in the Village. My father seemed upset, so I took him out to a bar. When we'd had a few, he told me he was leaving my mother. I couldn't believe it. As far as I knew, they had a perfect marriage. I asked him what was going on, but he wouldn't say. He was getting plastered, so I took him back to our place. Jessica made dinner and he spent the night on our couch. Nothing more was said about the problem. But the next day, when he left for work, I called my mother."

"And?"

"Her voice was shaky on the phone," Tom said, "so I went over there. When she saw me, she broke down in tears. Then she told me what happened—you know, why he left."

"What did she say, Tom?"

"It's too personal," he said. "Sorry, but I just can't talk about it. I've never discussed this with anyone. Even Jessica doesn't know."

"Well, I'm here now, and I'm listening."

"All I can say is she told me something I wish I'd never have known," Tom said. "I got upset. I mean, this concerned me directly. I was thirty-six, for Christ's sake. Why had she been hiding it all those years? She said it wasn't her fault—she hadn't known the truth herself until an hour before my father walked out on her. She begged my forgiveness, but I needed time to think things through. I left her there on her own, sobbing."

"You just walked away?"

"I had to," he said. "I had no choice."

"What did she tell you?" Sherry persisted. "Talking about it might help."

"No, it won't. Anyhow, that evening, when my father came back to our place, I told him I'd been to see my mother. He turned pale. He didn't have to ask what she'd told me—he could read it on my face. 'I'll be going now,' was all he said. Then he walked out the door and disappeared. That was the last time I saw him. He broke off all ties."

"Didn't you try to find him?"

"Yeah, of course," Tom said. "At first. But then I quit trying. He may even have left the country, for all I know."

"What about your mother?" Sherry asked.

"We're in touch, but we rarely see each other."

"So it's been seven years," Sherry said. "And for seven years, you've had writer's block. I guess what you're saying is that somehow this family drama blocked you."

Tom refilled their glasses as he searched for a way to express himself.

"Here's the thing," he said. "I write fiction. On good days, that can feel like the best way of getting at the truth. It depends on how you frame a story. You can tell it from any angle."

"Like a photographer," she said. "Except the lens doesn't lie."

"Ouch."

"That's not what I meant. Sorry."

"Don't apologize," Tom said. "It's an interesting concept—fiction as lies. I prefer to think of it as invention, or let's say a reinterpretation of reality."

"I know," Sherry said. "On good days, if I frame a shot right, I can capture a kind of truth that we'd miss otherwise. It's like a freeze-frame of reality—life viewed through a lens, more intensely."

"Now you're with me. So, for example, when a newspaper reporter writes about a napalm strike on a Vietnamese village, the story will talk about how many dead, how many houses destroyed, and so on. A novelist will take that same story and tell it differently. How did a mother feel when she saw her daughter running through the village, her back on fire? It will get closer to the truth of what happened—the brutality, the daughter's screams, the mother's terror, her hate for the attackers..."

"You're talking about the *AP* photo by Nick Ut," Sherry said.

"Was that his name? Well, yeah. It told a kind of truth no newspaper article could capture. But a photographer could, and so could a novelist. On a good day."

"And what about the bad days?"

"Yeah, well, I didn't use to have any bad days," Tom said. "But after the incident with my parents, I started questioning a lot of things."

"Like what?"

"Truth became a more elusive concept," he said. "I started doubting my judgment, even my legitimacy. When I sat down to write, I felt like a fraud. Was it fiction I was writing, or stardust? Or just plain bullshit?"

"Don't be so hard on yourself," Sherry said. "It's not bullshit. As you said, you reinterpret reality. And that's what makes it art."

"You talk a good line. I wish I could believe you."

"Tom—listen to me. Every day can't be a good day. That's impossible. You need to believe in yourself."

"Well," he said, "it's taken me seven years to get back to a place where what I'm writing feels true. And do you know what? I've got my doubts about this manuscript too."

৵১

When they'd cleared the table, Tom pulled an Otis Redding record from his vinyl collection and revved up the stereo, turning
the volume higher so they could hear it out on the deck. It was a
starry night, but the air was cool now. He fetched a blanket, and
they went outside. Tom pulled their lounge chairs together so the
edges were touching, just outside the pale pool of light shed by
the deck lamp.

"I've been talking too much," he said. "Your turn. Let's have
a story."

"About my parents?"

"For God's sake—no. Enough family. Tell me something
sexy."

"Ah, that," Sherry said. "Like what?"

"Something sexy enough to get me through a month without
holding you in my arms."

"Okay, let me think."

"I know," Tom said. "Tell me about Jerzy Gregorski. When
you left off, he was playing a solo at Tanglewood. 'To die for,' I
think you said."

"He's an incredible violinist."

"Have you heard him play recently?"

"Of course."

"You mean you're still in touch? Should I be worried?"

"No," Sherry said, thinking about Jerzy. She was looking forward to seeing him in Aspen.

"So there he was rehearsing," Tom said. "How did you meet
him? Wait, I know—you rushed onstage, he dropped the violin,
and the rest is history."

"Who's telling this story?"

"Sorry."

"I met him when the rehearsal was over," Sherry said. "Anouk
introduced us. She knew absolutely everyone."

"And this was back in 1980."

"Yes, sixteen years ago. God, that's a long time. Anyhow,
Jerzy was teaching a class that afternoon. He invited me to drop

by to get some pix. I shot the class, and afterward, we went out for coffee. We met up again after Jerzy's concert that evening."

"Just the two of you?"

"No, everyone," Sherry said. "All the musicians who'd just performed. We went to this French-style bistro. It felt out of place in the Berkshires, but they liked the ambiance. So when Anouk and I joined them, Jerzy made room for me beside him, and that's how it started."

"What—he picked you up at the dinner?"

"He was flirtatious. In fact, they all were. Musicians get kind of a high from playing together. The concert had gone well, the vibe carried into the dinner, and next thing I knew, Jerzy had his hand on my knee. I removed it, but there was clearly something going on."

"And?"

"Actually, he swept me off my feet. I loved his accent, his worldliness. And the fact that he'd be going back to Poland at the end of the summer made everything more intense."

"What was that about?" Tom asked.

"Jerzy was one of the rare Polish musicians allowed to leave the country to perform abroad at the time. The Communists were still in power back then. He said the country was like a giant prison, and he felt lucky to escape, if only for a couple of months."

"How long did it take him to get you into bed?"

"Not long," she said. "We slipped away the next day. It was a drowsy summer afternoon. He took me to a hotel..."

"Come here," Tom said.

They kissed under the stars, enlaced beneath the blanket. Sherry wasn't cold, but she was shivering.

"Tom," she said, "let's go upstairs."

"Not yet. First, the story..."

She touched his face, rough with the day's growth of beard.

"It's our last night," she said.

"We have time. You said it was sexy..."

"It was. Very..."

"At the hotel?"

"All the time. It was erotic in a way I'd never experienced before."

"What do you mean?" Tom asked. "Did he tie you to the bed or something?"

She smiled.

"Not at all. It wasn't like that. But I'd never slept with an East European, and it was, I don't know, a revelation."

"In what way?" Tom asked.

"Well, Jerzy was born in 1940, during the first months of the war, and he'd been through a lot. As a child, he was farmed out to relatives in the countryside."

"What does this have to do with sex?"

"I'm getting to that. So Poland was occupied by the Nazis when he was a little kid, and life was very hard. There wasn't enough food. When the war was finally over, Jerzy was reunited with his parents, but things didn't improve much. The bloodshed had ended, but when the Nazis were pushed out, the Russians took over. The Poles were nominally independent, but they were actually under Kremlin rule—you know, the thought police, political prisoners, all that. So Jerzy grew up in that atmosphere."

"Fascinating. But where's the sexy part?"

"Just wait," she said. "Jerzy's parents were intellectuals. They enrolled him in the conservatory, and he showed exceptional talent as a violinist. That made no difference. Like everyone else, he had to conform—in public. In private, people could say what they liked. This was true all across Eastern Europe. They mocked their masters around the kitchen table. You know the old joke: 'They pretend to pay us, and we pretend to work.' People developed a very strong sense of irony. It was a form of subversion. And with Jerzy, it played out in bed."

"You're kidding," Tom said. "What do you mean?"

"I mean he was totally unrepressed as a lover. Totally uninhibited. I thought it was because he was so much older than me—I was twenty-eight when we met, and he was forty—but when I told him that theory, he just laughed. '*Moja ukochana,*' he said—that means 'my darling' in Polish—'if I can't be free in bed, where can I be free?' He explained that under Communist rule, the state thought it could control every aspect of people's lives. But the state couldn't get into every bedroom. So just like irony, sex was a form of subversion."

"You mean they fucked the state by fucking."

"Yeah, sort of. It was the ultimate Polish joke."

"Love it," Tom said. "Let's go to bed."

They went inside, and Tom flipped the record over. He took Sherry's hand and twirled her as the first brassy notes came on, and Otis launched into "Keep Your Arms Around Me."

"Come here," Tom said. "Do as the man says."

They danced cheek to cheek, Tom gradually steering them back out to the deck.

"I thought we were going to bed," Sherry said.

"We are, my love," Tom said. Keeping one arm around her shoulder, he swung the other down behind her knees and scooped her up.

"What are you doing?" she laughed as Tom fumbled to open the screen door.

He bent his head down to kiss her.

"I'm carrying you over the threshold."

They kissed on their way upstairs, and when they reached the bedroom, they undressed each other, still kissing. They'd kept desire at bay during the hours they'd spent telling stories, and now, in the balmy night, they could give themselves over to passion.

Tom switched off the light.

"Let's be totally uninhibited," he said.

Chapter 12

Sherry slipped quietly out of bed at first light and went downstairs to make coffee. She carried her steaming mug out to the deck.

A month apart. It would be fine, she told herself. Yet she ached at the thought of leaving her lover. Her sweet, improbable lover. Like the night before, when he'd carried her over the threshold. So silly, but so touching...

By the time Tom came down, Sherry felt shipwrecked, reduced to flotsam at the thought of being without him.

Sensing her mood, he came and sat beside her.

"You were fabulous last night," he said quietly.

"I'm going to miss you so much," Sherry said.

"Me too," he said. "I've never felt like this before."

They sat in silence for a while, watching the waves lap at the shore.

"I was thinking," Sherry said. "Maybe you could come out to Aspen for a couple of nights so the month won't be so long."

"You know I can't," Tom said. "But we'll talk every day. We're cosmically linked, remember?"

He smiled, and Sherry felt her mood lifting.

"Come on," he said. "Let's take a walk on the beach before you catch your train."

They strolled barefoot along the water's edge, leaving footprints in the sand. By the time they turned back, wavelets had erased all trace of their passage. A metaphor for life, Sherry mused. A brief passage, and then no sign we were ever here.

As they neared the house, Tom stopped to skip a stone across the water, then another—as though wanting to delay the moment of separation, Sherry thought.

"I've got a question for you," he said finally.

"Yes?" she asked.

He took her gently by the shoulders.

"Will you be faithful?"

"And you?" she asked. With less than an hour before her train, she wanted to keep things light. But standing there in the morning sun, his bare feet planted in the warm sand, Tom looked more earnest than she'd ever seen him.

"I'll be writing nonstop."

"You didn't answer the question," she said.

"Neither did you."

"Is it important?"

"Yes," Tom said. "I'd be so jealous if you slept with another man, I'm not sure I could keep seeing you."

"That sounds serious…"

"This isn't a game, Sherry. I'm crazy about you. This past month has meant more to me than you can know."

He wrapped her in his arms and kissed her—not a passionate kiss, but deep, tender.

I remember this feeling, Sherry thought, as she lost herself in the kiss. It's almost like…

"Love," Tom said, stroking her hair. "I think we're in love."

Those words.

Even covered by the roar of the sea, they were impossible not to hear.

Sherry felt swept away. It's almost like drowning, she thought, as a warm rush engulfed her. Could she and Tom have a future together? He was married. End of story. Or was it?

She shook her head in the breeze, trying to cast away her thoughts. All she wanted now was to get to the station, to turn the page.

She took Tom's hand, and they began the short trek up from the beach.

Maybe they would have a new chapter together, maybe not, she thought.

Back at the house, they made small talk as she gathered her things. Tom parked at the station and walked her to the platform. They brushed lips when the train pulled in.

"Be good," he said, waving as she disappeared from sight.

PART II / THE BOOK

October 1996

Chapter 13

Tom was whistling as he strode down 39th Street, a sports bag slung over his shoulder. It was a clear October morning, and he was feeling on top of the world. In the bag were the corrected proofs of *The Rites of Man*—all three hundred pages of it. First stop: Fitzgerald & Fitzgerald, for the final strategy meeting on getting his book into print.

Uptown, Sherry was slipping prints into a portfolio. She was meeting Granville at a photo gallery in Soho whose owner had contacted them in Aspen. There had been a cancellation. Could they put a show together quickly? Only too happy to oblige, they'd come up with a theme—*Music in Black and White*—and had spent September scrambling to get ready.

Downtown, a party was in full swing at the *Voice* culture section. The special issue was finally ready, its front page emblazoned with a photo of Basquiat surrounded by graffiti-style lettering: "ART IN NEW YORK: BRINGING IT ALL BACK HOME." It was D-Day minus one, and Joe Reilly was pouring champagne for everyone. Jessica discreetly set her glass aside.

Helen Nussbaum was holding court in the conference room of Fitzgerald & Fitzgerald. Everyone was there: production, sales, publicity, advertising, promotion, and the creative director. They broke into applause when Tom came in. *The Rites of Man* was on track for an early December release, just in time for the Christmas shopping season.

Smiling confidently, Tom took a seat. This was it—at last, his comeback. He had put on a tweed jacket for the occasion. Next to him was Murray Thompson, who had negotiated the contract: a sizeable advance, international sales, book clubs, the whole enchilada.

A hush fell over the room as George Fitzgerald, patriarch of the publishing house, came in. It had been a slow year for Fitzgerald & Fitzgerald. With visions of dollar signs dancing in his head, he was not about to miss this meeting.

"Let's get started," Helen said, glancing up from her notes. "I'll take updates from all departments. Production."

"Right," Brenda Murphy said. "I have to hand it to my team. We're on a hugely accelerated schedule, but so far so good. Copy editing went smoothly, the book was typeset last week, and Tom has the proofs for review. When we get them back, we move on to final correction. That leaves enough of a margin to get the book into print on time."

"Tom? How are you doing on the proofs?" Helen asked, but he was already reaching into his sports bag. He brought out a sheaf of pages and handed them over to her.

"It's very clean," he said. "Thank you, Brenda."

As Helen examined an annotated page and passed it around the table, Tom's mind flitted back over the last couple of months. It had been totally nuts. The race to complete the manuscript. His elation when Helen liked it. Fine-tuning the contract with Murray, knocking the draft into final shape, all by mid-September. Then negotiating with the copy editor, and now revising the proofs. And in the meantime, seeing Sherry whenever they had time to meet.

"I like the look of the page," Cathy Cartwright said as the proof reached her. A dynamic thirty-six-year-old, she was in charge of promotion. This was her first Tom Paine novel.

"The Garamond gives it a certain elegance," Brenda said. "It's the same typeface we used in *The American Crisis.*"

"We wanted the continuity," Helen said. "Moving on. Sales. Joyce?"

"I'm happy to say that bookstores nationwide are taking a big position on *The Rites of Man,*" Joyce Chen said. "Thanks to Helen Nussbaum's efforts in particular."

There was more clapping, and George Fitzgerald nodded his approval.

"Let's get on with it," Helen said briskly. "Where do we stand today?"

"Helen set the wheels in motion back in July," Joyce replied, refusing to be rushed. At forty-five, she'd been sales director for Fitzgerald for fifteen years, and she was tough as elephant hide. "The chains went ahead and added Tom's book to their lists with a question mark attached. Nobody was going to pass up a potential bestseller at the height of Christmas buying. When Tom landed his manuscript on time, we gave them the go-ahead—knowing that our fabulous Brenda would get the book into production smoothly."

"This is turning into a love fest," Cathy Cartwright whispered to the creative director at her right. As the newest team member, she hadn't caught the tone of these meetings.

"Quiet!" Helen Nussbaum barked. "Joyce, how many copies in the first run?"

"Barnes & Noble and Borders expect to move at least 25,000 each in the run-up to Christmas," Joyce said. "There's also Waldenbooks. When we factor in the independents, we'd like to start with a hundred thousand."

"Can you handle that, Brenda?" Helen asked.

"No problem," the production manager said. "Of course, getting the book out to distribution points on such a tight schedule is going to cost us."

"We've already discussed that," Helen said tartly. She turned to Fitzgerald's stylish publicity manager. "Pia?"

"The challenge is to create buzz around a book that no one will see until it's actually on the shelves," Pia Franchinelli said. "No advance copies for the press, no reviews ahead of publication."

"No reviews?" George Fitzgerald asked. "Isn't that risky?"

"We're counting on the suspense factor," Pia said. "National Book Award–winning author emerges from seven years of seclusion with a hot new novel unlike anything he's done before. Guaranteed to have people flocking to the bookstores."

"Yes, but only if there's buzz," Helen said. "What are you doing about that?"

"I've reached out to my contacts in the media to let them know we have a new Thomas G. Paine book in the pipeline," Pia said. "They're already lining up, even if most will have to wait until the book is out to get a crack at the author. It won't be a total embargo. In the days ahead, Tom will break his silence with a couple of radio spots to whet the public's appetite. Then, on the eve of publication, *The New York Times* will publish an exclusive author interview and a preview of the novel. I've approached Marilee Dyer at the Book Review, and she's on board."

Pia handed Tom the schedule.

"Looks good," he said. "But about the radio gigs—what's the plan? Am I supposed to read or, you know, just shoot the shit?"

"Pia?" Helen said.

"It's up to you, Tom," Pia said. "I've made no commitments."

Helen turned to Neil Goodman, Fitzgerald's no-nonsense advertising director.

"Neil. Where do we stand on the ad campaign?"

"We'll roll it out a week ahead of publication, with ads in the major papers and panel displays on buses."

"Nationwide, I presume," Helen said.

"Coast-to-coast plus Canada. Then we follow up with TV spots just ahead of the launch."

"Fine," Helen said. "Moving on. Promotion."

Cathy Cartwright shot a nervous glance at Joyce Chen, her boss.

"We're on it," Joyce said. "Go ahead, Cathy."

"We're working with the chains and the large independents on co-op placements to ensure that *The Rites of Man* is prominently displayed in windows and on tables," Cathy said.

"It costs, but it will be worth it," Joyce added.

"We all agree on that," Helen said, exchanging a glance with George. She turned to Jim Steiner, Fitzgerald & Fitzgerald's bearded creative director.

"So now the moment we've all been waiting for," she said. "Jim, what have you got?"

"It's very late in the day to be choosing a cover," Jim Steiner said, "but we've narrowed it down to three simple designs."

He opened a folder and spread its contents on the table. An excited murmur rose as Helen passed the mock-ups around.

"We've done variations on the red-white-and-blue theme to link up with Tom's earlier books," Jim said. "The question is, how much fun can we have with this? Since the book is so different from the previous novels."

"I think we can take a certain amount of liberty," Helen said. "But let's hear from the author."

Tom couldn't suppress a grin. So far, the book had existed only as a loose bundle of typeset pages. Seeing the cover designs made it real.

"I think they're all great," he said. "Thanks, Jim. Now, if I were going to buy a book, I might be most tempted by this one."

The cover Tom picked bore a playful illustration up top of a woman's hand holding a heart, with a deconstructed American flag at the bottom. The red-white-and-blue images were set against pale gray, with THE RITES OF MAN and THOMAS G. PAINE in bold black lettering.

"Ingenious," Joyce Chen said. "Very modern."

"Other opinions?" Helen asked.

"What about this one?" Neil Goodman held up a red cover featuring a wavy flag set on the bias, its stars spilling out of the blue patch and onto the stripes. Beneath the flag was a couple kissing. "I like the energy, and it's closer to what we've done before."

"That's true," Pia Franchinelli said, "but it's not exactly edgy. Now, this is eye-catching."

She held up a bright blue cover with a hot-pink drawing of a woman's lips in the center. The lettering was in deep pink, with the title up top and Tom's name in large print at the bottom.

"Murray, any thoughts?" Helen asked.

"Whatever Tom wants," Murray said.

Helen stood to signal that the meeting was over.

"That will be all," she said. "Jim, please stick around."

As the team filed out, Helen and Jim Steiner returned to the table, where Tom, Murray, and George Fitzgerald were poring over the cover designs.

"George, would you like to weigh in on the cover?" Helen asked.

"I'd go with Tom's instinct," the publisher said.

"The one with the hand and the heart," Helen said. "Jim?"

"That would be a good choice," Jim said. "The gray gives it a certain sophistication to balance the playfulness of the image. And Joyce is right—it's modern."

"Then we've agreed," Helen said. "Jim, I'd like to see your mock-up of the back cover in the next couple of days. Anything else?"

"Yes," Jim said. "We're going to need a new author photo. The one we have on file dates back seven years."

"Could you set that up, please?" Helen said.

"I can take care of it," Tom said. "I know a photographer."

Tom and Murray walked in silence to the elevator. Once the doors had closed behind them, the normally restrained agent clapped Tom on the shoulder and did a little shuffle.

"Congratulations, Mr. Paine," he said.

Tom smiled modestly.

"Thanks, Murray," he said. "But save the congratulations until we've seen the reviews."

The elevator arrived at the ground floor, and they exited onto the street.

"You worry too much," Murray said as they headed east on 39th. "This book is a winner."

"Hope so," Tom said. "But it's hard to tell, given how few people have seen the MS. I can count them on one hand. You, Helen, the copy editor, Steiner, and maybe Fitzgerald."

"Fitzgerald? Are you kidding?" Murray said. "George doesn't give a shit about what's in the book. He only cares about what it's going to cost him and how much it's going to bring in."

"That means only four people have read it," Tom said nervously.

"You're forgetting about Ben Glazer," said Murray, who had already optioned the film rights to a producer friend in Hollywood.

"Right," Tom said. "But not even Jessica's seen it."

"Tom, for God's sake, don't show it to Jessica," Murray said. "If she lets something slip at the *Voice*, it'll be all over town."

They stopped amid a throng of pedestrians waiting to cross Sixth Avenue.

"Don't forget there's a secrecy clause in your contract," Murray warned.

The walk signal flashed on, and the human tide surged forward.

"Jessica won't see it," Tom said. "But there's someone else…"

"What?" Murray asked in alarm. "Another woman?"

"Yeah, I've been seeing someone," Tom said.

"Has she seen it?"

"No."

"Does anyone know about her?"

"Not until I just told you," Tom said.

He hadn't planned on mentioning Sherry. It just slipped out. But now that it had, he felt a sense of relief—at last, someone knew. And he could trust Murray to keep the news to himself.

"You know, Tom," Murray said, "I'm not sure you appreciate the magnitude of your return. This book is a big fucking deal.

Your adoring public has been waiting for seven years, and what you've written is going to create a sensation. The media will be after you like a pack of hounds. Your private life will go on display. And now you tell me you're seeing another woman."

"Yes," Tom said, "and I owe her a lot. She—well, she helped me break through. In fact, I'm meeting her now."

"So it's serious," Murray said.

They were approaching the 42nd Street-Bryant Park subway entrance.

"I'm heading downtown," Tom said. "You?"

"Back to the office, but I'll walk. I could use the air."

Tom caught the implication, and they stood uncomfortably for a moment, both of them aware that the conversation had drifted into uncharted territory.

"Listen, I have to go," Tom said. "If you've got something to say, please say it."

"All right," Murray said. "Then let me give you a piece of advice, my friend. I'm all in favor of romance, but as your agent, I have another opinion. You get your act together before the book comes out. The last thing we need is a scandal."

Tom's face flushed.

"This is my life, Murray," he said.

As he descended into the subway, Tom felt his mood darken. He'd been avoiding focusing on how his life would change when the novel was published. Yet Murray was right. Unless the book unexpectedly tanked, he'd be back in the limelight when it came out.

He'd been looking forward to it—interviews, invitations, the usual whirlwind with the Manhattan literary crowd, his standing restored as an author who mattered. But how did Sherry fit into that equation? Everyone would expect to see Jessica by his side—they were an item. If he turned up at a reception with Sherry on his arm, it would indeed create a scandal.

The only way to avoid it would be to clarify matters with

Jessica, but he didn't feel ready for a showdown. They'd hardly crossed paths since July, an estrangement that suited him perfectly. He'd been free to get on with the novel and, once Sherry came back from Aspen, to pick up where they'd left off. In his mad scramble to finish the book, they'd met less often, but that had only made each encounter more exciting.

He wasn't about to give up Sherry, if that's what Murray had been suggesting. He couldn't wait to see her now. They were meeting for lunch in Soho, their first date in a week.

The train clattered into the 34th Street station, and the crowd on the platform pushed inside. Tom gripped an overhead bar. As the train jerked forward, he decided that getting his act together could wait. The book wouldn't be out for a couple of months. He had time.

Jessica and Savannah left the *Voice* party together at noon, the entire culture section having been sprung for the rest of the day. Savannah's baby was tucked up in his stroller, sleeping contentedly. He'd made it through the festivities without waking.

As they walked toward Astor Place, Che trotting beside them, the baby stirred. Savannah tilted the stroller's hood back.

"Look at my Beau," she said. "Isn't he just gorgeous?"

Jessica peeked inside. The baby was wearing a tiny knitted cap. His eyes fluttered briefly, then he returned to dreamland.

"I can't believe he's nearly two months old already," Jessica said. "How's it going?"

"Well, I'm pretty tired, to tell you the truth," Savannah said. "This little fellow wants to eat all the time. Especially in the middle of the night."

"I don't know how you do it. It's like your life is no longer your own."

It had to be exhausting to raise an infant, she thought, yet Savannah looked positively luminous.

"I reckon that's what having children's all about," Savannah said. "You're still there, but part of you is outside yourself in this tiny little being. It's fascinating. I could watch Beau twenty-four hours a day if I didn't have to sleep."

"At least you have a husband. Has Phil been much help?"

"He's been great with the baby. I don't know how I'd manage without him. But you have a husband, too, honey. Bring me up to date. How are things going with Tom?"

"He's been out at the beach, finishing his book," Jessica said. Allegedly, she thought.

"Well, that's good, isn't it, sugar?" Savannah said. "Listen, I'd better go before my little guy realizes he's hungry. But stay in touch, okay?"

She was catching a train to Brooklyn, and Jessica helped her carry the stroller down the stairs into the subway. They air-kissed and said goodbye.

Back up on the street, with Che leading the way home, Jessica wondered whether all new mothers were as selfless as Savannah. Maybe it kicks in when you give birth, she mused.

With an hour free before his date with Sherry, Tom took the West 4th Street exit. He wanted to pick up some flannel shirts from his place in the Village. The days were still mild out at the shore, but the nights were getting colder.

It was a quick walk to the apartment. Tom entered quietly. The place was empty. Great, he thought, making for his closet. He stuffed the shirts into his sports bag and was heading for the door when he heard a key in the lock.

Jessica started at the sight of him.

"Tom—what are you doing here?" she asked as Che bounded forward, wagging his tail.

"I stopped by to pick up a couple of things," Tom said. "I didn't expect you to be here at this hour. Guess I should have called first. Is everything okay?"

"Everything's more than okay," Jessica said coolly. She reached into her handbag and pulled out a copy of the *Voice* special issue.

"It hits the newsstands at midnight," she said. "Joe thinks it'll make a splash."

Tom gave the front page a cursory glance.

"It looks good," he said. "What brings you home so early?"

"Joe gave us the afternoon off," she said, "and I've been tired, so I decided to take a break. I certainly didn't expect to find you here. I thought you were out at the beach."

Tom saw the challenge in Jessica's eyes. He'd enjoyed the respite from her barbs. Now, face to face with her, he figured he might as well bring her up to speed on his comeback.

"I just left Fitzgerald," he said. "Mind if I make some coffee?"

"Help yourself," Jessica said, slipping out of her shoes. Her feet were killing her.

"Whoa!" Tom said as he entered the kitchen, where a brand-new imported Nespresso machine stood on the marble counter. "How do you work this baby?"

"Coming. Let me do it."

She placed a small glass cup on the tray, inserted a capsule, and pushed the button. Instantly, the aroma of coffee filled the room. She made a second cup for herself, and they returned to the living room.

"So where do things stand, Tom?" Jessica asked as he settled into an armchair. "With the novel, I mean."

She had yet to see more than the first two pages. She'd asked him about the book, but Tom—who usually liked to talk about his work—had clammed up.

"It's all set," he said. "We chose a cover, and if all goes according to plan, it's coming out on December third."

"*The Rites of Man*—R-I-T-E-S?" she asked.

"Yeah, everyone loved that. I'm putting you in the acknowledgments."

"Thanks," Jessica said, thinking that this was the least he could do, given that tweaking the title had been her idea. Given, in fact, that his entire career had been her idea.

"When can I see it?" she asked.

"Sorry, Jess," Tom said. "Nobody sees the novel before its release. It's in my contract."

Her eyebrows shot up.

"Not even your wife?"

"My wife, the lead culture columnist on the *Voice*?" he said. "That would be like leaking Watergate to the *Drudge Report*."

"Now he thinks he's Woodstein."

"Look, this novel is pretty different from everything else I've written, and they want to maximize the surprise."

"You can't be serious. You mean there will be no publicity ahead of the launch?"

"No. Well, yes," Tom said. "A couple of radio spots and one exclusive interview."

"With?"

"*The New York Times Book Review*."

"Goddamn it, Tom," Jessica said. "You're giving an interview to that slut Marilee Dyer when you're married to me? Or maybe you've forgotten we're still married…"

"Come on, you know how things work. The *Times* has national reach. But don't worry—I'll make sure the *Voice* gets in on the action as soon as the book goes on sale."

Jessica pushed aside her coffee cup and rose.

"I think you'd better be going now."

"Right."

Relieved, Tom headed for the door, Che trotting behind him.

"Bye, old buddy," he said, tousling the dog's curly head.

"Hold on a second," Jessica said, inserting herself between Tom and the door. "How long do you plan to keep living out on the island? I presume you'll need to be in Manhattan when the book comes out. Do you think you can just move back in here?"

"We'll talk about it when the time comes," Tom said stiffly. In the ferment of the last three months, moving back in with Jessica hadn't crossed his mind. But Murray had reminded him that he needed to start thinking about his life post-publication.

"Jess," he said, hoping to mollify his wife, "this has been a hard time for both of us, and I'm truly grateful to you for giving me the space I needed to get back on track."

Sure, Jessica thought, and the space to get it together with some floozy with a pale blue toothbrush. She still hadn't told Tom she'd found it. In fact, she hadn't told him a lot of things.

"It feels like forever since my last novel," Tom said, "but this could be a new beginning." He flashed a grin. "Wait for it. I can already see the headlines—'Tom Paine Is Back.'"

"I'll believe it when I see it," Jessica said drily.

"You can believe it. This is going to be big—it could be huge." He checked his watch. "Listen, I have to go."

"No one's stopping you."

As he tromped downstairs, Jessica called after him: "Next time you plan to drop in, do me a favor and call first."

Jessica pulled the door closed and sank into an armchair. So Tom Paine is back, she thought. It's happening. Now what?

She reached for the phone and dialed Joe's private line.

"What's up?" Joe said.

"I saw Tom," Jessica said. "He was here when I got home from the party."

"And?"

"And I didn't see the book, but he says it's going to be huge."

"That's cool," Joe said testily. "I mean, isn't that what you wanted?"

"I don't know. It could change things."

"Look, let's have dinner tonight," Joe said. "We need to talk."

We sure do, Jessica thought, but she kept that thought to herself.

Sherry and Granville were at the Thurington Gallery on Sullivan Street, their portfolios lying open on the big table in the back room. They watched silently as the alarmingly chic owner, Selma Thurington, selected prints for the exhibition. Sherry realized she was holding her breath—after twenty years in the business, this would be her first show.

"We can do something dramatic with what you've got here," Selma said. "We'll hang the photos in pairs—one from each of you. I think the first space should be just hands. These, for example." She selected a shot by Granville of Herbie Mann on flute and set it beside Sherry's photo of Jean-Pierre Rampal. Both pictures zeroed in on the flutists' hands.

"Then we'll move on to longer-range shots of the musicians with their instruments, and then the conductors," Selma said. "At the back will be vocalists. And up front, I'd like large portraits of the two of you. Could you arrange that, please?"

"You want us to shoot each other?" Granville said, winking at Sherry.

Selma just looked at him, her kohl-rimmed eyes huge beneath a silk turban.

"That will be all for today," she said tartly. "Be back next Monday with the portraits."

Out on the street, Granville cocked his finger like a gun and pointed it at Sherry.

"Bang!" he said, and they both cracked up.

"That's one tough cookie," Granville said.

"Her bark is worse than her bite," Sherry said. "I hope."

"What do you think about the paired pix?"

"Fine by me," she said. "I still can't believe this is happening."

"Yeah, it's cool. Listen, I have to head uptown. Coming?"

"No, I have a lunch date," Sherry said. "I'll see you tomorrow night at the Liza Minnelli thing."

She gave Granville a peck on the cheek and turned the corner onto Spring Street.

Tom's face lit up when Sherry entered the back room at Aquagrill, a trendy new fish place. As she made her way to the table, Sherry wondered why he hadn't chosen the sunny veranda out front. Maybe he didn't want to be seen with her in a public place in Manhattan. A married celebrity lunching with his lover...

She leaned down to give him a kiss.

"How'd it go?"

They asked the question at the same time and burst out laughing.

"You first," Sherry said as she took her seat.

"It's all set," Tom said. "We chose the cover. It's got this sexy couple wrapped in the flag. And listen—I want to ask a favor. They need a new author photo. Could you do me the honor?"

"Sure. When?"

"They want it, like, yesterday, so I was wondering whether we could..."

"... go up to my place after lunch? Perhaps..."

Their eyes met, and a current passed between them.

When the waiter appeared, they chose Race Rock oysters on the half-shell and a mesclun salad. Tom ordered two glasses of Pouilly Fumé.

"Now you," Tom said. "Tell me about the show."

"I'm totally psyched," Sherry said. "Selma Thurington wants to get maximum mileage out of the black-and-white theme. She's going to hang the photos of the musicians in pairs—one by Granville and one by me—with portraits of the two of us at the entrance."

"Remind me—when does it open?"

"December fifth."

"That's two days after my book comes out!"

"You were right," Sherry said. "We're cosmically linked."

Tom touched his glass to hers.

"And how many of your lovers will be on display?" he asked. "Do I need to be jealous?"

"Tom—cut it out. We've been over that ground so many times."

Her mind wandered back to their reunion in September, when she'd returned from Aspen. Tom had bombarded her with questions. Had she seen Jerzy at the festival? (She had.) Were they still lovers? (They weren't.) Had she slept around? (She hadn't.) Meantime, he'd said precious little about himself, only that he'd spent August alone. Jessica had spent the entire month in Maine, he'd said. Jessica—the elephant in the room.

"If you want to talk about jealousy, let's talk," Sherry said. She was already feeling the wine, and it made her reckless enough to stray into territory she mainly avoided. "You haven't said much about Jessica lately. So where do things stand, Tom?"

"I just saw her," Tom said, wondering how two women as different as Jessica and Sherry could issue the same challenge in the space of an hour. "I dropped by at our place to pick up some shirts, and she appeared."

"And?"

"And nothing," he said. "We had coffee."

"Does she know about me?"

"I don't know how she could."

"Well, have you thought about telling her?"

Sherry knew it was irrational, but she couldn't help it. The thought of Tom seeing Jessica made her crazy. Back in August, when Anouk arrived at the festival to perform in a rock opera, they'd talked it over. How to be involved with a man who said he was free but stayed married?

"Try to slow it down," Anouk had said. "You need to protect yourself."

That had made sense at the time, but it was hopeless now that she and Tom were sleeping together again. The feelings were too powerful. She felt bonded to Tom—it was a physical thing. Every time they parted, she longed for him.

Tom shifted uneasily in his seat. He'd considered telling Jessica about Sherry many times, most recently an hour ago. But as usual when the thought arose, he'd buried it. He detested scenes, but that wasn't the only reason. It wasn't the right time to break up with Jessica—not on the eve of his comeback. It was absurd, given the state of their marriage, but he still felt the need for her support.

But he also needed Sherry. She wasn't just a creative, passionate woman who'd helped him turn his life around. She had reminded him what it meant to be happy. And she was sitting across from him now, waiting for his reply.

"Sherry," he said earnestly, "it's over between me and Jessica."

"But does she know that?" Sherry insisted.

"Listen, I know we'll have to make some decisions. But I can't upset the applecart right now, with the book coming out and everything. What matters is we're in love."

There it was again—the L-word. Sherry's heart reeled.

"Just hang on a little longer," Tom was saying. "Can you live with that?"

"I don't know," she said. "I think I'll have to try you out in bed to see if you're worth it."

Tom called for the check.

"Come on, let's get out of here," he said.

The autumn sun was slanting low through Sherry's bedroom windows on Riverside Drive. She gave Tom a kiss and rolled out of his arms.

"We'd better get started before the light disappears," she said.

But Tom was still basking in a satisfied haze.

"Hey," she said, shaking him gently. "Time to get up."

"I like it here."

"Fine. We can take the author pix another day."

At the word author, Tom snapped out of his trance.

"No," he said, bounding out of bed. "Let's do it."

Sherry slipped into her kimono while Tom dressed. She went to the living room, where her close-up of Tom's hands over the cutting board had found its place on her photo wall, between Leonard Bernstein conducting and Rostropovich with his cello. She'd kept the facing wall empty for portrait sessions.

Tom emerged looking tousled. He checked himself in the front hall mirror, ran a hand through his hair, and shrugged into his tweed jacket. Satisfied, he sat down to pose.

Sherry was all business, asking him to turn his head at different angles to catch the light. Working quickly, she shot two rolls of film—in color and black-and-white. By the time she finished, she could feel her stomach rumbling.

"Maybe we should have something to eat," she said.

"You mean go out? Let's stay here. I don't want to share you."

Again Sherry wondered whether he didn't want to be seen with her.

"There's not much in the fridge," she said. "Why don't we order in? Chinese?"

They ordered stir-fried shredded duck with scallions and ginger, along with spring rolls, sesame noodles, and a couple of Tsingtao beers. Sherry set the dining nook table, and when the food arrived, they sat down to enjoy it.

"Don't do this to me again," Tom said, biting into a spring roll.

"What? Order Chinese?"

"No. Make me wait like that. It was a very long week."

"You were busy," Sherry said.

"So were you."

"Well, I'll have more time now that Selma Thurington has made her selection," she said. "Although I still have to make the final prints."

"Tell me something," Tom said as they attacked the sesame noodles. "What made you decide to become a photographer? I've wondered about that."

"It's my parents' fault," Sherry said. "They gave me a Brownie when I turned eight."

"One of those big boxy things..."

"I went out with it right away. I found this beautiful pink flowering bush and shot my first roll of film. When the photos came back, I burst into tears—all I got was a bunch of gray flowers. I hadn't realized that the film wasn't in color. After that, I decided to be more careful. I tromped around the neighborhood looking for things that could work well in black-and-white. I shot windows and doors, the awnings of fancy buildings. Like that."

"At the age of eight, you shot awnings?" Tom asked.

"My mom came with me. We figured out that I could play with the shadows and angles to get some very cool shots. My parents eventually bought me some color film, so I played with that, too. But I actually preferred the challenge of black-and-white."

"When did you start shooting people?" Tom asked with a glance at the photo wall.

"That came later," she said. "When I was a teen. Do you remember when the protests broke out at Columbia in the spring of '68?"

"Vaguely. I was still in high school."

"It was after the assassination of Martin Luther King. The students occupied some buildings and went on strike. My father always watches the evening news—that's how I heard about it. I told a friend, and we decided to go up there to check it out. My parents said no, but we went anyway. It was probably the first time I disobeyed them."

"Weren't you scared?" Tom asked.

"I was curious," she said. "The students were protesting the Vietnam War and racial discrimination and Columbia's involvement in both. People were picketing and shouting, and the police were there. It was exciting. When we went back the next day, I brought my camera."

"You took your Brownie to the protest?"

"I had a Pentax by then. And when I saw the faces I'd captured, I never looked back. The photos magnified the intensity of the emotion—it was powerful. I decided that this was what I wanted to do in life. I'd opened up a new way of seeing the world."

"So your rebel spirit turned you into an artist," Tom said. "Come here, my love."

He stood up and extended a hand.

"It's getting late," Sherry said as she joined him. "Shouldn't you be on your way?"

"Maybe not just yet," Tom said. He tilted his head toward the bedroom.

"You'll miss the last train..."

"I was thinking I might spend the night," he said. "If you'll have me..."

In the darkened bedroom, he untied Sherry's belt, and her kimono dropped to the floor. They kissed as she helped him undress, kissed some more as Tom pushed aside the quilt, drew her down with him onto the bed, wrapped her in his arms.

"I'm in love with you, Sherry," he said. "I never want this to end."

Chapter 14

Sherry nestled deeper under the quilt. Tom was still sleeping. Just the two of them, in her bed, in the morning. Nothing had ever felt more right.

I never want this to end, she thought, but Tom was stirring.

"My love," he murmured. "What time is it?"

"It's early," she said, but he reached for the clock.

"Jesus, it's after seven. I have to get going."

He gave her a quick kiss and headed for the shower.

Just as well, Sherry thought. It would take time to print the author photos. She went to the kitchen to make espresso, smiling as Max turned circles around her legs.

Tom emerged in a T-shirt and jeans, and they carried their coffee to the dining nook.

"I've been wanting to ask you something," Sherry said. "Do we have time for a story?"

"No more stories, my love," he replied. "Game over."

"You're kidding."

He grinned. "Nope. It's time to move out of the past and into the future."

"Interesting," Sherry said. "And just what future did you have in mind?"

"Things will lighten up when the novel comes out. I bet you've never been out to the island in winter. I think you'll love it. Long nights in front of the fire…"

"But you never explained why your father walked out on you," she said. "I can't get it out of my mind."

"Please try to, because we're not going there. Besides, I have to leave."

"Tom, this has been haunting you," Sherry said.

"But you exorcised that ghost," he said. "Thomas G. Paine is back—or about to be."

"If you want us to have a future together, we can't have secrets."

Tom thought that over. She was right, of course. If they were going to make this work, he'd have to be open with her. But this was a story he'd told no one. First with Jessica, and then with Sherry, he'd always managed to skirt the issue. The hallmark of a professional liar, he thought—telling one story to obscure another.

"Let's take our coffee to the couch," Sherry said. "It's more comfortable there."

Tom followed her, cup in hand, weighing his options. He knew he'd be taking a risk if he opened up. Yet he also knew he'd kept the burden to himself far too long.

"Okay," he said. "But hear me out. And nothing I say leaves this room."

"Go ahead. I'm here for you, Tom."

Sherry sat cross-legged at one end of the couch, giving him space. He set his cup on the table and turned to face her.

"Here's the thing," he said. "I'm illegitimate."

"Very funny," Sherry said. "You're the most legitimate writer I know."

"I don't mean as a writer," Tom said. "I mean I'm illegitimate because the man who brought me up is not my real father. I'm a bastard."

"Your father's not your father?"

"Not genetically," he said. "I'm the son of another man."

"And that's what your mother told you when you went to see her?"

"Yes. Now please stop interrupting."

"I'm listening," Sherry said.

"This dates back to 1989, when my father was sixty-five," Tom said. "He developed a prostate problem and went in for tests. The results were good—he didn't have cancer—but the tests also showed he was sterile. He was very surprised by this news and decided to get a second opinion. So, without mentioning it to my mother, he went to see a specialist. This doctor not only confirmed it but told him it was a congenital problem—he'd been sterile from birth."

"So you couldn't be his child…"

"My father is an intelligent man. It didn't take him long to put two and two together. He went home and challenged my mother. He put it to her point-blank: 'Whose son did I raise?' My mother was shocked. They'd been happily married for forty years, and she'd intended to carry her secret to the grave. When he presented her with the test results, she said it must be a mistake. But he wouldn't accept that. He pressed her until she admitted the truth."

"Which was?"

"What she said—and I have to assume this is true—is that a man she'd known before she met my father had called up out of the blue one day to say he was passing through town," Tom said. "He invited her to lunch at his hotel. This was three years into the marriage. As it happened, my father was away on business, and my mother was lonely. So she accepted the invitation. The man was a Scot, over from Edinburgh. They'd had a fling in Boston when he was finishing his PhD and she was still single. Over lunch, they talked about old times, they had some wine, and one thing led to another. She swore this was the only time she'd been unfaithful—just that one afternoon."

"But she got pregnant," Sherry said.

"Yes, and she panicked. She didn't know whose baby it was. She and my father had been longing for children. They had an active sex life, so it could have been his—or not. After much soul-searching, she decided to keep the baby and say nothing about her indiscretion. She never told my father, and she never told the other guy either."

"Do you know who he is?" Sherry asked.

"No," Tom said, "and I don't want to know. Anyhow, upon hearing this, my father went berserk. That's when he came over.

I was at my typewriter when there was a knock at the door. My father looked terrible. He asked for a drink, no explanation. I poured him a whiskey. He knocked it back and asked for another. When I asked him what was wrong, he broke down. I didn't want Jessica to see him like that, so I took him out to a bar. After a few more drinks, he told me he was leaving my mother. I thought he was joking. They'd never had a fight, to my knowledge. He asked if he could stay at our place for the night, so I took him home. When he'd sobered up in the morning, I pleaded with him to tell me what was going on, but he wouldn't say. He went off to work as though nothing had happened. That's when I called my mother."

"I remember that part."

"When I went over there, she was a wreck," he said. "She told me my father had left her. Then she broke down sobbing and begged my forgiveness. Mine! I didn't know why. When she calmed down enough to talk, I asked her what was going on. She looked terrified, but I warned her that if she didn't tell me the truth, she'd never see me again. So she came out with it."

Tom smiled briefly.

"Of course, in hindsight, it doesn't really matter," he said. "I mean, I exist. What do I care who's responsible for that? It's not as though I'm going to begrudge my mother a roll in the hay."

"Seriously?"

"Yes. For me, Henry Paine is and always will be my father," Tom said, his voice cracking. "He's the man who raised me. He's the man who taught me how to skip stones when I was a kid. Who picked me up when I fell down. Who showed me through example how to be good to a woman. He loved me, and I loved him back."

"Did you tell him that, Tom?"

"When he came back to our place after work that night, I wanted to tell him. But as soon as he heard I'd seen my mother, he lost it again. It wasn't just that I wasn't his son—it was that I knew I wasn't his son. He had wanted to hide that from me. I tried to tell him that it didn't change anything, but he couldn't handle it. So he left. And that's the last time I saw him."

"But how could he just abandon you?" Sherry asked. "It doesn't make sense."

"You know, that's something I've spent seven years thinking about," Tom said. "I guess he must have felt so humiliated that he never wanted to see us again. I mean, my mother had not just betrayed him, she had deceived him. And I was the living proof of that deception."

"That's so hard."

"You know, I still hope he might knock on my door again one day. I thought he'd get over it eventually, that he'd come back and I'd have a father again. But he didn't, and it destroyed me. It was like a double whammy. I was illegitimate, and my father had rejected me."

"Tom," Sherry interrupted, but his words were tumbling out.

"I started to doubt my legitimacy in general," he said. "I stopped writing. I mean, I'd start, but nothing came together. It all felt like bullshit. Jessica didn't understand. How could she? She begged me to tell her what was wrong, but I was too shattered to say. It affected our sex life. I tried, but it was no good. Of course she felt rejected. We started fighting. And then I moved out."

He stood up.

"So that's the whole story," he said. "Are you satisfied now?"

"Where are you going?" Sherry asked, fearing he'd leave.

"To the kitchen. I need more coffee."

Tom returned with a fresh pot of espresso. He'd had time to collect himself, and he felt oddly relieved. At last, someone knew the truth.

"I guess I got carried away there," he said. "Sorry."

"No," Sherry said. "Thanks for telling me."

He sat down on the couch beside her.

"Anyhow, it's all in the past now," he said.

"Yes, but what a story. I really don't know what to say."

"Then don't say anything, my love. Just be with me."

Sherry studied him as he sipped his coffee. In the cool morning light, sitting there in his T-shirt, he looked vulnerable, a shock of sandy hair falling over his brow, his face unguarded. She reached for his hand.

"Now that I've bared my soul," Tom said, "I have a question for you."

Sherry felt a new pang of worry.

"Sure," she said. "Ask me anything."

"How does it feel, being in love with a bastard?"

She smiled in relief.

"It's not the first time."

"You'd better get used to it," Tom said.

"I think I can handle that."

It was time to get going. Tom wanted to wear one of his flannel shirts, but he couldn't find the sports bag. He must have left it behind during his confrontation with Jessica.

Before leaving, he scribbled Helen Nussbaum's address on a scrap of paper.

"Here's where to send the photos," he said.

"Don't you want to come back to choose?" Sherry asked. "I should be done by noon."

"No, I trust you. Call you later."

Out on the street, it was raining. He raised his umbrella and hailed a cab.

"West Village," he said, giving his home address. He'd have to stop back to pick up the shirts. With any luck, Jessica would be out.

The cabbie examined Tom in his rearview mirror.

"Hey, ain't I seen you somewhere before?"

"I doubt it," Tom said.

"Wait, I know. I seen you on television," the cabbie said. "What's your name, fella?"

"I'm Tom Paine."

"That's right, that's right. Tom Paine, the author. I seen you talking about one of your books, a good long time ago now. So, what you been up to? Ain't you writing anymore?"

"I've been in a dry spell," Tom said, "but that's over now."

At his apartment in the Village, Tom rang the bell this time before turning his key in the lock.

"Who's there?" Jessica called, but Tom was already striding into the living room.

"Should have phoned. Sorry," he said, looking around. "Have you seen my sports bag?"

"I'll get it," Jessica said, disappearing into the bedroom.

She returned and handed it to him. As he turned to leave, she stopped him.

"And what have we here?" she asked, brushing Tom's hair back from his collar. On his neck was a dark patch that looked suspiciously like a hickey. Was he still fooling around? Enough is enough, she decided.

"Tom, come sit down for a minute. We need to talk."

"I don't have a lot of time," he said, but the look in her eye gave him pause. Did she suspect he was seeing someone? Well, what if he was? They'd been separated for more than a year. But did they really have to have this conversation now? It would not be a quick one, and he had a lunch date with Murray at noon.

With Tom gone, Sherry headed into the darkroom. The contact sheets were ready within an hour. She took them into the living room and examined them with her photographer's loupe, using a red grease pencil to circle the shots she wanted to print. Seven made the cut. Then it was back into the darkroom with the negatives.

It was lunchtime when she emerged. She lovingly taped the prints to her living room wall. There was one in black-and-white that captured the duality of Tom's face as she'd seen it back in July, on one of their long, sexy nights out at the shore. She chose that one, along with two color prints: Tom with smiling eyes and a more pensive pose.

She rummaged through her desk for a hard-backed manila envelope, addressed it to Helen Nussbaum, and slipped the three photos she'd chosen inside.

Rain was still slashing down. Sherry put on her slicker and went out into it, shielding the envelope beneath an umbrella. It was a quick walk to the hole-in-the-wall messenger service she used. She waited while the clerk processed what seemed like a dozen packages for the customer ahead of her. At last, it was her turn.

"This is a rush order," she said.

"One-hour delivery?" the clerk asked, and Sherry nodded.

"Triple rush. That'll be $26.50."

Sherry paid and left, heading for the nearest coffee shop. She picked up a copy of the *Times* en route. It felt good to sit down, but she found it hard to concentrate on the paper.

Tom's story about discovering his origins was still playing in her mind. He'd been profoundly wounded, and that could derail a man. But now he seemed to be healing. She sincerely hoped his new book would finish that process.

Leaving his building in the West Village, Tom stumbled onto the street in a daze, Jessica's words ringing in his ears: "Move back in and at least act like a husband…" She hadn't finished the sentence, but her threat had been perfectly clear. In any other circumstances, he would have refused. But now, how could he?

He tucked his head down against the rain, his steps taking him toward Washington Square. Autumn leaves were dancing in the wind. He found a bench. His thoughts were ramming against each other like bumper cars on a midway. What would he say to Sherry?

From somewhere deep inside him, a strangled sound cut the air. He covered his eyes with the back of his hand as he broke down and cried.

❧

Back home after lunch, Sherry found Max in his favorite spot on the couch.

"How do you feel about Tom, Max?" she said, settling in beside him. "I think you may be seeing a lot of him. I wonder how you'll like it out on the island…"

Max purred as Sherry stroked him. She felt tired but content, remembering Tom's talk about long nights in front of the fire and his words: "I'm in love with you, Sherry…"

Slumped on his bench, Tom was still trying to make sense of his jumbled thoughts. He'd been sitting there for hours, unable to make up his mind. The situation seemed inextricable. Why had he and Jessica maintained the fiction that they were still married? Why hadn't they simply divorced? They should have made their separation official as soon as he moved out to the beach. But they hadn't, clinging to some misbegotten idea that they still needed each other. And now his life was in shambles. His wife had delivered an ultimatum, he was in love with another woman, and in the midst of this mess, his book was on track to come out.

Jesus, the book. Tom checked his watch. It was nearly three. What would he say to Murray? He'd missed their lunch—an essential strategy session ahead of his next appointment—and he'd have to hurry, or he'd miss that appointment as well.

He grabbed the sports bag and strode out of the park, looking for a phone booth, wishing he hadn't been so technophobic that he'd resisted buying a cell.

Chapter 15

Sherry awoke with a start. It was after four; she'd drifted off. She got up, made herself a cup of tea, and switched on NPR, where *All Things Considered* was running a newscast on the vice-presidential candidates. Al Gore and Jack Kemp were due to debate on TV that evening. The 1996 race for the White House was tightening, with the Republican camp hammering the first-term Clinton administration for failing to cut taxes.

"In the run-up to the debate," Rhonda Westerbrook was saying, "Bob Dole hit the campaign trail in New Jersey today, calling Bill Clinton a 'bozo' who should be booted out of the White House. Does his vice-presidential nominee agree with that description? Martha?"

"Dole—what a loser," Sherry said as Max stretched and yawned.

"I met Jack Kemp today while he was preparing for the debate," the reporter said, "and I asked him whether he thought 'bozo' was an appropriate term for the nation's commander-in-chief. Here's his answer, although he seems a little confused about where he comes from."

Kemp's voice boomed out of the radio: "I know that people in my home state of, well, New York and California, would have no problem with that description."

"New York, California, what's the difference?" Rhonda Westerbrook said. "We'll have more on the election later. And now a short interlude in honor of today's downpour along the East

Coast, with 'Overcast' by Simon Thoumire. This is National Public Radio."

The music had a Scottish lilt, and Sherry hummed along as she straightened up after her morning's rush to get the photos sent off. She took the four unused pix down from the wall and stacked them on her table, admiring both her lover and her work.

The music ended, and Rhonda Westerbrook was back.

"Now here's a surprise for our listeners," she said. "A special guest dropped in at our New York studio today, and I'll be speaking with him by phone. He's an author who may have slipped from your radar screens. But get ready, because after a seven-year absence, he's coming back with a new novel. Thomas G. Paine."

Sherry stopped in her tracks. *Tom, on NPR?*

Tom's gravelly bass came through loud and clear.

"Thank you, Rhonda. It's good to be back."

Sherry rushed to the radio and turned up the volume.

"So, Tom, tell us about your book," Westerbrook said. "It's due out in December?"

"Yes, December third," Tom said.

"And tell us about the title. You're sticking with your tradition of naming your novels after the works of Thomas Paine, the American revolutionary."

"That's right."

"But you've added a twist to the title this time."

"Yes," Tom said. "The novel is called *The Rites of Man* with a play on the word 'rites'—not rights as in human rights, but rites as in rituals. It's more contemporary."

"I see. Now, Tom, you set very strict conditions before agreeing to this interview, didn't you? I can't tell our listeners about the book because I haven't read it. In fact, as I understand the conditions, you won't be providing review copies until the book comes out. Why is that?"

"Good question, Rhonda. The publisher wants to keep this one under wraps because it's so different from my previous books."

"So you'll be keeping us in suspense," Westerbrook said. "But you've just agreed—unexpectedly, I might add—to read us a short excerpt. Is that right?"

"Yes."

Sherry settled down on the couch to listen. She'd been dying of curiosity about the novel.

"And from what you told me earlier," Westerbrook continued, "the interesting thing about this book, in contrast to your earlier work, is that it's entirely written in the voice of a woman. Over to you."

Sherry pricked up her ears.

A woman? He didn't say anything about that.

"*The Rites of Man*," Tom began. "From Chapter One. 'Revolutions Are Sexy.'"

Clearing his throat, he launched into the chapter.

"It all started with an anti-war demonstration," Tom read. "I was really young, eighteen. The police were out in riot gear. Everyone was shouting. You know, 'Ho Ho Ho Chi Minh, Vietcong are gonna win.' Like that. Some of the kids were throwing rocks, and it got ugly. I had my Pentax with me and started shooting."

Sherry flinched. *Pentax?*

"I didn't see the cops fall back to charge. There was a bang and a cloud of smoke, then more bangs. Everyone was screaming and running for cover. My eyes were burning. I couldn't see what was happening. Then someone grabbed me. 'Come on,' he said. 'They'll smash your camera!' We ran into a building—it was a dorm—and he led me to the men's room."

What the fuck?

"Tears were streaming down my face," Tom continued. "I was actually blinded. He doused my face, then his. I told him I'd caught some great shots if the Pentax wasn't ruined. 'Fucking pigs,' he said. 'That was pepper gas.' Then he stripped to his shorts."

It's my story!

"I could see by then," Tom went on, "so I asked what he thought he was doing. 'Just give me the camera and get out of your things or you'll cry all day,' he said. So I went into a cubicle and stripped to my underwear. I was still crying. 'By the way,' he said, 'I'm Josh.' He handed me some paper towels under the door. 'You can come out now,' he said. 'I won't bite.' But he did. Revolutions are sexy."

Tom paused, and Westerbrook cut in.

"Sexy indeed, and I'm sure our listeners will be asking for more. That's it for today from our special guest, the novelist Thomas G. Paine, reading from his forthcoming book. Next, a report on religion in Sierra Leone. We'll be back after a news update."

Sherry felt like she'd been punched. She couldn't believe what she'd just heard. Her story—in Tom's book? Head churning, she switched off the radio. It felt like a violation—her private life on the airwaves. And soon in print!

She wandered through her apartment in a state of shock. In the bedroom, she straightened the quilt, then recoiled as she realized what she was doing. Making the bed that Tom had left just a few hours ago.

Tom! Her sweet, vulnerable lover suddenly felt like a stranger.
He should have told me.

She returned to the living room, not knowing what to do, struggling to recall what she'd told Tom during their hours and hours of pillow talk. All those stories. As the implication sank in, she had to steady herself against the table.

What if the whole book is based on my stories?

Her pulse was racing.

No, he wouldn't have done that.

Panic engulfed her.

But what if he had?

Sherry tried again to reconstruct exactly what she'd told Tom, but her mind was numb. He'd said nothing about his radio appearance. Why hadn't he told her? If only she could talk to him—there must be some explanation.

Yes, that's it. I have to find him.

The telephone directory was in its place on the kitchen counter. She hurriedly flipped through, found the New York number for NPR, and dialed.

"I'd like Rhonda Westerbrook, please," she said, willing herself to sound normal.

"I'm sorry, she's in Washington," the operator said. "Can I help you?"

"She just interviewed a guest, Tom Paine. I need to speak with him. It's urgent."

"Mr. Paine left the studio twenty minutes ago."

Sherry checked her watch. Could twenty minutes have gone by already? She thanked the operator and hung up.

Now what?

Sherry tried to calm down enough to think clearly. What had Tom put in the rest of the novel? She had to find him. He was somewhere in New York, but where?

Maybe he's heading back to the island. Maybe I can catch him at the station.

She checked the schedule. The next train out was the 5:51. It was just after five. She threw on her slicker and rushed out of the house.

The packed subway ride from 96th Street to Penn Station seemed interminable, but she made it by 5:30. She checked the departures board and hurried to the platform, scouring the rush-hour throng in hopes of a glimpse of Tom.

Time seemed to crawl as passengers strode briskly along the platform, men with briefcases heading home from the office, secretaries tottering along in high heels. Sherry's eyes swept the moving mass, but there was no sign of Tom.

"The 5:51 is about to depart," the loudspeaker crackled. "Service to Jamaica and points east. All aboard."

Sherry checked her watch. It was 5:49. Two minutes. As the seconds ticked by, her hopes sank. Tom wasn't coming, and there was no way to find him, unless he'd boarded the train before she arrived.

She started to run, scanning the train's dirty windows, jogging past car after car. She kept running as the train began pulling out of the station, kept running until the last car had passed. Gasping for breath, she stopped as the train disappeared from sight.

Sherry decided to walk home. A light drizzle was still falling, but she didn't mind the rain. She had time, and she needed the air. Tom's train wouldn't arrive until after nine, if he was on it.

At Broadway and 72nd Street, she entered a bar. The dim light felt comforting. She chose a stool facing the bar's array of bottles, setting her damp coat on the stool beside her.

"Still wet out there, I see," the gray-haired bartender said amiably. "What'll it be, dear?"

"Jack Daniel's, please," Sherry said. "No ice."

With the flick of an experienced wrist, the barman poured the drink and passed it across the mahogany counter. He watched her take a small sip, then a longer one.

Sherry let the alcohol warm her. Feelings welled up. She drained her glass and asked for another. Fighting back tears, she rummaged in her handbag for a Kleenex but came up empty.

"Bad day, dear?" the barman asked as he passed her the second drink. "What's the matter? Boyfriend troubles?"

"Is it that obvious?" she murmured.

"Here," the barman said, handing her a cocktail napkin. "Why don't you tell me about it?"

Sherry cast a glance around the room. There were only a couple other customers in the place, and they were engrossed in conversation. Why not talk to a barman?

"You probably won't believe me."

"Try me." The barman poured her another shot. "It's on the house."

Sherry gratefully accepted the drink as he busied himself polishing glasses, creating a space where she felt she could speak freely.

"Imagine you meet a guy," she said. "You're swept off your feet, and it's fun. Great sex, everything. You start telling him about your life and all. You know, people you've known, old lovers—intimate stories."

"Sounds believable so far."

"He encourages you, wanting to know more," Sherry continued. "He tells you he loves you—he never wants it to end. And you believe him, even though he's married."

The barman looked up from his work.

"Married?"

"Well, separated. But here's the thing. He's not just any guy. He's a writer, and he's writing a new novel. It's all very hush-hush. He won't tell you about it, won't let you see it. You figure this is part of the creative process, you don't worry about it, until..." She paused.

"Yes? Go on."

Sherry took a breath, and the words came tumbling out.

"Until one rainy day you turn on the radio and bingo—there he is, reading from his new book. But it's not new, at least to you, because what he's reading is something you told him, pretty much word for word. It's something you told him in confidence, while you were beside him in bed. And now it turns out he's taken your story and used it in his novel."

"Without telling you? What a schmuck," the bartender said.

"Yeah. But I'm in love with that schmuck!"

The tears came now.

"I've been blind," she said.

"Don't cry, dear," the barman said gently. "We're all blind in romance. If you're still in love, maybe you can work it out. And if you can't, you'll get over it. Just give it some time. You know what they say. 'Better to have loved and lost than never to have loved at all.'"

Touched by his kindness, Sherry dabbed at her eyes.

"That's from a song by the Eurythmics," she said. "But the words go like this: 'Better to have lost in love than never to have loved at all.'"

"It's by Lord Tennyson, actually, and I got the words right," the bartender said.

Sherry glanced up at him. A barman quoting Tennyson?

"Uh… okay," she said. "So you're tending bar now, but I'm guessing you had a different career in a previous life. Were you maybe an English teacher?"

"You're very perceptive. Guess again."

"I don't know. Maybe you used to drive a cab in London and picked up Tennyson along the way?"

"Now it's my turn to say you probably won't believe me," the barman said, glad to have taken her mind off her troubles. "The truth is, I'm a psychoanalyst."

"You're a shrink?"

"Yes."

"Then what are you doing tending bar?" Sherry asked.

"As you suggested, it was a career choice," he said. "I switched when I turned sixty. Tending bar, the clientele's more interesting, and you get better stories."

Sherry smiled in spite of herself.

"People say shrinks and barmen have a lot in common," she said.

"We're good listeners. Now why don't you run along, dear? It's getting dark, and I think you've had enough to drink."

Sherry paid, thanked the barman, and headed out into the night.

The last twenty-five blocks up Broadway went quickly. As she made her way home, Sherry felt better, buoyed less by the three stiff drinks than by her conversation with the man behind the bar. At least not all guys are schmucks, she thought, rounding the corner at 97th and heading toward Riverside.

As she inserted the key in her door, she remembered that Tom had said he'd call. Maybe there would be a message.

But her hopes sank when she saw the answering machine. No blinking light.

It was incomprehensible. How could a man who loved her just disappear like that? She paced the apartment, trying to make sense of it all, fighting the qualms in her belly.

Maybe it's all a misunderstanding, she thought, recalling the barman's words: "If you're still in love, maybe you can work it out." If only she could reach Tom to find out.

It was 7:30. Should she call him at the beach house? He wouldn't arrive for a couple of hours if he was going there, but she could leave a message.

The phone was beside her, challenging her like a silent enemy. She picked up the receiver, then set it down. A moment later, she picked it up again and dialed.

She held her breath as the answering machine clicked on: "Hey, it's Tom. Talk to me."

Tom's voice—so familiar, so strange.

"Tom, it's Sherry," she said evenly. "I heard you read on NPR today. Call me."

She hung up, relieved that she'd managed to sound noncommittal. No questions, no accusations. He was sure to return the call.

But within moments, her anxiety came galloping back.

Worst-case scenarios darted through her mind. Had he made love to her the night before, knowing he planned to leave her? The memory of his touch crashed through her, leaving a wreckage of anguished yearning as the bottom fell out of her world.

What if it was the last time? What if I never feel his touch again?

The thought was unbearable.

Desperate to talk to someone, Sherry picked up the phone again. But who could she call? Anouk sprang to mind. She'd call Anouk.

But no, it was going on two in the morning in Paris. Anouk would be asleep.

Who else, she thought, still cradling the receiver. Maybe Granville…

Granville—shit. She'd forgotten about the Liza Minnelli benefit at the Beacon. He'd be waiting for her. Well, she wasn't going.

The minutes ticked by. At eight-thirty, Sherry opened a can of soup, but after she'd heated it through, she didn't feel like eating. At nine o'clock, she began her vigil beside the phone, hoping that Tom would call, uncertain what to say if he did.

There was no point in issuing recriminations. He'd probably just hang up on her. She needed to hear his voice, to sense how things stood between them. And then to find out what was in the rest of the book.

Tom was wandering through the city, lost in his churning thoughts. He'd been roaming since he left the radio studio, but the hours had brought no deliverance. Now, as he turned south from 12th Street, he felt both furious and aggrieved. He didn't know what to do. He'd told Sherry he'd call, but he didn't know what to say.

A pang shot through him at the thought of their night together, how her lips had parted in pleasure, how she'd called his name. And then, in the morning, her compassion as he unfolded his story. He'd been on the verge of opening up to her about his book, but she'd pressed him about his father, so he'd opened up about that instead.

She'd be waiting for his call. He didn't want to hurt her. Or was he fooling himself? Maybe he'd hurt her already. He knew she listened to NPR. Had she heard the broadcast? He hadn't planned to read that excerpt, but his talk with Jessica had derailed him. He'd done it on impulse. Why hadn't he just talked about the novel? Had he subconsciously found a way to ensure that Sherry would never want to see him again? The coward's way out.

Well, he wasn't about to be a coward now, he thought, as he climbed the steps to the apartment. He knocked and turned his key in the lock.

"Jess," he said, "it's me."

By midnight it was clear that Tom wouldn't be phoning. Sherry made herself a mug of chamomile tea. She took it to her room but again recoiled at the sight of the bed. Better to sleep in the living room, she thought, taking the quilt with her.

Max bounded onto the couch as she settled in for the night. But sleep wouldn't come. After tossing for more than an hour, she turned on the light. It would be 7:30 a.m. in Paris.

"Sherry, this is an unexpected pleasure," Anouk's voice trilled down the line. "Isn't it the middle of the night over there?"

"I need advice, Anouk. I'm in trouble. It's Tom."

"What? Are you pregnant? That's fantastic."

"No," Sherry said sharply. "Now listen to me. This is serious. You know how I told you about the game we played in bed? Telling stories to each other?"

"Yes, I remember. You called it foreplay."

"That's what I thought, but it's not that simple. You remember he was writing a new book, but he refused to show it to me? Well, he was on NPR today. He read an excerpt, and it was something I told him."

"You mean, something you told him in bed?"

"Yes, about meeting Rick at Berkeley. It sounded nearly verbatim."

"*Ooh-là*! How is that possible?" Anouk asked.

"You know about people with a perfect memory for numbers?" Sherry said. "Well, apparently Tom has a perfect memory for the spoken word. He must have written it down after I left."

"And you never suspected it?"

"No," Sherry said. "And here's what I'm worried about. What if it's not just that one story? What if he used everything I told him? In the book, I mean."

"Why don't you ask him?"

"That's the thing. I can't reach him. He doesn't have a cell, and he's not answering his phone at the beach house. He left here this morning saying he'd call, but he didn't."

"I see," Anouk said.

There was a pause on the line.

"Last night, Tom was talking about the future. He told me he loved me, and I believed him. I thought we were happy together. And now, the idea that he may have used me—well, it's too much to bear."

"*Chérie...*"

"The worst part is not knowing what's going on. And it's not just about losing Tom, if that's where this is going. It's bigger than that. I mean, if he publishes everything I told him, it will implicate other people."

"You mean, people like Rick?"

"Yeah. I mean, he changed Rick's name to Josh, but even so. Rick has a big job in government now. He's an adviser to Clinton in the War on Drugs. I'm not sure he'd want his past as a marijuana-smoking campus radical paraded in public."

"But if Tom changed his name, how could anyone connect the story to Rick?"

"I don't know if they could," Sherry said. "The point is, it's so dishonest. It feels like plagiarism! I mean, if he wanted to use my story in his book, why didn't he tell me?"

"He must have been afraid you'd say no."

"I'm freaking out. He said I'd inspired him. I didn't realize he meant it so literally. And then to just walk out on me..."

"*Chérie*, don't jump to conclusions," Anouk said. "He's sure to get in touch."

"Somehow I don't think so."

Anouk hesitated before replying.

"Well, you asked for advice, so here's what I think. Forget about Tom. He doesn't deserve you."

"I can't just forget about him," Sherry said. "I can still feel him inside me!"

"I understand, but try not to think about that. You can worry about your relationship later. First, you need to find out what's in the rest of the novel."

"You're right. But how?"

"Why don't you try phoning the publisher?. You could point out that there may be a problem with the book and ask to see the manuscript."

"That's an idea," Sherry said. "I could call in the morning."

"Yes, I think you should."

Sherry felt a wave of gratitude. She had a plan.

"*Merci*, Anouk. I knew I could count on you."

"Always, darling. Now try to get some rest. And keep me posted."

"I will."

Chapter 16

Blinking in the morning brightness, Sherry scrambled to find the jangling telephone. Hope and dread collided as she realized it might be Tom.

"Hey Sherry," a man's voice said. "You standing me up again today?"

It was Granville.

"Oh, I'm so sorry," Sherry said. "Something came up last night."

"You're gonna pay for this," Granville said cordially. "First round of drinks is on you. If you show up…"

"Oh God. What time is it?"

"It's ten. The rehearsal starts in half an hour, then lunch with Lou."

"There's no way I'll make the shoot," Sherry said. "I'm not even up."

"What's going on with you, Sher? This isn't like you."

"Long story."

"You can tell us over lunch, if you're coming," Granville said. "I'll be there."

"Good. But standing me up twice? Bring along some extra cash. You can buy all the drinks, and I'm feeling mighty thirsty."

Thank God for friends, Sherry thought as she hung up. But on her way to the kitchen, her eye fell on the leftover photos of Tom stacked on the table. Her mood darkened. It felt like a black cloud descending, sapping her energy. Even making espresso felt like a chore.

Max was there, demanding to be fed. He turned circles around Sherry's legs while she rinsed his dish and refilled it.

When the espresso was ready, she poured herself a steaming cup and returned with it to the couch. The coffee jolted her memory. She had a plan.

Rummaging through her wastebasket, she found the scrap of paper where Tom had noted his editor's name and address. She looked up Fitzgerald & Fitzgerald in the phone book. Steeling herself, she dialed the number.

"Fitzgerald. May I help you?" a chilly voice said.

"Helen Nussbaum, please," Sherry said.

"May I ask who's calling?"

"Sherry McManus."

"Does she know you?"

"No. It's a personal matter."

"Just a moment."

An irritating burst of cheerful music poured into Sherry's ear—"Spring" from Vivaldi's *Four Seasons*. Wrong choice, she thought darkly. "Nuclear Winter" would have been more appropriate. The voice broke into her thoughts.

"Mrs. Nussbaum's in a meeting. Would you like to leave a message?"

"Yes," Sherry said. "Please tell her there may be a problem with the new novel by Thomas G. Paine. *The Rites of Man*."

"A problem?" the voice asked, rising sharply. "What kind of problem?"

"He may not hold a rightful claim to the content."

"Hold on, please."

Vivaldi came back on the line.

In her office, Helen Nussbaum reached for the phone. She hated being disturbed during a meeting.

"Yes?" she barked.

"Sorry to bother you, Helen," the receptionist said. "I have a woman on the line who's talking about some problem with *The Rites of Man*. Something about rights to the content."

Helen frowned. Across from her sat her golden boy.

"Get rid of her," she said. "And no more interruptions."

Banging down the receiver, Helen returned her attention to Tom.

"Is there anything I should know about rights to the content of your novel?" she asked.

Tom's pulse quickened.

"It's a work of fiction," he said. "I own the rights."

"Then we're set. Marilee is expecting you on Monday at nine. And one more thing. The author photos. We'd like to see a few more shots. Can you get them for us?"

"We need to find a new photographer," Tom said.

After what felt like an interminable spell of Vivaldi, Sherry was told to buzz off. Not in those words, but the message came through loud and clear. Helen Nussbaum would be tied up all day, in fact all week and the rest of the year.

Feeling deflated, Sherry headed for the shower. As the hot water pounded down, she fought to keep the cloud at bay. The plan hadn't worked, but there must be another solution. She needed information about Tom's novel. If that Nussbaum woman wouldn't talk to her, she'd have to try something else.

Flushed and warm from her shower, wrapped in a towel, Sherry returned to the phone. Maybe Tom was back at the beach.

But his answering machine clicked on again: "Hey, it's Tom. Talk to me."

She hung up without leaving a message. So much for Plan B.

"Talk to me. Talk to me." The words seemed to mock her.

Frustration rising, Sherry considered Plan C. It was risky, but what did she have to lose? Tom might still be in the city. She had his unlisted number somewhere. She found it and dialed.

"Yes?" a woman said coolly.

It had to be Jessica. Nonplussed, Sherry hung up.

She dressed mechanically, berating herself for missing a chance to reveal her existence to Tom's wife. There was no Plan D.

She needed to get out of the house. On her way out, she stuffed the leftover author photos into her running bag and grabbed her Walkman.

It was a quick jog to Central Park. The tape was playing Jimmy Ruffin's Motown hits. As she entered the park, pounding along a leaf-strewn path, a new song came on: "What Becomes of the Brokenhearted." How ironic, she thought. She knew it by heart—broken dreams, the illusion of happiness, sadness and confusion. And the need to find peace of mind. Maybe…

Peace of mind—what a joke, Sherry thought, as her confusion of the past day crystallized into anger. She'd been focusing on Tom's book, and not on Tom himself. But now the truth hit home. If he hadn't called, it could only mean one thing. He'd used her.

She slowed as she reached the tennis courts, coming to a halt beside the bench where they'd sat together back in July. She'd jogged there unthinkingly, and the memories came flooding back. The rose. The kiss. Their tryst at her place.

She reached into her running bag. There they were, the photos of Tom. One by one, she pulled them and tore them to shreds. Some pieces scattered in the wind, lost amid the autumn leaves. The rest she tossed into a waste bin.

Gone.

Three frosty beers were on the table when Sherry arrived at Mort's. She took a seat and touched glasses with Granville and Lou.

"Sorry I'm late," she said. "How was the rehearsal?"

"Nothing special," Granville said. "We ordered for you. Now tell us, what's going on?"

"Yeah," Lou said. "We're worried about you."

"It's complicated," Sherry said.

"Tom?" Lou asked.

She nodded.

"I knew it," Lou said. "I never should have taken you to that barbecue."

"It's not your fault, Lou."

"Writers are shits," Lou said. "I ought to know."

"Come on, spill," Granville said. "Tell us what happened."

The men listened intently as Sherry gave them a quick run-down of her last twenty-four hours, culminating in the savaging of the photos.

"You just tore him up?" Granville asked.

"It was liberating," Sherry said. "But it doesn't solve the problem."

"Bottom line," Lou said, "you need to see the manuscript, but you don't know how to get hold of it. What would you do if you found it?"

"Well, at least I'd know where things stand. If he used just that one story and the rest of the book's about something else, I'd still be upset, but maybe I could get him to change it. If he used everything I told him—well, I don't know what I'd do. But I'd do something."

"I have an idea," Granville said. "What if you went out to his place on the island? There's got to be a copy of the manuscript there. Confront him. Make him hand it over."

Sherry shuddered at the image of Tom opening the door to the beach house. What would she do? She pictured herself pummeling him, battering him to the ground.

"He might not be there," she said. "He could still be in the city."

"Doesn't matter," Lou said. "You go out there and give him hell. And if he's not there, you can break in and steal the manuscript."

As she thought it over, Sherry warmed to the idea, just outrageous enough to appeal.

"Only if you'll come with me," she said.

Granville and Lou exchanged a look.

"Why not?" Granville said. "Tomorrow?"

❧

Sherry and Granville met at Penn Station in the morning. Lou had begged off—he couldn't get away on a Friday. On the ride out, Sherry buried herself in the *Times* crossword puzzle, too nervous to talk. The closer they got to their destination, the worse she felt.

By the time the train pulled in, her pulse was racing. She scanned the platform anxiously. Tom had always been there to greet her. But of course he wasn't expecting her now.

"Whatever happens, just be cool," Granville said. "Remember, I've got your back."

They found a cab. Granville kept up a steady patter on the ride to the beach house, but Sherry couldn't concentrate. She drew into herself, not noticing the familiar sights.

"This it?" the driver asked, slowing the car in front of Tom's house. When Sherry answered in the affirmative, Granville paid.

"Nice place," he said, leading the way to the front door.

He rang the bell. Silence.

"Looks like the dude's not home. You want me to break a window?"

"No, don't. There's a spare key."

She led him around the house to the herb garden in back. The sage was drooping now, and the basil had died. Sherry bent over the sprawling rosemary bush, pushing the branches aside. Beneath the spiky leaves, she caught a glimpse of silver.

"Got it," she said.

The weather-beaten deck looked forlorn in the autumn, the barbecue wrapped in a plastic cover, the lounge chairs stripped of their cushions. Sherry hesitated at the kitchen door. What if Tom was in there?

"Give me the key," Granville said. It turned easily in the lock.

Inside, all was as she remembered: the butcher-block counter, the sofa, the fireplace. The place looked pristine. Tom's neighbor must have been in to clean.

They toured the ground floor, finding Tom's stash of grass but no manuscript. Granville paused to examine Tom's vintage record collection. He pulled out an album.

"Want to hear *Magical Mystery Tour*?" he asked. "Music to hunt by..."

"Quit it," Sherry said. "I just want to find the damn book and get out of here. Let's go upstairs."

In Tom's study, a sheaf of blank paper sat on his desk beside the Olympia. They rifled through the desk drawers but found nothing. They tried the closet and dresser in Tom's bedroom next, then the guest room, and finally the bathroom.

Sherry winced as she noticed her toothbrush still in the bathroom cup with Tom's. She slipped it into her handbag.

"Nothing up here, far as I can see," Granville said. "Does he have a basement?"

They were starting back downstairs when the kitchen's screen door banged.

Sherry stopped dead, but Granville moved and the stairs creaked.

"Who's in here?" a woman called sharply. "Tom? Is that you?"

Footsteps were approaching the staircase.

"Say something," Granville whispered.

"Hello?" Sherry called, praying it was the neighbor. She motioned to Granville to go back up, but it was too late.

At the foot of the stairs stood Mrs. Johnson, clutching a shotgun.

"What's going on in here?" she demanded, squinting up at them through her glasses. She unlatched the safety and tightened her grip on the gun. "Who are you? Where's Tom?"

"Mrs. Johnson, it's me, Sherry! Tom's friend, remember? We met last summer."

"What are you doing here?" Mrs. Johnson snarled. "What have you done with Tom?"

"He's in the city," Sherry said nervously. "He asked me to pick something up for him."

"Tom always lets me know when someone's coming out," Mrs. Johnson countered. "What did you do, break into the house? I'll call the police!"

Sherry took a step toward the woman, hoping to placate her.

"Mrs. Johnson, please calm down."

"Who's that man?" Mrs. Johnson asked, eying Granville suspiciously. "I never saw anyone like that here before."

"He's a friend of mine," Sherry said, indignant at the racist implication. "And nobody broke in. Tom told me to use the spare key. Now please put the gun down—you're scaring me."

Sherry took another step toward Mrs. Johnson, then another. When she reached the foot of the stairs, the woman backed off, looking flustered.

"Let's put the gun in the kitchen," Sherry said firmly. "Everything's fine."

"You gave me such a fright," Mrs. Johnson said, setting the shotgun on the butcher block. "I saw a cab drive up but didn't see Tom, so I came over to take a look."

"Could you close the safety please, ma'am?" Granville called from the staircase.

There was a click as the woman complied, and he came gingerly down the stairs.

"We were just leaving," Sherry said. "Could you lock up for us, please?"

"I sure will," Mrs. Johnson said, looking relieved to see them go. But as the screen door banged shut, she came after them.

"Wait a minute," she said. "Did you get what you came for?"

"We did," Sherry said quickly, rummaging in her bag. "Tom forgot his toothbrush."

Waving the item at Mrs. Johnson, she grabbed Granville's hand, darted across the deck, and flew down the steps before the woman could ask more questions. When they reached the road, they broke into a trot, not stopping until the house was out of sight.

"Whew, that was a close one," Granville said.

They looked at each other and burst out laughing.

"Did you see that look in her eyes?" he said. "Hoo hah!"

"Hee hee! She could have killed us!"

"That's not funny," Granville said, and they laughed even harder.

When they'd caught their breath, they started back off toward the village. The road, crowded with vacationers in summer, was deserted in the off-season.

"Could you believe the size of that gun?" Granville said, shouting to make himself heard over the roar of the surf.

"Locals," Sherry shouted back. "They're all hunters. They shoot ducks."

"Yeah, well for a moment there, I thought we were dead ducks ourselves."

They cracked up again, laughing in the empty road.

"We didn't find the manuscript," Sherry said morosely as they set off again.

"Yeah, but we found the toothbrush!"

They howled in laughter.

"That was some pretty quick thinking, lady," Granville said when he'd calmed down enough to speak. "Now where do we get a cab around here?"

"There's a phone booth at the grocery," Sherry said. "It's just up the road."

Chapter 17

After the excitement of the trip to the island, being home was a letdown. A long, lonely Saturday loomed. Sherry spent the day trying to come to grips with her new situation. Curled on the couch, alone with Max, she had all the time she needed to rerun the story of Tom.

He hadn't called. No blinking light on her answering machine. Apart from the framed photo of his hands chopping rosemary in his kitchen, there was no sign he had ever existed.

Bursts of memory came and went as Sherry sought to construct a narrative that made sense. It was like piecing together a jigsaw puzzle. But however she turned the pieces, they didn't fit. The story was too complex.

What had he meant that last morning in bed when he'd said, "It's time to move out of the past and into the future"? A future without her? It hadn't felt like that at the time, with his talk about long evenings in front of the fire. But now that he'd disappeared, it just felt cynical.

What had been real, and what not, in their relationship? Tom's passion for her hadn't been fake—she was sure of that. He'd been a wonderful lover, wanting her, generous in giving her pleasure. But ultimately, could that, too, have been a game?

No, she thought, the physical part of their relationship had been real. But what about the rest? How much did she know about Tom, really? Thinking back over their conversations, she realized how little he'd told her about himself. Had that been spontaneous, or part of some odd master plan?

She'd opened up far more. And each time she'd told him a story, he'd pressed her for details. About Jimmy, for example. Time after time, Tom had asked about Jimmy, and she'd fallen for it, telling him private things about Jimmy's family in Harlem, sharing her thoughts about what it must have been like to grow up Black in America.

At what point had he started writing it down? The more she thought about it, the more she feared that he had simply picked up everything she'd said. It was such a rip-off! Her ideas about how the sexual revolution had affected her generation of women, for example. Had he used that, too? Those were her thoughts, not his!

But no, he wouldn't have done that.

Or would he? His words came floating back to her, his toast on their last summer night at the beach house: "To you—my inspiration." She'd taken it as the innocent enthusiasm of a man in love, but now the words took on a sinister cast. She could picture Tom laughing inwardly, making a fool of her.

And their last morning together, when he'd opened up about his father—about how learning that he was illegitimate had thrown his life off the rails. She'd been touched by Tom's story, but suddenly she was seeing it in a whole new light.

Illegitimate—darn right he's illegitimate, Sherry thought. Pirating somebody else's words and pawning them off as his own. She should have seen from the start that there was something fundamentally dishonest about Tom. Like his gimmick, using the titles of works by the other Tom Paine. And that hadn't even been his idea. He'd admitted it. Jessica thought that up, and afterward he'd proposed to her.

Jessica! The thought of Tom's wife made her hair stand on end. Jessica had been the power behind Tom's career. It was only when he stopped writing that they'd separated. And just how separated were they? She thought back to Jessica's trip to the shore in July. The memory still hurt. What had gone on that weekend?

Sherry had never considered herself part of a triangle. That's how confident she'd been of Tom's affection for her. She'd believed him when he'd said it was over with Jessica. Was that also a lie? She revisited the scene. They'd been lunching at Aquagrill when she'd challenged Tom, asking whether he'd considered telling his wife about their affair. He'd waffled, saying he couldn't upset the apple cart before the book came out.

What a coward, she thought. Why couldn't he have been straight with her? And then to walk out like that. She'd been through breakups before, but never had a man been so crass as to leave with no explanation—no phone call, no note, not even a Post-it.

As her fury mounted, she ticked through the men she'd told Tom about—Rick, Raphael, Jimmy, Jerzy. Beyond the pain he'd inflicted on her, what kind of damage would he do to others? Would their lives, their thoughts, be on display too?

How could she have allowed this to happen? She'd viewed Tom as a man of integrity, a talented writer who happened to be going through a rough spell. She'd found him intelligent and charming. She'd not only loved him, she'd admired him. But now she saw him for what he was—lower than low, a liar, a thief, a rapist of the heart.

He'd pay for it. She'd see to that—someday, when she was stronger. But first she needed to regain her perspective, to empower herself to move on.

Were there any positives at all? At least she hadn't told Tom every chapter of her life, she thought. Some stories she'd kept to herself. Her relationship with Jacques, for example. Now there was a man she admired. She could picture him as he was when they last saw each other, grinning zanily as he showed off his latest artistic creation.

If only she could go to Paris and get away from this shit, she thought. Jacques knew a thing or two about love. They could go back to the Closerie des Lilas, where they'd lingered so often. Maybe he'd find a way to make her laugh about her talent for romantic catastrophe.

But she couldn't run off to Paris now, not with the show to prepare...

The show!

Sherry felt as though she'd been thrown a life buoy. In the craziness of the last few days, she'd forgotten about *Music in Black and White*. The show was a major event in her life, and Thomas G. Paine had nothing to do with it. She needed to get to work.

She bounded up off the couch, heading for the kitchen.

No use denying reality any longer. Tom had left and he wasn't coming back. He'd used her, stolen from her, lied to her, abandoned her. She wanted him out of her sight.

On the kitchen counter stood an unopened bottle of red. She grabbed it. The photo wall was just a few steps away. Wielding the bottle with cool determination, she took aim at the framed shot of Tom's hands and smashed the glass to smithereens.

That felt good.

Gingerly, she extracted the battered photo from the wreckage. She took it to the kitchen, held it over the sink, and lit a match. When it had been reduced to ash, she ran the tap, washing the remnants down the drain.

Next stop: the telephone.

"I think I'm having an 'aha' moment," Sherry said when Anouk picked up.

"What's happening?" Anouk asked. "Have you heard from him?"

"No. And I'm not going to. I'm sure of it now. It's been four days. If he was planning to get in touch, he would have called or stopped by or something."

"Did you get hold of the manuscript?"

"Not yet," Sherry said. "Tom's editor gave me the brush-off. Then Granville and I went out to Tom's place on the island, but he wasn't there. So we broke in with the spare key, but the neighbor showed up with a shotgun, and we had to get out of there."

"A shotgun? *Mon dieu!* Please be careful!"

"Yeah, it was real. But that's not what I wanted to tell you. I've been turning things over and over in my mind, trying to wade through all the bullshit, and I think I'm getting a better picture of what's going on."

"Which is?"

"You remember what I told you about Tom saying he loved me the night before he disappeared?"

"Of course."

"Well, that's not all he said. The next morning—actually, it was our last morning, but I didn't know that yet—Tom told me he was illegitimate."

"Like, an illegitimate child?"

"Yes. He actually said, 'I'm a bastard.' That may be the only true thing he ever told me."

Anouk's laugh rang down the phone line.

"Yeah," Sherry said, "it would be funny if it weren't so pathetic."

"What about the 'aha' moment?" Anouk asked.

"I'm getting to that. Back in July, Tom told me he had this hang-up about his legitimacy as a writer. He said he'd developed writer's block when his father went missing after a family bust-up. This had been seven years earlier, and he hadn't seen him since. I asked why, but Tom wouldn't say at the time. He said he'd never told anyone, not even his wife."

"And?"

"And it turns out the father never knew he wasn't Tom's actual progenitor," Sherry said. "When he found out, he went berserk. He was apparently embarrassed or humiliated or something. So he walked out on the family."

"What a story."

"Yeah. It sounds pretty incredible, doesn't it? But I actually believe it. Because otherwise, there's nothing that explains why Tom would suddenly stop writing. He already had a complicated family history, and when he learned he was illegitimate, it paralyzed him. It was like an identity thing. He started questioning everything about himself. He said he felt like a fraud. This went on for seven years, and then I came along. Wait a second."

The bottle of wine was on the floor beneath the photo wall, intact amid a thousand shards of glass. She picked it up and went to find a corkscrew.

Tom was running late. He had no desire to go to dinner with Marilyn and Steve. But Jessica had insisted, and he was doing his best to keep the peace. The three of them were waiting for him at a French place in Soho, around the corner from Aquagrill, where he'd lunched with Sherry. No way did he want to go back to that neighborhood. The memory was too fresh.

He'd been trying not to think about Sherry. But now his yearning for her swept through him like a tidal wave. Images flashed through his mind. Her laugh, her touch. The way she'd smiled in the dark that last night as her kimono dropped to the floor. With each image, he felt a pang of longing. Too late for that, he thought ruefully. Way, way too late.

She'd tried to reach him; this he knew. When he'd phoned his answering machine at the beach house after seeing Helen on Thursday, there was a message from Sherry. She had indeed heard him on NPR. What demonic impulse had possessed him to read that excerpt? He could only imagine how she'd felt when she recognized her Berkeley story. She'd asked him to call back, but he hadn't. What could he possibly say?

Then there was the disagreeable call from Mrs. Johnson on Friday. Why had Sherry broken into his house? Apparently, she hadn't taken anything but a toothbrush. He didn't plan to pursue the matter. She must have been pretty upset, though, to go that far.

If only he hadn't read from the novel. It would have put off the moment of truth, and maybe he could have found a way to make things work. But he'd lost his moorings. He'd arrived at the NPR studio in a daze and had read like an automaton. And now he'd lost her.

As nostalgia gripped him, Tom checked his watch. He was late—so late, in fact, that it probably didn't matter if he stopped to make a call. He found a booth, inserted a quarter, and dialed Sherry's number. Just to hear her voice. But the line was busy. He waited a few minutes and tried again. Still busy.

Giving up, he walked another block and entered the Blue Ribbon Brasserie.

"Still there?" Sherry asked when she returned to the phone with a glass of wine.

"Yes," Anouk said, "and I can't wait to hear what comes next."

"What comes next is that, thinking this all through, I've finally figured it out. When I came along, and we started telling each other stories in bed, it somehow unblocked Tom. He started writing again. It never occurred to me that he was writing down my stories, but now I'm convinced that's what happened. He's written a book that's allegedly fiction but in fact is based on my life. That's why he dropped me. I'm the only one who knows the truth. I'm the only one who knows it's pirated—that it's illegitimate and he's a fraud."

"If this turns out to be true, you have to nail him to the wall," Anouk said. "But you don't know yet, do you? I mean, what if he just took what you told him about Rick to set the novel in motion and then moved on to something else?"

"No," Sherry said, "I'm sure he lifted everything I told him. But you're right, I don't have proof."

"But why would he have done it in the first place? He had a good thing going with you, or do you think that was all a fraud too?"

"Call it twenty-twenty hindsight, but I'm reevaluating everything he ever told me. He called me his inspiration. It's like he was trying to warn me, but I was too infatuated to hear what he was saying. When we were telling stories, I thought we were playing a game—you know, a lovers' game. I talked him into it, which I now profoundly regret."

"*Chérie*, are you still in love with him?" Anouk asked.

"He can go to hell."

"Hell's too good for him. But you didn't answer the question."

"It's fucked up," Sherry said. "I don't love him. I detest him. But then there's the physical thing. I mean, it probably sounds crazy, but even now I still desire him. He was passionate and tender, right up to the last moment. I actually think he believed it when he said he loved me. But—aha!—that was less important for him than getting back into print. He had, like, a visceral need to prove he could still make it as an author. Ambition trumped love. So he sacrificed me."

"What do you mean?"

"He figured out that he could use my stories as a springboard for his writing. I don't know how he negotiated with himself about exploiting me like that while we were sleeping together. It's so cynical. Maybe he repressed it. Maybe he actually fantasized that we could have a future together. Things could go on like that as long as I didn't know what was in the book. But now I know, and he knows that I know, or will know, and he's too humiliated to face me. Just like his father, he preferred to walk away."

"Aha," Anouk said. "So what do you plan to do about it?"

"I don't know yet," Sherry said. "I'm thinking it over."

"Tom, over here," Steve called. They had a table near the front of the restaurant and were halfway through a bottle of Stony Hill Chardonnay.

"You're late," Jessica said as Tom took his seat.

"Sorry," he said. "I had to make a call."

"Have some wine, Tommy," Marilyn said, passing him the bottle.

As Tom poured himself a glass, Jessica studied his face. Who had he been calling at this hour on a Saturday night? That woman, presumably. Or worse, had he been with her?

She threw him a poisonous glance, then turned to Steve and Marilyn.

"Tom's been obsessing about his book," she said. "I'm sure that explains why he's late."

Tom buried himself in the menu.

"I hear the Blue Ribbon shellfish platter is a knockout," Steve said.

"Fine," Tom said. "We could share that for starters."

"The waiter's already been here twice," Jessica said.

"I said I was sorry," Tom said.

Steve and Marilyn exchanged a here-we-go-again look. Now that Tom had moved back to the Village, they'd been expecting a pleasant evening. Jessica had called it a celebration when she'd phoned to make the date.

"I'm so excited about your book," Marilyn said, determined to head off a confrontation. "Jessica's been telling us all about it."

"Not very likely," Tom said, "since she hasn't read it."

"You haven't?" Marilyn asked in surprise.

"Tom won't let anyone see it," Jessica said. "There's some sort of secrecy clause in his contract."

"But we can still celebrate," said Steve, who was wearing his Yankees cap. "Hey, man—have you been following the action?"

Tom looked at him blankly for the split-second it took him to realize he'd forgotten about the pennant race between the Yanks and the Orioles.

"No," he admitted. "How are we doing?"

A look of utter disbelief crossed Steve's face.

"Are you shitting me?" he said. "The whole city's talking about it! We're up two-to-one, and if we take them tonight, we're just one victory from the Series."

"No way," Tom said. "I should be paying more attention."

"Yeah, you've got to get your head out of that book," Steve said. He had badly wanted to see the fourth game, but the women had vetoed that, specifically choosing a restaurant without a TV. And now, given the hour, it looked like he'd miss the whole thing. He wished he'd brought his transistor radio, but Marilyn had vetoed that, too.

She was chatting with Jessica now, girl talk of some sort presumably.

Steve returned his attention to Tom.

"Look," he said, "why don't we meet up tomorrow to watch the game? They're playing in Baltimore. We can go to the sports bar at Union Square."

"Sure," Tom said. "What time does it start?"

"It's at four, but come early," Steve said. "I'll save us a couple of seats."

Chapter 18

Sherry's place was a mess, shattered glass beneath the photo wall, her empty wine glass on the floor beside her. After another night on the couch, it was time to clean up—and move on, she thought. First stop, her bedroom.

She stripped off the sheets she'd slept in with Tom. Over the bed, her banner from Paris seemed to mock her: "*La beauté sera CONVULSIVE ou ne sera pas.*" For the first time, she dismissed the saying for what it was: surrealist.

Of course, there can be beauty without passion, she thought, piling the sheets into her laundry basket. Flowers are beautiful. Blue sky is beautiful. She opened the windows to air out the room. It was a bright, cool October Sunday.

Sherry fed Max and put on her running clothes. She took the laundry down to the basement, inserted enough coins to start the washer, and headed out into the day.

She jogged across Riverside Drive and into the park, then south to the *Sailors and Soldiers* monument, a place she'd never been with Tom. Running past kids playing softball and couples with baby strollers out to enjoy the sunshine, Sherry struggled against thoughts about what might have been. Visions rose up of her and Tom together, walking hand in hand, dining out with no fear of being observed, maybe even—if luck smiled on them— starting a family. Rounding the monument, she ran faster, and eventually the effort drove Tom from her mind.

When she reached Grant's tomb, Sherry slowed to a trot and headed up the hill, winded but refreshed, feeling better than she had since she'd heard Tom reading on NPR. She turned south at the soaring towers of the Riverside Church and made her way home, picking up coffee and a bagel en route. She popped down to the basement to transfer the sheets to the dryer, then sat on the stoop to have her breakfast.

A short while later, she found herself humming in the shower, something about washing that man right out of her hair. After toweling off, she inspected herself in the bathroom mirror. Her summer tan had faded, but her body looked fine, its angles and curves convening harmoniously. Not bad for a woman of forty-four, she thought. Now if only she could bring her psyche into harmony with the rest.

Tom was glad to get out of the house. It was only two, but he needed the air. As he made his way toward Union Square, he ran through the events of the past week. He was finally back on the author track, and that was huge. NPR was receiving calls from listeners wanting to hear more. The book was a reality now. But the rest of his life had gone off the rails.

He wondered whether to confide in Steve. It might be good to talk things through—his heartache over leaving Sherry, his troubled return to his wife. But Steve didn't know Sherry existed. How would he take it if he found out? Would he tell Marilyn— or, worse, Jessica?

Sherry slipped on a lightly embroidered white Indian tunic. She chose her long, filigreed silver earrings—they'd stand out nicely against her hair. She had a date with Granville to shoot the portraits for their black-and-white show, and she wanted to look her best.

Armed with her Pentax, she began the short walk uptown to his place, hoping the photo session would take her mind off the whole horrible mess with Tom. How long would it take to forget about him? Or, if he was putting her life into print, could she ever forget about him?

Granville answered the door to his loft wearing a black tuxedo.

"You're looking mighty fine," Sherry said as he ushered her in.

"You too," he said. "Come on, let's shoot each other."

The loft had an airy feel, with a large Italian black leather couch as its centerpiece. Granville had set up a wooden stool and a backdrop screen near the windows to take advantage of the natural light.

"You first," Sherry said, and he sat to pose. But as soon as she aimed her camera at him, he started camping it up.

"Gotcha," she said. "Selma's going to love it."

"Very funny. Now take a real one."

Sherry shot three rolls of film, and then it was her turn to pose. She felt remarkably calm being photographed, giving herself over to the gaze of the camera. With Granville shooting, she felt relaxed, admired.

"Have a beer?" he said when they'd finished.

"A quick one. My parents are expecting me. My dad wants company watching the Yankees."

"Yeah, it's a biggie," Granville said. He got a couple of Buds out of the fridge and handed one to Sherry.

"You doing okay?" he asked as they settled onto the couch.

"Not too bad, I guess. I went for a run today and managed to forget about everything for about a minute. That felt good."

"Any word from Tom?"

"Nothing. But I'm not expecting to hear from him. It would just be good to get some kind of closure."

"I hear you," Granville said. "So what are you going to do about it?"

"What can I do? Just wait, I guess. I mean, until the book comes out."

"That sounds kind of passive. Is this the same badass woman who faced down a shotgun?"

"Okay, then you tell me," she said. "What can I do?"

"What do you want from him?"

"From Tom? I guess I'd like an explanation. I mean, we were in my bed having this transcendent sexual experience. He told me he loved me. And the next morning, he walked out the door and never came back."

"Then ask him for an explanation," Granville said.

"How?"

"Why don't you write him a letter?"

"A letter? What good would that do? Unless there's some way to make sure he answers."

"You can just spell it out. You know, something like, 'Tom, you told me you loved me, and then you disappeared. I'd like an explanation. You owe me that at the very least.'"

"Do you think it would work?" Sherry asked.

"I do," Granville said. "You'd be challenging him. Guys can't resist a challenge."

"I don't know. Maybe."

Sherry finished her beer and stood to go.

"So I'll see you tomorrow at the gallery, right?" she asked.

"Yeah. With the portraits. Eleven o'clock."

The bar at Union Square was packed with exuberant Yankee fans when Tom arrived. Steve had saved them ringside seats at a table facing the wall-mounted TV. The Yanks had creamed the Orioles 8–4 the night before, and it seemed that every New Yorker and his brother wanted to watch what they all hoped would be the final showdown.

With Steve glued to the pregame chatter from Camden Yards, Tom let his mind wander. It was good to be in the company of men. Hardly a woman in sight.

Somebody turned up the volume, and the sportscaster's voice filled the room:

"It's gonna be a classic matchup, Bob, between the Yankees' pitching, their defense, and their aggressive base running, versus the power of the Baltimore Orioles, along with their pitching."

Tom didn't hear it. His thoughts had returned to Sherry. It

was hard to keep the guilt at bay. He'd walked out on her. She must be devastated…

On the TV, the Yankees' pitcher was warming up as the sportscaster rumbled on:

"Andy Pettitte is back on the mound after heading off this championship series on Wednesday."

Cheering broke out in the bar, nearly drowning out the telecast:

"Will he be able to deliver a ticket to the Series for all his fans back home in the Big Apple? Joe?"

Tom felt a ping of worry. What if she was not devastated, but angry? His mind flashed to Sherry backlit by fire, wielding the tongs like a virago. If she'd been incensed by the ways of her previous men, how must she feel about him? She'd already broken into his house. What else was she capable of? And why had he opened up to her? She knew too much…

Sherry arrived at her parents' place to find her dad in his armchair, a beer on the table beside him and the TV going full blast.

"How're we doing?" Sherry asked, leaning down to give him a kiss.

"Terrible," Bernie said. "It's zilch-zilch at the bottom of the second."

Rose emerged from the kitchen, wiping her hands on her apron.

"He's been moaning and groaning," she said. "Hello, dear."

"Can't the bums get one little run?" Bernie said as the teams changed sides.

But as Sherry settled onto the couch beside him, there was the crack of a bat, and the New York fans in the crowd erupted as the ball cleared the scoreboard for a homer. 1–0.

Soon they were roaring again.

"Are we winning?" Rose asked.

"Quiet!" Bernie said. "Sit down and watch. We're on a roll."

"Careful, Dad," Sherry said. "It ain't over till it's over."

But Bernie was right. By the end of the inning, the Yanks were up 6–0. Baltimore went on to score four runs, including two in the ninth, but they couldn't stop New York.

"And what a way to win this game!" the sportscaster exulted as Bernie punched the air, shouting, "We're going to the Series!"

The crowd in the bar on Union Square went wild. As they poured into the street, Steve whooped and threw his cap in the air. All along the block, people were streaming outdoors in a spontaneous outburst of love for their home team. Everyone was cheering. Everyone but Tom. He stayed inside, oblivious to the celebration.

He'd had time during the game to rewrite the script of his break-up with Sherry. He'd opened up to her, she'd heard him read, and she was smart enough to connect the dots. Illegitimate bastard... illegitimate writer. She knew too much. He'd been right to walk away.

"Goodness, it's after seven," Rose said. "Let's eat."

Sherry went to help her mother. The game had been a welcome diversion, but now it was over. Rose carried a platter of lox to the table, and Bernie opened a couple more beers.

"How's my favorite girl?" he asked, passing one to Sherry.

"Not too bad, I guess," she said.

Rose looked up sharply. It wasn't like Sherry to guess.

"Is everything okay, dear?"

"Well, the show's moving ahead. Granville and I just took portraits of each other. I'll have to leave early, by the way. I need to get home to develop and print."

"What about that beach bum of yours?" Bernie asked.

Sherry looked away.

"It's over."

"Oh! I'm sorry to hear that, dear," Rose said. "Did you have a fight?"

"It's not that simple. He actually left without saying goodbye."

"I always knew he was a bum," Bernie said. "Good riddance."

"Oh my," Rose said. "Tell us what happened."

"It's complicated," Sherry said. "You wouldn't understand."

"Try us," Bernie said.

"Maybe someday," she said, standing to leave.

She fetched her camera and kissed her parents goodbye.

"Well, just remember we're here for you, kid," Bernie called as the door clicked shut.

When they'd cleared the table, Rose put on her apron, filled the sink with hot water, and squirted in detergent, creating a mound of foam. Bernie picked up a dish towel, and they set to work.

"It was easier in our day, wasn't it, dear?" Rose said as she washed a glass. She handed it to Bernie to dry.

"Yeah, I guess," he said. "If you call it easy to go off to war overseas, not knowing whether the girl you love will wait for you."

"I missed you so much," Rose said. "Two whole years. And after D-Day, when your letters stopped coming. Oy, it was terrible…"

"I know. I wanted to let you know I was okay, but after Omaha Beach, we were fighting hedgerow to hedgerow. I sent you a letter as soon as I could. I wrote it in my foxhole, with the pounding all around me."

"I still have it," Rose said. "I saved all your letters."

"Come here," Bernie said, holding out his towel so she could dry her hands.

"But we haven't finished the dishes," Rose said.

Before she could protest further, he took her in his arms, kissing her wiry gray hair.

Rose felt his love flooding into her as she nestled against him. It hadn't all been easy, she thought, and not just the war years. She remembered the battle she'd waged with her Russian Jewish parents when Bernie came home from the front and she'd announced that she intended to marry an Irish Catholic. There had been other obstacles, too, but they'd surmounted them. And now he'd been her husband for fifty-one years...

As emotion welled up, she gave him a peck on the cheek. "You go relax," she said. "I'll finish this up."

"The dishes can wait," Bernie said gruffly.

Putting his arm around her shoulder, he led her to the piano. "Play for me tonight. My darling girl."

How lucky we are, Rose thought as she sat down at the keyboard. She closed her eyes, her fingers hovering over the keys as she decided what to play.

Bernie was watching her from his armchair. He nodded as the first mysterious bars of Chopin's "Mazurka in A Minor" filled the room, his heart swelling as the music lilted and danced. How lucky we are, he thought. How lucky we are.

Back at her place, Sherry set to work. She printed a contact sheet, got out her loupe, and chose a couple of shots. Then it was back to the darkroom, where she printed two portraits of Granville on large matte paper.

It was midnight by the time she finished. She poured herself a glass of wine and sat down on the couch to think. Granville was probably right—a letter to Tom would be a challenge he couldn't resist. But how to phrase it?

She went to her desk, chose a sheet of pale blue stationery with a matching envelope, and sat down, trying to reconstruct what Granville had said.

"Tom," she wrote, "you were in my bed. You said you were in love with me. And then you left. I haven't heard from you. I'd like an explanation. You owe me that, at the very least."

Sherry sealed the envelope, undressed, and climbed into her freshly made bed.

Chapter 19

Tom dressed carefully for his interview at the *Times* on Monday morning. He knew they were planning to photograph him. Should he wear a suit? No, he didn't want to look like a businessman. Instead, he chose a blue Oxford shirt, his tweed jacket, and a new pair of jeans. Moving stealthily to avoid waking Jessica, he left the apartment in search of coffee.

It was still quiet at the *Times* when Marilee Dyer arrived. She had some business to take care of before her interview with the mysterious Thomas G. Paine. She'd never met him. What could she ask, given that she hadn't seen the new book?

She sat down at her desk and phoned the archives to ask for the paper's clips on Tom. The librarian brought her a folder containing thirty-seven items, including three longish pieces. The first was from 1986, when *Common Sense* came out. After a favorable write-up in the Book Review, it had gone on to hit number three on the *Times* bestseller list. Not bad for a neophyte. The other two were from 1989—a rave review of *The American Crisis* and a portrait of the author in the Style section when he won the National Book Award. That novel went to the top bestseller spot and stayed there for half a year.

Marilee quickly scanned the rest of the clips. The only recent item was a small report from *Publishers Weekly* on Tom's radio appearance on NPR. It noted that his forthcoming novel, *The Rites of Man*, had been written in the voice of a woman.

ও

Tom arrived at 229 West 43rd Street at two minutes to nine. Honking cabs clogged the street, slowed by trucks delivering huge rolls of newsprint to the building. After a short wait at the security desk, he was ushered upstairs to Marilee's eighth-floor office. She rose to greet him.

"Mr. Paine. An honor to meet you."

"Likewise," he said, grinning. "I'm a big fan."

"Let's take a quick tour," Marilee said. "I'd like to introduce you to my deputy and some of the editors. Then we'll get started."

The newsroom was a jungle of books. They were piled everywhere—on desks, on top of filing cabinets, in stacks on the floor. Editors sat flipping through new arrivals. They didn't actually write the reviews, Tom knew, instead deciding whether a new book was worthy and, if so, assigning it to a reviewer. But they had to edit the reviews when they came in, and some of them were diligently typing away at their computers.

"I feel like a dinosaur in here," Tom said as they made their way among the desks. "I still work on a typewriter. Haven't bought a computer yet. The technology terrifies me."

"A lot of writers are dinosaurs, from what I hear," Marilee said. "Look at Kerouac. He wrote *On the Road* in notebooks and then typed it out on a taped-together scroll of paper."

She approached a bearded man in glasses who was reading a desk copy of a new book.

"Seth? Meet Thomas G. Paine," she said. "Tom, my deputy, Seth Parkman."

As they shook hands, Marilee picked up the desk copy.

"The new Crichton," Seth said. "*Airframe*. It's a pretty good read. I'm planning on handing it to Chris."

Tom figured he meant Christopher Lehmann-Haupt, one of the *Times*' star reviewers. He wondered who would get *The Rites of Man*.

Back in Marilee's office, they settled into armchairs beside a small table where a cassette recorder sat waiting.

"I'll record this if you don't mind," Marilee said. "It's a back-up. I take notes, but I never learned shorthand."

"That's fine," Tom said. "Fire away."

"Okay," Marilee said, switching on the recorder. "Now this will be about you, not the book, because I haven't seen it."

"Yes, I know. They're playing this one pretty close to the chest, but my editor will send you a desk copy in due course. They're not printed yet."

"Much appreciated. So tell me. What have you been doing for the last seven years? It seems you've been living the life of a hermit."

"Not really," Tom said. "But I did take a break from writing. It's not unusual, you know. I've had considerable time over the last seven years to look into other writers who paused, either temporarily or for good."

"Such as?" Marilee asked.

"Take Rimbaud. He blazed onto the literary scene at the age of sixteen when he published his first poem. At twenty, he quit writing. He never published another line of verse, but he was hardly a hermit. He traveled the world, went to Java with the Dutch colonial army, worked in a stone quarry in Cyprus and as a coffee trader in Ethiopia. Then there was E.M. Forster, who took a break of fourteen years between *Howard's End* and *A Passage to India*. Sometimes novelists need time to recharge their batteries."

"So this is your comeback. Fair enough. Now, moving on, I was rather surprised to hear that your new novel is written in the voice of a woman. Tell me about that."

"Women are the new men," Tom said.

Marilee raised an eyebrow.

"Excuse me?"

"I mean, my generation of women. They're the future. They're seeing everything in a new light. I wanted to try to get inside a woman's head in order to bring that to the page."

"Interesting," Marilee said. "And was that difficult? How did you go about it?"

"Not too difficult," Tom said. "Let's just say, I got by with a little help from my friends."

The interview lasted a full hour, followed by a thirty-minute session with the paper's top fashion photographer, a rare honor. It was 10:45 by the time Tom left the paper. He caught a train back to the Village. The interview had gone well, he thought. Marilee had tried to catch him off guard a couple of times, but he had parried. Helen would be pleased.

Sherry arrived on time at the Thurington Gallery carrying her portraits of Granville in a large white envelope. The small blue envelope was tucked inside her bag. She didn't plan to mail it. She'd drop it off at Tom's apartment later. She wanted him to receive it right away.

Granville was waiting for her outside the gallery, and they entered together.

"Let's see what you've got," Selma Thurington said, escorting them to the back room. Sherry extracted her two portraits of Granville and handed them over. Granville had brought three portraits of Sherry, printed on identical matte paper.

Selma placed the photos on the viewing table, moving them around and matching them up to see what worked best. She chose a full-front portrait of Granville, eyebrows raised, the play of light and dark capturing the sensitive curve of his mouth. Next to it, she set a three-quarter view of Sherry looking into the lens with a broody smile, her hair swept back over her shoulder, the filigreed silver earrings lending a glamorous touch.

"We'll decide where to place them later, when we hang the show," she said. "I'm thinking of setting them side by side on pedestals at the front, framed in Plexiglas."

"Sounds good," Granville said.

Selma's condescending glance made clear that his opinion mattered not at all. She gathered up the portraits.

"That's it for today," she said. "I'll need your final prints for framing by mid-November, and please set aside December fourth for me. I'd like you to be here for the hanging."

They thanked her and left.

"Did you hear that?" Granville asked as they turned the corner. "First she asks us to shoot each other, and now she wants us to come back for the hanging!"

"We should rename the exhibition. *Photography: A Deadly Art.*"

"I like it, I like it," Granville grinned. "Hey, want to ride uptown together?"

"I would but I can't," Sherry said. "I have to run an errand."

Nervously, Sherry checked inside her bag to make sure her letter to Tom was still there. It was a straight shot up Sullivan Street to the Village and a nice day for a walk.

When she reached Washington Square, she found a bench beside the playground and sat down to consider her strategy. She quickly rejected the idea of going up to Tom's apartment and slipping the letter under the door. The best plan, she decided, was to drop it in his mailbox downstairs and depart quickly. She only hoped the building didn't have a door code.

The excited shrieks of toddlers punctuated the air as they braved the perils of the slide, reveling in the intoxicating rush downward. Sherry watched them play. Around noon, their moms and nannies herded them off for lunch.

Sherry steeled herself. It was time to leave the safety of the square and complete her mission. Feeling a mix of anticipation and dread, she stood up to go but stopped in her tracks. Approaching from across the park was a man who looked remarkably like Tom. Bounding ahead was a poodle attached by a leash to a stylish dark-haired woman. It had to be Jessica.

Sherry reached into her bag and extracted the letter. She stepped forward as they neared.

"Tom, this is for you," she said, holding out the blue envelope. But he walked on by as though he didn't know her.

"Tom!" she called sharply.

He neither stopped nor looked back.

Shaken, Sherry just stood there. It was as though their love affair had never existed.

"Who was that?" Jessica asked, glancing over her shoulder to see whether the woman was following them. But with Che straining at his leash, she kept on walking.

"Never saw her before," Tom said. "She's probably a member of my fan club or something."

"Well, she certainly seemed to know you."

"Where are we going for lunch?" Tom asked, eager to change the subject. "I'm starving."

"I thought we could try this new place I heard about in Chinatown. Joe's Shanghai. They do dim sum."

"That sounds far," Tom said, "but let's do it."

The farther, the better, he thought.

Sherry sank back down on the bench. It wasn't just that Tom had ignored her. It was seeing him with his wife. She'd aged well, Sherry thought, remembering Jessica's photo in the spread *Time* published when Tom won the National Book Award. Apart from a gray streak, she did not appear to have changed.

So they're back together, she thought. Tom had walked out on her five days earlier, and now here he was gallivanting around town with his wife. The more she thought about it, the angrier she got. She could hardly see straight.

Sherry exited the park onto Waverly. She'd never been to Tom's place, but she'd memorized the address. She slowed as she approached the building. It was an elegant red-brick townhouse with ironwork railings and neatly trimmed boxwood plants at the top of the stoop. Wielding the blue envelope, she started up the steps.

But she halted midway. No, she would not deliver the letter. She wasn't about to ask that—well, that bastard!—for an explanation. She had other options.

Clutching the envelope, she ran down the steps and made her way to the subway at Christopher Street. When she emerged at 96th, she was still fuming. She stopped in at Gristedes to pick up some food. Her fridge had been empty for nearly a week. One more stop, at the liquor store, and she was home, ready for the hours to come.

She hadn't seen Susan in months, but that didn't matter. Susan Katz, her former roomie at Berkeley, now in Washington as a senior partner at Herzen Leibowitz, one of the capital's most prestigious law firms. Depositing the shopping, she got out a shot glass. She filled it with Jack Daniels, downed it, and went to the phone.

"Sherry!" Susan's throaty voice came down the line. "It's been ages."

"Thanks for taking the call," Sherry said. "I know how busy you are."

"Never too busy for you, girl. What's up?"

She knew Sherry wouldn't have called during office hours unless it was important. Not that office hours meant much in her line of work.

"I need advice about a possible lawsuit," Sherry said. "Not now, but I thought we could talk later, when you get home."

"Want to give me a hint?" Susan asked.

"It would be kind of a plagiarism case."

"Plagiarism? Of your photos?"

"It's complicated," Sherry said. "When can I call?"

"I should be home by nine."

It would be a long wait. Sherry returned to the kitchen and poured herself another shot of Jack. With Susan on board, she could sue the bastard. But what did she want to sue for?

"Sherry, it's over between me and Jessica." Tom's words rose up, mocking her. He must have known when he spoke them that it was a lie. How cruel was that?

But she couldn't sue Tom for lying to her. Or could she? As they say, all's fair in love and war. Why couldn't the brokenhearted win recompense in a courtroom?

Sherry made herself a salad, tossing it angrily, trying to eject from her psyche the image of Tom and Jessica out for a happy walk.

Her rage only intensified as episodes of deception churned through her mind. Tom had led her on, and then he'd dumped her like a piece of garbage. Criminals get life, or worse, for premeditated murder. Why was there no law against premeditated jilting?

She pictured Tom before a jury of his peers as the judge brought down the gavel and read out the verdict: "Guilty!" She would be there in the courtroom relishing the moment, she thought with a satisfied smile. But the image burst like a soap bubble.

She was being irrational, and she knew it. She couldn't sue Tom for deceiving her. But what about the deception he was about to perpetrate on the rest of the world, taking her words and passing them off as his own? There must be a law against that, surely.

At the stroke of nine, Sherry dialed Susan's home number.

"Hey girl," Susan answered. "What's going on?"

"So there's this writer," Sherry said. "We were having an affair, and while we were having it, he started a new novel. It's coming out in December."

"And?"

"And to make a long story short, I heard him read an excerpt on NPR. What he read was something I'd told him, virtually verbatim."

"Who's the writer?" Susan asked.

"I'll tell you, but this has to stay between us."

"Of course. Who is it?"

"Tom Paine."

"You had an affair with Thomas G. Paine?" Susan said. "You're kidding."

"No."

"Isn't he married?"

"Yeah," Sherry said. "Like I said, it was an affair."

"Was?"

"Yeah, it's over. It is so over."

Sherry poured herself another dose of Jack. She was drinking it on the rocks now.

"He was flavor-of-the-month a few years ago from what I remember," Susan said. "But I haven't heard anything about him for a while."

"No, I know. He had writer's block. But while we were seeing each other, he started writing again."

"Okay, but I'm not seeing a lawsuit here," Susan said. "What's the issue? He remembered something you said and used it in a novel? Writers are scavengers. They do that all the time."

"It's not just something," Sherry said sharply. "It's my whole life."

"What do you mean? I need details."

"The thing is, we told each other stories. So I told him about some of the people I've known. Men I've known, let's say, biblically."

"Come on. You boasted about your conquests? That's not like you."

"No! Of course not. We talked about our lives, and any number of things came up. It was kind of political. I talked about the women's movement, and Vietnam, and racism, the Cold War, that sort of thing. And in the telling, I mentioned a number of men I've been involved with. Including men in the public eye."

"Have you seen the book?" Susan asked.

"No," Sherry said. "He refused to show me the manuscript. But I'm convinced he lifted everything I told him."

"What makes you think that?"

"Well, for one thing, they said on the radio that the book is written in the voice of a woman," Sherry said. "For another, he pumped me for information. I mean, like he's had writer's block for seven years and suddenly he goes back to his typewriter? And knocks out a novel in a couple of months? Without realizing it, I gave him the material."

"I see..."

"He called me his inspiration, but unfortunately, I didn't take it literally. I trusted him. He told me he loved me. And now he's cut me out of his life. I saw him walking through Washington Square today with his wife. He actually pretended not to know me."

"That's revolting," Susan said. "But I still don't see a lawsuit. It sounds like you're mainly out for revenge."

"Yes and no," Sherry said. "If he wrote down what I told him, then he'll be making my private life public, and that would have consequences. Not just for me, but for the men I talked about. It could hurt them, and I don't want that. But I'd be lying if I said I didn't want to pay him back for the way he's treated me."

"How could it hurt them?" Susan asked. "He presumably changed the names..."

"So what? In the excerpt, he changed Rick's name to Josh. Big deal. All someone needs to do is to establish the connection between me and Tom, and it will be seen as a *roman à clef*. Anybody and their Aunt Fanny will be able to figure it out."

"I get it. Although that seems highly unlikely if you don't provide the information yourself. And you view this as plagiarism?"

"Yes," Sherry said. "He took what I told him and used it without my consent."

"You don't know that," Susan said. "But even if he did, plagiarism means literary theft—in other words, the theft of something written. Tom Paine didn't steal anything written, according to what you've told me. In any event, we don't have a plagiarism law in this country."

"Really? That's outrageous."

"Plagiarism is an ethical concept, not a legal concept. If you sue someone for stealing your work, you sue for copyright

infringement. But we wouldn't have a case, because you don't
hold a copyright to what you told him. And not to put too fine
a point on it, I doubt there's copyright or any other intellectual
property protection for things that you told your lover in bed."

"Yes, but he stole my stories. And now he's going to use them
to reestablish himself as an author. If the book sells well, he'll
make money from them. It's just wrong."

"I don't know," Susan said. "I'm not an expert in this area,
but just off the top of my head maybe you could go after him for
invasion of privacy, or maybe for intentional infliction of emotional distress."

"That sounds good," Sherry said.

"Do you have the publication date?"

"December third."

"Okay. Well, I'll have to look into it. There are precedents
for this kind of thing. I remember reading about a case where
the Hemingway heirs sued because someone published a memoir
quoting extensively from private conversations with the author.
The family claimed the conversations were covered under common law copyright, and if I recall correctly, they lost. Checking
through cases like this is going to take time. In any event, there's
not much we can do until the book comes out."

"Could you maybe subpoena the manuscript?" Sherry asked.

"No, not really. We have no basis for that. So what's your
bottom line?"

"My bottom line is, I'm consulting a lawyer because I have a
question. Can you sue someone for stealing your life?"

PART III / THE CASE

December 1996

Chapter 20

Rain was drumming down. Sherry curled up under the quilt, willing herself back to sleep. And then she remembered. It was Sunday, December 1. The *New York Times* preview of *The Rites of Man* would be out today, along with an interview of the author. They'd run promos all week. And Tom's book would be out on Tuesday. At last, she'd know.

For weeks, she'd been waiting. Every day, she'd struggled with questions she couldn't answer. How deep was Tom's deception? Had he merely broken her heart, or would there be more? Every day, she'd lived with doubt, and it had been torture. Not knowing whether he'd put her life on the page. Hoping he hadn't, fearing he had.

Now the waiting was nearly over. She dressed quickly, threw on her coat, and went out into the stormy half-light. Ten minutes later, she was back.

She tossed the bulky Sunday paper on the couch, startling Max. He licked a paw resentfully as she hung up her coat and sat down to read.

At the bottom of the front page was a teaser to the *Book Review*. She rifled through the paper and pulled out the section. On the cover was a full-length portrait of Tom alongside a bold headline: "Women Are the New Men." Snorting, she skimmed the opening blurb:

> *Has Thomas G. Paine lost his verve as the voice of our times? Far from it.* The Rites of Man, *his riveting new*

*novel, is virtually guaranteed to spark a national conver-
sation about how the last 30 years have redefined relations
between the sexes.*

Steeling herself, Sherry flipped to the preview inside. A fac-
simile of the book cover showed a naked couple wrapped in an
American flag, the smiling woman tempting the man with an
apple. It made her want to gag. She scoured the article for clues
about Tom's novel, but the preview carefully shrouded the contents in what amounted to a panegyric on the eve of the author's
comeback. An endnote promised a full review on Tuesday, the
date of release.

She turned to the interview, presented as a Q&A. Tom's answers were jarringly cynical. What had he been doing for the
last seven years? He managed to sound self-effacing even as he
compared himself to Rimbaud. How hard had it been to write
the book in the voice of a woman? "I got by with a little help
from my friends."

Indignant, she reached for the phone and dialed Susan's
number.

"It's me," Sherry said. "Have you seen the *Times*?"

"No, sorry. I'm not up yet."

"The preview's bullshit. There's nothing in it. But wait till
you see the interview." She picked up the Book Review. "Here's
the headline: 'Women Are the New Men.'"

"You're kidding."

"He actually said that."

"I'll go get a copy," Susan said.

The day passed in a blur. In the late afternoon, Sherry headed
back out into the rain. Her umbrella buffeted by the wind, she
made her way to the bus shelter at 96th and West End. Her parents were expecting her for an early supper. She had considered
canceling but came to her senses. She couldn't stay pent-up inside, waiting. In less than forty-eight hours, she'd be first in line

to buy Tom's book, and the waiting would end. The butterflies in her stomach would either quiet or transmogrify into some more menacing beast—a mad wolf, perhaps, or a raptor.

Lost in thought, she didn't notice the crosstown bus pulling up until it splashed her. She recoiled at the sight of the ad along its side. It showed Tom's grinning face beside the words: "Coming Tuesday, Dec. 3. *The Rites of Man* by Thomas G. Paine."

Bernie was in his Eames chair watching the news when Sherry arrived. She gave him a quick kiss and went to join her mother in the kitchen. It was her last visit with them before their annual month in the Florida sun over the holiday season.

"Are you all set for the opening, dear?" Rose asked. "I'm so sorry we'll miss it."

"The show will still be on when you get back," Sherry said. "And yeah, we're ready."

She helped Rose carry dinner to the table. Bernie muted the sound and joined them.

"Can you believe this rain?" he said. "I can't wait to get out of town."

"I know what you mean," Sherry said.

"So come on down to Florida for a visit," Bernie said.

"I'd love to, but I have to stick around while the show is up."

"Sherry, dear, you're not touching your food," Rose said.

"Sorry, Mom. I'm a little on edge today."

"What's the matter?" Bernie asked. "Is it the show? Don't worry, you'll knock 'em dead."

Sherry forced a smile as the butterflies did their dance. No way was she going to unburden herself to her parents.

When Rose went to the kitchen to make coffee, Bernie moved back to his armchair to catch the end of the sportscast, and Sherry joined him. It was wrapping up with an item about France beating Sweden in the Davis Cup. Then it cut to a commercial.

A man sat on a stool typing, his back to the camera. Each click of a key retorted like a gunshot. As the man typed, the camera zoomed in and a word appeared: *T-H-E.*

"Coming Tuesday," the voiceover said as the man kept typing: *R-I-T-E-S...*

"Oh my god," Sherry said.

"Thomas G. Paine rescripts..."

O-F...

"...the war of the sexes."

M-A-N

As the camera zoomed out, the man looked over his shoulder and winked.

"*The Rites of Man* by Thomas G. Paine," the voiceover said. "Unputdownable."

Sherry grabbed the remote and fired it at the TV. The screen went black.

"Fuck," she said. "Fuck, fuck, fuck."

"Language, dear," Rose said as she arrived with the coffee.

"Hey, it's just a book ad," Bernie said.

"It's not just a book ad," Sherry snapped. "It's an ad about a book about my life!"

Rose nearly dropped the coffee.

"Your life?" she asked. "Do you know the author?"

"I do. That so-called author just happens to be my beach bum."

Sherry's parents exchanged a startled glance. Her father spoke first.

"Your boyfriend was Thomas G. Paine? You're kiddin' me."

"I'm not. Tom is the man I was seeing this summer out on the island." The words came tumbling out. "He had writer's block, but then he started writing a novel. I heard him read an excerpt on the radio, and it was something I'd told him about Rick. He stole that story. And I'm afraid he's stolen everything else I told him and published it in the book."

"You mean you haven't seen it?" Rose asked.

"No."

"I don't get it," Bernie said. "If the bum was writing about you when you were with him, didn't he show you the manuscript?"

"No. He said he was afraid it could jinx him."

"So he's rewritten the script of the sex wars, based on your life?" Bernie said. "Hey hey. I can't wait to read that book."

"Don't joke about it, Dad," Sherry said sharply. "This is a huge fucking problem, and I don't know what to do about it."

"Haven't you asked him about it, dear?" Rose said.

"No. He cut me out of his life."

"That's no way to treat a lady," Bernie said.

"Sherry, dear," Rose said, "go find him."

As soon as Sherry got home, she put through a call to Washington.

"I read the interview," Susan said. "You're right, it stinks."

"Yes, but did you see the TV ad?" Sherry asked.

"No."

"Tom is sitting there typing out the title of his book. Then he turns around and winks."

"He winked?"

"Yeah. He rips off my life, and then he goes on TV to gloat about it. I'm so mad I could spit. I can't wait to sue the pants off him."

"I hear you," Susan said. "But for the moment, we don't even know if we have a case."

"What about invasion of privacy?" Sherry asked.

"Maybe," Susan said. "We have to see what he wrote. An invasion of privacy suit would only be possible if Tom identifies you. Otherwise, there's a catch-22, because if you sue, you'll be linking yourself to the book, which would make a private matter public."

"I can't think straight right now," Sherry said. "You do the thinking."

"In any event, there's nothing we can do before the book comes out. Just try to relax until then."

"Relax until Tuesday? I don't know how I'm going to make it through the next hour. By the way, my mother thinks I should track Tom down and confront him."

"I wouldn't suggest that," Susan warned.

"Yes, but he stole my life."

Sherry stayed in bed all day on Monday, aided by the sleeping pill she'd taken around three a.m. when she realized there was no other way to stop her thoughts from spinning. When she finally rose, she'd come to a decision. She would take her mother's advice.

Protected by the early evening darkness, she exited the subway at Christopher Street and made her way to Tom's apartment. She found the building and, relieved that there was no door code, slipped inside. The registry indicated that Paine/Franklin were in 3A. She climbed the stairs and pushed the doorbell.

"Yes?" a woman's voice called. Sherry heard footsteps approaching.

"I'm here to see Tom," she said.

The door was pulled open a crack, stopped by a chain lock.

"You!" Jessica exclaimed. She unhooked the chain and pulled the door wide. "Who are you? What do you want?"

But Sherry was too startled to reply. Her eyes were fixated on Jessica's form-fitting black cocktail dress, which stretched prettily over her extended belly.

"I, uh… uh… never mind," Sherry said, turning on her heel and flying down the stairs. As she left the building, she glanced up and saw Jessica staring down at her from the window. She quashed the impulse to run away and left at what she hoped was a dignified pace. But inside, she was a mess. Her nerve had failed her.

Jessica was running late. The visit from that woman had unsettled her. She checked herself in the mirror, slipped into her coat, and, leaving Che behind, went quickly down the stairs. At seven-fifteen, she breezed into the Gotham Bar & Grill, where Tom, Helen, and Murray were already seated for a pre-launch dinner.

As she joined them at the table, a waiter appeared with a chilled bottle of bubbly. They were in the mood to celebrate. Excitement generated by the *Times* interview had exceeded their expectations. Murray lifted his glass.

"Here's to you, Tom," he said. "May you receive all the success you deserve."

Tom grinned broadly.

"Thank you," he said, touching glasses with each in turn. "Murray, Helen, Jessica—this book is yours, too. I could never have done it without you."

Jessica murmured something under her breath. To Tom, it sounded like she'd said, "Damn straight."

Now what's got into her, he was wondering, when a man with a camera approached.

"Mr. and Mrs. Paine," he said. "Guillermo Green, *New York* magazine. For our piece on your comeback. May I?"

Tom glanced at Helen, a question in his eyes.

"It's legit," she said. "They want to run a spread on you and Jessica in the next issue. Murray gave them the green light."

"Do you mind?" Tom asked Jessica.

"It's okay," she said.

Tom gave the photographer a cordial nod, and Guillermo Green fired off a round of shots of the author and his party. Even Helen tried to smile.

"Now, one with just you and your lovely wife," the photographer said. Jessica obligingly slid her chair closer to Tom's, close enough to say a few words into his ear.

"You've got some explaining to do, mister," she said. A puzzled look flashed across Tom's face, but he quickly regained his composure.

"Big smile. That's good," the photographer said, snapping away.

Still smiling, Tom leaned over and whispered, "What do you mean?"

"That woman from the park," Jessica said. "She came to see you."

On the subway ride home, Sherry tried to process what she'd seen. Tom's wife was pregnant. And just how pregnant was she? She made a mental calculation. It couldn't have happened since the day Tom departed without leaving a note. That had been less than two months ago, and Jessica was more than showing. Had it happened in August, while Tom was allegedly alone at the beach house? Or worse, in July, at the height of their affair?

By the time she got home, Sherry's shock had turned to anger. When she and Tom first started seeing each other, he'd sworn he wasn't sleeping with Jessica. A lot of crap that turned out to be. He was such a liar!

Fuming, she poured herself a glass of wine and went to the phone.

"I've got news," Sherry said when Susan picked up. "And it's not good news."

"Did you get hold of an advance copy somehow?" Susan asked.

"No." Sherry had to struggle to keep her voice steady. "It's not about the book."

"What is it then? Tell me."

"I ignored your advice and went over to Tom's place. I just got home."

"And?"

"His wife is pregnant."

There was a pause on the line.

"You're joking," Susan said.

"No. It must have happened this summer."

"While you and Tom were seeing each other?"

"Yes," Sherry said. "I'm going out of my mind."

"Hang on," Susan said. "Let's think this through. How pregnant is she?"

"How should I know? Maybe four or five months. She went out to the beach one weekend in July, when Tom and I had been together for a couple of weeks and he'd just started writing again.

Maybe it happened then. Maybe she figured that having Tom's baby was the best way of getting him back."

"That sounds pretty far-fetched," Susan said. "Can anyone be that calculating?"

"I don't know her, so I don't know. I don't even care. What matters is, Tom slept with her while we were together. He made love to her! And now she's having his baby."

"Well, she is his wife..."

"For fuck's sake, Susan. He told me the marriage was over. Otherwise, I would never have spent one nanosecond with him."

"No, I know. I shouldn't have said that."

"I feel like I'm back to square one. I mean, I thought I was over him, but this is tearing me apart. Why did I ever trust him?"

"You opened your heart," Susan said, "and apparently he doesn't have one."

"Ha," Sherry said. "Now you're with me."

"Will you be okay tonight?" Susan asked. "Because tomorrow's a big day."

It took Sherry a moment to realize what she meant.

"Oh my god," she said. "The book."

"Get up early," Susan said, "and call me when you've got it."

Chapter 21

A couple of early shoppers were waiting outside Barnes & Noble when Sherry arrived at 8:45 on Tuesday morning. *The Rites of Man* was prominently displayed in the window under a bold banner proclaiming: "The book America has been waiting for."

When the doors opened at nine, Sherry entered briskly. She snatched up Tom's novel from a display table and opened it as she paid.

The dedication made her choke: "To my wife and muse, Jessica Franklin."

She left the store, found a bench, and sat down to read.

The Prologue led off with a quote from the original Thomas Paine's *Rights of Man*, published in 1791:

*"Every age and generation must be as free to act for itself,
in all cases, as the ages and generations which preceded it."*

Sherry imagined Tom feeling clever by including this tip of the hat to his literary forebear—yet another rip-off. She launched into the text:

*When in the course of human events it becomes necessary
for one sex to dissolve the rites which have connected them
with another, and to assume among the powers of the earth,
the separate and equal station to which the Laws of Nature
and of Nature's God entitle them, a decent respect to the*

opinions of humankind requires that they should declare
the causes which impel them to the separation.

Sherry paused. So now he's plagiarizing the Declaration of Independence? Steeling herself, she read on:

Thus begins my story. And who am I? My name is not
important. Let's just say that I'm a warrior in the battle of
the sexes—bruised, but still standing. A woman warrior.
I came of age at the start of the sexual revolution, and the
rites of men have defined my existence. Or should I say the
rites of man? For man as an individual is also an animal,
with animal needs. For the span of a generation, women
have tried to alter the animal patterns of man in the name
of equality between the sexes, but have we succeeded? I offer
my life as a case study. You can judge for yourself.

Sherry snapped the book shut. You bet I'll judge for myself, she thought. The animal patterns of man? Where did he dream that one up?

She walked home in a daze and sank onto the couch to continue.

It was all there, and then some. The unnamed narrator described herself as a woman of forty-four who knew a thing or two about seduction. The physical details matched Sherry's—"freckles" and "a certain way of smiling that men seem to like." But the tone was mocking, even snarky:

If you want to get a man interested in you, tell him a story.
Make him laugh.

It felt like Tom was taunting her. Then:

When I'm telling stories, I don't always reveal everything
I'm thinking. A little truth can hide the big lie.

Or maybe he was taunting himself. She skimmed to the end of the Prologue:

We stand at the threshold of a new millennium, and relations between the sexes are undergoing a seismic shift. Women are demanding new liberties, and men are losing their bearings. Their rites are under threat. Rites, not rights. They think they have all the rights, but that's where they're wrong. That's what gives us our power. I'm going to start with the most fundamental of human rites. The subject, of course, is sex.

Sherry got up to make coffee. She needed to fortify herself before going on. So Tom would tell the world what gives women their power?

When she returned to the couch, she checked the Table of Contents and saw that the book was structured into three parts. Here goes, she thought, as she turned to Part One.

Again, it led off with a quote from the 1791 original:

"When it becomes necessary to do a thing, the whole heart and soul should go into the measure, or not attempt it."

Fair enough, she thought. But she winced as she read the opening lines of Chapter One:

Picture me lying in bed with my current lover. He's a bit of a rogue, but a likable rogue. He likes to hear my stories as a kind of sex play. They excite him.

A likable rogue? Yeah, until he stabs you in the back, Sherry thought.

So, one day we're lolling about in the early morning—you know, just before daybreak—and he asks me why I never settled down. As though it's any of his business. But it's kind

of hot, tantalizing him with tales of other men, so I go
along with it. I tell him I tried.

Again Sherry paused, bristling at Tom's portrayal of her tender storytelling as an attempt to tantalize him. But was he right? Was she so unconscious of her motives that he knew them better than she did? She read on:

He asks who I tried with, and I play him along, making
him wait. But he insists, so I say, "Well, there was the
revolutionary…"

The rest of the chapter was a from-the-horse's-mouth rendition of the narrator's relationship with "Josh." Her first sexual experience. The way the women's movement had played out for men. Vietnam and the fault line through the heart of America. All liberally sprinkled with comments from the narrator about her "current lover," apparently Tom's take on himself:

He loves the ocean. I think in a previous life he could have
been a sailor—no, a mariner, spending long days at sea
and spinning stories at night with his mates.

You wish, she thought, wondering how Tom really felt about spinning her stories, not his, into a novel. And then, when Current Lover says, "I want to know you," Narrator comments:

As you can see, he's a total con artist. But I fall for it.

How cynical is that, Sherry thought. He's putting it right on the page—he's a con artist. She wondered whether any reviewer would be shrewd enough to pick that up.

She flipped ahead to Chapter Two and, sure enough, there were her Paris stories about Raphael, only he'd been renamed as "Ari." Chapter Three took readers through Harlem in the company of Jimmy, now "Scott," and Chapter Four went to Tanglewood with Jerzy ("Roman").

She skimmed the pages, rising from time to time to go to the window and check that the world as she knew it still existed— the traffic on Riverside Drive, the leafless trees of December. At lunchtime, she made a sandwich to ready herself for Part Two.

It opened with yet another quote from *The Rights of Man* by Thomas Paine:

"But such is the irresistible nature of truth, that all it asks, and all it wants, is the liberty of appearing."

Oh, wonderful, Sherry thought. So now the great deceiver is tackling the nature of truth. This should be good.

But her mouth fell open as she started on Chapter Five. It began with the Narrator's reflections on how the sexual revolution and feminism had altered the man/woman equation:

As you can see, men in an age of sexual revolution may appear to embrace the new situation created by women's demand for equal rights. But ultimately, they duck the challenge every single time. They can't handle it. The perceived hit to their empowerment bruises their sense of manhood. So they resort to secret stratagems as a form of rebellion.

Sherry paused. Secret stratagems? What could the conjuror have cooked up now?

Take Josh for example. He played the revolutionary when we were together, and in some ways, he was. Just like me, he was in the vanguard of the revolutionary new ideas of our generation. But as I mentioned, a little truth can hide the big lie. When we split up and Josh got married, he cast himself in a different role—the happy family man, with a respectable job as a history professor. What nobody knew, not even his wife, was that he had a sideline.

The rest of the chapter related how "Josh" got involved in a fringe group dedicated to the legalization of marijuana, the Grass Is Greener Party. How he attended secret meetings in "smoke-filled rooms," stoned out of his mind. How he put his consider-able intellect to use designing hilarious publicity campaigns that brought the group a steadily growing following. How he rose through the ranks to become a major underground organizer, always managing to avoid the attention of the police. All in some misguided attempt to compensate for copping out on his youth-ful radicalism, and in particular for buying into an institution like marriage.

Sherry cringed as she imagined Rick reading these lines. Rick Silverstein, the esteemed academic, who advised President Clin-ton in his National Drug Control Strategy, portrayed by Tom as a professional druggie. If Rick recognized himself in Tom's book, he'd be furious. And if anyone else tied Josh to Rick, it would destroy him. Bracing herself, she finished the chapter:

> You may be wondering how I know about this. Not a prob-
> lem. I'll tell you. A couple years into his marriage, Josh gave
> me a call. He wanted to see me. He said there were things
> I'd understand that nobody else could. So we reconnected.
> Not very often, but from time to time we met for drinks. It
> was all very innocent, in theory. He opened up. We'd shared
> so much that I guess he thought he could trust me. But I
> hadn't forgotten the way he dumped me. Which is why I'm
> spilling his secrets now. Purely in the interests of allowing
> the truth to appear...

The next chapter demolished "Ari" in similar fashion. He'd made his name in television journalism with an exclusive inter-view of Yasser Arafat, only the interview was a fake, the narrator said. The wily Ari had re-edited the tape of a press conference to make it appear that he'd been alone with Arafat, whose comments were actually replies to questions from other journalists. And this was not Ari's only venture into falsified news, the narrator said, embellishing the tale with lurid details of alleged plagiarism in his newscasts, all in the name of proving he could get away with it—i.e. proving he had balls.

Sherry hadn't seen Raphael Bensimon since their break-up. He had his faults, but dishonesty was not one of them. Again, she flinched as she imagined him recognizing himself.

In Chapter Seven, "Scott" was said to have moved to Europe with his saxophone not to escape the racism of the United States but because he was a heroin addict facing jail time for possession. Totally false! Jimmy Robinson may have smoked the occasional joint, but he never touched hard drugs. The problem was that the story sounded plausible. But a Black fugitive from American justice? Jimmy would go crazy if his name was linked to the book.

But worse was to come for "Roman," said to have worked as an informant for the Polish secret police in exchange for permission to perform abroad. His visa for Tanglewood had allegedly come with an offer he couldn't refuse—cooperate, or you will never see your wife and children again. But Roman had cooperated willingly, the narrator said, describing the various ruses he used to elicit information from the Americans he met, effectively spying on them.

As she read, Sherry felt a ping of doubt. Could Jerzy Gregorski have actually been an informant? He had, in fact, asked her many questions about her life, but they were innocent questions, surely. She thought back to her time with Jerzy, trying to remember what she'd told him. If he'd been a spy, and it became known, he'd be finished as a musician. But seven years after the collapse of the Soviet empire, the Poles were taking their time about uncovering collaborators with the Communist-era secret police.

She set the book aside. The worst thing was that all of the stories in Part Two were at some level believable. They could have happened. And while Part One used her stories, Part Two was pure invention. It was fiction. How could she sue for that?

She rose to feed Max, who was purring hopefully at the foot of the couch. On her way back, she found her bottle of Jack

Daniel's and filled a tumbler.

Part Three started off, as had the others, with a quote from the original *Rights of Man*:

> *"As revolutions have begun, (and as the probability is always greater against a thing beginning, than of proceeding after it has begun), it is natural to expect that other revolutions will follow."*

In the light of her previous relationships, the narrator said, she faced a dilemma with her current lover. Could she trust him? As her reckoning had shown, each of her previous love affairs had both a text and a subtext, and it all had to do with a man's need, when faced with a challenging woman, to boost his fragile ego:

> *Simone de Beauvoir may have launched the women's revolution, but the second sex? Don't make me laugh. Anyone who still believes that females are the weaker of the species can just take a look at my life and rethink the matter. The men I loved couldn't take the heat. They parroted the rhetoric of liberation but capitulated to the values of previous generations. And then, to restore their sense of self, they resorted to gambits from fringe politics and fake reporting to drug abuse and counterintelligence. Duplicity is at the heart of each of these stories. So now, let me ask you: Is dissemblance the ultimate rite of man?*

Good question, Sherry thought. She was reading quickly now, eager to reach the end.

The narrator said her relationships had taught her that trust was impossible at a time of sexual revolution—but this did not mean that love was impossible. She issued a call for a new era in relations to coincide with the coming millennium. In this "human revolution," men and women would stop pretending to be equal in every way and would enjoy each other as human beings with separate strengths and weaknesses. Her conclusion? Her current lover might not be the perfect man. He was more probably a dishonest scoundrel like the rest of them. But he was her scoundrel, and this time she wouldn't let him get away. Reader, she'd marry him. *Et vive la différence.*

It was already five p.m., and what remained of the day was fading. Sherry poured herself another Jack, reached for the phone, and dialed Susan's office.

"It's even worse than I thought," she said when Susan picked up. "Have you got it?"

"I bought a copy at lunchtime, but I haven't had time to look at it yet. But I did read the *Times* review by Sakura Tanaka."

"Oh God, I forgot about the review," Sherry said. "I don't even have the paper. What did she say?"

"I wouldn't call it a rave, but it's pretty positive. Hang on. I'll get it."

The butterflies did somersaults while Susan fetched the paper.

"She calls it, quote, 'a refreshing new take on the war of the sexes,'" Susan said.

"Fuck."

"Listen, I'll read it to you." Susan chose an excerpt:

In his new book, the author Thomas G. Paine delivers a gripping narrative as we see behind the facade of romance and into the dark recesses of post-feminist sexual politics. This is a story that will encourage all readers to reevaluate their own lives and emerge the wiser. Its message? Acceptance.

"What is she talking about?" Sherry said. "If the truth comes out, she'll regret it."

"So tell me about the book already."

"Okay. So, just as I feared, Tom ripped off my stories. That's in Part One. But then he embroiders in Part Two. He invents a dishonorable secret life for each of the men I told him about. Like, his Rick character becomes a pothead working for some group called the Grass Is Greener Party, and the Jerzy character signs up as an informant for the Polish secret police."

"What?"

"Yeah. You have to read it," Sherry said. "So, like he stole my stories and then he twisted them to promote his own agenda. The narrator is this snarky woman who tells stories about her past affairs to her so-called current likable rogue of a lover. The guys are portrayed as bastards, but it's not their fault. It's the fault of women! Basically, the thrust of the book is that feminists may have tried to change women's destiny, but we failed. The guys will always outsmart us because—wait for it—dissemblance is the ultimate rite of man. The narrator says we need to accept this. Forget about trust, but love the bastards anyway. I mean, give me a break."

"Sounds complicated," Susan said. "Okay, I'll read it tonight."

"The problem is that it's half rip-off and half invention."

"Well, you can forget about anything resembling an intellectual property claim if he made it all up. Do you still want to sue?"

Sherry's face flushed in anger.

"Are you out of your mind? He seduced me into thinking I meant something to him and went on to betray me in every possible way. I'll do whatever it takes."

"How soon can you get down here?" Susan asked.

"I'd like to get on a plane right now," Sherry said, "but we're hanging the show tomorrow and it opens on Thursday. I'll fly down on Friday."

As she placed the receiver back in its cradle, Sherry felt like her mind was exploding. What was worse? The surreptitious way Tom had used her for her stories? His bold-faced lies about loving her when he was actually still with his wife? Or what the book revealed about the way his mind worked? She needed to do something, anything, to drown the noise inside her head.

She turned on the television and sound filled the room, but it wasn't enough to chase away the images of the past two days. Jessica standing pregnant in the doorway. Tom winking as he advertised his book. Now he'd have it all—fame, fortune, and family. The bottle of Jack was nearly empty. She poured the last of it into a tumbler and went to run a hot bath.

From the living room, she could hear the evening news roundup. President Vaclav Havel was doing as well as could be expected after surgery for lung cancer the previous day. Serbian protesters were challenging President Milosevic. The reports from Eastern Europe brought Jerzy back to mind. Had she told him anything that could possibly be of value to Poland's Communist authorities? As unlikely as that seemed, she felt the need to call him. Yet she'd never called Jerzy in Warsaw. She didn't even have his number.

Sherry was so wrapped up in her thoughts that she lost track of the newscast until she heard the words "literary phenomenon of the year."

"And with us in the studio," the anchor was saying, "is the author Thomas G. Paine, whose new book was released today and is already selling like hotcakes."

Sherry scrambled out of the tub and grabbed a towel.

"Good to be here, Roger." It was Tom's gravelly voice.

"Now, Tom, *The Rites of Man* is generating a lot of buzz, in part because the narrator is a woman. You're already being compared to William Boyd, who performed a similar feat a few years back with *Brazzaville Beach*."

Wet footprints followed Sherry to the TV.

"I picked up your book this morning," the anchor went on, "and I have to say that the way you got inside a woman's mind is just uncanny. How did you do it?"

Tom smiled humbly into her living room.

"Well, Roger, I spent seven years on this novel, and that gave me time to consider how the women engaged in social change might be feeling at this juncture. Of course, we'll have to wait and see how women themselves appreciate this story."

Tom camping the modest hero. She returned to the bathroom and retched.

Chapter 22

Tom was back on TV in the morning, on *The Today Show* promoting his book. Sherry knew she shouldn't watch it, but she couldn't help herself. She felt like a moth drawn to a flame, flying toward self-destruction. Byron Hazelworth was reading from reviews that had come out in the Wednesday morning papers, and Tom was lapping it up.

"Here's what they have to say in the *Los Angeles Times*," Hazelworth said as the camera zoomed in on the paper's headline: "Just Like a Woman." He picked up the review and began to read: "'What is most striking about *The Rites of Man* is its authenticity. The narrator may be irreverent, but she's also vulnerable. She could be any woman, or maybe everywoman.'"

Tom grinned, looking every bit the modern author in his tweed jacket and jeans.

"Can't argue with that," Hazelworth said.

Oh yes, you can, Sherry thought.

"Although at least one reviewer begs to differ," Hazelworth went on. "Here's Erica Jong in *The Washington Post*: 'Thomas G. Paine has written a startling novel that challenges the notion that women's rights are worth fighting for. Mr. Paine appears to believe that the sexual revolution didn't revolutionize anything. His narrator contends that men are as they've always been, and that women must accept this. We would like to challenge Mr. Paine in turn. Are the rites of man really so immutable? Are they rights?'"

Sherry was suddenly glad she'd tuned in.

"So, Tom," Hazelworth said, "would you like to reply for our viewers?"

"You know, Byron, I've always been an admirer of Erica Jong, and she is, of course, entitled to her opinion. My response is simple. Let's let the readers decide."

The two men were shaking hands when Sherry's doorbell rang. It was Granville.

"Come on," he said. "Let's go to a hanging."

As they left the gallery a few hours later, Granville allowed himself a last look inside. Selma Thurington was adjusting their framed self-portraits, which stood on pedestals up front to the left of the door. On each side wall were photos of musicians' hands. It had taken Selma ages to line everything up to her satisfaction. She looked up and nodded a curt goodbye.

"Where to?" Granville asked as they headed up Sullivan Street. "Want to grab a sandwich?"

"Sure," said Sherry. "I'm actually starving."

She was feeling better, she realized as they strolled along. Concentrating on the show had briefly driven Tom's book from her mind. She was wondering whether bringing it up would ruin their lunch when she stopped short at the sight of a newsstand.

The owner was putting up posters billing the next issue of *New York* magazine. "The Comeback," the headline read over a smiling photo of Tom and his wife.

Sherry took a step back, stumbling into Granville.

"Hey, are you okay?" he asked, catching hold of her.

"No, not really. Look at them, the happy couple."

"I thought you said they'd split up."

"That's what he told me."

Granville steered her away from the newsstand. There was a deli on the corner, and he ushered her inside.

"Sherry, we've got a show opening tomorrow," he said as they settled into a booth. "You need to pull yourself together."

Sherry didn't seem to hear. She reached for a menu.

"You're not listening. Look at me."

Sherry glanced at him resentfully.

"You've got to deal with this," Granville said.

"Yeah? And how do you propose I do that?"

"Why don't you just go confront him?"

"I already tried that," she said. "I went to their place in the Village. The bitch is pregnant. Can we order now?"

Granville just looked at her.

"You mean, like he was two-timing the both of you?"

Sherry nodded.

"You've got to be kidding," he said.

"I saw her, Granville. She's pregnant. She's having Tom's baby."

Struggling to keep her cool, she returned her eyes to the menu.

Granville signaled to the waiter, who arrived with his pad.

"Bring us a couple of Cokes please," he said. "No, hang on a sec." He turned to Sherry. "Maybe you'd like something stronger. We could go to a bar…"

"No, that's all right. Coke is fine."

They sat in silence until their drinks arrived and the waiter departed.

"Now give it to me straight," Granville said. "How are you dealing with this?"

"Not very well. I've been obsessing about the book, probably because it's less painful than thinking about the way Tom lied to me. That magazine cover was just the icing on the cake. I mean, he told me he was free, and now he and his pregnant wife will be plastered all over town. I just don't know how to get past this. I need to move on, but I can't see how."

"Hey, Sher. He's only a guy."

Sherry stared at him blankly.

"That's not the issue," she said. "The issue is me. Why did I fall for it? I told myself from the beginning not to go running after happiness with a man again, but I got swept up and forgot about that. And now I'm paying the price."

"Listen," Granville said. "I know all about running after happiness with a man. I've had my share of hard falls, too. It's part of life. A lot of people wouldn't risk it. They prefer to play it safe, to settle for less. They're afraid to fall in love. But that's just not us, Sher."

It took Sherry a moment to realize what he was saying.

"You never talk to me about your lovers," she said.

"You never ask."

"Maybe I've been too discreet. The thing is, you're always so solid. How do you do it?"

"The same way you do. Look, you've got a whole lot of shit going on that has nothing to do with Thomas G. Paine. No matter how hurt you're feeling right now, he's only a guy. He and his wife and his book—they're going to fade away in time. You're going to have to tough it out until that happens."

"I can't," Sherry said. "I'm a human wreck."

"You can," he said. "And I mean, starting right now. Because you're my partner, Sher. We've got a show opening tomorrow, and we've worked hard to get there, and you're going to shine, and you're going to show this town just how much talent you've got. So, love? Yeah. It's important. But you and your camera— you've brought beauty into the world. Truth and beauty. No one can take that away from you."

Sherry felt like hugging him.

"I still don't know how I'll get through the opening," she said.

"You'll be a star. Now, if you're feeling better, how about we order some lunch?" He looked around for the waiter.

"You're on," she said.

Murray and Tom were chatting animatedly as they walked to Fitzgerald & Fitzgerald. It was only a block away from the fashionable restaurant where they'd lunched. Both of them were in good spirits, fueled by half a bottle of the excellent house white. Murray generally didn't indulge at lunchtime, but he didn't want his star author to drink alone. And although Tom had straightened out his private life, he'd seemed edgy since moving back to the city.

As they waited for the elevator, Murray decided to broach the subject.

"How's it going at home, Tom?" he asked. "Is Jessica doing okay?"

"She's fine," Tom said. "In fact, pregnancy seems to suit her. She's in a better mood these days."

Most of the time, he thought, remembering Jessica's hostile questions after Sherry appeared at their door. He'd managed to deflect them. At least he hoped so.

"Remind me, when's the baby due?" Murray asked.

"Around mid-April," Tom said as the elevator doors creaked open, discharging a cluster of people. Several more had gathered for the upward journey, enough to make conversation impossible in the antiquated cubicle, Tom thought with relief as they stepped inside.

It wasn't that he didn't want to open up to Murray about his personal life. He didn't want to open up to anyone. Ever since Jessica had informed him that she was expecting, he'd been grappling with the prospect of fatherhood.

As the elevator slowly rose, stopping at every floor, Tom's mind flashed to the moment back in October when Jessica had announced her pregnancy. She'd cornered him as he was about to leave the apartment, saying they needed to talk. Then she'd sat him down and informed him that she was two-and-a-half months pregnant.

"How... how is that possible?" he'd stuttered. His mind had galloped back to July, when he'd taken Jessica into his bed. It had been madness! Why had he done that? And why had she gone along with it?

Then he'd asked the wrong question: "It's probably a non-issue, but do you plan to keep the baby?" Jessica had looked at him as though he was insane.

"I'm going to be a mother, Tom," she'd said. "It feels like a miracle that this happened now, at my age. You can decide what you want to do about it. If you've moved on and want to split up, I'll raise the baby on my own. But if you want to be a father to this child, you're going to have to move back in and at least act like a husband…"

He'd left in a daze. Why hadn't this happened when they were still happy together? When the news would have made his heart soar in elation? It was too late. And yet, how could he not be a father to his child? His own father had deserted the family. He would never do that…

The elevator finally reached the twenty-fifth floor.

"Let's go," Murray said as the doors opened.

Jessica had been right, Tom mused as they walked briskly down the hall to Fitzgerald & Fitzgerald. After all those years of putting off having children, and then not succeeding when they tried, it was a fucking miracle she got pregnant. A miracle at the wrong fucking time.

The receptionist escorted them to the conference room, where Helen Nussbaum was chairing a meeting on upcoming events for *The Rites of Man*. As they took their seats, George Fitzgerald poked his head in.

"Mind if I join you?" the publisher asked. "Hello, Tom. Murray."

"We're going over the dates for Tom's book tour," said Helen, who was flanked by Joyce Chen of sales and Pia Franchinelli of publicity.

"Joyce, what's the latest?" George asked as he took a seat.

"We're going through the roof," Joyce said, passing him a spreadsheet. "We should hit fifty thousand nationwide in the next couple of days. We'd better start thinking about another print run. There's a lot of buzz, and if sales accelerate, we could be looking at 150,000 by Christmas."

Tom allowed himself an inner smile. Seven years of nothing, and then a breakout bestseller.

"That's going to fix our balance sheet for this year," George Fitzgerald said, giving Tom a friendly nod.

"Mine, too," Murray said softly, mentally calculating his share of the profits. The money would come in handy next year when his six-year-old started private school.

"Let's move on," Helen said. "Pia, could you run us through Tom's schedule?"

"Of course," Pia said. "So, our favorite author will spend the rest of this week doing interviews with the national media. *The Today Show* went well, and we have a gig with CNN airing tomorrow for international reach. The book tour starts next Tuesday with a signing at Barnes & Noble. Tom goes on to Washington for a signing at Politics and Prose, and then he flies out to Chicago to tape with Oprah. The last stop will be San Francisco on Monday, December 16, with Tom reading and signing at City Lights."

"Isn't that a rather small venue?" George Fitzgerald asked.

"It's historic," Pia said. "Ferlinghetti will be there, and we're in touch with the local networks. We expect the coverage will sell more books than the actual signing."

"That's a pretty tight schedule, Tom," Helen said. "Can you handle it?"

"Can't wait," he said, a huge grin illuminating his craggy features.

The short December day was already fading when Sherry got home from the deli. The blinking red light of her answering machine caught her attention. She pushed the button.

"Sherry, it's Rick."

She hit the pause button. Rick! She'd figured he'd call, but not so soon. Bracing herself, she pressed the button to hear his message:

"We haven't talked in a while, so this is kind of out of the blue, but I need to ask you something. Have you seen the new Tom Paine book by any chance? *The Rites of Man*? It's been in the news, and I picked up a copy. Anyhow, this may be just a coincidence, but there's a character in the book who meets a woman at Berkeley, and they sound just like us. I mean, remarkably like us, with details like when we got gassed together and ran into the men's room. And then later it all goes to hell, with the guy getting involved in some stoned-out political group. So I'm wondering, what's the deal? You don't know the author, do you? Call me back."

Sherry shrugged and turned her back on the phone. Max was watching her.

"You must be hungry, little guy," she said, and Max followed her to the kitchen. She filled his dish distractedly, some of the pellets falling onto the floor.

"Granville's right, isn't he, Max?" Sherry said. "I need to pull myself together."

She went to her bedroom and opened the closet.

"Now let's see, what can I wear to the opening tomorrow?"

She pulled out a black Calvin Klein dress with an asymmetrical neckline, slipped it on, and put on a pair of heels. The dress flowed swishily to her knees. She added her filigreed silver earrings and a fine silver necklace, and checked herself out in the mirror.

No way was she going to call back.

Chapter 23

The jangling of the telephone jolted Sherry from sleep. The sun was already up. By the time she made it to the living room, the answering machine had clicked on.

"Hey, Sherry, it's me, Jimmy. You there?"

She didn't pick up.

"Guess you're not there. So, well, I'm calling from Geneva, Sher. Hey, how're you doing? Just checking in. Well, actually, I wanted to ask you about something…"

He paused, and the transatlantic static crackled into the room.

"Well, it's like this," he said. "I was watching CNN, and they were talking about this new book called *The Rites of Man*. Hot-shit author and all that. I guess it's getting a lot of press in the States. Anyhow, they read an excerpt about this dude named Scott, only he sounded a lot like me. He plays the sax, and he's involved with a white woman. Takes her to Harlem to meet his folks. And you know? She sounded a lot like you. In fact, everything she said sounded just like what you said when we were seeing each other. It was weird, Sher. I'm going to have my mom send me a copy. You know, it just brought it all back. The old days—you and Lou and Granville Macks. How is that son-of-a-bitch? Haven't heard from him either. So call me, right?"

Sherry looked at the phone like it was radioactive. Under other circumstances, she would have loved to talk with Jimmy, but today? Forget it. She was heading to the kitchen to make coffee when the phone rang again. She let it ring until the answering machine clicked on.

"Sherry, it's Rick. You didn't get back to me. So maybe you're out of town? But I know you pick up your messages, so listen. I'm concerned about that book. Please call me as soon as you get this message. By the way, in case you're away, I'm calling on Thursday, December fifth."

Thursday. Sherry struggled to clear her head. That means the opening is tonight.

Desperate for coffee, she made it as far as the kitchen this time before the phone rang again. Steeling herself, she returned to the living room as the answering machine clicked on.

"Sherry, it's Susan. Are you there?"

Sherry snatched up the receiver.

"Sorry. I'm screening my calls," she said. "The phone's been ringing off the hook."

"What's going on?" Susan asked.

"My exes are after me. They're asking about the book. Rick has phoned twice since yesterday, and Jimmy called from Geneva this morning."

"Did you talk to them?"

"No. But the phone is driving me crazy. What if Raphael calls? Or Jerzy?"

"Don't answer," Susan said. "In fact, unplug the phone."

"Great idea, but then how would you call me?"

"Just kidding. Now, moving on, I finished *The Rites of Man*, and I've had some thoughts about how to approach this. We'll go over it tomorrow. Have you booked your flight to Washington?"

"No, not yet," Sherry said. "I'll take care of it this morning."

"Good. I'll book a table for lunch if you can make it by then."

"I plan to. If I survive the opening tonight."

Loud chatter filled the Thurington Gallery as an elegant crowd drifted from room to room admiring the photos on display. Granville moved easily among them, looking smart in his tux, telling anecdotes about the musicians he'd captured in his lens. Selma Thurington reigned over the proceedings from the front of the gallery, welcoming visitors, the price list set discreetly on a pedestal by her side. She had reason to look satisfied beneath her African silk headdress. *Music in Black and White* was clearly a success.

Lou Karmitz had been among the first to arrive, and Sherry had not left his side. Many musicians had turned out, and she nodded to those she knew as she and Lou wove a path through the throng. Waiters with flutes of champagne on silver trays circulated among the guests, and Sherry gratefully accepted a glass.

"Here's looking at you, kid," Lou said as he touched his glass to hers, a note of concern in his voice. Granville had brought him up to date, and he knew this was an ordeal.

Snatches of conversation floated up from the crowd.

"… and the Polish violinist turns out to be a spy!"

Sherry flinched. It seemed everyone was talking about *The Rites of Man*.

She turned to see who was speaking. It was a plump, middle-aged woman in bright red lipstick and a fur stole, her eyes brimming with the smug excitement of an insider who had already read the hottest book of the season.

"I wonder who his model was for that one," the dapper man beside her remarked drily. "Either Thomas G. Paine has one hell of an imagination, or we should be keeping closer tabs on foreign musicians."

Sherry cast a distressed look at Lou, and he steered her away from the couple, toward the back room where Granville was holding court before his portrait of Miriam Makeba.

"She's even more of a fireball offstage," he was saying. "You should hear her talking about her time with Stokely."

Lou cleared his throat, and Granville excused himself to join them.

"How are you holding up?" he asked Sherry.

"Would it be gauche if I slipped away?" she said. "I've got an early flight."

Lou looked surprised.

"You skipping town or something?" he asked.

"I'm meeting my lawyer in Washington. It's just a quick trip."

"Better stick around for a while," Granville said. "I think Selma's making a speech. You'll be back in time to shoot the concert tomorrow night, right?"

"Avery Fisher Hall, eight p.m.," Sherry said. "I'll be there."

Chapter 24

Sherry barely noticed as her cab swept through the monumental center of Washington on Friday morning. The Lincoln Memorial flitted past, looking drab in the late-autumn drizzle, then the Washington Monument and the White House—she'd seen them all before. Her mind was elsewhere. What did Susan have in mind as payback for Tom Paine? The cab swung left onto M Street and pulled up at Vidalia, the restaurant where they'd hold their working lunch.

Susan was already there, at a table for two beside a pillar, far enough from the other tables to provide a modicum of discretion. She rose as Sherry approached, and they hugged. A bottle of sparkling water stood on the table.

"We don't have a lot of time," Susan said as Sherry took her seat, "so let's get straight to the point. You're sure you want to pursue this?"

"I am, absolutely," Sherry said.

"Then we need to consider the options. And of course, given the nature of Tom's book, the situation has changed since we first spoke. Because we were talking about a book in which he pirated your words, but there's more than that in this novel."

"I know," Sherry said. She had forgotten how intense Susan could be.

"So the first part is based on your stories, correct?" Susan asked.

"No," Sherry said. "It's not based on my stories—it *is* my stories. They're my thoughts, and my words, not his words."

"Right. Although there are places where he's written around your words with original content."

Susan reached into her handbag and pulled out *The Rites of Man*.

"Here, for example. I mean, I can't imagine you saying this." She opened the book to the Prologue and, lowering her voice, read a passage:

> *I have charm, and that's a magnet for men. It obscures my faults. A man will forgive a lot in the name of charm. Of course, sooner or later he's going to discover your faults and tell you all about them.*

"Yeah, that's the narrator speaking," Sherry said. "In the parts where she's not using my words, she's not at all like me. At least, I hope I'm not like that."

"Don't worry, you're not. The point is, we can't pursue an intellectual property claim—not just because stories told out loud are not protected, but also because Tom included original content, even in Part One. And then, from what you told me, Part Two is pure invention?"

"Yes."

"So we need to take a different approach."

The waiter appeared and Sherry opened her menu, but Susan stopped her.

"Let me order for you. I know what's good here." She turned to the waiter. "We'll have the crab cake sandwich."

"What about wine?" Sherry asked as the waiter departed.

"We need to keep it together," Susan said. "So, getting back to the lawsuit, another approach could be to sue for intentional infliction of emotional distress. This is a tort that can make it possible for people who suffer real damage from the misbehavior of another person to recover in court."

"Fine," Sherry said.

"But I can't imagine it would work in your case," Susan continued. "I don't think a lover outside a marriage would have

much success persuading a jury that she was the object of inflicted emotional distress."

"So that's how people will see me, a lover outside a marriage.
But that's not how it was. Tom convinced me he was free."

"Sure. It's an old story. They string the mistress along with
promises while taking care not to jeopardize the relationship with
the wife."

"Did you see he called her his muse in the dedication?" Sherry said.

"That's so cynical."

"It's just ironic. The way I see it now, they deserve each other.
Anyhow, do we have a plan?"

"I'm not sure yet," Susan said. She pulled a steno pad from
her handbag and flipped to a page of notes.

"I've looked into invasion of privacy. It's a tort with four
possible claims," she said. "One, intrusion of solitude. Two,
appropriation of name or likeness. Three, public disclosure of
private facts. And four, false light. If you were somehow revealed
as Tom's source, then I think the first three could potentially be
applied to your situation, and the fourth could be used by the
men portrayed in the book if they ultimately decided to sue. The
problem is that none of these would apply unless you were pub-
licly linked to the book."

"I see," Sherry said. "That doesn't sound very promising."

"So another possible approach is breach of confidence," Susan
said. "This is also a tort. It protects private information conveyed
in confidence if the disclosure of that information is harmful to
the litigant or is used for unfair gain or advantage."

"Well, it's definitely harmful. I mean, it's turned my life
upside down. Not to mention the fact that Tom is making big
money off of the stories he stole from me."

"I understand that you're angry. But in order to claim in a
court of law that the confidential information Tom used was
harmful to you, you would first have to prove that you were the
one who supplied it."

"But that would also mean going public," Sherry said.

"Honey, let's face facts. If you sue on any grounds, you'll be going public."

"I'm not sure I want to do that."

"But you do want to go after Tom?" Susan asked.

"Yes."

"Then we'll have to think it through. In any event, we don't have to make a decision today. You have the facts at your disposal. Take all the time you need. In the meantime, I'm going to brief the partners this afternoon, and we'll see what they say about taking the case."

"Brief the partners?" Sherry asked in alarm. "No, I'm not ready for that. My name could leak out."

"No, it couldn't," Susan said. "The firm is airtight. Nothing leaks out."

They made small talk over lunch. When they finished, Susan signaled to the waiter to bring the bill, and Sherry pulled out her credit card.

"Don't bother," Susan said. "I'll expense it. So do I have your go-ahead to brief the partners? Because this has been between just you and me, but I can't take things any further without the firm's approval."

"Go ahead, then," Sherry said. "But please make sure it stays private."

It was 3:15 p.m. when Sherry's cab pulled up at National Airport, leaving her forty-five minutes to catch the next shuttle back to New York. She would land at LaGuardia in plenty of time to stop home, pick up her camera bag, and get over to Lincoln Center for the concert.

At four p.m., as the shuttle took off, the Herzen Leibowitz team was gathering in the conference room to go over upcoming cases. All the partners were there, along with a couple of associates. At the head of the table, Sam Leibowitz, the firm's grizzled surviving co-founder, brought the meeting to order.

"Susan, please get us started," he said. "I understand you have a potentially interesting case for the firm."

"Interesting, yes," she said. "In fact, it could cause a sensation due to the identity of the defendant."

She paused to ensure that she had their full attention.

"Which I will reveal in a moment, providing you assure me that nothing said here today leaves this room."

"Everybody on board?" Sam asked as the attorneys exchanged expectant glances. He took a visual tally of the table, and they nodded in turn.

"If you're satisfied, Susan, please go ahead," he said.

"Our potential client alleges that the author Thomas G. Paine pirated her stories in his new novel, *The Rites of Man*."

A collective gasp went up around the table.

"Tom Paine? That's dynamite," exclaimed Jerome Coe, the youngest and most junior of the associates.

"Quiet, please," Sam Leibowitz said. "Susan, please continue. Who is the potential client, and does she have proof?"

"It's complicated," Susan replied. "The potential client is a photographer and personal friend named Sherry McManus. She had an affair with Tom Paine over the summer that he broke off when he finished writing the book. According to Sherry, Part One of the novel consists mainly of stories she told Tom, largely verbatim. Four men she was previously involved with are mentioned, under pseudonyms, and if identified, they may also wish to sue."

She ran through the details of the case, interrupted from time to time by questions. If there was no proof of Sherry's piracy allegations, was there even proof that she'd been involved with Tom Paine? How could they protect themselves from a countersuit by the author? And would a claim of any sort hold up in court?

It was nearly five-thirty by the time the meeting broke up.

"Let's do some research over the weekend and convene again on Monday," Sam Leibowitz said as the attorneys gathered their things. "If we take the case, we'll be working in conjunction with our New York office. I'll be in touch with them in due course. And please remember, not a word leaves this room. Susan, I'll see you in my office."

～

Cocktail chatter filled the subtly lit Hay-Adams bar as Jerome Coe ushered his date to a table and helped her settle onto the red upholstered banquette. Joanne Simpson was blonde, sleek, and new enough to D.C. to be impressed by the clubby ambiance— at least he hoped so. She was a just-out-of-college congressional aide he'd met at a party the previous weekend. They'd talked on the phone during the week, and if he had his way they'd be talking in bed by midnight.

It was six p.m., and the bar was packed with the usual crowd of Washington insiders out to relax after another hard week. As Joanne consulted the cocktail menu, Jerome glanced around the room. No one he knew, and that was just fine. He didn't want any interruptions.

They ordered martinis, straight up, and when the drinks arrived, Jerome plucked the olive from his glass and offered it to Joanne. He'd seen an actor do that in some old movie—who was it? Bogart? Cary Grant? He hoped he appeared as suave.

"Tell me about your week," he said smoothly. "What does a congressional aide do when Congress isn't in session?"

She smiled wryly.

"I'm still learning the ropes. It's mainly answering the phone for the moment."

Joanne was working for a Democratic representative from her home state of Oregon who had been easily reelected in the November vote that swept Bill Clinton into his second term in the White House. The lame-duck Congress was now in recess.

"I expect things will pick up next month," Jerome said.

"Yes, that's what I'm afraid of."

Jerome loved the way she wrinkled her nose when she smiled. With a wave of his hand, he summoned the waiter and ordered another round of drinks.

"And what about you?" Joanne asked. "It must be so exciting working for Herzen Leibowitz. I used to be addicted to *L.A. Law.* Especially Jimmy Smits. Do you get to handle any hot cases?"

Jerome leaned forward across the table.

"Funny you should mention it," he said, lowering his voice. "You won't believe what I heard today."

"What?" Joanne said brightly. "Tell me."

"Shh, not so loud," he said. "This is top secret. Come here."

As she leaned in, her peach silk blouse gaped prettily, exposing a hint of curve. The sight was too much for Jerome. Any reservations he might have had about revealing secret information flew out of his mind as he mentally undressed his date.

"You've heard of the author Tom Paine?" he asked.

Joanne looked unsure.

"His new book just came out," Jerome said. "It's been in the news. *The Rites of Man.*"

"Oh, right. I saw an ad for it on a bus."

"Well, what would you say if I told you he ripped off the stories in that book?"

Her eyes widened.

"You mean, like, plagiarism?"

"Kind of," Jerome said. "He apparently had an affair with a woman who claims she told him about her life, and he used her exact words in his novel. I think we're taking the case."

"That's awesome. Who's the woman?"

Jerome glanced around the room again. At the next table, two men were engrossed in conversation, holding hands discreetly under the table. He refocused on Joanne.

"She's a New York photographer named Sherry McManus," he said quietly.

"I'm impressed," Joanne said. "Do you think it's true?"

"I don't know," Jerome said, downing the rest of his drink. The two men were looking their way now.

"Hey, let's get out of here. Want to get a bite to eat?"

Joanne wrinkled her nose and smiled.

"Sure," she said.

Most of the AP city desk staff had already left the Rockefeller Center newsroom for the weekend when the duty editor spotted an emailed item marked "Exclusive." It was from the *Drudge*

Report. He strolled over to the Coke machine, wondering what they'd dredged up now. When he returned to his desk, he opened the item. It was time-stamped seven-thirty p.m.

"THOMAS PAINE TO FACE PLAGIARISM CHARGE," the headline said.

He skimmed the item, printed it out, and went to see the deputy bureau chief, who was still in his office straightening up his desk.

"Take a look at this. Some crazy dame wants to sue Tom Paine," he said, handing over the printout. It said:

WASHINGTON, Dec. 6—The DRUDGE REPORT has learned that author Thomas G. Paine is being sued by a woman who claims she provided the content for his new book, "The Rites of Man." The woman, Sherry McManus, a New York photographer who allegedly had a relationship with the author, has hired the Washington law firm Herzen Leibowitz to represent her, sources with the firm say.

"What do you make of it?" the duty editor asked.

"Well, they sourced it," the deputy bureau chief said. "Could be bullshit, but you'd better follow up. Put a reporter on it. You won't reach the law firm at this hour. Try to get to the author. If you can't get hold of Tom Paine, try to track down the woman."

The audience at Avery Fisher Hall erupted in rapturous applause at nine-thirty p.m. as the New York Philharmonic concluded its performance of Beethoven's *First*. Kurt Masur brought the musicians to their feet, shook hands with the first violinist, then turned to face the audience, nodded twice, and bowed. Crouching before the stage, Granville and Sherry caught the moment on camera.

"Want to stick around for the encore?" Granville whispered.

"No, let's go. I'm hungry."

They crept along the aisle and entered the lobby. Sherry

extracted a scarf from her camera bag and fastened her leather jacket against the cold.

"Mort's okay with you?" Granville asked.

"Perfect," said Sherry. She was looking forward to telling him about her meeting with Susan. She might even have a steak.

As they exited onto the plaza, a man approached.

"Sherry McManus?"

She stopped, startled.

"Roy Hutchinson, Associated Press," he said. "Do you know Thomas G. Paine?"

He raised a camera, and Sherry was caught in its flash.

"The *Drudge Report* says you were his muse," he said. "Care to comment?"

"Back off," Granville snarled, grabbing Sherry's hand. They raced across the plaza to a taxi stand, the reporter following on their heels.

"Where to?" the driver asked.

"Uptown," Granville barked. "Go, go, go!"

Sherry was trembling.

"Your place?" Granville asked.

She nodded.

"97th and Riverside," he said, shooting a glance through the rear window to see if they were being followed. Apparently not. He turned back to Sherry.

"The *Drudge Report*," he said. "What the fuck?"

"I just don't believe it," Sherry moaned. "My lawyer swore the firm was airtight."

"What do you want to do?" Granville asked.

"I don't know. I've got to call Susan."

They sped up Amsterdam Avenue, the driver skillfully weaving a path through the Friday night traffic. He swung left on 97th, pulling to a halt at the corner of Riverside.

"Here or around the corner?" he asked.

"Around the corner, please," Sherry said, relieved to be home and safe. But as he pulled up to the entrance of her building, she gasped. More paparazzi were gathered.

"Keep going!" Granville commanded, and with a screech of tires, the cab wheeled away.

This time, a couple of paparazzi revved up their motorcycles to give chase, and the cabbie stepped on the gas.

"Hey, this is just like in the movies," he said, keeping an eye on his rearview mirror. The motorcycles were two blocks behind. He made a sharp right onto 100th, raced through a yellow light, and swung left onto West End, then right again at 102nd.

Granville watched out the rear as Sherry gripped the seat.

The tires squealed as the driver veered south on Broadway, joining a stream of identical yellow cabs. He slowed to a normal pace and checked his mirror.

"Get down," he barked as a motorcycle roared up from behind, and Sherry and Granville crouched onto the floor. But the cab had become anonymous in the yellow tide. The cycle shot on past.

The driver continued down Broadway amid a throng of cabs, protected by the safety of numbers. At 94th Street, he swung left and checked his mirror again.

"You can get up now," he said. "I think we lost them."

Granville slowly rose, peering into the night. No motorcycles in view. He helped Sherry back to her seat.

"Pull over, please," he said, and the driver brought the cab to a halt just shy of Columbus Avenue. Granville turned to Sherry.

"What do we do now?" he asked.

Sherry's heart was still pounding.

"I've got to get out of New York."

"What are you talking about?" Granville said. "You live in New York."

"I can't live with that rat pack on my back. And if I was linked to Tom on the *Drudge Report*, they're not going to let up. We'd better go to the airport."

"You mean, like, take a plane?"

"I can go to my parents in Florida," she said. "They're in a rented condo. No one will find me there."

"Okay," Granville said. "If you're sure, let's go."

He tapped the cabbie on the shoulder.

"No, wait," Sherry said. "I can't leave Max. Could you go get him? You can take another cab, and I'll wait for you here. If that's okay, sir," she added for the cabbie.

"No problem," he replied. "Just tell me there's nothing criminal going on here."

"No, no, it's nothing like that," Sherry said. She reached into her handbag and handed her keys to Granville.

"There's some money in an envelope in my desk drawer, about five hundred dollars. Bring that too, please. The cat basket's beside the door."

"What about clothes?" he asked as he stepped from the taxi.

"No, I'll deal with that down there," she said. "Please hurry."

But Granville was already waving down another cab.

The paparazzi were waiting when Granville's taxi pulled up at Sherry's building. They crowded him as he made his way to the entrance.

"What's up, man?" one shouted. "What did you do with the lady?"

Granville pushed his way through to the door. He turned Sherry's key in the lock and entered the building. A few moments later, he was back, with Max safely tucked inside the basket. Cameras flashed, and more shouts rang out.

"Where's Sherry McManus?"

"You her new boyfriend?"

"Hey, cat got your tongue?"

Granville stopped at the top of the stoop and struck a pose like a catwalk model.

"Boys, boys," he said. "Now what's got into you? You be jealous?"

He strutted down the stairs, raised his middle finger, and ducked into the waiting cab.

&

It was twenty past ten when Granville's taxi pulled up beside Sherry's in the dark December stillness. He paid his driver and climbed in beside her, cat basket in tow.

"Where to?" the cabbie asked.

"Hang on a second," Granville said. He turned to Sherry. "You know, I was thinking. It's getting late. How do you know you'll find a flight to Florida at this hour? Maybe we should go back to my place, and you can take a plane in the morning."

"Thanks, but I'll risk it," Sherry said. "I'll spend the night in the airport if I have to. I'm freaking out, and I just want to get out of town."

"Okay. If you're sure."

The cabbie had been following the conversation in his rear-view mirror. He turned the key in the ignition.

"Which airport, lady?" he asked.

"LaGuardia, please," Sherry said. "And hurry."

As the cab crossed Central Park, she lifted the lid of the basket to stroke Max's head.

"Listen," Granville said, "why don't you leave Max with me? I'll take good care of the little fella. You've got more than enough on your plate as it is."

"Leave Max?" Sherry said, but even as she asked the question, she saw there was no reason to object.

"You're right," she said. "Thanks."

The cab turned north onto FDR Drive, heading for the Triborough Bridge.

Sherry reached into her camera bag for her Pentax.

"Could you do me another favor?" she asked Granville. She removed the film she'd shot at the concert and handed it to him. "Take this down to *Musiques* on Monday. Nan Gillette will be expecting it. She can have a staff photographer make the prints."

"Sure thing."

As they neared the airport, Sherry pulled her sunglasses from her handbag, not that they'd offer much of a disguise. Inside, they scanned the departures board. The last flight to Miami was leaving in half an hour, and the plane was already boarding. They rushed to the ticket counter, bought Sherry a seat, and raced to the gate.

"Here," she said, scribbling down a phone number on a scrap of paper and passing it to Granville. "I need you to phone Susan tonight. Tell her what happened, but don't say where I'm going. You're the only one who knows, and it has to stay secret. Promise you won't tell."

"I swear," he said. "Now you take care."

Sherry lifted her sunglasses and gave Granville a peck.

"Thank you," she said. "Thanks for everything."

The attendants were closing the gate.

"Don't try to find me," Sherry added. "I'll call you."

She turned and slipped through the gate, disappearing down the passageway toward an uncertain future.

Chapter 25

The nine a.m. meeting at *The New York Times* was usually a model of decorum, styrofoam coffee cups lifted in silence as editors read out their early news skeds, but today the day editor had to shout to call the meeting to order.

"Quiet!" he bellowed. "Okay, we'll start with Metro." He pointed the remote at the TV bolted into an upper corner, muting the sound. "Run us through it, Mike."

"Well, you already know what's happening," said Mike Mallett, who as editor of the Metro section handled news out of New York. "The *Drudge Report* posted an item last night alleging that Tom Paine is being sued over his new novel."

"Yeah, the *Drudge Report*," the day editor grumbled. "A reliable source…"

"We can't ignore it," Mike said. "It's been picked up by the wires, and the AP has pix of the woman alleged to have been his muse."

He held up a photo showing Sherry looking startled outside Lincoln Center, a deer caught in the headlights.

"Let's keep the woman's name out of it for the moment," the day editor said. "We need to get Legal involved. Put a reporter on the story, and I'll contact Marilee."

"Look," the sports editor interjected. "They're running it on the morning news."

The day editor waved the remote at the TV and turned up the volume.

"Reports that a woman was the source of Tom Paine's new book, if true, put his authorship in question," the anchor said. "Did he write a novel, or did he simply transcribe her words?"

Tom was in the kitchen making Nespresso when the phone rang.

"Hey man," Steve said. "Have you seen the news?"

"No," Tom said. "I just got up. What's going on?"

"You'd better take a look," Steve said, but Tom had already switched on the TV.

"So, to recap," the anchor was saying, "the *Drudge Report* alleges that Tom Paine wrote his best-selling new book, *The Rites of Man*, with the help of a muse who intends to sue. We are withholding her identity pending checks with our legal department. We'll have more later."

"Holy shit," Tom said.

"Is it true?" Steve asked.

"Hell no."

Jessica emerged from the bedroom wearing one of Tom's Oxford shirts.

"Hey, gotta go," Tom told Steve.

"I heard that," Jessica said. "Some woman helped you write your book. Nice one, Tom."

"It's bullshit," he said, glaring at her. "I wrote the book."

The phone was ringing again. Jessica grabbed it.

"It's for you." She handed Tom the receiver.

"Tell me there's nothing to it, Tom," Helen Nussbaum said.

"Drudge?" he said. "It's libel! We need to sue."

"Take it easy," Helen said. "I'm calling Murray to set up a meeting. Be over here at eleven."

Russell Hartzman, editor-in-chief of *The New York Times*, was alone in his office with a shaken-looking Marilee Dyer for a brief tête-à-tête ahead of the main morning news meeting at ten.

"Looks like we blew it in the interview," Russell said. "I mean, 'I get by with a little help from my friends?' Didn't any alarm bells go off?"

"I'm so sorry," Marilee said. "He seemed sincere."

"The big question being, what are we going to do about it?" Russell said. "Let's go."

He rose and escorted Marilee to the conference room, where chatter subsided as the paper's top editors realized that their normally affable chief was fuming.

"Okay, everybody," Russell said. "We've got a situation here. This newspaper went out on a limb for Thomas G. Paine, and if it turns out he plagiarized, we're going to have to backtrack. Mike, bring us up to date."

"The editor of *The Rites of Man* is Helen Nussbaum at Fitzgerald & Fitzgerald," Mike Mallett said. "Her office is closed on Saturdays. We're trying to reach her."

"Marilee, can you get a statement from the author?"

"No," she said ruefully. "His number's unlisted, and he never gave it to me."

"What about email?" Russell asked.

"He told me he doesn't own a computer. He called himself a dinosaur."

"That's unfortunate," Russell said. "Then call his agent, his mother, his Aunt Fanny, whoever you can find. We need to get to him. And get someone to check out Tom Paine's previous work for any hint of plagiarism. We'll need a fresh author portrait, but keep it short. Mike, what have we got on the woman?"

"Sherry McManus," Mike replied. "She's a New York photographer specializing in musicians. She's not answering her phone, but she's got a show on now down in Soho. I assigned Sally Sykes to follow that up. She's on her way there."

"Good," Russell said. "So, do we name her? What does Legal say?"

"They're being cautious as usual," Mike replied, "and the networks haven't named her yet, but the wires are out with it, so it's only a matter of time."

"Right," Russell said. "So by the time we put the paper to bed, she'll be in everybody's living room. Put another reporter on it."

He turned to Peter Steinberg, the bespectacled business editor.

"What are the ramifications for the publishing biz, Pete?"

"Too early to say, Russ, but it's bound to make waves. This book was on track to set sales records. Now it could go either way. I mean, think about the publicity factor—more people may want to buy the book to see what the fuss is about. On the other hand, if there's plagiarism and the publisher pulls the book, the industry will get a case of the shivers."

"Okay, let's wrap this up," Russell said. "Metro will handle the main story and a sidebar on the woman. We'll take a news analysis from Pete on the publishing angle, and Marilee will produce a short sidebar on Mr. Paine, keeping it balanced. We don't want to take sides."

"With all due respect, Russ," said the national editor, who usually stuck to politics, "it seems obvious that this story would not have come out if there weren't some element of truth. No smoke without fire, you know? He's a fraud. We need to hang him out to dry."

The culture editor shot him a withering glance.

"But Tom Paine wrote the book, even if it's somebody else's story," he said. "That's what we call literature."

Tom was in the shower when the phone rang again. Jessica was in no mood to answer, so she let it ring. The voice of Joe Reilly came through the answering machine.

"Jessica? Are you there?"

She picked up, casting a furtive glance toward the bathroom door.

"I told you not to call me at home," she said. "Have you heard the news?"

"That's why I'm calling. Is this for real?"

"Tom's denying it."

"Who's the woman?"

"Jesus, Joe. How the hell should I know?" Jessica said. "You think my husband's going to tell me about another woman?"

"Whoa! It was only a question. So, listen. How soon can you get here? I'm calling an emergency meeting."

"On a Saturday?"

"Yeah. This is hot. We've got to update our piece on the book."

Jessica hung up and sighed. The last thing she needed was to be dragged into a *Voice* assault on Tom's book, if that's what Joe had in mind. Of course, if there was any truth to the newscast, the *Voice* would have to deal with it. But if there was any truth to the newscast, she realized, her life with Tom was about to go back off the rails. They'd found a modus vivendi that suited her well enough. Tom was doing what she expected of him, playing the part of husband and father-to-be. She hadn't mentioned her suspicions about his love life. Why should she? Whatever had happened was over. Tom was back home, and now he was back in print. In the few days since the book came out, he'd recovered his former swagger, his confidence boosted by the positive press. He was more like the man she'd married, and she'd been enjoying the public attention. But now he was about to be dragged through the mud.

"I heard the phone ring," Tom said as he emerged from the bathroom wrapped in a towel. "Who was it this time?"

"It wasn't for you," Jessica said.

"Well, who was it?"

"I've been summoned to the *Voice*. Joe Reilly seems to think I may have an inside track on the woman who helped with your book."

"There isn't any woman, Jess," Tom said, but she wasn't listening. Her eyes were riveted to the TV. Granville's glamorous portrait of Sherry filled the screen.

"No woman, huh?" she said.

"We are now in a position to reveal the name of the woman who allegedly played a role in the writing of Tom Paine's new novel," the anchor said. "She is Sherry McManus, a forty-four-year-old photographer based in New York."

Jessica's eyes blazed.

"That's the woman who came here looking for you!"

"But where is Sherry McManus?" the anchor continued. "We can't find her."

The white sand seemed to stretch for miles as Sherry wandered along the shore, the sun hot on her shoulders. No one would recognize her here—she'd made sure of that when she'd stopped on the drive up from Miami and had her hair cropped short, Jean Seberg style. She felt safe hidden behind her sunglasses, her legs bare beneath her mother's tropical beach dress, the sand warm beneath her feet. The ocean's roar was a comfort, each crash of waves drowning the tumult inside her head until the water ebbed and the question came pounding back: What to do? What to do?

A dozen reporters were waiting when Tom exited his building.

"Mr. Paine!" one called. "May we have a word?"

"Tell us about your muse," another shouted.

Resisting the temptation to give them the finger, Tom ducked his head, walked briskly down the street, and hailed a cab.

"West 39th between Seventh and Eighth," he said as the cab pulled away.

He wasn't looking forward to seeing Helen Nussbaum, but there was no way out of it. He only hoped she'd come up with a way to deflect the unwanted attention.

The small crowd gathered outside the electronics store on Sixth and 23rd didn't notice as Tom's cab sped by, although they might have wanted to glimpse the author had they known he was coming their way. Their eyes were glued to a giant TV in the window that was tuned to coverage of the latest celebrity scandal. On the screen was the portrait of Sherry.

"Look at her, what a babe," a man in a gray overcoat said to the fellow beside him.

"Yeah, no wonder he fell for her."

The image switched to the *New York* magazine poster of Tom and Jessica.

"That must be the wife," said a young woman in a parka. "I'd hate to be in her shoes today. Tom Paine, what a jerk."

Helen Nussbaum and Murray Thompson were huddled in conversation when Tom arrived. They looked up darkly as he came in and took a seat.

"This is a very unfortunate turn of events," Helen said. "We're going to have to put out a statement."

"I wrote the book," Tom said. "That's all you need to say."

"Fine, if that's how you want to handle it, in public," Helen said. "But we need the fine print. So talk."

Tom met her gaze but said nothing.

"Let's start with the woman," Murray said. "Do you, or did you, have a relationship with Sherry McManus?"

"I wrote the book, Murray."

"You didn't answer the question," Helen said. "Do you know her?"

"I wrote the book. I'm the author. Period."

"Tom, as your agent and your friend, I'm asking for an honest answer," Murray said. "I haven't forgotten our conversation back in October. You told me you were seeing someone, and you said she'd helped you break through. Was it Sherry McManus?"

The only sound in the room was the buzz of the fluorescent lighting.

"This isn't going away, Tom," Helen said. "It's time to come clean."

"Look," Tom said, "I know her, okay? We had a flirtation during the summer. It got my author juices flowing again—after seven years, for Christ's sake—and I owe her for that. But she's out of my life now. Nobody knows we saw each other, and I defy them to prove it."

Helen smiled grimly.

"Well, they say there's no such thing as bad publicity," she said. "Maybe this will help sales. But they said on TV that she's planning to sue. You'd better talk to your lawyer."

"Right," Tom said, standing to leave. "I'll do that."

Jessica fastened the black wool maternity coat she'd bought at Lord & Taylor, put on her floppy felt hat, and looked out the window. The press was still there. She pulled the hat lower over her eyes, attached Che's leash, and threw an oversize leather tote bag over her shoulder. As she left the building, she slipped on her sunglasses and squared her shoulders.

"Mrs. Paine, is it true there's another woman?" a reporter called as she stepped outside, met by a burst of flashbulbs.

Jessica marched down the steps, ignoring them.

"Is your husband a fraud?" another shouted as she made for the nearest cab, Che strutting beside her.

"Get me out of here," she said as the cab pulled away. "Village Voice."

Russell Hartzman had Marilee Dyer back in his book-lined office. He had positioned the small TV on the side of his desk so that they both could see it.

"Did you get to the editor?" Russell asked.

"Yes, finally," Marilee said. "She says there's no story. Tom Paine wrote the book. It's his original work. Period."

Jessica appeared on the TV screen, her face hidden by the floppy hat as she descended the steps of her building. The camera zoomed in on her tote bag.

"And now the latest twist in the Thomas Paine affair," the voiceover said. "Amid the reports that another woman may be the voice behind Mr. Paine's new novel, his pregnant wife was seen leaving home today, looking like she might be gone for a while."

Russell sighed deeply.

"Jessica Franklin is a columnist at the *Village Voice*," the voiceover continued. "She may simply have gone to work this morning. On the other hand, the way she left home carrying what appeared to be an overnight bag is feeding rumors that the couple may split."

Russell muted the TV and turned to Marilee.

"We're going to have to splash it," he said. "You'd better drop what you're doing. You can hand off the author update to one of your staffers. I'd like you to work up a think piece on the literary angle. If Tom Paine wrote his novel based on somebody else's words—and we don't know that yet—is he a fraud, or is he a legitimate author? Is it plagiarism, or is it literature? Give it all you've got. We'll decide whether to front it when we see the copy."

Sam Leibowitz was wearing a pale yellow cashmere sweater and tan slacks instead of his usual suit and bow tie. He often came into the office on Saturdays, but usually he was alone. Today he had company, and Susan Katz was seething.

"It's a disaster," she said. "How did this happen?"

"That's what I'd like to know," Sam said. "Let's find out."

He took Susan's arm and led her to the conference room, where the firm's attorneys had been hastily gathered. A hush fell when they entered.

Sam held Susan's chair for her and took his seat at the head of the table.

"I've called this meeting to discuss what appears to be a leak of confidential information provided by a woman who sought the help of this firm," he said. "You all know what I'm talking about. This is not only a very serious breach of ethics. It also complicates matters immensely if we decide to pursue the case. We will discuss that in a moment. But first, who is responsible?"

The people around the table glanced at one another, but no one said a word.

Sam's eyes narrowed beneath his hoary eyebrows. The attorneys knew that look. They'd seen it in court when Sam was hammering the witnesses, and he never lost a case.

"Now we can stay here all day," Sam said, "but I'd rather get this over with so we can concentrate on the case. Who leaked it?"

He rose, looming over the table, and pointed a finger at the newest associate.

"Jerome, let's start with you."

Jerome Coe seemed to shrink into his chair. His face bore traces of fatigue. Joanne had been terrific in bed, riding him like a cowgirl. They really know how to raise them in Oregon, he mused. He had only just gone to sleep when the call came summoning him to the firm.

"Jerome," Sam barked. "I'm waiting."

Jerome was having a hard time thinking.

"Yes, sir?" he said.

The thing was, Joanne had tempted him. It would have been beyond the capacity of a mere mortal to resist. But had it been worth it?

"I'll repeat my question," Sam said sternly. "Did you tell anyone about the Thomas Paine affair?"

"No, sir," Jerome said. "Not really. I mean, I may have mentioned it to my date last night, but she couldn't have told anyone. We were together all night, and she's still in my bed."

"Your sex life is of no concern to this firm, young man," Sam said coldly. "Now get out of here and clear out your office. You're fired."

Jerome looked stunned. The others watched as he slunk out of the room. His exit set off a volley of muttered epithets rarely heard in that temple of propriety—"dickhead," "asshole," "stupid little shit."

"That's enough," Sam said. "Let's move on. Now that this matter is out in the public arena, we need a rethink. Susan, what's our next step?"

Susan had gone pale.

"We need to contact Sherry McManus and find out what she wants," she said.

"Well, what are you waiting for?" Sam said. "Please get in touch immediately."

"I can't," Susan said. "She left town last night. She's gone to ground."

Chapter 26

Sherry brushed the sand off her feet outside the entrance to her parents' four-story Florida-modern condo building. Carrying her flip-flops, she took the elevator to the top floor.

"Is that you, dear?" Rose called when she heard the door click shut.

Sherry found her parents out on the balcony having iced tea.

"Would you like some lunch?" Rose asked. "I made shrimp salad. We left some for you."

"No thanks," Sherry said. "I'm not hungry."

She padded into the guest room where she'd dumped her things on arrival, found a notepad, and dialed her home number in New York. When the answering machine clicked on, she punched in the code to access her voicemail.

"December seventh. You have twenty-eight new messages," the receiver said in her ear. "Message one."

A man's voice came through: "Ms. McManus, this is Philip Asmundsen of CNN. We'd like to hear your side of the Tom Paine story. Could you give me a call, please? Here's my number."

Sherry jotted down the details and erased the message, repeating that action after hearing each call. There were messages from the AP, CBS, the *Times*, the *Post*, every news outlet in America it seemed, and also the BBC. All looking for her. Sandwiched in the middle was an angry call from Rick.

"Okay, now that you've ruined my life, what do you plan to do about it?" he said.

When she'd heard all the messages, she merely sighed, put on her flip-flops, and headed back outdoors.

Tom knew that Jessica would be out when he came back from Fitzgerald & Fitzgerald, but he hadn't expected to find the white envelope she'd left on his desk, his name inscribed in her bold cursive. He tore it open.

"I won't be home tonight," the note said.

That was it—no signature, nothing. He crumpled the note and tossed it into the waste basket. After all I've done for her, he thought.

Tom checked his address book for his lawyer's home number. Dudley Melville was an old friend, and he needed friends now. He began dialing, then thought better of it and hung up.

Maybe he could reach Jessica at the *Voice*. He couldn't have her walking out on him at a time like this.

Joe Reilly noticed the flashing red light on his office phone but didn't pick up. He had instructed the switchboard to hold all calls while he was talking with Jessica. She had maintained her composure during the emergency staff meeting, even agreeing— maybe—to write a column on her life with Tom for the following week. There was no urgency, as they already had plenty on the agenda for the upcoming issue. Their review of *The Rites of Man* was being torn up and rewritten. Savannah would produce a quick sidebar on Tom's literary career. But now that Joe had Jessica alone with him in his office, she looked more shaken than he'd ever seen her.

"Talk to me," Joe said from across his desk. "How are you doing?"

"Are you serious?" Jessica said. "How do you think I'm doing? He was cheating."

Joe gazed at her evenly.

"But so were you, my love…"

Jessica glared at him.

"You can't compare us to what I've had with Tom. He's been my whole life."

"Until now, you mean."

"Actually…" Jessica looked away.

"Actually what?" Joe demanded. "I thought the happy couple routine was just for show."

"I'm almost five months pregnant, Joe," she said. "And Tom has always wanted a baby."

Joe looked at her in disbelief.

"But it's not his baby!" he said.

"It could be."

"What the fuck is that supposed to mean?"

"That weekend back in July," Jessica said, "when I went out to the island…"

"You slept with him?"

"Only once," she said.

"In July? But that's when we started seeing each other!"

Joe shoved his chair back and went to the window. A light snow was falling. Fighting to keep his cool, he turned to face Jessica. Her rounded belly seemed to mock him.

"So whose baby is it?" he asked.

She met his gaze.

"I don't know," she said.

"You don't know?" he bellowed. "How could you be so careless?"

"Joe, please. I never thought I'd get pregnant. I thought I was past it. Christ, I'm forty-three."

"I don't believe this is happening," Joe said. "You let me think it was my baby."

"I'm sorry," she said, adding limply, "It might be."

"That is so pathetic! You said you were finished with Tom."

"Yes, but the book changed things. I thought we could work it out."

"When you were pregnant with another man's baby?"

Jessica's eyes flared.

"Don't pressure me, Joe," she said. "Not at a time like this. I thought I could count on you for support."

But when Joe remained silent, eying her resentfully, her nerve faltered. She had never seriously considered single motherhood. But Tom's dalliance with another woman was now on public display. How could she go back to him? And if Joe deserted her, she'd be alone.

Jessica's head began to throb. She stood up, wobbled, and sat back down.

"I'm not feeling very well," she said. "Do you have an aspirin?"

Her face was ashen, Joe saw with alarm. He rummaged in his desk drawer and found the aspirin bottle.

"Can you take this when you're pregnant?" he asked nervously as he handed it over. "Wait a sec, I'll get some water."

As she waited for Joe to return, Jessica ran through the events that had brought her to this pass. She'd been so surprised when she learned she was pregnant that she'd said nothing about it to either man. Her first reaction had been the irony of the situation. After trying for years to make a baby with Tom and not succeeding, they'd had one quick roll in the hay in July. It was a fluke. She didn't love him anymore. Finding the toothbrush the next morning had been the last straw. Back in New York, she'd phoned Joe Reilly. He'd been flirting with her forever. They'd gone out for drinks, then dinner, and she'd let it happen.

She'd been in Maine with Joe when she skipped her period in August, and she'd kept quiet about it, figuring it was a sign of early menopause. Tom was holed up on the island, immersed in his writing, and she'd said nothing to him, either. When her pregnancy was confirmed in September, she hadn't known what to do. She was enjoying her dalliance with Joe, but she was still married to Tom, and either could be the father. She'd met Tom for dinner, but he'd been preoccupied with his book and their brief sexual foray had gone unmentioned. Obviously, it hadn't crossed his mind that he could have impregnated her. And, uncertain about how to handle the situation, she'd left Joe in the dark as they continued their secret affair.

Matters had come to a head in October when she'd run into Tom at the apartment. She'd again said nothing. But the next morning when he reappeared, having clearly spent the night with his paramour, she'd flown off the handle and informed him that she was pregnant.

Tom had no grounds for suspecting that he might not be her child's progenitor. And when she'd finally told Joe she was pregnant, he'd simply assumed that the baby was his. But could she count on him? While Tom, despite all their accumulated resentments, had proven his commitment to fatherhood by returning to her. Their relations were rocky, but he was still there.

Joe had initially accepted her explanation that Tom was back in Manhattan to promote his novel, but his questions about the future had become more pointed recently. She'd asked him to be patient, implying that she would play the devoted wife until the hoopla around Tom's book died down, and would then clarify matters regarding the baby.

But now things had spun out of control. Tom was apparently about to be sued—for plagiarism?—by the woman who'd come to their house, presumably his lover. The scandal would take over their lives. She'd be in the spotlight as the pregnant wife of a cheater. And now she'd managed to upset Joe, the one man she could turn to. How could she blame him for being confused? It was her fault.

And her head was pounding.

Joe returned from the water cooler and quietly closed his office door. Jessica's face was a train wreck. He handed her the plastic cup.

"Take two," he said, hovering over her as she complied. He felt nonplussed for making a scene. He'd been so distraught by her news about the baby's uncertain paternity that he hadn't remembered about her condition. Not to mention the pressure she must be feeling due to the news coming over the airwaves.

"Are you all right, Jess?" he asked.

"I'll just sit here for a minute," she said.

He perched on the edge of his desk, watching her with concern.

As the color returned to her face, she met his eyes.

"I'm so sorry for putting you through this," she said. "I should have told you sooner."

"Don't think about that now," he said. "You have to take care of yourself and the baby."

Touched, she reached for his hand.

"I know you're upset, but it's hard for me, too. And I do need your support."

"Look, I need time to absorb this," Joe said gruffly.

"I do, too," Jessica said. "I'm not going home tonight. I need some space."

Steadying herself, she rose to leave.

"Where are you going?" he asked. "Will you be okay?"

"Yes," she said. "Savannah is waiting for me."

Tom went to the kitchen and poured himself a beer. The *Voice* switchboard had been no help at all. They didn't know if Jessica was there, and if she was, she couldn't be disturbed.

He carried the beer to his desk and dialed his lawyer's number. At least he could trust Dudley Melville. They'd been tight since they met as freshmen at Columbia.

Dudley picked up right away.

"I've been expecting your call," he said. "You're all over the media."

"Christ, what a day," Tom said. "They're out to kill me."

"Hey, take it easy. We'll get you through this. Now let's start from the top. What's the main issue, as you see it? That the woman is planning to sue?"

"No! For God's sake, Dudley. My reputation as an author

is at stake. We've got to stop this before it gets anywhere near a courtroom."

"Tom, take a breath," Dudley said. "It may never get to a courtroom. I don't have all the facts yet, but it's hard to imagine on what grounds she could possibly sue. In the meantime, you know what they say—the best defense is a good offense."

"And what is that supposed to mean?"

"Can anyone prove you had a relationship with Sherry McManus?"

"No."

"Then it's very simple," Dudley said. "Deny, deny, deny. Attack her as a mythomaniac nymphomaniac groupie, whatever. The point is, she had nothing to do with your novel. Right?"

Tom struggled to repress a vision of Sherry smiling seductively as she spun out a tale for him during their sex play at the beach house. He forced himself back to reality.

"I wrote the book, Dudley."

"Good. And what about Jessica? Will she stand by you?"

"She got mad and left," Tom said. "I haven't been able to reach her."

"Doesn't surprise me," Dudley said, "but you're going to need her. By the way, I understand you're going to be a father. She won't be gone long."

"Frankly, it's easier with her out of the house."

"I hear you. And what about Fitzgerald? Are they going to bat for you?"

"You need to get in touch with Helen Nussbaum," Tom said, remembering the purpose of his call. "They want to put out a statement for the media."

"To keep the hounds at bay. Fine. I'll take care of it."

"Thanks, old buddy."

"Now listen," Dudley said. "You're going to need to lie low until things die down. And they will. Tomorrow, or the next day, the media will move onto the next hot story, and everyone will forget about Thomas G. Paine. In the meantime, as your lawyer and your friend, I'm counseling you to take your phone off the hook. Do not speak to anyone. Especially Sherry McManus."

Pink and gold reflections danced on the Atlantic as evening fell. Sitting on the sand, gazing out at the waves, Sherry felt alone in the world. Alone and hunted. How many more messages would she find when she went back to the condo? Should she talk to the press, or shouldn't she? The adrenaline of a night on the run had given way to fatigue.

"There you are, dear."

Sherry hadn't heard Rose arrive, but now her mother was standing over her.

"Come inside," Rose said. "You can't sit on the beach all night."

"Why not?" Sherry said. "I like it here."

"You have to eat something. Your father's waiting. Besides, you have to deal with this."

Sherry got up and brushed the sand from her legs.

"I'm not ready to deal with this," she said as she followed her mother across the beach to the condo.

When they came in, Bernie was watching a report on CNN about the safe return to Earth of the Columbia space shuttle. Mission specialist Story Musgrave, still in his space suit, was waxing rhapsodic about watching the heavens fly past.

"It was kind of a spiritual thing," the astronaut said.

"At least they've stopped talking about Tom's book," Sherry said.

"It's not a bad book," Bernie said. "I learned a lot."

"You read it?" Sherry asked, wishing he hadn't.

"Of course. Picked up a copy when we landed in Miami and raced right through it. Very unreliable narrator, though."

Rose carried their dinner to the table.

"Turn the volume down, dear," Rose said.

As Bernie reached for the remote, an image of Tom flashed onto the TV.

"Now back to our continuing coverage of the Thomas Paine affair," the anchor said. "The publisher of *The Rites of Man* has just issued a statement. As our viewers will know by now, at the center of this fast-moving story is a New York photographer named Sherry McManus."

Sherry flinched as her portrait came up on the screen, inset beside the anchor.

"I will now read the statement from Fitzgerald & Fitzgerald," the anchor said, lifting a dispatch from his desk:

The Rites of Man by Thomas G. Paine is an original work of fiction. Any insinuation to the contrary is libelous and will be treated as such. Mr. Paine, one of the nation's most beloved authors, is baffled by the allegations and can only presume that the woman said to be at their source is suffering from delusions. He respectfully asks Sherry McManus, wherever she may be, to cease and desist.

"Delusions!" Sherry said. "He is such a liar."

An image of customers crowding into Barnes & Noble appeared on the screen.

"Meanwhile," the anchor said, "the controversy over *The Rites of Man* has apparently set off a buying spree."

The image switched to customers leaving the store clutching Tom's book.

Rose switched off the TV.

"I think that's enough news for tonight," she said.

"This is just unreal," Sherry fumed as she joined her parents at the table. "He's in New York making a fortune, and I'm holed up here like some sort of criminal."

"You're right, dear," Rose said. "You can't go on hiding for the rest of your life."

"But what can I do? If I come forward, I'll be exposing other people."

"You're letting the media use you," Bernie said. "Use them. Tell a story. Get your lawyer friend to help you."

"Susan?" Sherry said. "But she's the one who leaked it!"

Rose shot her a concerned glance.

"Sherry, dear," she admonished, "you're not thinking straight. Susan Katz is one of your oldest friends. She wouldn't have leaked it."

"Yeah," Bernie said. "You should call her."

"Maybe I should," Sherry acknowledged. She excused herself and went to her room.

By the time she returned, her parents were finishing dinner.

"So?" Bernie asked.

"Susan's coming down tomorrow," she said. "She'll be on the first flight to West Palm."

Chapter 27

On the drive to the airport, Sherry lowered the top of her rented Golf convertible to take advantage of the morning sun. In her crop cut, with no long mane whipping around in the wind, she felt light, and it felt good. She parked in the palm-lined pickup area. A few minutes later, Susan appeared, the Sunday *New York Times* poking out of her handbag.

"Good flight?" Sherry asked as Susan hopped in.

"Uneventful," Susan said. "The best kind."

Sherry pulled out of the airport and swung north onto I-95.

"Love the haircut," said Susan. "Where are we going?"

"There's a seafood joint up the beach from the condo," Sherry said. "We can stay there all day if we like. We won't be disturbed."

"I brought you something," Susan said, extracting the paper. "They fronted an article that may interest you. It's by the woman who interviewed Tom for the 'Women Are the New Men' piece in the Book Review last week."

"Marilee Dyer? Can you read it to me while we're driving?"

"Yeah," Susan said. "Here goes. The headline is: 'An Uncommon Story.'"

Sherry kept her eyes on the road as Susan began to read:

In February 1855, in the depths of a Russian winter, Ivan Goncharov returned from a long trip abroad and met up with his fellow author Ivan Turgenev. During his travels, Goncharov told his friend, he'd come up with a great idea

*for a new novel. Turgenev listened raptly as Goncharov
outlined the story. Five years later, the two met again, this
time before a court of their peers. Turgenev had published
a best-selling new novel, and Goncharov had accused him
of plagiarism. Turgenev, he said, had stolen his plot, his
characters, even his words.*

"Really?" Sherry interrupted.
"It gets better," Susan said. She resumed reading:

One week ago, on the eve of publication of The Rites of
Man *by Thomas G. Paine, this newspaper published an
interview with the author in which he was asked, among
other things, about how he had managed to write his book
from the point of view of a woman. It has since emerged
that Mr. Paine is allegedly being accused—by a woman—
of basing his new novel on content provided by her.
The two situations are not identical, and yet the question
remains the same: What is fair use? If all art is derivative,
when does a writer's use of borrowed material cross the line
of legitimacy? If Mr. Paine did indeed appropriate stories
told to him by a woman, is he to be damned for plagiarism
or praised for turning them into a great American novel?*

"Uh-oh," Sherry said. "I can see where this is heading."
"Don't be so sure," Susan said. She picked up the thread:

*The situation is all the more ironic given that Mr. Paine
has built his career on the basis of another man's fame,
borrowing titles from his American revolutionary namesake
for each of his novels. And like the original Thomas Paine,
whose 1791 book* The Rights of Man *sparked such an uproar in England that he was sentenced to death for sedition,
Thomas G. Paine finds himself caught up in a scandal—although no one is yet proposing that he be hanged.*

"At least Marilee Dyer's got a sense of humor," Sherry said. Susan smiled and kept reading:

In the case of Goncharov and Turgenev, the court of their peers—literary critics and other writers—effectively dismissed Goncharov's complaint, ruling that it was only natural for works by two authors living in the same time, on the same soil, to have "similarities and coincidences, in ideas and even phraseology," as one recalled in an account of the session. Goncharov, whose breakthrough novel had been titled A Common Story, *went on to write a bitter memoir about the incident that was published only after his death, under the title* An Uncommon Story. *His point was that the appropriation of his ideas, however skillfully done, was unfair.*

"Exactly," Sherry said. She slowed and turned east off the freeway.

"Do I have time to finish?" Susan asked.

"Go for it," Sherry said.

In the case of Mr. Paine, who has been unavailable for comment, it is too early to say how the court of public opinion will rule on The Rites of Man. *But given his newly revived status as America's literary darling, there's a good chance that his fans will give him a break—even if it turns out that he poached somebody's stories. After all, as T.S. Eliot once said, "Good writers borrow, great writers steal." Or, as Oliver Goldsmith put it, "In most cases we are disposed to pardon the want of originality, in consideration of the exquisite talent with which the borrowed materials are wrought up into the new form."*

And yet, if Mr. Paine did borrow his materials, and even if such borrowing is considered acceptable in the name of art, there remains the question of fairness. Did Mr. Paine betray a woman's confidence? Did he put her private life on the page? This is an issue not of plagiarism, but one of ethics. It is to be hoped that Mr. Paine will break his silence and tell the public what went into the making of The Rites of Man. *This is only fair. This is only right.*

Sherry pulled into the parking lot of Conchy Joe's, at the edge of the broad Indian River lagoon. They got out and stretched their legs. A weathered blue sign stood balanced on a wooden railing: "Ladies must be clothed," "All feet must be shoed."

Susan followed Sherry to the waterfront, where a rickety pier extended out from the thatched bar area. They walked to the end of the pier, squinting into the sun. To their right, an egret paddled and rose from the shimmering lagoon.

"This sure beats December in Washington," Susan said.

"Thanks for coming down," Sherry said.

"I would have come sooner if I'd known where you were. Why didn't you get in touch?"

"I was upset about the leak. But last night my parents convinced me to call you. They said you wouldn't have leaked it."

"Of course I didn't. It was a young colleague—who's been fired, by the way. But I feel responsible. What else did your parents say?"

"My dad said I was letting the media use me," Sherry said. "He said we should use them instead—you know, turn the story around."

"I've always liked your dad," Susan said as they strolled back along the pier, heading toward the bar for a pre-lunch mojito.

Tom was making a sandwich when he heard the front door bang. Che bounded into the kitchen, tail wagging. Jessica stalked in behind him.

"No woman, huh?" she said, flinging a copy of the *New York Post* onto the counter. Splashed across the front page was a photo of Tom and Sherry sitting together in deck chairs at the beach house. The giant headline read: "Gotcha."

Tom just stared at it, trying to figure out where the photo had come from. He scanned the blurb at the bottom of the page: "Delusional? Really? Tom Paine with Sherry McManus at his Long Island getaway."

"You said you didn't know her," Jessica said. "How many other lies have you told me? I mean, I found her fucking tooth-brush in the bathroom."

Tom recoiled.

"It was a fling," he said, trying not to sound lame. "I ended it as soon as you told me about the baby. I'm sorry."

"Sorry? Sorry?! How can we raise a child together if I can't trust you? And what about the book? Is it true she fed you her stories?"

"Fuckin' A, Jess. No!"

She glanced at the *Post*, then back at Tom, fixing him in a cynical stare.

"You're denying it?"

Tom took a tentative step toward his wife.

"Come on," he said. "We've been down a long road together, and I need you now."

She turned her back on him.

"We're making a family together," he said. "That's all that matters."

He reached his arms around her, gently placing his hands on her belly.

"Hey!" he said, jumping back as his face lit up. "Was that a kick? Is that our baby?"

He gently touched her belly again.

"It's the baby," Jessica said curtly. "Now take your hands off me."

She turned to face him, cold fire in her eyes.

"This is how it's going to be," she said. "I'm not walking out on you now. But it's not for you. It's for the sake of the baby. I'm pregnant, and I can't deal with a major disruption."

The implication wasn't lost on Tom—she wasn't leaving him "now." Resentment welled up. He had to struggle to keep his tone even.

"I'm facing a crisis, Jess," he said. "Will you stand by me?"

"You're a cheat and a liar and a philanderer," she said, "and you're asking me to stand by you? That takes a lot of nerve."

"You're not so perfect yourself. You can't imagine how much shit I've put up with all these years."

"Then why did you move back in?"

"You ordered me to, for Christ's sake. And we're having a baby. Isn't that what you wanted? I thought we could make it work."

Jessica looked at him stonily.

"I'll protect you in public, but that's it," she said. "As far as I'm concerned, this is over."

A waiter arrived with a second round of mojitos for Sherry and Susan. Their table at the edge of the bar looked out over the lagoon.

"Now where were we?" Susan asked as the waiter departed.

"You asked if I still wanted to sue," Sherry said. "The answer is, I don't know. Going public isn't a problem anymore. I mean, my name is already out there, so the catch-22 thing about privacy isn't an issue. Thanks to your colleague…"

"We should never have hired that jackass," Susan said. "I'm so sorry."

"Forget it. The point is, my name's out there, but I haven't acknowledged being Tom's source. As soon as I do, people will try to link everything in the book to me. There will be a stampede to figure out who the men are."

"It's already happening," Susan said. "I heard someone speculating on the radio last night that the sax player could be James McCoy Robinson."

"Oh fuck. Jimmy's gonna kill me."

"I was thinking there might be another way to approach this," Susan said. "Without actually taking Tom to court."

"Really? Tell me about that."

"I will. But first, let me ask you something. Whatever possessed you to tell him all those stories in the first place?"

"Oh God," Sherry said. "I never should have."

She looked out over the water. A small white cruiser was gliding past, cutting a trail of froth through the dazzling aquamarine.

"I saw it as foreplay," she said. "When we were together and, you know, in the mood to make love, we'd tell each other stories. About our lives. It was totally hot."

"I don't get it."

"It was kind of a sex game. We'd start when we were already aroused, and the longer we had to wait during the storytelling, the more exciting it got."

"This was in bed?" Susan asked.

"Usually. So, like, I'd be telling a story, and Tom would be asking questions, and the goal was to drive each other crazy with desire so that when we finally made love it would be more intense. When things got too hot, I'd break off in the middle and finish the story afterward. Tom always wanted to hear the ending."

"That sounds kind of like Scheherazade," Susan said.

Sherry looked puzzled.

"Scheherazade?"

"Well, wasn't that the whole point of *A Thousand and One Nights*?" Susan said. "She told tales to a sultan, but she always broke off in the middle so he wouldn't kill her when morning came—because he wanted to hear the end of the story."

"So he spared her," Sherry said thoughtfully. "Maybe you're right. I guess in a way I was also telling stories to save my own life."

"What do you mean?" Susan asked.

"It wasn't a conscious thing, but I must have felt that the stories would protect me from getting hurt again. By keeping Tom waiting, anticipating the ending, I'd make him want to stay."

"That's kind of twisted. Don't you think that if he were a normal person instead of an asshole, he might have wanted to stay because you're worth it?"

"You know, I've been doing a lot of thinking about how I got into this mess," Sherry said. "Plenty of love affairs, but they always stopped short of commitment. Ever since Rick. I've been too worried about getting burned in love to allow a relationship to develop. It's as though my whole life has amounted to foreplay."

She fell quiet as the waiter arrived with their lunch.

"Let's eat," Susan said. "We can get back to this later."

By the time their coffee arrived, Sherry had moved on to the irony of her predicament.

"I was trying to save my own life, and look what's happened," she said. "I've been forced into hiding for who knows how long. Maybe it's God punishing me for getting involved with a married man."

"No," Susan said. "You're being punished for living your life as a free woman. Society can't handle that. But your father's right—you need to take control of the situation. Now pay attention, because I think this could work."

Sherry listened intently as Susan outlined her plan. If they pulled this off, she realized, it would separate truth from fiction. She and the men portrayed in *The Rites of Man* would clear their names, while Tom would get what he deserved.

The sun had dipped low over the horizon by the time they paid their check. On the drive back to the airport, they worked out a schedule for executing the plan.

"Stay in touch this time," Susan said as Sherry pulled up to the departures area.

"I will," Sherry promised. "This is going to be good."

Rose and Bernie were out on the balcony when Sherry came home. She joined them, feeling calmer than she had in weeks. It was a starry night, bright pinpoints in a black velvet tropical sky, the waves lapping the shore as a soothing backdrop.

Sherry gave them a quick rundown of her discussion with Susan. Then she went in to check her voicemail in New York. The recording clicked on: "December eighth. You have fourteen new messages." Among calls from the usual suspects—the *Times*, the AP, CBS, and on and on—was an angry message from Raphael, all the way from Israel, a furious rebuke from Jimmy in Geneva, and a call from Granville assuring her that Max was doing just fine.

"Message twelve," the recording announced.

A French-accented voice came through the earpiece.

"*Alors*, Sherry."

It was Jacques, from Paris.

"I saw a report on CNN about a book about men, and they say you are the woman behind it. So I have a question for you. Am I in this book? I hope the answer is yes!" Sherry had to smile. "And I want to tell you, when they showed your picture, I nearly fell out of my chair. You are just as beautiful as you always were. Call me."

Sherry hung up thoughtfully. She hadn't spoken with Jacques since July, yet as soon as he'd heard about the scandal, he'd called. She was touched. And not only that—she found it refreshing that instead of commiserating, he'd made light of the situation. It made her long to see him again. She needed friends like that. But this was hardly the time to fly off to Paris. On the other hand, now that she and Susan had a plan, she'd soon be free...

Chapter 28

The morning news was on when Sherry padded into the kitchen in search of coffee. She poured herself a cup and settled into an armchair. She could hear her father singing in the shower. Her mother had already gone out for her morning swim.

Sherry got out her notepad to make a to-do list: phone Nan Gillette at *Musiques*, check in with Susan, buy some clothes. She was wondering where she could go to expand her wardrobe—driving up from Miami, she'd picked up only a swimsuit and flip-flops—when the anchor launched into the Monday morning press review.

"It looks like the critics are forgiving Tom Paine," he said.

Sherry looked up in dismay.

"Two days after a plagiarism scandal engulfed Mr. Paine over his best-selling new novel," the anchor continued, "today's papers conclude that it's his exceptional talent as an author that gives *The Rites of Man* its merit, regardless of the origin of its content. Now I ask you, folks, don't all writers take their material from life? Mr. Paine, who is beginning a book tour tomorrow, has so far declined to comment. In other cultural news, America's poet laureate says the country is facing a literacy crisis..."

Putting aside her to-do list, Sherry took her coffee back to her room and closed the door. She consulted her address book. It would be early afternoon in Paris.

"*Allo?*" Jacques's familiar voice came across loud and clear.

"*C'est moi*," she said.

"Sherry," he exclaimed. "I was hoping you'd call. Where are you?"

"I'm somewhere. It's not important."

"But you are very much in the news. You are now famous!"

"Actually, I'm in hiding," she said. "It's not really a lot of fun."

"They say you are a *femme fatale*, but of course I knew that already."

"I don't know if I'm fatal, but the situation is killing me."

Jacques laughed down the line.

"I see you haven't lost your sense of humor," he said. "But seriously, Sherry, how are you doing? I'm concerned. It can't be easy."

"You're right, but I think it's almost over. And Jacques, when it is, it might do me good to get some air. Like get on a plane."

"You mean, like, Air France?"

"Yes," she said. "I'd like to come over for a while, until people forget about me."

"Sherry, you are making me very happy. It will be like old times."

"I haven't told Anouk yet, but I'm sure she'd let me stay."

"*Mais non*, stay with me," Jacques said.

"What about Sophie?" she asked. "Wouldn't she mind?"

"Sherry, I need to bring you up to date. Sophie moved out at the end of the summer. She left me for a woman."

Sherry was momentarily speechless.

"For a woman?" she asked.

"I'm afraid so."

Sherry found the notion astonishing, given Sophie's penchant for flirting with every man in the room, charming them with her sexy laugh, her arty Parisian sophistication.

"You must be shattered," she said. "I always saw you as the perfect couple."

"Maybe we were, once," Jacques said. "But things happen, you know? Life doesn't always work out the way one intends."

"I know," Sherry said wryly.

"So when are you coming? I'm so looking forward to seeing you. We'll go back to the Closerie des Lilas."

As she gazed out her window at palm trees, Sherry saw herself, twenty years younger, sharing a platter of oysters with Jacques at the Closerie. They'd been to see an exhibit of paintings by Robert Delaunay, and over the last of a crisp Sancerre, Jacques had told her about the great love affair and passionate artistic collaboration between Robert and Sonia Delaunay.

"Sherry? Are you there?" Jacques asked.

"Oh, sorry. I was remembering our last lunch at the Closerie."

"But I asked you a question. When will you come?"

"I have some business to attend to here," she said. "I'll come as soon as I can."

Back at her office in Washington, Susan Katz was briefing Sam Leibowitz on the Sherry McManus case. In private. The firm's other attorneys, they had agreed, did not need to know. In fact, Susan had decided, even Sam didn't need to know all the details.

"I think the best approach would be to threaten an invasion of privacy suit on all four claims, including false light," she said. "Then, if all goes well, we can settle out of court."

"Yes, but there has to be proof," Sam said. "We need to be able to prove that Tom Paine's novel actually portrays Sherry Mc-Manus and her friends—well, lovers—in a false light. It doesn't sound like you're there yet."

"We're working on that," Susan said.

Helen Nussbaum and George Fitzgerald had convened Tom to a meeting about his book tour, the first question being whether to cancel it. They'd asked Fitzgerald & Fitzgerald's lawyer about it, but he'd waffled, saying the book tour was a business decision, not a legal matter.

"We don't want to send the wrong signal," Helen said. "If you bow out of the tour, the public won't understand. They might jump to the wrong conclusion and stop buying."

"Yes," George said. "It could hurt sales."

"But you'll have to deal with the media," Helen said. "There will be questions."

"Don't worry," Tom said. "I'll tough it out."

Helen buzzed her secretary and asked her to get Murray Thompson on the line.

"At least the papers are giving you a break this morning," Helen said as they waited for the call to come through. When her secretary buzzed, she turned on the speaker.

"Helen, what can I do for you?" Murray said.

"I'm here with Tom and George," Helen said. "Tom's going ahead with the reading at Barnes & Noble tomorrow. I'm assuming you'll be there to help fend off the press."

"Absolutely," Murray said. "You there, Tom?"

"What's up, Murray?" Tom said.

"I'm being deluged with interview requests," the agent said. "What do you think?"

"Whoa," Tom said. "One thing at a time. Let's see how things go on the tour."

"I second that," Helen said. "The media crucified Tom over the weekend. No interviews until we've ensured his resurrection."

Murray sighed and hung up. Snow was drifting down outside his window. No interviews meant another bleak day of saying no to people who wanted to hear yes, he was musing, when his secretary buzzed him.

"Ben Glazer's on the line," she said.

Glazer, his producer friend in Hollywood.

"Ben, old buddy," Murray said as he took the call. "How's life in sunny California?"

"There's no easy way to say this, so I'll give it to you straight," Ben said. "We're putting the movie on hold."

Murray felt a chill run through him, cold as the snow.

"You're kidding," he said. "Last I heard, you thought you could line up Susan Sarandon and Tim Robbins, or maybe even Redford. You said *The Rites of Man* was a sure hit."

"Maybe. But we talked it over last night and we're not moving ahead until this Tom Paine mess is cleared up."

"He wrote the book, Ben," Murray said.

"Yes, but if this Sherry McManus woman sues, it could cloud the issue of rights. We're not dropping the project, but it's on the back burner for now."

"Right," Murray said. "Okay, thanks for letting me know."

Fucking Glazer, he thought as he hung up. He's sitting out there in Hollywood drinking margaritas with starlets while I'm stuck here babysitting an author and freezing my ass.

Murray put on his coat and headed for the door. Agent schmagent, he thought as he departed for lunch. I've got to get out of this line of work.

The sun was warm on Sherry's face as she walked across the sand to the water's edge. She waded into the waves and dived under, her body tingling at the cold shock of the water. Staying parallel to the shore, she swam hard until the condo had nearly disappeared from view. The effort drove all thinking from her head.

When she turned back, swimming an unhurried breaststroke, she allowed her thoughts to resurface. Jacques had asked her to stay with him in Paris. The prospect was enticing, but would it be wise? They'd always been attracted to each other. The only thing that had stopped them from acting on it had been his marriage, and now that was over. If they started something together, it would be more than a dalliance. Was she strong enough to handle that now, when she was still damaged from Tom's betrayals? She swam harder as she made for shore.

Back on the beach, Sherry sat in the sun for a long time wrestling with her feelings, and as she sat there her spirit began to revive. She thought back to her conversation with Granville, what he'd said about people playing it safe. "But that's just not us, Sher," he'd told her. Well, she thought, Tom Paine may have deceived her, but just how damaged was she? His book was just a book, and he was just a guy. He hadn't touched the core of who she was, an independent woman who wasn't afraid to take risks. Jacques was waiting for her in Paris, she was free, and she already loved him. She was strong enough to get on a plane.

But first she'd have to set things in motion.

Sherry got to her feet and headed back to the condo, stopping at the outdoor shower to rinse off before going inside. She found Rose in the kitchen making sandwiches.

"Good swim, dear?" her mother asked.

"Great," she said. "I'll come help in a minute."

She went to her room, closed the door, found her notepad and dialed a number.

"Rick?" she said. "It's Sherry."

Chapter 29

An overflow crowd was waiting when Tom and Murray arrived at the Barnes & Noble flagship store on Fifth Avenue. It was Tuesday, December 10, exactly a week since Tom's book had come out. Every seat for the reading was taken, and the aisles between the bookshelves were jammed. A hush fell as the manager helped Tom and Murray pick their way to a table stacked with copies of *The Rites of Man*, ready for signing. TV crews started recording as the manager took the floor.

"Barnes and Noble is proud to welcome Thomas G. Paine on the first stop of his book tour for *The Rites of Man*," he said, eliciting a smattering of applause. "When we scheduled this event, we knew that Mr. Paine had written a provocative book. But just how provocative, nobody knew at the time."

Titters ran through the crowd.

"Please," the manager said. "Let us accord Mr. Paine the respect to which he is due. At his first book signing in seven years, Mr. Paine will read a passage from his novel, followed by a short question-and-answer session. Mr. Paine."

Tom stood and cleared his throat. The crowd was watching expectantly. This was a chance to restore his good name—maybe his only chance—and he didn't want to blow it.

"Hello," he said. "I'm Tom Paine. That's Thomas Geronimo Paine, and as I look out into this sea of faces, I kind of want to shout 'Geronimo!'"

Laughter rippled through the audience.

"But don't worry, I'm not about to jump," he said with a self-deprecating smile. "And by the way, in case you haven't heard, I wrote the book."

"Sure you did," someone called out, and a low murmur rumbled through the crowd.

"What about Sherry McManus?" another man shouted.

"Let him speak!" a woman said. She began to clap, and others joined in.

Tom waited for the noise to subside.

"Whew!" he said, pretending to wipe his brow. "This is off to a great start. You over there, and you"—he pointed to the men who had shouted catcalls—"I'll take your questions later. First, I'd like to read a passage from Chapter Two of the novel, in which the narrator tells her lover about her affair with a Frenchman in Paris. It's adults-only—you know the French—so anyone under eighteen, please leave the room."

People laughed, and Tom flashed a grin. At least most of them were on his side. He opened his copy of the novel to a bookmarked page and began to read:

Ari was the kind of guy who insisted on separate bedrooms but always wanted to know what was going on in mine...

As he uttered the word "mine," a commotion caused Tom to look up. Heads turned as a knot of women pushed their way toward the table, waving signs and shouting slogans. The manager tried to intervene, but the women pushed past him, brandishing their posters: "Rip-Off Artist!" "Sexist Fraud!" "Justice for Sherry!" One grabbed a copy of *The Rites of Man* and held it up, shouting, "Boycott this book!" The others chimed in as security arrived to hustle them away, their chants audible as they were escorted out of the store. The television cameras had caught it all.

Tom, flustered, looked to Murray for guidance, mouthing the words, "What do I do?"

The agent smoothly took the floor.

"Ladies and gentlemen," he said. "This unfortunate incident

will make it difficult for Mr. Paine to continue his reading. I'd like to propose that we take a short break, after which he will be available to sign your copies."

As Tom sat back down at the table, a few members of the audience approached to offer their support. A few picked up the book and went to pay, coming back for Tom's dedication. A few remained in their seats, but most gathered their things and drifted away.

Beads of perspiration pearled on Sherry's forehead, and it wasn't because of the sultry Florida weather. Three down and one to go. Her talk with Rick yesterday had been easier than she'd feared, his anger fading as she told him the story behind Tom's book. Then this morning, talking with Jimmy had felt like old times. But the conversation had drained her. Nonetheless, she'd put a call through to Israel, and after thinking it over, Raphael had agreed to her proposal. But she still didn't have Jerzy's number. Maybe the Aspen festival people could help.

Helen Nussbaum had heard about the disruption at Barnes & Noble even before Tom and Murray phoned in—it was already on the airwaves—and now they were in her office for a hastily organized meeting on damage control.

"Why don't you take Jessica with you to Politics and Prose tomorrow?" she asked.

Tom frowned. Was Helen messing with him? She knew perfectly well that Jessica wasn't the kind of woman to smile and forgive now that his affair with Sherry was out in the open. Yet he could see Helen's logic—if any female detractors turned up, having Jessica beside him would send a powerful signal. After all, if she supported him, why should other women be so bothered?

"I'll ask her," he said, although he hardly relished the prospect of a three-hour train trip to Washington in the hostile company of his wife.

"You're sure you want to go through with it?" Helen asked.

"For God's sake, Helen," Tom said. "I'm not going to let a few rabid feminists scare me off."

"Murray? Your thoughts?" she asked.

"Maybe it's time for Tom to write a piece giving his side of the story," Murray said. "We need to turn things around, and quickly."

Tom prickled.

"Saying what?" he asked.

"You're the writer," Helen replied. "You'll figure it out."

"I think the book speaks for itself," Tom said. "I don't know what I could add."

Helen rose to signal that the meeting was over.

"Write the article, Tom," she said.

Tom and Murray proceeded to the elevator in glum silence, each of them lost in thought. Tom's anger at having been ordered to write an article justifying himself was morphing into worry about how to do it. He wouldn't be able to avoid mentioning Sherry, but anything he said about her would just raise more questions. Murray was fretting about the feminists who broke up the reading. Boycott this book? It was outrageous. But what if the idea gained steam?

"Do you have time for a drink?" Tom asked as they exited onto the street.

"I'd like to, but I can't," Murray said. "I have to get back to the office." The storm over the book had left him exhausted, and he didn't feel up to providing the kind of morale-boosting camaraderie that Tom apparently desired.

"By the way," he said, "and sorry to break it to you this way, Tom—I got a call from Ben Glazer in Hollywood yesterday. They're putting the movie on hold."

Tom looked shocked.

"They can't do that," he said. "We signed."

"I'm afraid they can," Murray said. "It's in the morality clause."

❧

Two weeks to Christmas, and George Fitzgerald didn't want any more bad publicity. He'd been furious when he heard about the incident at Barnes & Noble and had asked Helen to report back to him as soon as Tom and Murray departed. He looked up as she entered his office.

"So?" he asked.

"Tom's going ahead with the tour," she said.

"Helen, my dear. I know Tom is a particular favorite of yours, but I think we may need to contemplate Plan B."

"Which is?" she asked.

"Cutting our losses."

Jessica agreed to go to Washington, honoring her pledge to support Tom in public. But as their train pulled out of Penn Station the next afternoon, she reached into her bag and pulled out the latest edition of the *Village Voice*, hot off the presses.

Splashed across the front page was the headline: "The Rites of Mean."

Tom ripped the paper from Jessica's hands, his face flushing as he read the teaser: "Some say Tom Paine is a phony. Some say he's legit. Savannah Banks investigates."

He scanned the story as the train rattled through the tunnel under the Hudson. It was a clever hatchet job that damned him with faint praise while at the same time insinuating that he'd built his career, and his name, at the expense of a woman—his wife.

He turned on Jessica, cold fury in his eyes. "How could you let this happen?"

But she didn't answer. She was too busy watching the unlovely Jersey suburbs flit by.

Tom spent the rest of the trip regretting that he hadn't brought along a bottle from the case of J&B he'd had delivered after yesterday's meeting with Helen. He buried himself in *The New Yorker*, thinking ruefully that he should have considered the potential for disaster when he first began forming Sherry's stories into a novel without her consent.

The mid-December light was already fading as the train crossed a broad, silvery branch of Chesapeake Bay. When they disembarked shortly after six at Washington's Union Station, they had hardly exchanged a word. But as their cab approached Politics and Prose, Tom swallowed his pride. He needed Jessica now.

"Thanks for coming along," he said. "I think we can nail this."

"Think so?" Jessica said as the cab pulled up to the bookstore. Outside, a handful of women bearing "Boycott Tom Paine!" signs had formed a loose picket line.

Catcalls rang out as Tom emerged from the taxi. But as he helped his pregnant wife from the cab, the women stopped shouting. Jessica held her head high as they made their way inside.

The audience sat politely through Tom's reading, but when he finished, he faced a barrage of hostile questions.

Jessica felt her mood shifting as forgotten feelings of loyalty surfaced from the dark place where they'd been buried the last couple of years. When someone asked Tom who was really his muse, his wife or Sherry McManus, her eyes blazed, and she sprang to her feet.

"You've got a lot of nerve—all of you," she said. "Thomas G. Paine is an author. Maybe you don't understand what that means, so I'll spell it out. He creates literature. He's got more talent in his little finger than you, I, or Sherry McManus could ever hope to have. He doesn't need a muse, and our private life is none of your business."

She turned to Tom.

"Let's get out of here," she said.

A dozen people had bought the book before the reading, and Tom quickly signed their copies. Then it was back to Union Station.

To Jessica's surprise, her empathy persisted during the train ride home, and she listened attentively when Tom confided that he'd been asked by Helen and Murray to write an article on the making of *The Rites of Man*.

"That's ridiculous," Jessica said. "What do they expect you to say?"

"I have no idea," Tom said.

"So will you refuse?" Jessica asked.

Tom shrugged.

"I guess I'll spin something out about the nuts and bolts of writing. Sitting down at the typewriter every day. Ninety percent perspiration. That kind of thing."

"Focus on the other ten percent. Inspiration. Did that woman merely inspire you, or did she write the book for you? The question everyone's asking is whether you're a fraud. Actually, that's a question I've been asking myself."

Tom paused before replying. As usual when it came to his writing, Jessica had hit the nail on the head.

"To tell you the truth, I never know what inspires me. When I sit down to write, the words take over, and if I'm lucky, a novel appears. It's a mysterious process. The story is based on life, but I reinterpret reality. That's what makes it art."

As he said the words, he had the impression that he'd heard them before.

"Go with that," Jessica said, "although you still haven't answered my question."

Tom glanced apprehensively at his wife, but she was observing him mildly. Yes, now he remembered. Sherry had said those words to him at the beach house.

He felt a jolt of guilt-tinged desire at the thought of Sherry. If only he'd told her what he was writing, she might have headed him off at the pass or even helped him find a different approach to the novel that she could accept. And they might still be together. But that was then, and this was now, and his wife was beside him, carrying their child.

"You know," he said, "none of this really matters. Of course I'm a fraud, but so is every other writer who's ever lived. We pretend to know the truth, but it's an illusion. What's real is that there are three of us on this train—you, me, and the baby. We're creating a new life, Jess. That's a kind of creativity no book can match."

Jessica looked out into the night, the train's clickety-clack a comfort as she wondered when she'd work up the courage to inform Tom that he might not be the baby's father. He'd most likely be devastated, but she couldn't postpone it forever.

Chapter 30

It was Thursday by the time Sherry finally got through to Warsaw. A woman answered, and there was a moment of confusion as neither spoke the other's language. Sherry did her best to pronounce Jerzy's name the Polish way, saying "*YER-zhi*" over and over until the woman at last said, "*Ah. YEH-zhi. Minutka.*"

Sherry was sincerely astonished when Jerzy asked why she was calling. Clearly no enterprising reporter had yet sought him out to ask whether he was the fictional violinist named "Roman," the informant.

"I'm afraid we have a problem," Sherry said, unsure how much to spell out over the phone. She knew that the telephones of prominent Poles had been tapped in the old days, but were they now? She managed to convey the gist of what had happened, speaking in parables, certain that Jerzy would understand. After all, living under Communist rule had made him an expert in deciphering double meaning.

"Sherry, of course I will help you," Jerzy said when he'd grasped the plan. "When does this take place?"

"I'm not sure yet," she said. "Someone will be in touch."

At his desk at the Village townhouse, Tom tore a page from his typewriter and crumpled it into a ball. His side of the story—what a laugh. He tossed it at the waste basket but missed.

"Shit," he said, getting up from his desk to retrieve it. The basket was spilling over with crumpled pages. He crammed the new one in and went to the kitchen to pour himself a J&B.

The problem was that his article wouldn't come together. Every time he wrote a paragraph, he felt like he was incriminating himself. He needed to find a way to salvage his reputation without providing more ammunition to destroy it. But it just wasn't working.

The uncomfortable thought flashed through his mind that maybe he was getting what he deserved, but he quickly rejected it. For Christ's sake, he was an author. He shouldn't have to justify himself for creating a work, even if some people found it objectionable.

He reached for the phone and dialed Dudley Melville.

"Hey, old buddy, I need your help," Tom said when his lawyer picked up.

"Sure thing, Tom. What's up?"

"I'm being skewered by the press—did you see the *Voice* article?—and now a bunch of feminists are on my case. They keep turning up at my book events."

"So I hear. What are they on about?"

Tom took a slug of his drink.

"Come on. You know these women. Fuck, we supported them back at Columbia when women's liberation was just getting started. They don't trust male authors to begin with. We're 'phallocrats.' They detest it when a man presumes to write from the point of view of a woman, and the publicity around Sherry McManus has made them detest me even more."

"Okay, how can I help?" Dudley asked.

"My agent wants me to write a piece putting a different spin on the story behind the book," Tom said. "He thinks it could improve my image, but I can't get my head around it. I mean, if I'm facing a lawsuit, what can I possibly say that won't be used against me?"

"Don't sweat it, dude," Dudley said. "No one's filed suit yet. I've been asking around discreetly, and there's no sign that Herzen Leibowitz is even taking this case."

"So you think I should write the piece?" Tom asked.

"Yeah. It could help. But why don't you take a few days off first? You've been under a hell of a lot of pressure."

"I can't take time off. I'm due in Chicago tomorrow to tape with Oprah, and then I fly out to San Francisco for another book gig. I'll work on the piece on the road."

"Is Jessica going with you?" Dudley asked.

"Not this time."

"But she did move back in, right? How are things going?"

"She's like the fucking sphinx," Tom said. "I can't tell what she's thinking. She kind of threatened to leave me. She said she couldn't deal with a major disruption now, repeat now. In other words, once the baby is born, all bets are off."

"Heavy."

Tom knocked back the rest of his whiskey.

"If things die down, she might stick by me," he said. "But if there's a lawsuit, she could just walk out and slam the door."

Evening was falling when Tom and Jessica arrived at the bar, a small East Village joint festooned with Christmas lights. It was Tom's first social venture since the *Drudge Report* turned his life upside down, and before going out he'd put on his fedora.

As they entered the bar, he pulled the hat lower over his eyes.

"You can cut the cloak-and-dagger routine, Tom," Jessica said. "Nobody cares."

He shot her a resentful glance. The grace period was apparently over.

Steve and Marilyn were at a table in the back. They'd already started on a pitcher of eggnog, the usual drink at their annual holiday outing with the Paines.

Tom had considered canceling, but he knew he couldn't stay cooped up forever. Besides, he didn't have to fake it with Steve and Marilyn—he could be himself, and they'd understand.

"I think I need something stronger than eggnog this year," Tom said when they'd exchanged the usual pleasantries. He hailed the waiter.

"I'll have a Manhattan," he said, "and for the lady…"

"A Virgin Mary," Jessica said.

The waiter looked at her belly and rolled his eyes.

"A Virgin Mary," he repeated, oozing irony in a Brooklyn accent.

Tom and Steve chortled as he departed.

"Ignore them, Jess," Marilyn said. She was determined to have a good time, or at least be there for her friends. She wondered how Jessica was handling the situation. Had she known about Tom's affair with Sherry McManus when it was happening? If so, she'd done a very good job of concealing it.

She and Steve had discussed it more than once since the scandal broke. Marilyn was convinced that Jessica's pregnancy dated back to their July weekend out at the shore, when Tom was starting his novel, apparently with the help of that McManus woman. Whether Jessica had known then of Sherry's existence or not, it must be excruciating for her now that everything had come out in public.

Steve had counseled Marilyn not to broach the subject with Jessica, just as he had avoided bringing it up with Tom. In fact, he and Tom hadn't had a personal chat since the final game of the World Series back in October. He'd scored some seats via his law firm and had invited Tom to join him. Before the game started, he'd asked Tom how things were going with Jessica now that they were living together again. But Tom had been uncharacteristically terse, so he'd backed off. And the Yankees' awesome victory had ended all other discussion.

When the drinks arrived, Marilyn was advising Jessica on the best places to shop for maternity clothes. Tom knocked back his Manhattan in two long gulps.

Marilyn looked at him with concern.

"Are you okay, Tommy?" she asked.

"For god's sake, Marilyn," Tom said quietly. "What do you think?"

To his chagrin, he felt a lump in his throat. For weeks he'd been carrying his burden alone—the wrench of leaving Sherry, his regret over his lack of candor with her, his turmoil over becoming a parent with Jessica, and now the uproar over his book. But he didn't want to display his feelings. Instead, he hailed the waiter and ordered another drink.

"Take it easy, man," Steve said. "Don't forget, we're here for you. So's Jess."

The mention of Jessica ended Tom's moment of introspection.

"Sure," he said, allowing anger to swamp his remorse. "That's why she had her friend Savannah publish that Tom-Paine-is-a-phony piece in the *Village Voice*."

Jessica swirled her Virgin Mary.

"I can't control what Joe puts in the paper," she said.

"Bullshit," Tom said. "I wouldn't trust that guy as far as I could throw a stone. And you're in cahoots with him, don't think I don't know it."

Steve and Marilyn exchanged a worried glance as Tom's tone mounted.

"I saw the piece in the *Voice*, Tommy," Marilyn said. "It was totally unfair."

"Was it?" Jessica said. "People have the right to ask questions, starting with me. Imagine how it feels to know your husband was having an affair right under your nose."

"It wasn't under your nose," Tom said. "It was out on the island after you kicked me out of the house, or did you forget about that?"

The table fell silent as the waiter arrived with Tom's second Manhattan. When he'd downed it, a warm glow spread through his body. He decided to pursue the matter.

"So tell us about Joe Reilly, Jess," he said. "What's up with the two of you?"

"I have no idea what you're talking about," Jessica said neutrally.

"Sure you do," Tom said. "I wouldn't be surprised if you were next up on his list to write a piece destroying me."

Jessica was taken aback. Surely Tom couldn't know about the exposé Joe had asked her to write about their home life. But she quickly regained her composure.

She smiled apologetically at Steve and Marilyn.

"I'd better get him out of here," she said, rising. "He can't hold his liquor."

Marilyn began to object, but Steve stopped her. He knew the Paines well enough to realize that things could only go downhill from there.

Chapter 31

Tom felt a jolt as his plane dipped downward for the descent to O'Hare.

"The captain has turned on the seatbelt sign," the chief flight attendant announced. "Please return to your seats and stow your tray tables in their original upright position."

Tom shoved a legal pad into his briefcase and clicked his tray into place. It didn't matter that he couldn't work anymore. He'd written only one paragraph during the entire two-hour flight.

He gazed out the window as the plane left the sunny stratosphere for the thick clouds blanketing Chicago. He was dreading the session with Oprah. Why did they have to schedule it for Friday the fucking thirteenth, he thought as the plane dropped toward Earth.

Jessica was sitting across from Joe at a deli around the corner from the *Voice*. It was a small place mainly frequented by students from NYU. No one they knew was around, but she lowered her voice all the same.

"Tom suspects you've asked me to write a piece about him," she said.

"Did you tell him?" Joe asked.

"Of course not. He pulled that out of nowhere. It's like he's got this sixth sense."

Joe sighed. He wished Tom Paine would disappear off the face of the Earth.

"So how about it?" he said. "Will you write the column? We need it by Monday."

"I'm still thinking about it. I've had a lot on my mind."

Seeing an opportunity, Joe mustered his nerve.

"I hope I'm still part of that equation," he said.

"Even if the baby's not yours?" she asked.

"Yeah. I've been doing some thinking too. I mean, this thing with Tom's book isn't going away. If you stay with him, you're going to have to live with that. Close the chapter, Jess, and start a new one. With me."

Jessica thought that over. If Joe was prepared to bring up a child that might not be his, he must care for her more than she realized. But she wasn't ready to let down her guard.

"I can't make any big decisions now," she said.

"Have you thought about seeing a divorce lawyer?" Joe asked.

"I've thought about it."

Joe knew better than to press further. He called the waitress and ordered a couple of coffees.

"I'd like you to write the column," he said. "Keep it nice and simple. A day-in-the-life kind of thing. It doesn't have to be bitchy."

Jessica looked at him in surprise.

"But bitchy is what I do best."

Sherry stretched, got up, and shook out her towel. Time for lunch. She was enjoying her Florida routine now—up early and down to the beach for a run and a swim, then a leisurely rest in the sun. Sometimes she left the beach early to help with the grocery shopping, but today her mother was taking care of it. She'd had the whole morning to herself.

When she went inside, Bernie was watching the news, but there was nothing about Tom Paine. A week had passed since the scandal broke, with new scoops usurping the airtime. Still, when Sherry passed the TV, the butterflies she'd lived with since Tom's book came out began fluttering nervously, reminding her that she still had work to do.

She went to her room to call Susan.

"I got through to Jerzy yesterday," she said. "That's four for four. Everyone's on board."

"Perfect," Susan said. "In that case, we can go ahead and announce that we plan to sue."

"Today?" Sherry asked.

"No," Susan said. "Sam wants to wait till Monday. He thinks we'll get better coverage if the news breaks after the weekend."

"So when do I mobilize Granville?" Sherry asked.

"Let's wait and see what happens when Tom hears about the lawsuit," Susan said. "If he reacts, it could give us a springboard for setting the rest of the plan in action."

Tom understood why they called Oprah Winfrey the queen of media as soon as the cameras started rolling at Harpo Studios. It wasn't just her regal bearing. It was her ease beneath the gaze of the lens, the ambience of intimacy she created.

The interview began well enough, with Oprah praising *The Rites of Man* as one of the year's most important novels. She quickly moved on to more personal questions.

"So, Tom," she said, "this is the first time we've met, and my producers tell me your middle name is Geronimo. All this time I thought the 'G' in Thomas G. Paine stood for something more common, like Gregory or George. Tell us about that."

"You know, Oprah," Tom said, "my mom studied the history of the Apache, and she took a particular liking to the story of Geronimo. She thought he'd been unfairly portrayed by historians, and I guess she wanted to honor his memory. I'm actually proud of the name."

"Has your mother read the book?" she asked.

"I'm not sure, but I hope she's watching," he said.

"What about your father?"

Tom suddenly felt hot under the television lights.

"I'd rather not discuss my father," he said.

Oprah raised an eyebrow but quickly moved on.

"Tell me, Tom, you won the National Book Award seven years ago, and it's taken all that time for you to produce another book. Was it because you felt under pressure to match that performance?"

"It wasn't so much the book award but, yeah, I did feel a kind of internal pressure," Tom said. "I wanted to write something completely different—well, similar, too, because *The Rites of Man* is about America at a specific moment in time, the same as my other novels. But different because I wanted to write from a woman's perspective."

"And why is that?" Oprah asked.

"Well, I think women today have replaced men as the vanguard of original thinking," Tom said. "I mean, you yourself are an example."

"Thank you, Tom. I'm sure many women among our viewers will applaud that thought. But at the same time, I hear you've run into some trouble with protesters at your book events. Tell us, what's all the fuss about? Why has *The Rites of Man* created a sense of outrage among some women?"

Tom prickled even though he had prepared for that question.

"I'd like to ask you, Oprah, what are they protesting about?" he said. "Are they outraged because a man dared to imagine what a woman might be thinking? If that's the case, then they may as well write off Shakespeare, too, because he did the same. His plays are full of outspoken women—I'm thinking of Rosalind in *As You Like It*, Cordelia in *Lear*, Kate in *Taming of the Shrew*, and the list goes on. I have to admit I'm perplexed about all the fuss, as you put it. What troubles me is that the message of my novel is being drowned out by these voices. And that message is that we need a revolution in human relations in order to move from confrontation to harmony."

"I see," Oprah said. "Now from what I hear, a lot of the opposition has to do with the notion that you may have been, let's say, inspired by a real woman named Sherry McManus. Would you like to tell our viewers about your relations with Ms. McManus?"

"Why don't you ask her?" Tom said curtly.

"We of course tried to contact Ms. McManus when preparing this program, but she has unfortunately dropped off the radar screen," Oprah said. "So do enlighten us, please."

Forgetting about the media coaching he'd received, Tom rose to his feet.

"I have nothing to say about Sherry McManus," he said. Without a backward glance, he strode off the set and out of the studio.

As he left the building, Tom started at the sight of a crowd of women. Across the street, bundled against the cold, they were brandishing placards saying, "Not Fair! Not Right!" and "Oprah, Interview Sherry Instead!"

"It's him!" one shouted, and the crowd surged forward. A tumult of voices rang out.

"No more lies! "No more lies!" they chanted as Tom, mortified, looked in vain for a cab. As he scanned the street, he saw a second group of women arriving from around the corner.

"There he is!" one cried.

They rushed to encircle him, excitedly shouting his name: "Tom Paine, Tom Paine." Two of the women unfurled a banner saying, "The Thomas G. Paine Fan Club."

Tom struggled to understand what was going on. Did these women actually support him? But before he could wrap his mind around it, the first group of women had moved in on the second, their competing slogans clashing in a riot of noise.

"Are you insane?" one of the protesters yelled. "Tom Paine is no friend of women."

A woman from the fan club pushed her.

"Get out of our way," she shouted. "Tom Paine's book is brilliant. His message comes from God! We must accept each other as different, not equal."

"Yeah, that's what it says in the Bible!" another chimed in as the encounter turned into a scuffle. The women were grabbing each other by the collar, by the hair. Tom's opponents threw the fan club's banner to the ground and stomped on it.

With a shrill blow of his whistle, the security guard from Oprah's building ran out to try to end the melee. A moment later, a couple of Chicago's finest were at the scene.

Tom took advantage of the confusion to slip away, jogging until he spotted a cab. He collected his wits as the taxi sped off. A fan club—that was something he hadn't expected. It was a promising turn of events. But being compared to God? Over the top, even for him.

Jessica had the apartment to herself for the first time in ages. Well, Che was there, but he wouldn't bother her. Determined to make the most of her evening, she took a leisurely bath, splashing warm water over her belly, enjoying the sensation of floating, feeling in harmony with her unborn child. When she'd toweled off, she put on one of Tom's sweatshirts, a new pair of maternity leggings, and her fuzzy slippers, and made herself a cup of tea.

Then she sat down at Tom's typewriter, inserted a clean page, and began typing quickly. Yes, she thought, bitchy is what I do best.

Chapter 32

Tom awoke in San Francisco on Monday morning feeling groggy after a weekend holed up at the Fairmont trying to get to grips with the article he'd promised Murray. He rubbed his eyes, and when his hand brushed his cheek, he could feel the three-days' growth that had sprouted.

He got up and opened the curtains to a spectacular view of the Golden Gate. It was a cool, pleasant day, perfect weather for a stroll around town before his appearance at City Lights. He dialed room service to order breakfast, switched on CNN, and went to the bathroom to shower and shave.

Warm and clean, wearing only a towel, he was running his razor down the last strip of lather when he heard his name emanate from the TV. He nicked himself in his hurry to go see.

"In the latest development in the controversy over *The Rites of Man*," the anchor said, "the New York photographer Sherry McManus is filing suit against Mr. Paine and his publisher, Fitzgerald & Fitzgerald, for invasion of privacy, her lawyer announced this morning. Here's attorney Susan Katz of the Washington law firm Herzen Leibowitz."

The screen flashed to Susan in her office.

"My client, Sherry McManus, had a brief relationship with Thomas G. Paine last summer," Susan said. "During that time, and without her knowledge, he transcribed stories she told him in private and went on to publish them in *The Rites of Man*. Acting with reckless disregard, he appropriated her likeness and then distorted those stories to portray her and her acquaintances in a false light. On behalf of Ms. McManus, Herzen Leibowitz will ask Mr. Paine and the publisher of his book for three million dollars in punitive damages."

The anchor reappeared on the screen.

"There has been no comment from Mr. Paine nor from his publisher," he said. "Stay tuned for updates."

"Christ," Tom said, dabbing at the blood on his cheek. He was en route back to the bathroom to clean up the cut when the phone rang.

As he went to answer, there was a knock on the door.

"Room service," a voice called.

Tom scrambled to open the door and grab the phone at the same time. He motioned to the waiter to set his breakfast on the desk as Dudley Melville's voice came over the line.

"This looks bad, Tom," Dudley said. "They say they're suing."

"Yeah, I just saw it," Tom said. "What do we do now?"

"Frankly, they don't have a leg to stand on, legally speaking. I mean, the book is fiction, right?"

Tom felt the knot in his stomach tighten.

"Right. Hang on a sec."

The waiter was still standing there. Tom signed the check and fumbled for change for a tip. He poured himself a cup of coffee and returned to the phone.

"But then there's the court of public opinion," Dudley said. "We may need to settle."

"Uh, settle?"

"Yeah, pay Sherry Fucking McManus some money to shut the fuck up."

Tom sighed deeply. He remembered fucking Sherry McManus. If only things hadn't turned out this way, he thought. A vision rose up of Sherry posing for him on her bed, nude save for the quilt over her loins.

Dudley's voice shattered the vision.

"Tom? Are you there?"

"Yeah, sorry," he said. "Let's discuss this tomorrow when I'm back in town."

"When are you getting in?"

"Early. I'm catching the red-eye after my reading."

"Okay," Dudley said. "You're the boss."

Tom left his breakfast on the desk uneaten. He stretched out on the bed and allowed himself a moment of escape from reality. He remembered pushing the quilt aside, and everything that followed. If only, he said to himself. If only…

Joe Reilly was smirking when he looked up from his reading. He was back at the deli with Jessica.

"You nailed it," he said, glancing around to make sure they weren't being observed. "What about the art?"

"I brought some snapshots you may be able to use," Jessica said, reaching into her bag. She extracted three photos, their edges yellowed with age. One showed Tom grinning in front of the Paris plaque commemorating Thomas Paine, another was a baby pic of him in diapers, and the third was from their wedding day, Tom in a tux and flowers in Jessica's hair.

Joe reached across the table for the photos, holding them up in the dim afternoon light.

"They'll do," he said. "Come on. Let's get this into print."

He helped Jessica into her coat, resisting a proprietorial temptation to brush his hand over her belly. Now that she'd been to see Ophelia Friedman, known as the hottest divorce lawyer in town, there could be no displays of affection in public. No one could find out about their liaison, at least not yet. It could jeopardize her case. But no one appeared to be watching.

He opened the door for her, surreptitiously planting a kiss on her cheek as they stepped into the wintry day.

Lawrence Ferlinghetti was on the doorstep to greet Tom when he arrived at City Lights. There were no picketers, Tom saw with relief. A uniformed policeman stood guard.

"It's an honor to meet you, sir," Tom said as the white-bearded poet shook his hand and ushered him inside. The place was surprisingly empty, only a few customers and a couple of staffers at work in the shelves. There must be a special room somewhere, Tom thought as Ferlinghetti led him to his office.

"Where are we holding the signing?" Tom asked.

Ferlinghetti motioned to Tom to sit and drew up an armchair beside him.

"I'm afraid we've had to cancel your appearance," he said. "We can't hold the signing when you're facing a lawsuit."

Tom stared at him in stunned disbelief.

"Is this some kind of joke?" he asked.

"No, sir. My staff is pulling your novel from our shelves right now. We got in touch with Fitzgerald & Fitzgerald this morning when we heard about the suit, but apparently they couldn't reach you."

Of course they couldn't, Tom thought dejectedly. He'd been wandering the hills of San Francisco, worrying about the lawsuit.

"So I came all the way out here for nothing," he said.

"It's a tough break, I know," Ferlinghetti said, "but other writers have faced worse." His eyes migrated to a photo on his desk of himself with Allen Ginsberg.

As Tom's eyes followed Ferlinghetti's, he remembered what the Beats had endured. Ginsberg put on trial for obscenity after publishing *Howl*. Ferlinghetti arrested for publishing it. They had defended the work in court and won. But that work had been attacked for what was viewed at the time as outrageous originality, and not, as in his case, for want of it.

Tom stopped back at the hotel to pick up his bag before catching a cab to the airport. He donned his fedora and added a pair of shades. As he made his way to the check-in desk, he saw a knot of people gathered around a television monitor and, telling himself not to be paranoid, went to take a look.

He had forgotten about *Oprah's Book Club*. It had aired earlier in the day, and the newscast was running a clip. There she was in her cool majesty—"So do enlighten us, please"—and there he was, rising from his seat in anger—"I have nothing to say about Sherry McManus."

Murmurs went up as the airport viewers saw Tom stalk off the set.

"He's walking out on Oprah?"

"The man's got no spine."

The voices followed him as he slunk away.

"Yeah. And Sherry McManus is suing."

"I hope she takes him for every cent he's worth."

At the check-in counter, the clerk did a double take when Tom presented his ID.

"Thomas G. Paine, the author?" she asked.

"I'm afraid so," he said.

Chapter 33

The first indication Tom had that something was wrong was the quiet when he turned his key in the lock of his townhouse in the Village on Tuesday morning. No excited barking to greet him. It was seven thirty a.m., and Che should have been there wagging his tail.

The apartment was dark. He switched on the light, deposited his suitcase in the living room, and went to check the bedroom. Jessica wasn't there.

She's probably freaking out about the three frigging million dollars, he mused.

He went to check his voicemail. A message from Helen Nussbaum telling him to get his ass over to her office, another from Dudley suggesting they meet for lunch. He showered, returned the calls, and fearing the worst, set out for Fitzgerald & Fitzgerald.

"We're in consultations with our lawyer, Tom," Helen said when he'd joined her in George Fitzgerald's office. "In the meantime, we've halted the Christmas run."

"A week before Christmas? That sounds a little extreme," Tom said.

"I'm afraid not," George said, "given that the stores are pulling your book."

"All of them?" Tom asked, his voice rising in disbelief.

"That's what we hear," Helen said. "This lawsuit has spillover potential. If you're found liable for invasion of privacy, anyone who sells *The Rites of Man* could be affected."

"Jesus Christ," Tom said.

"Yes, it's very unfortunate," George said. "Furthermore, I'm afraid you'll be liable for any damages, including our attorneys' fees, if the book is found to violate the privacy of any person."

Tom felt like he'd received a body blow.

"Is that legal?" he asked.

"It's in your contract, Tom," Helen said. "I hope you're in touch with your lawyer."

"Yes, I'm meeting him now."

Mustering what was left of his dignity, Tom shook hands with them and departed.

Back in the West Village, he recounted the conversation to Dudley over lunch at the Knickerbocker Bar & Grill, their usual watering hole. He tried to joke about it—"Hey, it's only money"—but something in his friend's demeanor stopped him.

"Let's talk about Sherry McManus," Dudley said. "You said no one could prove anything. Then the *Post* fronted a photo of the two of you together. What's the story?"

"I have no idea who took that picture," Tom said ruefully. "Will it hurt me in court?"

"That's not what I meant. What I'm asking is, what's the story with you and Sherry McManus?"

"We saw each other over the summer. It was a fling. No more, no less."

"What about the invasion of privacy part?" Dudley persisted.

Searching for a way to answer, Tom glanced across the restaurant to the arty posters arrayed on its wood-paneled walls.

"You know how it is," he said. "A writer's a sponge. I absorb everything I hear, everything I see, and it naturally works its way into my writing. But to go from there to saying I actually used her words..."

"Yes?"

"I can't say," Tom said feebly. "The truth is, I don't know."

"You have to know," Dudley said. "It's the first thing you'll be asked if this goes to court."

Surprised by Dudley's tone, Tom realized he'd have to open up, at least to his friend.

"Sherry was, you know... well, she was fantastic," he said. "She's the kind of woman who lights up a room. Heads turn. When we were together, she recharged my batteries. She'd come out to the beach for a night, and when she left, I found myself pounding away at the typewriter. Maybe I lifted some of her words. But I didn't do it on purpose."

"All right," Dudley said. "I'll try to work along those lines. Meantime, I've been in touch with Herzen Leibowitz, and it looks like they hope to settle out of court. Unless you want to fight Sherry McManus, in which case we can countersue for libel."

"No," Tom said. "I don't want to attack her."

"Because?" Dudley asked.

"Because maybe she has a point."

He couldn't acknowledge the other reason. It was absurd to think he could somehow patch things up with Sherry. Yet he wished he could push the rewind button and go back to where things had been during the summer—their long, sweet nights, their playful courtship. But there was no point in fantasizing about it, he realized gloomily.

Dudley called for the check.

"Anything else I should know about?" he asked.

"Yeah, maybe," Tom said. "Jessica didn't come home last night."

Dudley frowned.

"Not good," he said. "I thought she said she'd support you."

"She said 'for now,' but that was then. Before the lawsuit."

"Have you tried to reach her?" Dudley asked.

"I don't know where she is. She could be anywhere."

"She'll be back. You're having a baby."

"I'm not sure," Tom said. "She's been pretty upset, and the lawsuit may have driven her over the edge."

As he spoke, he felt a prick of dread at the idea of facing the collapse of his world alone.

"Look, why don't you buy her something nice for Christmas?" Dudley said. "It's only a week away. You can give her an early present when she comes home."

"If she comes home," Tom said.

Chapter 34

Tom didn't shave before setting out for Van Cleef & Arpels the next morning. Ferlinghetti had inspired him. A writer looked good in a beard.

The scruffier, the better, he thought as he lingered outside the shop's elegant window display, his fedora pulled down low. A gold-and-ruby necklace with matching earrings caught his eye. But when he opened the door of the venerable establishment and entered its dazzling interior, it was the diamonds that beckoned, glittering in glass cases.

A saleswoman approached, sizing up her customer with a practiced eye.

"How may I help you, sir?" she asked coolly.

Tom was examining a V-shaped necklace formed by a double strand of diamonds set in platinum. There was no price tag.

"I'm looking for something special," he said. "How much is the necklace?"

"Eight hundred thousand."

When Tom recoiled, the saleswoman smiled condescendingly.

"Perhaps something less extravagant?" she said.

In the end, he escaped for a mere nine thousand dollars, choosing a small heart of tiny diamonds on a fine platinum chain. Jessica was sure to like it, he thought, as the saleswoman set the necklace against black velvet in an elegant pale green box.

On his way home, he passed a row of Christmas trees for sale out on the street and, on impulse, chose a small one. He was approaching the apartment, dragging the tree behind him, when he saw Jessica and Che arriving from the other direction.

Tom waited for them on the sidewalk, reaching furtively into his pocket to make sure the box from Van Cleef & Arpels was still there.

Jessica tightened her grip on Che's leash.

"It's good to see you, Jess," Tom said as she brushed past him.

He lumbered up the stairs behind them, the tree slowing his progress. By the time he reached the apartment, Jessica had disappeared inside.

He found her in the bedroom, rummaging in a dresser drawer.

"I've got something for you," he said as he placed the pale green box on the dresser. "It's an early Christmas present."

Jessica merely glanced at the box and returned to her work.

"What are you doing?" Tom asked.

"I'm leaving you," she said.

The worst hadn't been watching Jessica pack. He'd groveled, begging her to stay for the sake of the baby. The worst hadn't been watching her walk out the door without telling him where she was going. No. The worst had been her parting gesture.

She'd reached into her handbag and thrown the *Voice* on the table. On the front page was a teaser: "Paine in the Ass: Jessica Franklin Tells All."

"It's an early Christmas present," she'd said. And she was gone.

Alone in the apartment, Tom picked up the paper and slumped onto the couch to read. Nothing she'd written was false, and yet it made him out as the ultimate loser. Jessica claimed credit for his entire career, up to but not including his new book. Getting him started as a writer? Her influence. Using Thomas Paine's titles? Her idea. In short, he'd never had an original thought in his life. She accused Tom of duplicity, saying she now knew he'd been having an affair when she got pregnant. And the other woman? She pitied her for having been taken in by such a lamentable excuse for a man.

Tom got up and rammed the *Voice* into the waste basket. He felt like punching someone. The tree was still lying where he'd left it on the living room floor. He kicked it into a corner and went to the kitchen to pour himself a J&B. When he'd downed it, he went to the bedroom and opened the pale green box. The diamond heart seemed to mock him. He snapped it shut.

What a fool I've been, he thought. He poured himself another tumbler of Scotch, pacing around the apartment as he considered the wreckage. When he'd crawled back to Jessica in October, with the book due to appear and a baby on the way, he'd felt that he had no choice. His relationship with Sherry was doomed in any event. Whether or not she'd heard the NPR broadcast, she was bound to read the book, and it was certain to outrage her. He hadn't merely pirated her stories. He'd twisted them, making villains of the men she'd loved and creating a narrator so unlike Sherry as to be laughable. The only true thing he'd written was to portray himself as a con man. He'd even conned himself. He'd tricked himself into believing that it was possible to carry on a love affair while secretly exploiting his lover. He'd tricked himself so well that he'd fallen in love.

While walking the streets of Manhattan after reading on NPR, he'd realized that Sherry would never forgive him. He'd broken her trust. He'd lost her, irremediably. And he'd been devastated. But at the same time, intoxicated by the prospect of a return to literary stardom, he'd convinced himself that there could be an upside to returning to Jessica. If the book did well, she'd believe in him again. He'd win back his renown, he'd make serious money, and, most of all, he'd have a family. Now that had all turned to dust. Any last shred of self-esteem he'd managed to cling to was gone. Jessica had seen to that. He felt like tearing her eyes out, but he couldn't lie to himself any longer. He knew he had only himself to blame.

Tom refilled his tumbler. He needed to dull his senses, but oddly the whiskey was having the opposite effect. Suddenly

everything seemed perfectly clear. He went to the phone and
punched in a number. He didn't need to look it up because he
knew it by heart.

After five rings, Sherry's answering machine clicked: "This is
Sherry McManus. Please leave a message."

Tom mustered his courage.

"Sherry, hi, it's Tom. Are you there?" He paused. "Okay,
guess you're not there. So yeah, it's me. Hey, I miss you, Sher.
Well, that's probably not what you want to hear, right? So I'll get
straight to the point. Things didn't work out so well, did they?"

He paused again, working up the nerve to continue.

"Sherry, I owe you an apology," he said. "In fact, many apolo-
gies. I should have shown you the manuscript before I published
my book. Well, I probably never should have written the fucking
book. You're right, I used your stories. I thought they'd make
a good novel. I didn't stop to think how it would affect you. I
was only thinking of getting back into print and rebuilding my
reputation. And now everything's falling apart. Jessica's gone, the
stores are pulling my book, and I don't even want to think about
my reputation."

Tom realized his voice was quavering.

"So here's the thing," he said. "My lawyer wants us to sue you
for libel, but I won't do it. I want to make things right with you,
Sherry. This whole thing is my fault. I've ruined things for both
of us. And all you did was tell the truth. Call me."

Bernie was downstairs grilling a T-bone on the condo's commu-
nal barbecue. Rose was setting the table, and Sherry was helping
her. When they finished, she went to her room for a quick check
of her voicemail before dinner.

There were a couple more messages from reporters who hadn't
given up trying to find her. Then Tom's voice came through.

She played his message three times to make sure she'd heard
right. The start of it made her wince. Had he really said, "I
miss you"? After dropping her like she was radioactive? After

pretending he didn't know her when they'd crossed paths at Washington Square? Well, she thought, at least I don't miss him anymore. Then came the good part: "You're right, I used your stories." And the cherry on top: "And all you did was tell the truth."

She hung up and went to the window. The palm trees were dancing in the wind, bending and swaying. When she'd calmed down enough to speak, she dialed Susan in Washington.

"Tom called," she said. "We've got him."

After dinner, Sherry returned to the phone in her room. Susan had instructed her to launch the plan. First on the list was Granville.

"Hi, it's Sherry," she said when he picked up. "I need you to run an errand for me tomorrow."

When she'd brought him up to date, she checked her notes from her first frantic day in Florida. She found the number of Philip Asmundsen at CNN, took a breath, and dialed.

"This is Sherry McManus," she said. "You said you'd like to hear my side of the story…"

Chapter 35

Marilee Dyer was waiting in the lobby when Granville arrived at
The New York Times on the morning of Thursday, December 19.
She ushered him up to her office and closed the door.

"Thanks for contacting me," Marilee said. "You say you have
a message from Sherry McManus?"

"That's right," Granville said. "For your ears only. I need your
word on that."

"Of course."

"Okay then. Sherry would like you to send a reporter to Florida tomorrow."

Marilee raised her eyebrows.

"Florida?"

"Right. She's ready to speak out about her role in the making
of *The Rites of Man*. You can run the piece on Christmas Eve as
an exclusive."

"Fantastic," Marilee said, making a quick mental calculation.
Christmas Eve was five days away; plenty of time to organize the
column space.

"But where in Florida?" she asked.

"Put the reporter in touch with me," Granville said, handing
Marilee his card.

"I expect I'll go myself," she said. "We have a photographer
in Miami. I'll have him join us, if that's okay."

"Fine," Granville said. "Then please book a flight to Palm
Beach and give me a call with the arrival details. We'll have a car
waiting at the airport. The photographer can meet you there."

❧

Sherry put through two calls to Paris before lunch. First, Anouk, to make sure she'd be around over the holidays. Then Jacques. He picked up on the second ring.

"Is your offer of a place to stay still good?" she asked. "Because I'm coming."

"*Fan-tas-tique*," Jacques said. "I am so happy. When do you arrive?"

"I have a few things to wrap up, but I hope to make it by Christmas."

"Perfect. That's in less than a week! I am waiting for you."

As she hung up, there was a knock on her bedroom door.

"Come out and take a look," Bernie said. "They say they're running a Tom Paine update after the ad."

Sherry joined her dad in the living room.

"Levi's wide-leg jean," came the message from the TV as a handsome man and a sexy woman in jeans exchanged a sulfurous look. "It's w-i-d-e open."

CNN switched to its home screen and the anchor reappeared.

"And now the latest on the Thomas Paine affair," he said. "With Christmas coming, things are looking grim for the author…"

Tom was sprawled on the couch, an empty bottle of J&B on the floor beside him. He hadn't left the place since phoning Sherry, hoping that she'd call back. In vain. He had the TV on but wasn't paying attention—until he heard his name.

"… With *The Rites of Man* no longer on sale at bookshops," the anchor said, "a black market is taking shape. Mr. Paine's novel is reportedly selling for a hundred dollars a copy and more, but he won't get a penny of it."

Tom sat up.

"Jesus Christ," he said.

"Meantime, a groundswell of support for Sherry McManus is growing across the country as women take to the streets to denounce Mr. Paine's alleged pirating of her stories," the anchor said. "They have been fighting off forays by a small but vocal fan club of women who adore Mr. Paine to the point of comparing his book's message to the Bible. No comment on that. And now we learn that Mr. Paine's pregnant wife has left him."

The image cut to a reporter interviewing Jessica outside the *Village Voice*.

"Jessica Franklin, you say you've moved out of the apartment you share with your husband, Thomas G. Paine?" the reporter asked.

"That is correct," Jessica said.

The camera zoomed out to show Jessica in her black maternity coat.

"Will you be seeking a divorce?" the reporter asked.

"I'm considering my options."

The reporter tried to draw her out, but she declined to say more.

Joe Reilly was waiting in Jessica's office when she came in from the interview. He didn't look happy.

"We need to talk," he said.

Jessica closed the door and hung her coat on a wall peg.

"Is there a problem?" she asked, taking a seat at her desk.

"Yes, there's a problem," Joe said crossly. "You're considering your options? What the fuck is that supposed to mean?"

"Don't use that tone with me," Jessica said.

"I thought this was a done deal. I mean, you talked to the lawyer. What were you talking about? The weather?"

"Cool it, Joe," Jessica said, her eyes flashing a warning.

"What about us?" he asked, a plaintive note creeping into his voice. "When you turned up at my place with your suitcase, I thought you were planning to stay."

Jessica sighed. She'd just told the world that she'd left Tom, and now Joe was pressuring her.

"Let me spell it out for you," she said. "The lawyer warned

me not to show my hand too early. It's enough for Tom to know that I'm thinking about a divorce."

"So that was just for the TV?" Joe asked.

"It's not that simple. I've got a lot on my mind. It's not just about you or me—I've got my child's future to consider. And besides, maybe Tom's telling the truth about his book. Nobody's proved that his stories came from that woman."

"Are you saying you might go back to him?" Joe asked, his temper rising again.

"Come here," Jessica said, swiveling her chair as he moved to her side of the desk.

She stood up and took his hands.

"It's like this," she said. "I'm coming home to you tonight, and I'm grateful to you for taking me in, but we've never lived together before. Let's just see how it goes."

Joe gave her a grudging nod of acceptance.

She rose to her toes and kissed him on the cheek.

"Jessica," he said, "if you only knew how much you mean to me…"

"I do," she said.

Chapter 36

On the morning of Friday, December 20, with the team from *The New York Times* turning up, Sherry sent Rose and Bernie to West Palm to buy her a ticket to Paris. They decided to make a day of it, sticking around for lunch at an oceanfront resort.

By the time they returned to the condo, Sherry had finished her interview with Marilee Dyer and was posing for the photographer.

"Perfect timing," she told her parents. "They want some pix of the three of us."

After the shoot, the photographer was in a rush to get back to Miami. Marilee had time before her flight, so Sherry offered to drive her down to Palm Beach International a bit later. On the way there, they went over the terms of the interview one last time. It would run on Tuesday, December 24, as an exclusive. The photographer had been sworn to secrecy. No leaks.

"You're a very impressive woman," Marilee said when they pulled up to the airport. "I think what you have to say will make a tremendous impact."

Sherry smiled warmly.

"I hope so," she said.

After extracting herself from the convertible, Marilee reached back inside to shake Sherry's hand.

"Thanks," she said. "And good luck."

᪥

Tom was back at his Olympia. He typed a few lines and frowned. It was useless. His side of the story? What the hell was he supposed to say? When the phone rang, he tore the sheet from the carriage and crumpled it up.

It was Murray.

Tom cut him off before he got past "hello."

"Please don't pressure me, Murray," he said. "I'm working on the piece right now."

"That's not why I'm calling," Murray said.

"Yeah? Sorry. I'm having a bad day. How can I help?"

"Tom, this isn't easy. We've been down a long road together, and I've been proud to represent you. But the problems with *The Rites of Man* are out of control. I'm letting you go."

Tom sat for a moment in stunned silence.

"Are you serious?" he asked.

"I'm afraid so," Murray said. "You've become too much of a liability for the agency."

Sherry was waiting outdoors at ten a.m. on Saturday, December 21, when the white CNN van pulled into the condo's parking lot. She walked over to greet Philip Asmundsen as he emerged from the van, followed by a cameraman and a sound man.

"Are you ready to film your statement?" the reporter asked as Sherry led them inside.

An hour later, another CNN van was winding through the streets of Minneapolis toward a leafy neighborhood near the largest of the city's lakes. It pulled up to a handsome gray-green house on Humboldt South, its windows decorated with festive lights.

"Looks like this is the place," said the cameraman, who was at the wheel.

"Okay, let's go," the reporter said.

They gathered up their equipment and went to ring the bell.

Rick Silverstein opened the door and ushered them inside to meet his family: his wife, Jacqueline, and their two teens. The kids tried to act nonchalant, but their eyes brightened when the cameraman set up his lights in their living room.

"Here, you can help me out," the sound man told them. "Let's do a test."

While the teens made silly noises into the mike, Rick and his wife chatted quietly with the reporter, and the cameraman ran some checks with his light meter.

"Can I get you all some coffee?" Jacqueline asked.

"Maybe later, thanks," the reporter said. "Professor Silverstein, are you ready to film your statement?"

Around the same time across the Atlantic, similar CNN vans found the homes of Raphael Bensimon in Tel Aviv, James Robinson in Geneva, and Jerzy Gregorski in Warsaw. Each time the men were there to greet the team. Each time they were asked the same question: "Are you ready to film your statement?"

Chapter 37

Sherry made herself a cup of tea on Sunday morning and went out to the balcony to commune with the ocean. She felt she could never get enough of the sound of the waves against the shore. Could it possibly be December 22? You wouldn't know it in Florida, she mused. The morning air was as fresh and gentle as in Paris in the spring.

As she lingered, the sound of the waves took her back to the summer. It felt like a lifetime ago—her steamy affair with Tom, the thumping of the surf forming a backdrop to their sex play. She'd thought that she could carry on a love affair while erecting barriers to expectations—as though her desire for happiness in love wasn't legitimate. She'd had time in Florida to come to terms with certain truths about herself, and she felt like a new woman. Never again would she let her fear of losing love prevent her from daring to find it. No, it was time to move beyond foreplay.

She rose from her deck chair, went inside, and dialed Paris.

"Jacques?" she said.

"I've been waiting for your call," Jacques said. "*Tout va bien?*"

"Everything's great. I'm leaving tomorrow."

"Perfect."

"So I get in on Tuesday morning. If I hop in a cab, I can be at your place by noon."

"*Mais non,*" Jacques said. "I will be there to meet you."

Sherry read him her flight number and promised to bring him a guava or three, to paint or to eat, as he preferred. When she hung up, she was smiling.

❧

Tom inserted a clean page into his typewriter. There was no point in killing himself over the article now that Murray had ditched him. But he felt the need to write something. Anything. He thought that he could maybe put together some notes about everything that had happened—notes toward a future novel, perhaps—but the words wouldn't come.

The Christmas tree was still lying forlorn in the corner. It had been shedding its needles. As he got up to fetch a broom, he turned on the TV. The news at noon was wrapping up with a promo.

"Be sure to tune in tomorrow evening for a CNN special report," the anchor said, "as the mystery woman behind the Tom Paine scandal finally breaks her silence."

Inset on the screen was Granville's portrait of Sherry, her long hair cascading behind her silver earrings.

Tom winced at the sight of her. He switched off the TV. Mystery woman indeed, he thought. She still hadn't called back.

He decided to try again.

"Sherry?" he said when her answering machine clicked on. "I need to talk to you. Where are you? Speak to me…"

But no one spoke, so he hung up and went to the kitchen. Time for lunch. Only a couple of bottles were left in his case of J&B. Christ, I've been drinking too much, he thought as he opened one up and filled a tumbler.

He carried it to the living room, set the glass on the bookcase, and swept up the needles. When he returned for his glass, his eye lit on a stack of copies of *The Rites of Man*, abandoned on a shelf, as forlorn as the Christmas tree. He picked one up and sat down on the couch.

Without Jessica and Che around the apartment, the silence was oppressive. He opened the book at random and began to read:

As you can see, men in an age of sexual revolution may appear to embrace the new situation created by women's demand for equal rights. But ultimately, they duck the challenge, every single time.

Tom snapped the book shut.

"Jesus," he said aloud in the empty room. "How could I have written such shit?"

He took a slug of whiskey. The more he thought about it, the more he resented the very existence of that book.

He reopened the novel, found the passage he'd read, and ripped out the page, watching with satisfaction as it fluttered to the floor.

He read a few lines from the next page and tore it out. By the time he'd finished his tumbler, the living room floor was littered with pages.

Russell Hartzman wasn't happy about being summoned to the paper on a Sunday, let alone the Sunday before Christmas. He'd had to abandon his family as they were trimming the tree. The afternoon news meeting was already underway when he arrived. A hush fell as he entered.

"Why isn't Marilee here?" he asked.

"She's on her way in," the night editor said.

Russell sighed and sat back to listen as the editors ran through their skeds for the Monday paper. It sounded like a thin day for the front page. National was billing a piece on the FBI's search for clues in the crash of TWA Flight 800, which had blown up and plummeted into the Atlantic back in July. From Foreign, there was a scene piece from Rome about the funeral of Marcello Mastroianni.

The door to the conference room opened and all eyes turned as Marilee came in and took a seat.

"Sorry I'm late," she said, although she wasn't on the meeting's usual roster.

"Thanks for joining us," Russell said curtly. "So let's get straight to the point. Your Sherry McManus piece isn't running till Tuesday, right?"

"Right," Marilee said.

"Then what's this bullshit about a CNN special tomorrow? The day before we publish your so-called exclusive interview? Is she trying to screw us or what?"

"No," said Marilee. "Let me explain. We…"

Russell cut her off.

"Maybe we should slam your piece into the paper tonight. Is it ready?"

"It is, Russ. But we have a deal with Sherry McManus, and we have to stick to it."

Groans went up around the table.

"Just listen to me," Marilee said. "It's okay. We planned it like this. She's only reading a statement on CNN. In our interview, she tells all. And CNN has agreed to pitch our story at the end of their broadcast. It will work as a springboard."

Russell turned to the Page One editor.

"Well, for Christ's sake, get a promo out there tonight," he said.

Joe brought a couple of pizzas home to his place in the East Village, cheese and sausage for him, gourmet vegetarian for Jessica. She was on the couch watching the evening news when he came in, just in time to hear CNN run its promo again.

"Mystery woman breaks silence," he said. "Great line. I wish we'd had it."

"There's no mystery about that woman," Jessica said. "She's after Tom's money."

Joining Joe at the table, she eyed her pizza suspiciously.

"I said no peppers." She picked one out with a fork and held it out to Che, who delicately removed the morsel.

"I wonder what Sherry McManus will say," Joe said.

"Who knows?" Jessica said, picking out another pepper. "But if she proves she wrote Tom's book for him, I'm done with that loser for good."

Joe's face lit up. At last, the future he'd hoped for seemed within reach, a future with Jessica and the baby.

"You mean...?" he said, letting the question hang in the air.

"I mean I'm out of there," she said, stabbing her fork into her pizza. "I am so out of there."

Chapter 38

It was mid-afternoon on Monday, December 23, and Sherry was at the wheel of her convertible en route to the airport, her father beside her, Rose in the back. She'd put the top down for her last drive in the Florida sun for... well, she didn't know how long. The wind felt great as she barreled down the palm-lined express-way to Miami, a smile in her eyes.

Then it was all business—returning the car, finding a trolley for the suitcase, checking in at Air France, locating the security checkpoint. Her parents stayed with her, keeping up a running patter. She would have preferred to do the goodbye thing back at the condo, but they'd insisted on coming along, assuring her they wouldn't mind the bus ride back.

As the loudspeaker called her flight, Sherry set her camera bag on the conveyor belt.

"Take care of yourself, dear," Rose said, hugging her daughter. "We love you."

Sherry kissed them both, walked through the metal detector, slung her camera bag over her shoulder, and turned back to wave.

As she disappeared from view, Rose felt her eyes well up.

"Paris is so far away," she said, reaching into her bag for a Kleenex.

Bernie took her arm and led her toward the exit.

"Don't worry," he said. "The kid'll be fine."

⚘

The last light of evening had faded by the time Rose and Bernie got home, just in time for the CNN special. With two minutes to go to the broadcast, Bernie turned on the TV and fetched the bottle of champagne he'd set to chill for the occasion.

"And now," said the anchor, "our special report on the Tom Paine scandal, with a statement from the woman he scorned, Sherry McManus."

Sherry appeared on the screen. She wore no makeup but looked striking in her cropped hair, a light glow on her cheeks, her freckles deepened by the sun.

"My name is Sherry McManus," she said, her voice calm and deliberate. "Much has been said about me recently, and the time has come to separate fiction from truth."

She paused for a beat.

"Yes, I was Tom Paine's lover. We had an affair during the summer. While we were together, I told Tom about my life. That much is true. What I didn't know was that he was writing down every word. You can read those words in Part One of *The Rites of Man*. I cannot begin to speculate on why he did this, or why he chose to use the rest of the novel to smear four men who are dear to my heart. Because after Part One, *The Rites of Man* is pure fiction. I would like to apologize to those men and also to express my gratitude to the women throughout this country who've come out to support me in the name of fairness. Thank you."

There was a loud pop as Bernie opened the champagne.

"Brief and dignified," he said. "Nice going, kid."

As her plane veered out over the dark Atlantic, leaving the lights of Miami behind, Sherry checked her watch. Yes, they'd be airing the broadcast now.

Bernie touched glasses with Rose as the TV cut back to the anchor:

"For any viewers just tuning in, Sherry McManus has now confirmed that she was indeed the inspiration—more than the inspiration—for *The Rites of Man.* Or should we call that 'The Rites of McManus?' Well, Sherry has arranged a little treat for any of you who may still doubt the veracity of her version. She sent us to see some of the men she mentioned to Tom Paine when she had no idea that her life would end up in print."

In Washington, the Herzen Leibowitz partners had gathered in the conference room to watch the broadcast. Susan turned up the volume.

"Here it comes," she said.

"If you've read *The Rites of Man,*" the anchor said, "you may recall that the narrator's first lover is described as a Berkeley student named Josh. In real life, he is Professor Rick Silverstein of the University of Minnesota's Humphrey School of Public Affairs. He welcomed us into his home a couple of days ago to talk about his relationship with Sherry McManus."

As the image cut to Rick surrounded by his family beside their holiday tree, its lights glittering, Sam turned to Susan, his eyes twinkling beneath his hoary eyebrows.

"Well done," he said.

"I recognized Josh as my fictionalized persona when I read *The Rites of Man,*" Rick said, "and I would like to state for the record that most of what Thomas Paine wrote about me is false. I am not now, and never have been, a member of the so-called Grass Is Greener Party. In fact, I've had groups like that in my sights as an adviser in President Clinton's War on Drugs. But the rest is true. I was surprised when I read the novel to see how clearly Sherry remembered our time together. Every word about our romance is exactly as it happened. It was a wonderful, passionate time. And afterward"—he smiled and took his wife's hand—"if I found love, Sherry found adventure. She's a terrific woman who has always stayed true to herself. I love her dearly."

In the East Village, Joe and Jessica were on his couch watching the report. When Rick finished speaking, Jessica reached into her bag for her Filofax.

"That does it," she said. "How could that son-of-a-bitch claim he wrote the book when the characters are real people and it was that woman who told him about them?"

She went to the phone and dialed Ophelia Friedman's home number.

"Please get things started," she told her lawyer. "I want a divorce."

A satisfied smile spread across Joe's face as Jessica escaped with the phone to the bedroom. He returned his eyes to the screen.

"Next we went to see the man portrayed by Tom Paine as Ari," the anchor said. "In real life, he is Raphael Bensimon, an award-winning television producer with Israel's Channel One. Here he is, speaking from his home in Tel Aviv."

Raphael appeared with his wife and their four children. He calmly denied having ever faked a news report. But the rest of what Tom wrote about Ari, he said, was true.

The TV cut back to the anchor.

"And what about the other men who dallied with the narrator in Tom Paine's book? Well, they have come forward, too. First, James McCoy Robinson."

Jimmy made his statement from his home in Geneva, flanked by his wife and their three girls. Then Jerzy and his wife appeared from Warsaw. With them was a senior official from the Polish Interior Ministry who declared that Mr. Gregorski's record was clean. He had served the state with honor as a distinguished musician and had never been an informant.

As Jerzy concluded his statement with warm words for Sherry, Jessica returned to the living room. She attached Che's leash, put on her coat, and brought Joe his jacket.

"I think we've heard enough," she said. "Let's go out."

Joe linked his arm through hers as they exited onto the street. There was a new bounce to his step. They were out together in public, and it didn't matter if anyone saw them.

They proceeded together toward Broadway, an anonymous couple with a baby on the way. As Che bounded forward to inspect a fire hydrant, Jessica gripped Joe to steady herself.

"Do you mind if I take over?" he asked, and she readily relinquished the leash.

As Joe leaned down to steal a kiss, Jessica felt a strange feeling come over her. It was something she hadn't experienced in months, or years.

As she remembered what it was, she looked up at Joe and smiled.

She felt at peace.

Across town in the West Village, Tom was watching the broadcast, a bottle of J&B in his hand, the floor still littered with pages torn from his book. There were no more clean glasses, he hadn't changed clothes, he hadn't washed, his face was scruffy. And he was sloshed.

"To conclude this special report," the anchor was saying, "Sherry McManus has provided a sound bite from the author himself, who left her the following telephone message."

Tom choked as his voice came through the TV: "Sherry, I owe you an apology... You're right, I used your stories... This whole thing is my fault... And all you did was tell the truth."

"Yes," the anchor said, "you heard right. That was Thomas G. Paine acknowledging to Sherry McManus that he did indeed, shall we say, borrow her stories in *The Rites of Man*. So there you have it—a story of truth and lies, love and betrayal, and the way ambition can poison the human heart. We would like to thank Sherry McManus for having the courage to come forward and confirm to the world that the penetrating insights in Part One of *The Rites of Man*—insights that won such remarkable praise when the novel first came out—were not the original thoughts of Tom Paine, but her own."

Tom snorted. He set aside his bottle of scotch, lit a match, leaned down to the pages at his feet, and set one on fire.

"And now that the men portrayed in the book have also come forward," the anchor said, "I wouldn't be surprised if these honorable gentlemen brought a case against the author for defamation. These men readily agreed to speak up for Sherry McManus even though it meant putting themselves and their families in the public spotlight. Theirs was a gesture proving that love is stronger than deception, a wonderful message as we head into the Christmas holiday."

Tom lit another page, and another. He raised the bottle to his lips as flames danced around his feet.

"And as for Mr. Paine," the anchor said, "we can only wish him better judgment in the future if he decides to write—if he dares to write—another novel. Happy holidays, and good night."

Chapter 39

Jacques was waiting at the airport when Sherry emerged with her suitcase in the morning. He broke into a wide smile when he saw her, his eyes crinkling beneath tousled salt-and-pepper hair. As she approached, he held out his arms and gave her a bear hug. Then they stood back and looked at each other.

"Can you forgive me?" Jacques said. "I'm going gray. But you…"

"Stop right now," Sherry said. "I'm surprised you even recognized me in this new cut."

"I'd know you anywhere. Besides, I saw you on CNN last night."

"You watched it?" she asked in surprise.

"I stayed up till midnight and saw it live. You were amazing."

Sherry smiled and took Jacques's arm.

"So what's the plan?" she said.

"The plan is very simple," he replied, taking her suitcase. "We go to my place, I make us some coffee, and you tell me what's been going on in your life for the last twenty years."

"I feel like I saw you yesterday," Sherry said. "Can it really have been that long?"

"*Mais oui, ma chérie.*"

On their way to the exit, they saw people gathered in front of a monitor and went to take a look. It was the daily French TV review of the international press. On the screen was that morning's edition of *The New York Times*, with a front-page photo of

Sherry under the headline, "The Real Author Tells Women: Dare to Be Free."

"*Voici un message pour vous, mesdames,*" the anchor said. "*Osez être libres!*"

"You didn't warn me about your new career as a TV star," Jacques said as they departed, causing a woman to turn her head.

The woman nudged her husband.

"*Regarde,*" she said, pointing. "*C'est elle!*"

Back at Jacques's place, Sherry explored the apartment while he made coffee. Paintings were stacked in the room Jacques used as his studio, and the walls were adorned with his work. He'd hung a large new painting in the living room. Executed on corrugated cardboard in tones of gray, black, and white, it showed a nude man leaping, or maybe dancing. The man's face bore no expression, but the feeling was of pure joy.

After breakfast, Jacques watched as Sherry unpacked a few things in his study, which doubled as a guest room.

"These are for you," she said, handing over the guavas.

He picked one up, ran his hand over the nubbly, pale green skin, and tried to bite into it.

"No," Sherry laughed. "You have to cut it open."

She fetched a knife from the kitchen and sliced the fruit in half, revealing its deep pink interior.

"It's beautiful," Jacques said. "So sensual."

"Taste it."

"No, first I must paint it. I want to show the world this beautiful fruit brought to me all the way from Florida by a beautiful woman."

Sherry's smile was engulfed by a yawn.

Jacques set the guava aside and led her to the sofa bed.

"You must be tired," he said. "Why don't you take a little nap? And then later we'll go out and do Paris."

"That sounds good," she said. She had slept little on the flight, she realized, as she stretched out and closed her eyes. Within moments, she was asleep.

Rose skipped her morning swim, instead going out to get the December 24 edition of the *Times* from the newsstand downstairs. She skimmed Sherry's interview on her way back.

Bernie was waiting for her on the balcony.

"So?" he asked.

"Look," Rose said, holding up the front page so he could see the headline.

"She said, 'Dare to be free?'" he asked.

"Let me read it to you," Rose said. She sat down in a deck chair and launched in:

I asked Sherry McManus…

She broke off and turned to Bernie.

"That's Marilee Dyer speaking."

"I get it," he said. "Go on."

I asked Sherry McManus, now that her life is an open book, whether she would change anything if she could live it over again. Her reply was a resounding no.

Rose looked up at Bernie over her reading glasses.

"Go on, already," he said.

"Okay. Now here's Sherry's answer."

It was a shock to see my words appear in The Rites of Man, *and I have to admit I was angry at first. But over the past few weeks, I've had plenty of time to think, and I've come to see things differently. In fact, I'm grateful to Tom Paine for giving voice to my thoughts about how my generation of women has had to negotiate our new reality—a reality where we are free, if we dare, to embrace life to the fullest. Today, anything is possible for women, if we meet the challenge of accepting that freedom.*

"Well put, kid," Bernie said proudly.

"Wait, there's more," Rose said:

As for my own life, I've made a lot of mistakes, and it hasn't always been easy. Like many free-thinking forty-something women in today's United States, I'm single and childless, and that is definitely a challenge. But would I change anything about my life? No, I would not. I feel remarkably privileged to be alive at this moment in time, when anything is possible, if you are ready for anything. Just open your heart to love, and it will find you.

Rose felt her eyes well up.

"Here," she said, handing the paper to Bernie. "You'd better read the rest yourself."

She was squeezing a grapefruit into the juicer when Bernie joined her in the kitchen.

"You left out the part where she says she's dropping the case against Tom," he said. "Why would she do that?"

"Why shouldn't she?" Rose said. "He's being punished enough already."

"But three million big ones? That's the least she should get from that bum."

Rose reached for his hand.

"It was never about the money, dear," she said.

Marilee closed her office door and checked her watch. She'd have to hurry to make it to the ten o'clock meeting on time. Russ had asked her to join them in case any follow-up was needed.

She took the elevator down to the main newsroom. As she made her way through the warren of copy editors, heads turned. One of the editors stood and began to applaud. The woman beside her joined in, men rose, and soon the sound of rhythmic clapping and foot stomping filled the newsroom, a rare ovation.

ಇ

Joe found Jessica making lunch when he came home from the
office at noon, Che watching hopefully beside her. He ruffled the
dog's head and grabbed a beer from the fridge.

"Did they phone you?" he asked.

"They did," she said.

"Well, come on, let's take a look."

Joe switched on the TV. The news had already started with
an update on frantic Christmas Eve shopping across the country.

"And now, in the latest on the Tom Paine scandal," the anchor
said, "his pregnant wife, Jessica Franklin, is suing for divorce."

Jessica joined Joe on the couch as her photo came up on the
screen.

"We reached Jessica Franklin by phone earlier today," the
anchor said.

The sound crackled as Jessica's voice kicked in.

"As hard as it is to turn my life upside down at a time like
this," she said, "I don't want my future child to live in a home
tainted by fraud, deceit, and corruption. I will be seeking a divorce. Any questions should be addressed to my lawyer, Ophelia
Friedman."

Joe was beaming as he switched off the TV.

"Now it's just you and me, honeybunch," he said.

"And Che," Jessica said.

"Aren't you forgetting someone?" he asked.

She smiled up at him serenely.

"Of course not. And our baby."

Helen Nussbaum had the TV on in her office. When the newscast finished, she went to see George Fitzgerald.

"Maybe we should wait until tomorrow," she said. "He's had
a lot of bad news already today."

"That's true," George said. "But I'm afraid we're going to have
to bite the bullet. Would you rather have me make the call?"

Helen frowned.

"No," she said, "I'll do it."

This was the part of the business she liked least, she thought as she returned to her office. And Tom Paine! His books had made a fortune for Fitzgerald & Fitzgerald, and she herself had benefited nicely. But there was more than that. She'd nurtured Tom for ten years. She liked him. It almost felt like she was losing a child. She sighed and reached for the phone.

"How are you doing, Tom?" she asked when he picked up.

"I've been better," he said, looking around the living room. There were scorch marks on the furniture and ashes everywhere. At least the place hadn't burned down, he thought.

"What's up, Helen?" he asked.

"I'm calling to let you know that we're issuing a statement to the media."

Tom's heart sank. He'd been expecting this.

"I'd like to read it to you," Helen said.

"Go ahead."

But Helen didn't want to be rushed.

"You know, Tom," she said, "I've always enjoyed working with you..."

"... but we've come to the end of the road. I get it. Please read the statement."

"All right then," Helen said. She lifted a typed page from her desk and read it out.

"Regarding the matter of Thomas G. Paine and his novel *The Rites of Man*, the house of Fitzgerald & Fitzgerald can no longer support this writer. We are canceling his contract and cutting all ties. At Mr. Paine's request, any future royalties from this book will go to a fund for women in the arts."

Tom nearly dropped the phone. If he'd expected to be dumped by his publishing house, he hadn't imagined they'd take away his earnings.

"You can't do that," he protested. "The royalties are mine."

"Think it through, Tom," Helen said. "We can go to court over this, and you might even win. But it would only further tarnish your reputation. If you'd like to publish another book someday, and I hope you will, then this is the honorable route."

Tom instantly realized that she was right.

"We don't need to go to court," he said. "I won't fight it."

"I'm sorry, Tom," Helen said, and the phone went dead.

Dusk was falling as Jacques and Sherry arrived at the Closerie des Lilas. The maître d' greeted them warmly and led them through the bar, where casually chic Parisians sat chatting at tables bearing small brass plaques commemorating former patrons of the establishment—Hemingway, F. Scott Fitzgerald, Lenin, André Breton. The pianist was playing a jazz melody. Undeniably French, Sherry thought, maybe a tune from a Truffaut movie.

Florida felt very far away.

The maître d' seated them at a table in the brasserie section, and a waiter appeared with the menu. When he departed, Jacques reached into his pocket, extracting a flat box the size of a postcard.

"A little something for Christmas," he said. "In exchange for the guavas."

Sherry peeked inside. The box held a miniature painting of a nude woman surrounded by the words: *La beauté sera CONVULSIVE ou ne sera pas.*

She looked up from the painting and smiled.

"You remembered. After all these years."

"So that you'll feel at home in Paris," Jacques said. "I wanted to write it in English, but I couldn't find the words. How would you translate that?"

"Without passion," she said, "beauty cannot exist."

For the first time in days, Tom went out to pick up some groceries. Even in New York, most of the shops would be closed tomorrow on Christmas Day. He needed to stock up. The fridge was nearly empty, and he was hungry. Besides, he thought as he trudged through the Village, his fedora down low, he'd need fuel if he was to make a new start.

Oddly, the phone call from Helen had energized him. To hell with Fitzgerald & Fitzgerald, he thought, as he entered Gristedes. He was glad to be rid of them, to put that disaster behind him. Everything was settled now. Sherry wasn't suing—in fact, she'd thanked him. Jessica was out of his life. Of course, that was going to cost him, and he'd have to fight to get time with their child. But he'd never been afraid to put up a fight, he thought.

The store was crowded with last-minute shoppers. Tom picked up a couple of steaks, some deli salads, tomato juice, and a lime. Next stop: the liquor store for a bottle of Stoli.

Back home, Tom found the Worcestershire sauce and Tabasco and mixed himself a Bloody Mary. He threw in a couple of ice cubes and took a taste. Bloody good, he thought, as he carried the drink to his desk. He sat down at his typewriter, inserted a blank page, and considered it for a moment. Then he raised his glass.

"To losers everywhere," he said. "Merry fucking Christmas."

He took a long drink, set the glass down, and began to type.

Chapter 40

When Sherry awoke, sunlight was slanting across the bed. She blinked, trying to remember where she was. Then she saw Jacques in bed beside her.

"Merry Christmas, *mon amour*," he said.

Sherry smiled, her mind revisiting the end of their evening— their kiss on the cab ride home, the fire in Jacques's eyes as he'd undressed her, the incandescent moment when old friends had become new lovers, when affection had ceded to passion, when they'd known each other totally, completely, for the first time.

"Maybe we should get up," she said.

"Maybe we shouldn't," he said, taking her in his arms. She kissed him tenderly. All felt calm, all felt bright. All felt right with the world.

When Jacques finally rose to make coffee, it was nearly noon. He brought it to her on a tray, and they had their breakfast propped against the pillows, talking about everything and nothing. Sherry was wearing one of Jacques's T-shirts, and as they chatted, he inspected her with his artist's eye. She looked radiant, and he felt blessed to have her beside him. It was like a miracle of fate, he thought, that they'd been able to reconnect, that desire had withstood the passage of time. A miracle especially that when he'd become free, Sherry, too, was single. That was the luckiest thing of all.

He turned to her, a thoughtful look in his eye.

"Tell me something," he said. "I've been wondering about it all these years."

"Yes?"

"You never settled down. Why not?"

Sherry burst out laughing. She grabbed her pillow and threw it at him.

"Hey," Jacques protested. "I only asked a question."

Sherry laughed even harder, gasping to get the words out: "Read. The. Book!"

EPILOGUE

December 1997

Sherry was strolling down the Rue des Ecoles on Christmas Day, arm in arm with Rose and Bernie. Her parents had skipped Florida this year and come over to Paris instead. Bringing up the rear, Jacques was pushing a double baby stroller. The twins were tucked up inside in snowsuits, deep pink and bright blue, their dark curls peeking out from pom-pommed hats.

Rose beamed as Jacques caught up with them outside Le Balzar.

"How are my angels?" she chirped. "Look at them. Aren't they precious?"

But the kids were asleep, lost in dreamland.

Sherry held the door for her parents, and they all went inside, choosing a table on the brasserie's narrow heated terrace. It was teatime, and the lunch crowd had largely departed.

"Can a man get a drink in a place like this?" Bernie asked, glancing nervously at the small china teapots on the neighboring tables. He was feeling a bit overwhelmed, not as much by the odd habits of Parisians as by the advent of granddadhood.

Sherry smiled at her father.

"Of course you can get a drink," she said. "But the hot chocolate is good here."

"I'd like to try that," Rose said as Jacques hailed the waiter.

He ordered hot chocolate all around, with cognac alongside for himself and his father-in-law.

Dusk had fallen by the time they trooped back to Jacques's place—Jacques's and Sherry's place now. Jacques had cleared one wall of his paintings to make room for Sherry's photos. At the suggestion of Nan Gillette, Sherry had switched to a Canon digital and was filing from Paris via her new Apple PowerBook. Of course, she'd had to slow down since the twins arrived.

They were babbling now as Sherry extracted them from their snowsuits. Leaving her mother in charge of bath time, she went to the kitchen to slice the roast turkey leftover from Christmas lunch as Jacques took Bernie down to the cellar to choose some wine.

The doorbell rang promptly at seven, and Anouk swept in with her usual flourish, overladen with gifts and a bottle of chilled Champagne. She dropped her packages on an armchair and went to admire the children, clean and rosy-cheeked in their matching pajamas.

"How's my little Robert," she crooned, pronouncing it the French way—*Ro-BAIR*. "And look at darling Sonia. They're so big already!"

"I know," Sherry said, taking her friend's coat. "Three months old, and they're growing like crazy. And I thought I was too old to have children…"

There was a loud pop as Jacques opened the Champagne.

"But many women these days are having children in their forties," Anouk said.

"Still, as far as I'm concerned, it's a miracle," Sherry said.

She was happier than she'd ever been, she realized. And the odd thing was that none of this would have happened had she not taken up with Tom. She thought back to the start of their affair, when she'd wondered whether to stay or slip away, asking herself whether the pursuit of happiness was worth the risk. She'd learned a lot since then, she thought, looking lovingly from Jacques to the twins and back to her husband. It was so obvious, but she hadn't seen it back then. True happiness only comes when we accept that we deserve it.

Jacques had filled five Champagne flutes and was handing them out.

"For you, *mon amour*," he said as he gave one to Sherry.

Rose sniffed back a tear.

"Here's mud in your eye," Bernie said gruffly, hoping his voice wouldn't crack.

"That's English for Merry Christmas," Sherry explained, and they laughed and touched glasses all around.

Sensing the festive mood, the twins cooed and wriggled in their baby rockers.

"We'd better get these two to bed," Sherry said, plucking up Sonia. "Mom, will you help?"

"You stay with your friend, dear," Rose said. "Your father and I will settle the children."

She picked up Robert, handed him to Bernie, and took Sonia from Sherry's arms. They disappeared into the former guest room, now converted into a nursery.

Sherry sank onto the couch beside Jacques.

"You two look so happy," Anouk said.

"You mean, we look so tired," Sherry said.

"*Oui*," Jacques said, "when you turned up on my doorstep a year ago, I hardly expected to find myself with two mini models to paint, and feed, and change, and..."

"Can you believe it's been only a year?" Sherry said. "I was such a wreck when I got here, but now it feels like that whole business happened a century ago."

"I wonder what Monsieur Paine-In-The-Ass is doing now," Anouk said.

"Frankly, I haven't given him a thought," Sherry said.

Only a few customers had braved the blustery cold to drive up to Montauk for Christmas lunch at Gurney's. Just as well, Tom thought as he straightened his apron. He walked to the table of a couple who'd just arrived, took their drink order, and strolled over to the bar.

"Two Champagne cocktails for Table Four," he said.

Tom gazed out to sea as the barman mixed the drinks. The waves were pounding the shore, their whitecaps dancing. He carried the cocktails to the couple, took their lunch order, and withdrew discreetly.

Being a waiter suited him. Nobody recognized him in his new look—beard, mustache, and hair swept back off his forehead. It felt good being anonymous. The job brought in a little money—it helped pay off his legal costs—and in off-hours, he could write.

The wind was howling, rattling the windows. As customers looked anxiously out at the crashing sea, the barman turned up the volume of the Christmas music. Nobody noticed when the door opened and a heavily clad couple walked in, their faces wrapped in wool scarves.

The man approached Tom and tapped him on the shoulder.

"Table for two?" he said.

Tom turned around, and the woman let out a gasp.

"Tom Paine?" she said. "Holy shit! What are you doing here?"

Tom did mental gymnastics trying to figure out who it was until the woman removed her scarf and he recognized Marilee Dyer.

"Everyone has to earn a living," he said wryly, wondering what on earth had brought her into his restaurant.

He escorted them to a table and held Marilee's chair for her.

"Now, what would you like to drink?" he asked. "I can recommend the house white. It's a New York chardonnay."

"Fine," said Marilee. "But will you please join us?"

"I'm afraid I have to work," Tom said, departing to fetch the wine.

When he returned, Marilee eyed him with concern.

"How are you doing, Tom?" she asked. "With everything?"

"I'm okay," he said, pouring the wine. "I've been living out here full time since the divorce. Jessica got the apartment in the Village, and I got the beach house. Which is fine by me. I get to see my son on weekends, and I do a little writing when I can."

"Are you working on a new novel?" Marilee asked.

"Hell no," Tom said. "I'm through with fiction."

❧

Jessica was setting the table, ignoring the squalls from the play-pen. This was her second Christmas with Joe, and their first to-gether in the West Village.

"Can't you get that kid to shut up?" Joe said, looking up from his laptop. "I'm trying to write, and I can't think."

"Don't blame it on the baby," Jessica said. "It's not Ben's fault if you can't write."

She scooped up her son, who continued to howl as she set him in his high chair. He calmed only when she began to feed him small spoonfuls of homemade carrot purée. She took her time, although Savannah and Phil would be arriving soon with little Beau.

"There's a good boy," Jessica cooed as the child followed the spoon with wide eyes beneath wispy dun-blond hair. She fed him another spoonful, wondering—as she had throughout his eight months of existence—exactly how his hair had turned out to be light, not dark like hers. Had he inherited it from Tom or from Joe? He looked like neither of them. It would probably remain a mystery, as they had collectively decided to forgo a paternity test. And Ben, they'd agreed, would bear his mother's last name, Franklin.

The dish of purée was empty. As Jessica removed it, distress flooded Ben's face, and he began to howl again.

"That does it," Joe said, snatching up his laptop and stalking into the bedroom. He slammed the door shut, sat down on the edge of the bed, and opened the computer. But the words wouldn't come. Half an hour later, when Jessica poked her head in to say that the guests had arrived, he was still facing a blank screen.

The light was fading when Tom came home from his shift, the beach house beckoning with a cheery glow from the windows.

"Hi, Dad," he said as he entered.

Henry Paine, seated on the couch before a crackling fire, set aside the manuscript he was reading.

"That's some mighty fine writing, son," he said. "Your mother will be proud."

"Thanks," Tom said, grinning. "That means a lot to me."

"Let's get the whiskey out," Henry said. "I expect they'll be arriving any minute now."

Tom walked around the butcher block to the kitchen area and fetched four highball glasses and a bottle of single malt.

"Are you sure you're ready for this?" he asked his father.

"I've had eight years to think it over," Henry said. "And now that your mother and I are back together, I think it's time for us to meet the man who brought you into our lives."

Gravel crunched as a car pulled into the driveway. Footsteps approached, and there was a knock on the door.

"You go," Tom said, suddenly nervous.

Henry pulled the door wide to his wife and the man beside her.

"Anne," he said fondly. "And you must be…"

"Ian Rowland," the man said, extending a ruddy hand.

"Come in, come in," Henry said.

As they entered, Tom gave Ian a shy smile.

"Hello," he said, approaching. "I'm…"

"You're Tom," Ian said. "Hello, my lad."

He wrapped Tom in a bear hug and held him tight, as if to make up for forty-four years of not knowing he had a son. When he released Tom, they stood back to look at each other.

Ian was tall and sandy-haired, with deep blue eyes and chiseled features.

Much like Tom's, thought Anne, feeling her heart would burst.

"Well, this is quite a moment," Henry said. "I'm actually at a loss for words."

"Come, let's sit down," Anne said, taking a seat in front of the fire. "It's so cozy in here."

Henry lifted the bottle of single malt.

"Can I pour you a whiskey?" he asked their guest.

"That would be smashing," Ian said. "It's been rather a long day."

Henry served them all and raised his glass.

"I'd like to propose a toast," he said, "but I have only one word to say: Welcome."

Tom smiled at his father, then at his mother and Ian, feeling proud to have brought them all together. It hadn't been too difficult once Henry resurfaced, turning up unannounced at the West Village apartment when Tom's world was falling apart. That had been a year ago. Within a couple of months, Tom had arranged for his parents to meet, and they'd soon taken up together again. They'd needed some time to accept the idea that he wanted to meet his biological father, but eventually they'd come around.

A gust rattled the windows.

"Look, it's snowing," Anne said, glancing outside. Caught in the light of the outdoor lamp, large flakes were dancing wildly in the wind.

Tom turned to Ian.

"Lucky this weather didn't get started until you were on the ground," he said. "Did you have a good flight?"

"Uneventful, straight in from Edinburgh," Ian said.

"My mother tells me you're a professor of archeology there?"

"Yes, quite right," Ian said. "And your mother says you've begun a new book."

"Here it is," Henry said, picking up the manuscript. "It's called *Geronimo Revisited: A Memoir*, by Thomas G. Paine."

Anne beamed proudly.

"Tom is writing about my family," she said. "Could you read us a bit?"

"Sure," Tom said as his father passed him the manuscript. He set aside the title page and launched in:

"Chapter One. I'm one-eighth Apache, and it's on my mother's side. She's actually descended from a Mayflower pilgrim, Peter Browne, but things happened…"

It was nearing midnight in Paris. Rose and Bernie were still at the table chatting with Anouk and Sherry as Jacques cleared away the remains of a chocolate Yule log. When the doorbell rang, Anouk suppressed a smile.

"Who can that be at this hour?" Sherry asked.

She opened the door and gaped at the sight of Granville.

"Oh my god! What are you doing here?" she said.

Smiling broadly, Granville held out a bouquet of roses. In his other hand, he was holding a cat basket.

"You've brought Max!" Sherry exclaimed.

"Merry Christmas, Sher," Granville said. "Aren't you going to ask me in?"

"Oh, sorry!" Sherry said. "Please."

Granville shook hands with Rose and Bernie and embraced Anouk as Sherry reunited with Max.

"I'm so glad this worked out," Anouk said warmly.

"Don't tell me you had something to do with it," Sherry said.

"We worked it out together," Granville said, looking around. "Now did you say something about a husband?"

Jacques emerged from the kitchen, wiping his hands on a dish towel. A smile lit his face.

"I am Jacques, and you must be Granville."

"Right. How're you doing, man?" Granville said. "Now let me see those twins."

"They're sleeping," Sherry said. But as if on cue, a small wail emanated from the nursery, followed by another one.

"I'll go," Jacques said, reappearing a moment later with one twin in each arm. He extended them to Granville.

"This calls for more Champagne," he said, heading for the kitchen to fetch it.

When he returned, Granville was settled in an armchair, cooing over the children.

"And what are you going to grow up to be, little lady?" he asked Sonia. "And you, little man?" he asked Robert. "Will you be a photo ace like your Uncle Granville? Or an artist like your dad? Or maybe a first-class, A-Number-One teller of tales like your mom?"

Everyone laughed.

"Don't go putting ideas into their heads, Uncle Granville," Sherry said. "Nobody's telling any more tales. That's finished now. End of story."

Acknowledgments

I would like to thank the many friends and colleagues who generously shared their insights with me as I completed this book, among them Susan Benda, Ron Blunden, Celestine Bohlen, Barbara Chudzikiewicz, Kristin Duncombe, Sylviane Dungan, Odile Hellier, Ann Mah, Reine Marie Melvin, Anne Penketh, Eleanor Randolph, Serge Schmemann, Janice Steinberg, John Tagliabue, and Martin Walker. Special thanks to my brilliant publisher, Michael T. Braun, and his team at Ten16 Press, notably Katie Ramos, who edited this novel with grace. I am also exceptionally grateful to James Eric Jones, who created the cover design. Posthumous thanks to Marguerite Duras, in whose garden in Neauphle-le-Château the inspiration for this novel arose. Finally, I would like to thank my daughter, Djeneba Rosa Bortin, who gave me the love and support I needed to see this project through to completion.

About the Author

Meg Bortin is an American writer based in Paris. Previous literary works include a memoir, *Desperate to Be a Housewife* (Mirabelle Books, 2013), and *Dear Djeneba*, a personal essay included in *Family Wanted: Stories of Adoption* (Granta Books, 2005; Random House, 2006). As a journalist she covered international affairs for 30 years. Her articles have appeared in many publications including *The New York Times*, which honored her with a Punch award in 2007. She also writes a cooking blog, *The Everyday French Chef*. Learn more at megbortin.com.